MUSIC SHALL UNTUNE THE SKY

THE CELWYN SERIES BOOK 2

MUSIC SHALL UNTUNE THE SKY

LOU KEMP

Music Shall Untune the Sky
The Celwyn Series Book 2
Copyright © 2023 Lou Kemp. All rights reserved.

4 Horsemen Publications, Inc.
1497 Main St. Suite 169
Dunedin, FL 34698
4horsemenpublications.com
info@4horsemenpublications.com

Cover by J. Kotick
Typesetting by S. Wilder
Editor Joseph Mistretta

All rights to the work within are reserved to the author and publisher. No part of this publication may be reproduced, stored in a retrieval system, or transmitted in any form or by any means, electronic, mechanical, photocopying, recording, scanning, or otherwise, except as permitted under Section 107 or 108 of the 1976 International Copyright Act, without prior written permission except in brief quotations embodied in critical articles and reviews. Please contact either the Publisher or Author to gain permission.

This is book is meant as a reference guide. All characters, organizations, and events portrayed in this novel are either products of the author's imagination or are used fictitiously. All brands, quotes, and cited work respectfully belongs to the original rights holders and bear no affiliation to the authors or publisher.

Library of Congress Control Number: 2022945572

Print ISBN: 979-8-8232-0065-3
Hardcover ISBN: 979-8-8232-0066-0
Audio ISBN: 979-8-8232-0063-9
E-Book ISBN: 979-8-8232-0064-6

Table of Contents

Acknowledgements:

MANY THANKS AND LOVE TO MY daughter Charmaine who supports me no matter what I dream up. Thank you to friends Nikki, Debbie, Peggy, and Karen for their support and advice. Authors, who are also friends, have improved my work beyond simple mistakes: Anita Dickason, Benjamin X. Wretlind, Bob Van Laerhoven. I am grateful to John Helfers of Stonehenge Editorial for his patience and expertise in editing the Celwyn series.

Cast of Characters:

Jonas Celwyn: Immortal magician and provocateur

Professor Xiau Kang: Automat,
medical man, scientist

Bartholomew: widower from Juba, friend to Kang
and Celwyn

Annabelle Pearse Edmunds: heiress and ward of
Uncle Celwyn

Captain Patrick Swayne: Friend to Celwyn,
loves Annabelle

Mrs. Elizabeth Kang: tolerant and beautiful
wife of Kang

Zander: an orphan rescued on the way to Prague

Telly: an orphan rescued on the way to Prague

Ricardo: Chef Ricardo of Tellyhouse

Mrs. Thomas: formidable Housekeeper of Tellyhouse

Jackson, Selkirk, and Stephen: porters on the train and in Prague

Edward Murphy: their driver and head of security

Sully: footman of Tellyhouse and a legendary bad chef

Francesca: head of Prague's notorious coven

Delgado: Vampire who killed Suzanne and Telly

Mrs. Karras: disciple of Delgado and enemy of Celwyn

Prince Leo: thief and old friend of Celwyn

Mary Giovanna Fioria: Prince Leo's crazy daughter

Prologue

WITHOUT TOUCHING IT, JONAS Celwyn yanked the knife out of Annabelle's hand, away from Zander's neck, and turned it on her, plunging the blade into her stomach and causing the crowd around them to erupt in screams. As Patrick rushed to her side, a thin stream of blue mist escaped Annabelle's lips and disappeared into the throng. Celwyn elevated himself, trying to see where the entity Jax had gone and failed.

The ethereal music quieted while the audience's clamor grew.

Shaking with horror and sorrow, Patrick cradled Annabelle's head in his lap while Professor Xiau Kang pushed everyone back.

Beside them, Bartholomew's anger exploded, and he shouted at Celwyn. "You killed her!"

"No—he did not!" Kang grabbed his arm and swung him around. "Think, man! Block the view of her while Jonas brings her back." He lowered his voice. "The wound was not intended to be fatal, only to scare Jax out of her."

Bartholomew's face contorted in relief.

As Kang spoke, Celwyn knelt and covered Annabelle with his cape. He removed the bloody knife and held a hand over the wound as he looked at the tall and distraught black man beside him.

"My friend, I would never kill her. The Professor showed me where I could stab someone to cause the most blood flow, yet the wound be one that I could easily repair." He watched Bartholomew's face relax and turned back to study Annabelle a moment more. "There. Good as new. Patrick, if you could help her stand?"

Captain Patrick Swayne licked his lips and, with a trembling hand, brought Annabelle to her feet. As Patrick bent her over his arm and kissed her thoroughly, the audience applauded. The crowd may have cheered because a beautiful woman hadn't died or because she was embraced in the arms of a gallant military man.

"Much better than a performance of King Lear," Kang said with a pointed look and smile at Celwyn. "I need to put a stop to all of this attention." He turned to the audience sitting on the ice stage and raised his voice. "This performance has been brought to you as just that, a performance, an illusion that tells a story. We hope you enjoyed the show." He bowed. "Good night."

Beside him, Annabelle clung to Patrick and said in a thick drawl, "I *do* declare, I am so grateful that disgusting thing is gone." She watched Celwyn lift the boy into his arms. Her voice broke. "How is Zander?"

"He isn't aware of anything that happened." The situation reminded Celwyn of how, once before, they had rescued the orphan. With a raised brow at Bartholomew, he asked, "Are we good again, my friend?"

"Yes, Jonas. But please never scare me like that again!" The big man paced back and forth. "Good grief."

Their driver, Edward, stepped up. "If you'll excuse me, I second that request." He lowered his rifle to his side. "I'll get the carriage. I've had enough society, and drama, for the night."

Kang lowered his voice. "Jonas, you might want to wipe the blood off your face. And what about him?" he pointed to their feet. Through the water of the Vltava River, the vampire Delgado's red eyes still glowed from the bottom of the illuminated cage. In the clear water, it looked like they could reach out and touch him.

The killing of Telly and Suzanne came back to him, bringing the magician's sadness too. With it came the unseen and spectral violins whose music surrounded them and the illusions on the edges of the stage began to fade. Celwyn said, "He is ready for the culmination of the evening."

"Are you sure?" Kang studied him as worry filled his eyes. "You are tiring now, correct?"

"Yes."

Bartholomew rejoined them and said, "As much as I want to see Delgado's demise, I'd best take everyone home. It is very late."

He removed Zander from the magician's arms and herded the others off the frozen stage and toward the street. The automat pointed at the dome of the Opera House. "Will the net up there hold the rest of the vampires until dawn?"

"It is made of metal, and I'll be here to be sure it does." Celwyn smiled a hard smile of revenge. "It will be a very bright dawn, wouldn't you say?"

Kang patted him on the back. "I'll stay with you."

Moments went by as the crowd dispersed. They chattered in excited voices, entertained and unaware of the truth of what they'd witnessed. As soon as they left the ice, heavy clouds rolled in overhead, obscuring the moon. An astute observer might wonder why the clouds waited until that moment.

"It doesn't appear that you brought your umbrella," Celwyn remarked as they gazed upward.

He produced a large one and handed it to Kang. "Join me for a moment, please." They walked away from the melting ice stage and onto the footpath paralleling the river.

Kang opened the umbrella and regarded the magician with an eyebrow up.

The magician turned, face upraised to the night sky.

The thunder began to the east, low and far away. Just a rumble, barely enough to notice. But within a minute, it covered Prague, boom after boom, shaking the buildings to their foundations.

The noise became deafening as the wind arose, competing with a joyous chorus of French horns announcing the storm's arrival. The pedestrians in the street scattered as the heavens opened and the rain poured down.

The electricity in the air sizzled, raising the hair on their scalps and arms. Even the automat, Kang, shivered in anticipation.

All of the emotion from Suzanne and Telly's deaths arrived, strengthening the magic, and Celwyn once more lifted his hands, sweeping them from side to side. Lightning illuminated the sky, turning night to day, seeming to crack the sky open. Directly overhead, one bolt separated from the rest, arcing high and coming down.

The smell of the electricity was overwhelming as the bolt went into the river, straight and sure into the cage holding Delgado. When it exploded, it sent waves of water flying upward. The lightning blossomed, unfolding like an enormous rose as it spread across the sky.

The music rejoiced as Celwyn opened his cape, letting Qing fly free into the night sky. The bird soared high and then dipped low over what remained of the ice on the river. He landed on the crystal pipe organ, pecking at the silver keys as they began to fade away.

Across the city, the spectral violins played forlornly, echoing triumphantly, in celebration of love, revenge, and ultimately music.

Out of the corner of his eye, the magician spied something white and diaphanous in the river.

Horror gripped him. With the last of his strength, he plunged into the water, fighting the current as he swam to the bottom. He slowed, already knowing what he would find. In front of him, Christina's hair flowed in the current as if a light breeze blew through it. Her sightless eyes were open, and her hands upraised as if imploring him to save her.

Twin punctures decorated her neck.

Chapter 1

THE SUN ROSE, GLINTING OFF THE ornate cornices and brass crossbeams of the Prague Opera House. A murder of crows hovered over the top of the dome, their plaintive cawing as articulate as words.

"Francesca is most angry. Somehow, she knew Christina had died." Kang shielded his eyes against the glare. "I believe she is the loudest one with the long neck."

Celwyn sat beside him on the rim of the fountain, shivering under the shadow of the dome and too shocked over Christina's death to even cry. He'd only begun to know her and her inner beauty. Later, he would ask himself if he was the reason she had been killed or because the witches of Prague had a longstanding feud with vampires. The way Christina was murdered would make it worse. Too exhausted to stand, he watched the crows for a moment.

"Agreed. She has every right to be angry at Delgado and the rest of them."

The magician couldn't help glancing across the street to the Vltava River running swift and dark through the city. In the last few hours, he had made sure Delgado would never hurt someone he loved again, but in the end, he had been too late to save Christina.

The sun rose higher, spreading light over the city. The aroma of cooking fires reached them as the residents prepared to greet the day, and a forlorn siren wailed in the distance, competing with the cawing of the crows who circled, pecking at the magically enhanced net dangling from the spire. It was filled with vampires, except for one: Delgado had deserved special treatment—his minions would just burn. A suggestion of faces and hands of the vampires could be seen inside the net, and their growls and snarls punctuated the clear morning air like wild dogs.

"It is unfortunate that you couldn't have gathered up Mrs. Karras, too." The Professor scanned the area. "I don't see her."

Celwyn barked a mirthless laugh. "She will lie low for a while without the other vampires to help her." He touched the scratches on his face. "Hopefully, she will stop jumping on my back, too."

As the sun struck the top of the spire, the snarls of the vampires escalated to bellows as flames engulfed the net, and they burned. Kang held his nose with two fingers, anticipating a rancid cloud to descend on them.

"That sight was worth it." The magician wallowed in his anger as he thought of the damage the vampires had done. "Francesca will appreciate my efforts, but she will still hunt down the rest of them herself. She is a vindictive witch."

"That she will." Kang hesitated before speaking again. "Were you smitten with Christina?"

The magician sighed deeply. "Yes, but it was so new, I wasn't sure. We will never know."

"Your performance last night was extraordinary; I'm not surprised you are tired." The diminutive, centuries-old automat helped the nearly six-and-a-half-foot-tall magician to stand. "We need to find a blasted carriage."

They headed to the street with the magician leaning heavily on the mechanical man. Celwyn glanced a last time at the spire above them. Nothing moved in the charred net, yet a few crows still soared and dived above the dome, cawing mournfully.

"I imagine Annabelle will be a mite sore this morning from the finale with Jax, but she will be fine with Patrick fussing over her," the magician said as they walked. Bartholomew represented an unknown factor. He worried more than anyone Celwyn knew.

"What do you think our friend's reaction will be after everything calms down?"

"Bartholomew will be fine." Kang leaned Celwyn against a lamp post and stepped into the street to look for a hire cab. Coal carts trundled by a few blocks away, but nothing else. As he turned back to rejoin the magician, the pounding of hooves on cobblestones approaching at speed reached them, and then a team of four pulling a sizeable black carriage rounded the corner.

Edward drew back on the reins, and the horses snorted clouds into the chilly air. As he jumped to the ground, he doffed his top hat. "Good morning again." Seeing Celwyn's condition, he helped bundle him into the carriage.

"Thank you, Edward. To Tellyhouse, please." The magician leaned back and let his eyes close. The Professor settled in the seat opposite and took out his pipe.

"To finish answering your question, Jonas," Kang said between aromatic puffs, "in my estimation, Bartholomew will do his best to accept that you had to stab Annabelle ... to save her. However, he would probably appreciate being taken into your confidence before experiencing something like that again. As would I." He drew on the pipe again and relit it.

The metallic bird with the silver-tipped feathers peeked out of Celwyn's coat and squawked at Kang.

The automat covered his pipe. "It appears Qing still dislikes it when we smoke."

Chapter 2

By the time Celwyn finished tying his tie and admiring his profile in the looking glass, it lacked a few minutes until luncheon at Tellyhouse. Only an hour ago, Qing had jumped on him to wake him. He felt refreshed and prepared for any vampire or other entertainment. Yet he couldn't get the picture of Christina's lifeless body out of his mind.

"As good as new and handsome as ever, eh?" he asked Qing, who waddled across the basin and back again. The bird hopped onto Celwyn's shoulder and burrowed inside his coat. "No chewing. Mrs. Thomas says my collars look like we have rats, and she considers that a personal insult."

They entered the dining room just before Kang and found Zander and Bartholomew already seated, deep in animated conversation. The boy showed the big man a drawing of a giraffe with dark hair and large green eyes.

"Perhaps it is a picture of you." Kang elbowed the magician.

Celwyn smiled. He explored the lad's thoughts, finding the usual mix of spiders and odd and questionable objects that he discovered in the yard, including a dead frog. Zander had no memory of the entity Jax. Nor did he remember how Jax had possessed Annabelle and used her to hold a knife to his throat or of her speaking in a guttural growl. Celwyn shook himself. He would prefer not to relive something like that again.

Bartholomew waited until they had sat down before saying, "Good afternoon. Last night was most successful and impressive, Jonas. However, I insist that you never scare me like that again."

"Noted. The Professor has already requested that I take both of you into my confidence in the future."

Bartholomew's lips twitched with suppressed amusement. "Will you?"

"When I can, and as time permits."

"That is reasonable."

"No, it's not," Kang huffed.

"And when I know you can accept what you see without impeding my plans." Celwyn wiggled his brows at them.

Bartholomew chuckled. Kang rolled his eyes. "If you had told me you intended to part that river and freeze it, I would not have thought it possible."

"Neither would I." Bartholomew sobered. "I would also have worried that the weight of that orchestra would cause it to fall through the ice." He smiled broadly. "No matter. I would have offered my best wishes for success. And requested an explanation."

"Of what?" Zander asked.

Kang snickered, knowing the magician hated to be put on the spot.

Celwyn regarded the lad. Months ago, they had found him on the streets of Pushkari, half-starved and threatened by a madman. He gazed at the boy with fondness, enjoying his childish good humor. Although he'd endured horrors and dangers no child should experience at eight, the magician doubted he was ready for a demonstration of magic, no matter how tasteful and artful.

"Just the orchestra's music. What did you do with the dead frog?"

Zander's eyes widened and he whispered, "It is a secret!"

Behind them came a shushing and then a giggle that preceded Annabelle and Patrick's entrance into the room. Annabelle's golden hair shone, and her eyes twinkled with romantic mischief. The Captain held the hand of his betrothed and made sure she arrived at the dining table without incident.

"Good afternoon." Patrick faced the others. It appeared he, too, had a speech prepared about the previous evening's festivities. "Last night's confrontation with our enemy was highly disturbing." He watched Annabelle as if she might disappear at any moment. "Nevertheless, when I heard of the destruction of Delgado, it made the final result most satisfying."

Years ago, the vampire had been responsible for the death of his sister, Suzanne. Patrick had waited a long time for his revenge. "I didn't get a chance to properly thank you last night, Jonas."

"No need," Celwyn assured him. "It was my pleasure. I loved your sister very much."

Patrick glanced at Annabelle, who'd put her napkin in her lap while waiting for their lunch to be served. "However, you scared the daylights out of me when you dealt with Jax."

Celwyn cleared his throat. "I had to make sure that he left her without hurting her."

"Which he did," the Professor said with a pointed look at Zander, who didn't need to hear the details. "We are all thankful. Let us talk of something more pleasant and enjoy our lunch."

As he spoke, Mrs. Thomas pushed the serving cart into the room. Celwyn had no doubt that, at well over six feet and built solidly, their housekeeper could have carried the cart into the room with a pinky finger. She ruled all four floors of Tellyhouse, and everyone from Sully, their footman, to Chef Lucien admired her. When he tried to woo her, Sully learned not to express his admiration after she boxed his ears.

"What is on the menu, Ricardo?" Bartholomew asked.

Ricardo, assistant to the chef, had followed the cart into the room and knew better than to admire, or cross, the housekeeper. As he removed the domed covers from the dishes, he said, "Quiche a la Lorraine and roasted potatoes with rosemary. For dessert, fresh peaches with brandy sauce."

"Do giraffes eat peaches?" Zander's eyes tracked each dish as they were placed on the table. He bounced in his chair, and his dark curls bounced too. "Are we going to the zoo today?"

Kang looked at Annabelle, who glanced at Celwyn. "It is Sunday."

The magician nodded. "I believe a spot of beauty and distraction are in order. We are finally free from danger."

Six months ago, he and Kang had embarked from San Francisco on a ship sailing west. After a violent storm, Celwyn intervened when Professor Kang was threatened by his brother, Talos. The magician's actions had saved both Kang and their ship. In discussions since then, they deduced this was the point at which the entity Jax had taken an interest in them. He had followed them out of Singapore to the Bengal region and beyond as they traveled west. To make things more exciting, at the same time, a pack of vampires had become as attracted to them with as much dedication and interest as Annabelle displayed to large, feathered hats.

"How do you know Aunt Annabelle?" Zander asked Bartholomew.

The big man finished chewing and said, "I met your Uncle Celwyn first. He and the Professor asked me to join them on their journey."

Celwyn enjoyed the memory. Bartholomew was from Juba near the White Nile and a world traveler. But when the ticket master for the *Royal Victoria* had denied him a ticket because of the color of his skin, the magician intervened. The ticket seller was lucky he hadn't been transformed into a stinky pig and sent squealing into the train yard. That same night, Bartholomew had watched as Celwyn tossed the first of the annoying vampires, Mrs. Karras, off the *Royal Victoria*, petticoats and all. It later became their misfortune that she tracked them to Prague, intent on vengeance.

"Shortly afterward, I met your aunt and Captain Patrick."

Patrick's handsome face brightened.

"Then me and Telly!" Zander shouted.

The moment he spoke her name, Zander's expression changed. As he relived Telly's death, a hush came over the table, each of them remembering the little girl they'd rescued the same night they'd found Zander, eventually taking both orphans with them to Prague.

"I miss her still."

"We all do, Master Zander," Bartholomew told him.

Celwyn looked at the boy. "To answer your earlier questions, last night I made all of the bad people who hurt Telly go away. You will never see the 'genie man,' as you call him, again. But if you see someone like him, what will you do?"

"Run to you!"

"Good." Kang patted him on the shoulder.

Luncheon continued to the peaches and brandy sauce, with ice cream instead for Zander. The Professor finished first and sat back to address them.

"I have an announcement."

A tiny thrill electrified Celwyn, and he stopped eating to regard Kang. Xiau looked the same with his elfin ears, intelligent eyes, and too-long hair. He was a friend, doctor, professor, and keeper of atomic secrets. The automat also existed from before the Renaissance and had seen much, yet was excited about something. The magician had caught the tremor of anticipation in Kang's voice.

"You have had a scientific breakthrough?" the magician asked as if it didn't matter.

"It is of a more personal nature." The automat shook his head. "Some of you were not with us in Singapore and did not meet my wife, Elizabeth." He added, "She stayed behind to be with her mother."

Annabelle said, "I enjoyed her company very much while we were on the ship. How is her mother?"

"Well enough. In her last letter, Elizabeth again asked when I will return for her."

Celwyn smiled. Now he understood the happiness in Kang's voice.

"As you remember, we'd been leery of exposing her to the danger from our enemies," Kang said. "This morning, I wrote her saying I would leave for Singapore soon."

"And bring her here." Bartholomew's eyes sparkled with proof of his romantic nature.

"I hope to. However, I must first convince her to come here."

Annabelle put down her spoon and turned to him. "I will write her and describe Tellyhouse and tell her of Prague, of Zander, and how Patrick and I want her at our wedding."

"That will help," the automat said.

Patrick told him, "It would be wonderful to have her here with us."

Zander watched the exchange, and his bottom lip trembled.

"You are leaving?"

"For a short time." The Professor hugged him. "Let's adjourn to the parlor so that we can finish our discussion in comfort."

As they entered the other room, Qing flew off the top of the armoire to Celwyn's shoulder, and after everyone made themselves comfortable, the bird chose his quarry and hopped onto the back of the sofa. His eyes glittered with intent as he approached Bartholomew sitting at the other end.

The big man's head swiveled on his bull neck. "No." He was well aware of the bird's affinity for jewelry and all things shiny. Qing fluffed his wings and waited. The magician made a private bet on how long it would take until the bird made his move.

Zander perched on Kang's lap. "Please explain."

"My wife Elizabeth is in Singapore. I must go to her. I hope to bring her back here."

"But who will give me my science lessons while you are gone?"

"I will," Bartholomew said and turned to the bird, who had taken another step toward him. "Don't do it."

"I will leave lesson plans for you, too," the Professor told the boy.

With lowered brows, Zander stared back at him. "How long will you be gone?"

"It probably depends on when the next train traveling east leaves," Annabelle said.

Qing had a tendency to come back to the magician when he was disappointed, and that could be where the Professor got the idea that Celwyn spoiled him. As the magician listened to the conversation, he stroked Qing's silky feathers. Celwyn had discovered that if he sat quietly and left a finger on the bird's neck, in his fancy, he could feel the mechanical workings inside. The magician wondered if he could do the same with Kang. All he knew about his mechanical friend was that he had been made in the 1500s, and when they ran fast, such as when escaping from enemies, Kang wasn't even winded.

"Zander, would you go and ask Ricardo for a pitcher of lemonade for us, please?" Celwyn assumed he would also take the time to request a cookie.

As soon as he was out of the room, Celwyn swept a hand at the wall beside the armoire. A holograph of a vintage train painted shiny black became superimposed on the wall. They could clearly see "*Elizabeth*" in beautiful gold script across the nose of the locomotive. Steam from the engine filled the parlor, and the floor vibrated. In front of the engine, a ghostly image of Kang seemed relaxed as he talked with Celwyn.

"Subtle, Jonas." Kang rolled his eyes.

It had been six months since Celwyn had enhanced the train with magic, and he would need to do little to reinforce the charms of the majestic machine now. She consisted of several cars that a visitor would pass through, eventually finding the well-appointed kitchen, refrigeration and water tanks, crew quarters and storage, and finally, the coal bins and locomotive.

"Of course. I propose we take the *Elizabeth* to Singapore." Celwyn heard Zander running back up the hall and waved a hand. The image faded away. As the boy entered the room and jumped into Patrick's lap, the magician told them, "It will be much faster than a regular train with many stops and layovers. And I promise it will be much more entertaining." He closed his eyes, imagining some things they would encounter.

Professor Kang laughed. "You don't say."

"I can only hope you won't take undue chances." Annabelle's brows drew together, and she frowned at each of them equally.

Celwyn opened his eyes at her. "Would I do—"

"Stow it, Jonas." Kang still laughed.

Bartholomew had been quiet, and now he said, "I can understand why I should remain here to continue Master Zander's schooling, but I can also provide reasons I should go with you."

"Perhaps I can clear this up." Celwyn asked Patrick, "Are you stationed in Prague permanently? Could you remain here to protect Annabelle and Zander?"

Patrick puffed out his chest. "I would consider it my duty. I hadn't told anyone yet, but next week I officially leave the Queen's army for good." He saw his betrothed open her mouth in consternation and rushed to say, "It was to be a surprise."

With a twinkle in his eye, Celwyn told Bartholomew, "Then it appears you are able to accompany us, and we will once again have many adventures."

The big man rubbed his hands together and turned to Annabelle and Patrick. "We'll leave the protection spell from Francesca in place. You'll also have Edward and the house staff."

"Oh no." Kang's expression turned to one of alarm. "We'll have to leave Chef Lucien behind."

Bartholomew frowned. "I'll find a new chef tomorrow … and kitchen and porter staff."

"While you do, I'll visit the train yard and arrange for a conductor and assistants." Kang added, "We'll need supplies too."

"The train will have to be readied. She has been sitting for months." Celwyn held a hand up. "We have a great deal to do, my friends." He watched as Qing flew to the ceiling to soar around the room, his form of celebration. He landed beside Annabelle and squawked in her face.

She covered her earrings. "You *will* take that damn bird with you."

"Aunt Annabelle cursed!" Zander shouted.

Chapter 3

EDWARD SMOOTHED HIS LONG MUStache, tilted his hat over his face, and leaned back atop the carriage to wait while Celwyn and the automat crossed the train yard to the *Elizabeth*.

"I've missed both Elizabeths."

"I have, also," the magician said as they gazed at the train. "It is nearly sundown. Let us walk through her before we must return."

"I hear we are having Trout Almondine for dinner." Kang climbed the stairs into the car.

Celwyn joined him and once again admired their train. To the left of the entrance door, stained glass lamps graced the ornate bar beside the oversized globe. Persian rugs lay under sofas and chairs, inviting visitors to sit and enjoy the view out the windows. To the right was their work and game table under a wall of maps. At the far end of the room, a well-polished dining room table awaited them. A glass observation bubble covered most of the ceiling. The entire car spoke of comfort and civility. The magician had remade the train from a derelict, and although old-fashioned, she remained most handsome.

"I want to move the pianoforte back here for our journey."

The Professor nodded. "I'll need help to pack and move my texts over also. You may not be aware of it, but I found a wonderful bookseller in town."

"I am," Celwyn said. "The bookseller's name is Ezekiel. He thinks you should read more classics."

The magician chuckled at Kang's expression and followed him across the room. They wandered down the hall toward the classroom and cabins, and as they entered the first room, Celwyn pointed to the dolls and stuffed animals on the shelves. "We should make a decision about Telly's things before we depart."

"I agree." Kang sighed. "Annabelle, Bartholomew, and Zander need to visit here and take what they want to remember her by."

"Excellent suggestion. Do..."

Celwyn held an arm in front of Kang and pointed toward the area in front of the beds.

"Those are not ours."

Several trunks lay before the children's beds, and another larger trunk had been propped against Annabelle's bed.

"We should have considered locking the train." Kang backed out of the room and continued down the hall. Celwyn remained in the classroom and examined the trunks, thinking there seemed to be enough of them for several people.

Kang returned, saying, "Nothing was disturbed in Bartholomew's room, or yours or my old compartments."

"I imagine whoever owns these trunks found the crews' quarters too basic for their needs. But we'd better check." As he left to do so, the magician called out to Kang, "This large trunk looks familiar."

When they met again in the cabin, Celwyn reported, "Someone made an attempt to fry eggs in the galley, but there is no other activity."

Kang stood again and approached the window, inspecting the pedestrians across the yard. Satisfied he saw nothing untoward, he pulled the largest case away from the wall and lifted the lid. "Yes, I recognized one of the trunks. Let's look inside this one."

Celwyn removed a slinky diaphanous shirt with tiny diamonds studded around the collar. Kang shook out a fluffy transparent nightgown with ruffles.

"Prince Leo has the most outlandish taste in his attire." Kang held up a purple boa. "I recognize this from when he traveled with us."

"Indeed. Look at this." Celwyn dangled a pair of high-heeled pink boots in the air.

"Since he is your acquaintance, what do you intend to do about him?"

"We'll return here after dinner." Celwyn imagined his expression could be interpreted as rather forbidding. "And surprise Prince Leo."

Chapter 4

AS THEY APPROACHED THE *ELIZABETH* later that evening, the Professor asked, "Do you think Patrick and Annabelle will hold it against us if we borrow Chef Lucien for the trip? We would bring him back."

"They would be annoyed." Celwyn clapped him on the back. "Just as I once made a copy of you, I could make a copy of Chef Lucien to leave behind. But it wouldn't last very long, and it wouldn't be capable of cooking."

"I remember. That effigy made me nervous, and I had to hide it from Bartholomew." Kang shuddered as he stepped over pieces of wood and around several empty crates. "You should also know that he reports he is having trouble finding a chef for our journey."

As they climbed aboard the train, Celwyn threw a limited amount of light around the dining room to verify Prince Leo had not yet arrived. Kang lit a candle and headed down the hall to check the cabins while the magician examined the kitchen and other cars. They met again in the dining room and settled down to wait. The magician waved a hand, blocking the windows to outside viewers.

"I have an alarm set out in front." He pointed to a fountain pen on the bar counter that he'd stood upright. "If anyone approaches, we'll know of it."

Kang looked at his pocket watch. "It is nearly ten o'clock. When is Edward returning for us?" He finished pouring drinks and handed a glass to the magician.

"Two hours. If I remember correctly, Prince Leo retires early. It shouldn't be too much longer."

They had just begun another whiskey when the fountain pen clattered to the floor.

"I believe we're about to have company." The magician dissolved the light beside them and removed the block on the windows. Two shadows approached the train, one as short as a child and round, the other a bit taller than Kang and willowy. Prince Leo's voice reached them.

"...it is only for another day or two—"

Prince Leo entered first, waddling across the darkened room and turning on the light. He froze.

A large, muscular tiger sat on its haunches in front of the dwarf, nearly at eye level. It lifted its head, and a low growl rumbled in its throat. Prince Leo yelped and then saw Celwyn.

"Jonas!" He stumbled backward into the wall.

The cat stood, and its feral breath washed over them as its tail swished the air.

"Jonas, I can explain..." Prince Leo whined.

The dwarf's companion stepped into the shadows, ready to run.

"I wouldn't leave if I were you," Celwyn said in warning. "Who is this, Leo? Ask them to remove their hood so that we can be properly introduced. Or I will." The magician gestured, and every light inside the car blazed to life. The tiger was gone.

Prince Leo's companion faced Celwyn, and a steady pale hand threw back the hood, revealing a young woman with a patrician nose and heavy brows. Her cropped black hair barely reached the top of her jacket, and she appeared to be wearing men's trousers.

The dwarf collapsed in a chair.

"Mary Giovanna Fioria." She turned to regard Kang. In a voice full of disdain, she asked, "Who are you?"

"To begin with, we are the owners of this train upon which you are trespassing." Celwyn studied Prince Leo. "You look a bit, ah ... distressed, Leo."

Sweat dripped off the man's chin, and the shirt under his arms appeared damp.

"*I do*? Jonas, you know that was terrifying and unnecessary." He shuddered. "Mary, this is Mr. Jonas Celwyn and Professor Xiau Kang. Months ago, they kindly brought me to Prague on this train." Turning back to Celwyn, he tried an ingratiating smile. "It would be a natural assumption that you wouldn't mind if I visited my accommodations again."

Kang snorted. “It appears to be more than a visit; otherwise, you'd be staying in a hotel.”

“Astute as usual, my friend.” The magician nodded at Kang. “Prince Leo must still be running from the Russians and using the *Elizabeth* to hide in.”

Mary Giovanna's stare at Prince Leo indicated she would shoot him if the Russians didn't.

The Professor saw her reaction. “Confirmed.”

Tonight, Prince Leo wore a white vest, lavender shirt, red boots, and a bright orange boa; the Russians wouldn't have trouble recognizing him. Leo straightened his cuffs and, with a snake oil salesman's charm, attempted to smooth over the situation. “That is not a criminal offence. A trifle. I would accept a glass of that whiskey, and Mary Giovanna would also.”

The magician gestured for the young woman to sit on the sofa next to the dwarf.

“Would you like something other than whiskey, Miss?”

“I prefer wine, but there isn't any...”

Celwyn brought up a bottle where there hadn't been one and poured a glass. As he handed it to her, he sent a whiskey glass to Prince Leo without touching it. The woman's eyes widened as she tracked the glass, but she didn't say a word. The magician watched her a moment more and then resumed his seat next to Kang.

“Now that you are comfortable Leo, tell me how close the Russians are.” When the man began to shake his head, the magician told him, "Don't make me scare the information out of you."

Prince Leo hesitated.

Kang asked, "Why don't you give them back their rubies? Then they would leave you alone."

"I tried, and they shot at me." The dwarf's lips tightened. "I wish to heaven I'd never taken the damn things. There is a price on my head, for some reason."

As Celwyn listened to him, he entered Maria Giovanna's thoughts, a much quicker way of finding out her story and status. He'd already eliminated the obvious guess that she was a prostitute, mostly because of how she was dressed. As he explored, the magician shook his head at life's circumstances. He always enjoyed surprises.

Kang tried again to reason with their guest.

"Could you answer Jonas' question, please? How likely are the Russians to attack?"

Prince Leo wiggled a hand back and forth. "I don't know."

"Damnation! That means they are probably following you around town and think you still communicate with us." Celwyn glared at him. "This could endanger everyone at Tellyhouse." If Bartholomew had been there, he would have had a few choice words for the state of affairs.

Mary Giovanna regarded Prince Leo like she would a pile of manure.

"So, it is Russians this time?" Her voice rose.

Celwyn's smile broadened when Prince Leo tried to explain himself, even looking to the magician for support.

"Now, Mary—"

"Shut up!" she spit at him.

"But—"

"Why do you *do* such dangerous things?" Mary Giovanna demanded. "I came here to visit you, not be chased through the streets or be shot at and knifed!"

Although amusing to watch the dwarf squirm under his daughter's wrath, Edward and the carriage had just pulled up in front of the *Elizabeth*. "We must depart." While Kang finished his drink, Celwyn shook down his pant legs. "It was nice meeting you, Miss, although as Prince Leo's daughter, I can only imagine the difficult and embarrassing predicaments in which you've found yourself embroiled."

Mary Giovanna's mouth fell open.

Prince Leo expostulated, spittle flying as he swiveled between his daughter and the magician, "Now Jonas—"

"Ah." Kang nodded. "Much more interesting than my guesses."

"How did you know?" She glared.

"I'll tell you later," Prince Leo said as Celwyn and Kang crossed to the door. The magician turned.

"You might want to pack up and find a hotel, Leo. Beginning tomorrow, there will be deliveries and various people visiting this train." He stared at the dwarf. "The *Elizabeth* departs Prague in two days."

When they had settled into the coach for the ride home, Celwyn said, "Mary Giovanna is a complex young woman."

"Oh?"

"I feel sorry for her, having Prince Leo as a father."

Kang laughed. "At least she can enhance her wardrobe as needed."

"Ha. An interesting tidbit for you: she is an actress by trade. A thespian. From my brief glimpse of her thoughts, I do not know if she has been successful or not." He considered Kang with amused speculation. "If you are in a betting mood, we could discuss the chances Leo will want to go along with us on our travels. If so, he will take Mary Giovanna with him."

"Why?"

"He won't leave her behind in the sights of the Russians."

Kang puffed on his pipe. "As I've often noted, my life is never dull in your company, Jonas." Qing poked his head out of Celwyn's collar and hacked at the smoke. Kang ignored him. "What else did you learn from Prince Leo's daughter?"

"Quite a bit," Celwyn replied. "She is Leo's only child. Years ago, she was arrested for public nudity several times. Perhaps an adventure by train to get away from her problems is what she needs."

"Public nudity?"

"So it seems."

Qing started a metallic tapping on the coach window as they drove up the street to Tellyhouse.

The magician patted the bird's head but didn't stop the bird concert as he said, "I have a luncheon scheduled tomorrow with Jules Verne, the author. You almost met him last night at the Opera House." As they pulled up the circular driveway to the front of Tellyhouse, he opened his collar, and Qing climbed inside. "Bartholomew has errands and can't join us. Would you care to?"

Chapter 5

A FEW MINUTES PAST ONE O'CLOCK the next day, Kang asked, "Is Mr. Verne a good friend?"

"Earl Grey, please," Celwyn requested of their baby-faced waiter. To Kang, he said, "An acquaintance, mostly."

The Hotel Marlborough's dining room displayed the conservative, old Continental atmosphere of white tablecloths, solemn waiters, graceful draperies, and well-polished silver. In an alcove near the entrance, an elegant woman played a viola, and the music floated like errant flowers in the wind above the hushed tones and murmurs of the diners. Across the room, a table of expensively dressed women huddled amid whispers and the occasional furtive look over the fox furs on their shoulders. One of Celwyn's talents included reading lips—a highly useful habit when he couldn't be close enough to enter minds. It was only later, much to his chagrin, that he found out the Professor could read lips also.

Kang spied where his attention had stopped and raised a brow in inquiry.

"Suffragettes from New York, Bern, and Seville. They are discussing women's rights. Thankfully in English." Celwyn read more. "I believe their table is a cauldron of unrest. The next few years should be lively."

"Not only in America, now that their civil war has stopped. I hear things are becoming interesting in England and France also."

"Indeed."

"By the way, if we settle the issue of our chef later today, we will be able to depart on our journey tomorrow." Kang checked the entrance of the restaurant for their luncheon companion. "I have promised to bring back a geisha doll for Annabelle, and for Zander, a toy monkey. He would prefer the real thing."

"Of course, he does. I will miss our charge. He is growing into a fine young man. Where is Verne?" He glanced out the door again. "Regardless, I think I have resolved the problem of finding a chef for our journey."

"Oh? You know what I think of your effigies."

"Ricardo." The magician waited for the Professor's reaction. Celwyn grinned with him. "Mrs. Thomas will find it easier to replace him than Chef Lucien, and he is already very experienced."

Kang sipped water slowly. "A suggestion. I would enlist Annabelle to tell Mrs. Thomas of our choice;

the reaction will be less noisy." After Celwyn's shrug, he asked, "What can you tell me about Verne?"

Celwyn pursed his lips. "A bit of an odd duck. Prolific and popular writer. His son hates him; why, I don't know." He tapped his spoon on the table for a moment and thought. "What I do wonder about is the man's source of inspiration."

"Because of the extraordinary details ... and the science ... behind his stories? I've read some of it."

"Yes."

A heavyset waiter pushed an elaborate dessert cart by them. It stopped at a neighboring table. "Temptation, temptation. The torte looks delicious," Kang said with the same admiration as if he'd seen a well-endowed woman in angel wings.

The magician leaned closer to the cart. "I disagree. The trifle looks like it would melt in my mouth."

"Jonas!"

A compact older man wearing a tailored grey suit, shrewd blue eyes behind spectacles, and well-tended and curled mustaches arrived. The maître d pulled out his chair, and once seated, the author beamed at them.

"Please introduce us, Jonas."

"Professor Xiau Kang, may I present Mr. Jules Verne?" Celwyn nodded at the author. "You should know that the Professor and I will be departing from Prague tomorrow for the Far East. I'm pleased that you and he have an opportunity to meet under such a congenial atmosphere."

"I'm honored." Verne studied Kang with one brow up.

His scrutiny went on long enough for Celwyn to interrupt it. "What brings you to Prague, Jules?"

"What? Oh. Research for my new novel. I am particularly interested in the secrets within Prague Castle." His eyes twinkled like jewels in the sunlight that streamed through the restaurant's mullioned windows. "I believe there are many hidden rooms and secrets in the castle." He continued to inspect Kang like a particularly fine bug under glass. "What is the purpose of your journey east?"

Celwyn coughed a somewhat oblique reminder to Kang to be discreet. He hadn't told him yet of Verne's network of reporters and even nosier publishers, not to mention Verne's reputation as a superior gossip as bad as any Fleet Street informant.

Kang signaled their waiter. "My purpose is to visit friends and sample a variety of cuisines." To the waiter, he asked, "By chance, do you have quail today?"

After they had ordered, Verne sampled the wine, eyed Celwyn like a horse that he didn't know whether to place a bet on and finally said, "Through friends, I heard of a most unusual occurrence at the Opera House a few days ago." He scowled. "I wish I hadn't left before the intermission."

"What did you hear?" Celwyn was beginning to understand Kang's point about the cost of his flamboyant tendencies. Before, when the magician became notorious, he left town. Sometimes, he left inventive and surprising momentos for his pursuers. Yet, because of his alliances with everyone at Tellyhouse, he enjoyed his new situation and the people in it.

Verne patted his lips with his napkin and didn't meet his eye. The magician immediately suspected Verne of hiding something.

"My good friend, the publisher of the Česká Novina, reports last night there was a grand display of magic. Of vampires, of music, and drama. On top of the Opera House dome, they found burned skeletons in an odd-looking iron net. They were identified as vampires. However, my friend seemed short on details." He turned to the magician sitting inches away and looked him in the eye. "You wouldn't know anything about it, would you?"

Kang snickered into his sleeve and blinked as innocently as a preacher squatting in front of a still.

"I'm sure your publisher acquaintance will investigate further." The magician shrugged.

Verne studied Celwyn openly. "As you say, he will do so. By the way, are you traveling on the *Eastern Star*? If so, you may want to adjust your plans: it does not depart for at least another week. And I believe it is stopping to the south in Vienna after it departs Prague."

"We'll keep that in mind," Kang said.

Their entrées arrived, and by the time they had ordered their coffees, trifle, and tortes, the magician and automat made sure Verne knew as little about their journey as possible. Like Kang said, they did not need the notoriety, and they still hadn't decided what they would do about the Singapore police once they arrived. It would be best to slip into town and slip out again just as quietly.

"Interesting chap," Kang remarked as they crossed Roska Street to where Edward waited with the carriage.

"He certainly was curious about the Opera House." Celwyn doffed his hat to Edward and climbed into the carriage after the automat. "Interesting. He even knew details about what they found in the net on top of the spire."

"I'm sure it was aromatic." Kang made a face.

"Did you notice that Verne wanted to know about you even more? By sundown, he'll have asked a dozen people about you and perhaps even have his newspaper friends send out inquiries."

"It is more serious than that: if the story is carried in other newspapers, in time, it could reach Singapore." The Professor studied the scene outside as they bumped along, passing a speeding carriage going the other way. "The police there could become curious." Kang sighed. "We need to stop him."

Celwyn looked outside to be sure Verne, or his publisher friends, hadn't hired anyone to follow them. "As long as he doesn't know about either of the Elizabeths, he will not cause us difficulties or be able to follow us."

Chapter 6

AN HOUR LATER, THEY PULLED INTO the train yard and up to the *Elizabeth,* where they found a great deal of activity. A team of overall-clad men and mechanics led by a large, white-haired man sporting fluffy sideburns walked the length of the train. Kang identified the man as their new conductor, Hannibal Smith. He also pointed out two of the much younger muscular men, the twins Abe and Andy, who would function as the conductor's assistants.

"I added a third assistant to help with the coal. See the taller one with the large nose and a slight limp?" Kang pointed. "That is Ludvik. He will also drive the train as needed or work as a porter. The train will be able to keep a good pace, and everyone will have longer rest periods from shoveling coal."

From beside him, Celwyn studied the scene and nodded. "Good approach. Who are they?" He pointed to an even younger man who unloaded vegetables and other foodstuffs from a cart.

"I think that is someone sent by Mrs. Thomas. I haven't been introduced, but Bartholomew pointed out the heavier blonde-haired one as Jackson, our new porter." The automat scanned the yard. "I don't see the third one. His name is Stephan, which is all I know at this point."

"We should make their acquaintance."

"Agreed." Kang indicated another cart containing more trunks and the pianoforte. "Are you keeping the instrument in the bar area? It would be wonderful to hear it in the evenings."

"Possibly. Remember our wager? Let's find Prince Leo."

They crossed the yard and entered the *Elizabeth's* dining room. As expected, Mrs. Thomas had sent over a small army of housekeepers who fluttered everywhere, tidying and dusting. None of them spoke English, and Czech was not one of his languages. Celwyn lifted his hat, bowed to them, and trailed Kang down the hall toward the sleeping compartments.

The door to the classroom and children's bedrooms stood open.

Every one of Prince Leo and his daughter's trunks still lay where they had been before. The chaos of clothing had been tidied, and from Zander's bed came delicate snoring reminiscent of a tiny forest animal with a stuffy nose. Celwyn kicked the bed.

"Jonas. Professor." Prince Leo sat up, rubbing his eyes. "I hoped that you'd return."

Celwyn relaxed in one of the chairs and crossed his legs. Kang did the same.

"Leo." The magician trained a stare on him. Seen in daylight, the man had changed little since they parted ways after arriving in Prague. The goatee looked new; the slicked-back hair and small, shifty eyes were old.

Prince Leo's feet dangled off the bed, exposing striped socks. Above them, he wore a rather wrinkled bright blue shirt and trousers and an orange rope tie that would make an excellent cat toy. Celwyn wondered how he could sleep in something so garish. The dwarf straightened his tie and patted his hair.

"To be sure. I have a proposal for you." Prince Leo's smile displayed an inordinate amount of goodwill.

Celwyn raised a brow at Kang.

"Really?" The Professor removed his wallet, extracted a note, and handed it over. "You probably cheated."

The dwarf's expression faded a bit like someone had pulled on the strings holding his smile in place. "What was that for?"

"I bet the Professor that you would want to go with us."

"Humorous, Jonas." Prince Leo caught himself, realizing he needed to remain in the magician's good graces. "However, it is true. Mary Giovanna and I wish to accompany you on your journey."

Celwyn got to his feet, pocketed his winning note, and headed to the door. "We have other errands." He did not plan to make this easy for the annoying imp.

"Where is your daughter?" Kang asked as they walked back to the dining room. Prince Leo trotted to keep up.

"Shopping for warmer clothing. It is nearly fall, and who knows how cold it will be where we're going?"

"You are assuming that you will travel with us." Celwyn held the door leading to the next car open.

"You wouldn't leave me here." The dwarf paled. "I'm—we're in danger!"

"Yes, I would."

"But Jonas," he whined.

"Does your daughter actually wish to journey with us?" Kang asked as he leaned against the sofa, out of the way of the maid sweeping the floor. She finished and headed outside with a dustbin.

Prince Leo shrugged and concentrated on tying his shoe. "She knows it is hazardous to remain here."

"Because of you." Celwyn crossed the room and inspected the fresh supply of whiskey and glasses above the bar. He aimed a thumb out the main window. "There she is now."

As the young woman entered the dining room, Kang and Prince Leo met her to take the parcels she carried. Celwyn noted that she wore a traditional dress and bustle, along with a simple, plain hat.

She regarded the three of them as warily as if they were jurists and she was on trial.

The rest of Mrs. Thomas' cleaning crew must have moved to the kitchen, judging from the noise emanating from the next room. "Sit here, my dear." Prince Leo patted the spot next to him on the sofa. "How did your shopping go?"

Celwyn produced a tray of coffee in front of them. Without hesitation, Kang poured and handed her a cup.

Mary Giovanna eyed them and then sipped. "It went well." To her father, she said, "What..."

He took her other hand. "I hadn't told you yet, but I've asked our friends here if we could accompany them on their journey. They are traveling east, as you know."

Prince Leo had lied when he said she wanted to go with them.

Her eyes, dark and heavily lashed, searched Celwyn and Kang for clues. "Thank you, but no." Then she switched back to her father. "Why are you telling me this?

"Mary, dear..." the dwarf began.

"A pet name won't influence my decision." She faced Celwyn and Kang. "Again, thank you for the offer, but I decline."

Beads of sweat decorated Prince Leo's domed head like a little crown. He held his hands out in supplication. "You can't stay here; it isn't safe."

"Why not?" She looked down her nose at him. "Because of your activities?"

"Please. Jonas says we are welcome to join his expedition."

He did? Celwyn thought but said nothing: graciousness when dealing with the fairer sex ruled.

They all watched as the girl who had been sweeping finished and studiously ignored them before continuing to the kitchen.

"Our route will be finalized this evening." The magician consulted his watch. "It is nearly three in the afternoon, and we must be on our way." As he got to his feet, he briefly entered Mary Giovanna's mind, this time finding opinions of costumes, jewelry, other actors, anger at her father, and very clear memories of stage scenes and her dislike of various plays.

Father and daughter continued to argue as he and Kang exited the train and crossed the yard to Edward and the waiting carriage. Kang eyed Celwyn. "There's another reason for your generosity, is there not?"

"You know me well." The magician tipped his hat to Edward and opened the carriage door.

With his hands on his hips, Kang blocked him from entering the coach.

"You plan to draw the Russians out, perhaps even entice them to follow us."

"Yes. It will guarantee that they do not stay behind in Prague to bother Annabelle and Patrick while they hunt Leo." He moved the automat out of his way without touching him.

"Another reason is a spot of fun, I presume," Kang surmised as he followed the magician into the carriage and settled into the seat. "On a more pleasant note, I spoke with Ricardo. He has agreed to become our new chef."

Celwyn rubbed his hands together as they drove out of the train yard. All their plans were coming together nicely. "Most pleasing news."

"Mrs. Thomas will be highly annoyed about that, but she will forgive us."

"Indeed." The magician tapped the glass and signaled Edward to hurry. "We should probably be there when she finds out."

Chapter 7

DAWN BROUGHT LIGHT SHOWERS and the first hints of fall to the city. He would miss Prague. By nine, Celwyn could smell the change in the air as he descended the steps of Tellyhouse and joined Bartholomew in the carriage.

"Good morning." The big man smoked a cigar and stifled a yawn.

"You look tired, my friend." Celwyn regarded him with an amused and sardonic eye. "Perhaps from a last-minute visit to the witches?"

"Droll, Jonas."

The local coven was paid handsomely to protect Tellyhouse, and they thought of Bartholomew as an adorable lusty toy when he visited with their fee.

Celwyn tapped his pockets, one dedicated to a tea supply and the other for his newly delivered supply of peyote buttons. Mrs. Thomas had been exceptionally curious about the box when it arrived from his source in Santa Fe, tied with dirty string and stamped "*Archeology Specimens. Do not open.*"

Bartholomew sighed, and the buttons across his coat threatened to go flying. At nearly seven feet tall and built solidly, the big man commanded respect from their enemies. In contrast, several times Celwyn had witnessed his friend's kind heart and had a feeling that even the most dastardly of villains would fare well unless they threatened someone Bartholomew loved.

He frowned at Celwyn.

"You should know that I found a carriage watching the house earlier. I chased it off."

With fear and even more anger, Celwyn asked, "Who was it?"

"I'm not sure, but from the look of the men, I suspect Russians." The big man lifted his hands and let them fall again. "My guess is they followed one of us here. God damn Prince Leo."

Celwyn verified no strangers lurked nearby, taking his time. "When we leave town, the Russians will also."

"This situation is unacceptable. What if they get beyond our security?" The big man looked mad enough to spit.

"The protection spells from the witches will hold."

"Hopefully." Bartholomew's glower could have lit a campfire.

"As a solution, I have been promoting the rumor that the rubies will leave Prague this morning." Celwyn blinked at him innocently.

A slow smile spread across the big man's face. "You want them to follow us."

"Yes. I suggest that we not speak of this, except to Xiau, until we're out of this city. I've left Edward and Patrick specific instructions on what to beware of."

Bartholomew nodded. Celwyn also calmed down as he gazed back at Tellyhouse, once more enjoying the tall windows and Georgian architecture. During last night's dinner, he'd overheard the enthusiasm in Annabelle's voice as she described the things she planned for the house.

However, time was a wasting.

"What do you think the Professor is doing? Looking for more books? I'm anxious to begin our journey."

Bartholomew smiled. "Either searching for one of his papers or in the kitchen holding a wake because we're leaving Chef Lucien behind."

"I think the latter." Celwyn tamped tobacco into his pipe and lit it. "You do realize the irony of your personal journey? When we met in Baghdad, you were on your way to Paris. Now, we're heading east again to Singapore." He puffed a moment. "Do you ever wish you had continued to Paris back then?"

The big man spread his hands open. "And miss your adventures?" He laughed. "Good grief, Jonas, you attract criminals like bees to honey." He stopped laughing and studied him. "What are you thinking?"

The magician verified Edward tended the horses and then opened his hand. On the seat beside Bartholomew, a toy-size train chugged across the velvet toward a squat set of mountains. The gold lettering of the *Elizabeth* could clearly be seen on the nose of the locomotive. From within the train, tiny glints of red light shone through the windows. A miniature Bartholomew rested a rifle out of one of the windows.

"The royal rubies that Prince Leo absconded with, I presume?" Bartholomew's eyes lit up in anticipation. "You're saying we might have a spot of action if attacked."

The magician nodded and dissolved the scene. "If the Professor would hurry, we will get underway."

"Uncle Celwyn! Bartholomew!"

Zander raced down the front steps and across the gravel with Kang, Annabelle, and Patrick close behind. He bounced into the carriage and hugged Celwyn. After a moment, the boy raised a teary face. "Please don't go." He buried his face in the magician's coat. Celwyn patted his back and inhaled deeply so he wouldn't cry, too. Qing's head popped out of Celwyn's collar and would have pecked the lad's nose if Celwyn hadn't stopped him.

Bartholomew patted Zander on the back, too. "We will be gone about four months and return before Christmas."

Zander climbed onto Bartholomew's lap and looked from one of them to the other. "I should go with you!"

Celwyn laughed and ruffled his hair as Annabelle leaned into the carriage and told him, "Young man, I need you here."

From over her shoulder, Patrick smiled at them. "I envy you this adventure, but after the war, a nice rest in Prague with my beautiful fiancé seems a better choice."

"It better be." Annabelle tried to sound stern but ended up kissing him. "All right, Master Zander, time to climb out and let the Professor in."

"I know." Zander swiped at his eyes as he backed out again.

The Professor scooped him up. "You will be surprised how soon it is until we return. And I know Elizabeth will love you as we do."

That did it; Celwyn had to look away and dry his eyes.

Patrick glanced back at Tellyhouse. "If it were me, I would get going. Mrs. Thomas is still mightily annoyed because you are taking Ricardo with you. I hear he is already on the train."

With a furtive look over his shoulder, Kang quickly handed Zander to Patrick and scampered into the carriage.

"I predict Ricardo will be a fine chef in his own right. And I volunteer to taste all of his creations along the way." The automat tried to sound virtuous, but Bartholomew grinned and elbowed him.

"Be sure you take care of everyone, Zander," the magician said.

"I will, Sir." Despite his sadness at being left behind, the boy couldn't suppress a giggle. "Uncle Celwyn."

Twenty minutes later, they embraced Edward and shook his hand, bidding him adieu.

As Celwyn unloaded their final bag out of the carriage, he stood in the middle of the train yard to scrutinize the *Elizabeth*. To the magician, she represented an elegant example of comfort, and, of course, good company. Except possibly for their guests, Prince Leo and his daughter.

"Do you know much about our new crew, other than what you initially told me?" Kang asked Bartholomew.

"Nothing except..." he indicated a plump, hamster-like individual who peered at them from the stairs of the train, "...that must be Stephen, the one we didn't see earlier."

The showers began again, driving the hamster inside. Almost immediately, another porter approached, his military gait as evident and precise as his speech. Like a wayward caterpillar, a thin mustache decorated his upper lip. The magician controlled the urge to make that impression more real.

"Gentlemen, I am Jackson, your porter. Professor? Allow me to take your bag." He handed them umbrellas and swiveled. "If you will follow me, please."

"Shall we?" Celwyn said as they tailed him onto the train.

Beyond the *Elizabeth,* a moderate-sized crowd of spectators had gathered, peering through a bank of smoke from engines that rumbled, heralding their departure. Even though she wore a veil, Celwyn felt certain that Mrs. Karras stood among the crowd, unsmiling and watching them.

The magician looked down and up again, trying for control.

Mrs. Karras was gone.

He cursed. "Damn vampire."

Chapter 8

As he waved a final goodbye to Edward, Celwyn ascended the steps and inhaled with satisfaction. They were finally underway. The steel wheels screeched, metal on metal, and the train started to move. With a jolt, the familiar bump and sway of the *Elizabeth* began.

"A toast to our journey," Kang called from the bar. He handed out whiskies, and they touched glasses as the train's whistle blew. Prince Leo entered the car from the kitchen wearing a cherry red suit and yellow boa, munching a carrot.

"Greetings, greetings everyone!" he said.

Bartholomew told Celwyn an aside, "His attire makes my eyes water."

Kang returned to the bar to pour another drink while Celwyn and Bartholomew occupied the chairs on each side of the man-sized globe, exchanging a tolerant look. Kang gazed beyond them, dropping the whiskey he just poured. He stared and quickly looked away.

Through the door from the sleeping car, Mary Giovanna walked toward them, naked as a jaybird.

"Oh my," the automat said as he knelt to retrieve the shards of glass.

Bartholomew shifted uneasily in his chair. "Jonas?"

The magician frowned. He hadn't encountered something like this before. Evidently, Prince Leo had.

"Really, Mary. I thought we'd agreed you would wear clothes on the train," he said. "Really, Mary."

She smiled like she was attending high tea at the palace and sat beside her father on the sofa, keeping her knees together in the prescribed manner of parlor etiquette. "Could I have a whiskey, too, please?" She folded her hands in her lap.

Kang looked at Celwyn and poured another glass.

Celwyn noted that in times of stress, of the three of them, he became the chosen spokesman.

"Miss, are you warm? We can open a window."

The train rumbled through a residential area in the Zizkov district, and the spire of St. Vitus Church could be seen ahead of them, around the next bend. Then there would be a crowded marketplace located very near the tracks. Knowing the inside of the train could be seen from outside, Celwyn lowered the shades for the entire car. He glared at Prince Leo.

"No, the temperature is very pleasant, thank you." She tilted her head and smiled at Bartholomew.

The dwarf tried again.

"Dear, I would appreciate it if you would put on one of those pretty frocks you bought yesterday. The blue one was quite becoming."

Bartholomew stared at his hands. Kang gulped whiskey and kept his eyes on his glass. The magician tapped the arm of his chair and waited.

"Oh, for god's sake," Mary Giovanna huffed. She dropped her glass in her father's lap and stalked out of the room toward the sleeper car.

When the door slammed, everyone breathed again.

"Leo," Celwyn asked, "what is this about?"

The dwarf pursed his lips.

"Don't lie to me," Celwyn warned him.

Again, sweat dotted Prince Leo's brow like tiny dew drops on a rose petal. He wiped it off with the end of his boa. "You need to understand."

Bartholomew sent the dwarf a disgusted glare. "Please explain it to us."

Celwyn noted the big man's opinion of Leo hadn't changed since their last encounter. The dwarf gazed longingly at the whiskey bottle. Celwyn brought it to him, poured, and sent it back to the bar. Without a naked woman in front of the windows, he opened the shades: he couldn't stand a dark room.

"Talk."

The train began the climb to Mount Kladno, the mountain overlooking the city. As they ascended, the clouds thickened, and the showers increased. The *Elizabeth* prudently blew her whistle in case another train descended from the other side of the mountain.

Prince Leo studied the contents of his glass as if looking for answers, then began pacing like a squat canary with a pointed beard.

He sighed. "I never married Mary Giovanna's mother, but at times I visited and sent money even though her family has been in Verona for hundreds of years and is obscenely wealthy."

"You'd think they would have bought her clothes at some point," Kang said and went back to his book.

Leo gave Kang a pained look. "Early on, I noticed a lack of respect in my daughter. I'd even wondered if I was truly her father." He stopped pacing long enough to verify the door between the cars remained closed. "I do not know for certain. Regardless, I have only seen her a handful of times since she came of age."

"Until Prague," Celwyn said.

The dwarf took off his boa and draped it over the bar.

"My, it is warm in here."

"Go on," Bartholomew told him.

"Last week, she arrived in Prague, out of the blue. A month before, she had written me back, which I found … surprising."

Kang asked, "Was she running from something?"

He shrugged. "No, not that I know of. She had been on stage in Vienna for months, and the play ended."

"Has it occurred to you that she may be affiliated with the Russians?" Kang asked.

Prince Leo blinked. He began licking his lips like a retriever after his dinner.

Celwyn blocked his trip to the windows and steered him back to the sofa.

"The Professor's question is of interest, but there is more, isn't there, Leo?"

"Yes." He checked the door again.

They had to lean close to hear him over the rumbling and clanking from the train.

"Her nickname at the theatre is 'Crazy Mary.'" Prince Leo swallowed several times. "In Rome, they found her lying next to a dead body in the catacombs. You know—the cemetery there. Other things have happened, but the nudity problem is relatively new."

"Why didn't you tell us about this before we departed?" Celwyn demanded.

"I was afraid you wouldn't take me with you." The dwarf grabbed the magician's hands. "Please, Jonas—they'll kill me if I stay in Prague."

The magician disengaged himself and rubbed his face. He had known the dwarf a long time and until now, had just been irritated at him. "All right." At this particular moment, he pitied him. "I propose we continue on our journey. Leo, you are responsible for the girl. Impress her with some examples of my displeasure if she should have the urge to appear nude again or do anything else rude."

"Or dangerous," Kang added.

The kitchen door opened, and Jackson, the muscular porter they had met earlier, pushed a cart through. He bowed.

"Good afternoon. Luncheon is ready."

"Excellent." Kang savored a bite of lamb. "I predict Ricardo will achieve great heights in the culinary world."

"Agreed. I love this sauce." Bartholomew dabbed his lips with his napkin. "Please pass the butter."

Mary Giovanna hadn't said a word since she joined them at the table. She was attired in a demure lace dress and had even added rouge to her cheeks. Her black eyes missed nothing as she sat between her father and Bartholomew at the end of the table.

Prince Leo lined up each piece of his silverware, hesitated, and addressed the Professor.

"How far will you be traveling?"

Kang finished a bite of fruit compote. "Unlike our journey here last year, we are in a bit of a hurry now. We have three helpers to shovel coal as needed and keep our speed steady. I will finalize the route soon."

"Excuse me." Stephen, the porter they hadn't formally met yet, moved between them, slopping coffee into their cups. Up close, he did little to dispel Celwyn's initial impression that he resembled a hamster. Of medium height, with a hunched stature and short dusty hair, he displayed unmemorable features. His English sounded perfect, but the magician suspected it wasn't his native language.

"It is good that you are traveling with us, Stephen. Where did you work before you joined our train?" Bartholomew asked.

"The Hotel Marlborough, and before that, I was at university in London."

A moment went by, then Bartholomew asked a question casually as if he didn't really care if the man answered.

"Why did you choose Prague?"

Celwyn had caught the connection to the hotel, as did Kang: Jules Verne was staying at the Marlborough.

"My aunt was ill," Stephen said as he finished the coffee service and prepared to leave the room. "She passed last month."

"I am so sorry." Mary Giovanna blinked her understanding at him.

Stephen seemed surprised as he raised his eyes to hers. "Thank you, Miss."

"Welcome aboard, Stephen," the magician said, wondering about their new crew member's intentions.

As they left the dining table, Prince Leo announced he had letters to write and requested that his daughter goes with him. The door to sleeping compartments closed behind them.

"Isn't it odd that we also met your friend, Mr. Verne, at the same hotel?" Kang asked as they settled in front of the windows.

"I noticed it too," Celwyn growled under his breath and glanced at Bartholomew. "You saw Mr. Verne at the Opera House the other night. He is an acquaintance of sorts. One of his habits is befriending reporters and cultivating publishers. Something we do not need."

The big man tapped his glass with an index finger. "Are we really that intriguing?"

"Yes. Jonas is." Kang teased the magician. It was a subject of an ongoing debate about which of them Jax had been after. There was no doubt who the vampires hated. "Especially after his Opera House performance the other night." The Professor continued and eyed the magician. "There is another possibility."

"Russians," Bartholomew guessed.

"It is possible. I made sure they knew of our departure and that we are taking Prince Leo with us," Celwyn said. "That reminds me. It is probably a good idea to find a few of our firearms and discreetly prepare for an attack."

"Before we reach Zlin?" Bartholomew asked as he crossed to the enormous map that covered the wall next to the windows. "They will want us isolated for an attack, and they'd have to stop the train to do so."

The Professor frowned. "I'll advise Prince Leo and his daughter to remain in their rooms with the windows closed."

Bartholomew sent a scowl toward the sleeping car and got to his feet. "Prince Leo should stop stealing." As he reached the kitchen door, he said, "I'll confer with Ricardo and give him a pistol."

"At least we will have drawn the Russians away from everyone at Tellyhouse," Kang said.

"Wouldn't it be interesting, not in a good way, if we have unintentionally brought a reporter or Russian criminal aboard?" the magician asked.

Kang rolled his eyes and headed to the sleeper car.

Chapter 9

FOR THE FIRST PART OF THE AFTERnoon, Celwyn kept Conductor Smith company in the cab of the locomotive. With enough white whiskers for a walrus and as rosy-cheeked and round-bellied as Saint Nick, the man looked the part as he pulled levers and called over his shoulder for more coal. He also watched the area around the tracks as they slowed into or out of each village. His predecessor last year had not handled the odd occurrences that befell them well and had quit them for London. Celwyn predicted that Smith would do much better.

Hour after hour, they passed through green fields, and in the far distance, the mountains grew closer. All the while, the Conductor maintained a running description of the destinations where he had skippered trains, including the planned southern route to Singapore.

"It isn't unheard of for trains to be stopped and robbed."

"Especially smaller ones, such as this one." Smith's grave expression indicated a personal experience.

"You have had that occur?"

The Conductor pointed to an old-fashioned Enfield Pattern rifle leaning in the corner.

"That is why I carry my little Lou Lou."

Celwyn felt better. "Good. We will also be prepared."

Smith blew the train's whistle as they slowed to cross a trestle and then resumed their speed. "If it were regular robbers, they would probably engineer a landslide to stop the train. But that isn't usually a good plan because after we crashed, they'd have a hell of a time finding valuables under tons of steel." He chomped on his cigar. "To avoid that, I need to be able to see a problem from miles away to have room to stop this train."

"On this route, is there a particular village they would wait in and attack as we slowed down going by?"

The Conductor shrugged. "Zlin, or between there and Murska Sobota, but they also might—hold on." He turned. "Andy, relieve Abe and get to shoveling!" Back to Celwyn, he said, "Sorry, those boys need to watch the level of coal."

"And then rest while the other shovels?"

"Yes."

"How long is it in between the times that they shovel?"

"Maybe twenty minutes ... if they pay attention and don't let it get low." Smith blew the *Elizabeth's* whistle before they passed a collection of cows and a now-alert shepherd who shook a fist at them. "Anyhow, if the robbers know the mountains ahead, they might block the tracks with trees or drop onto the train from other trees. But again, if they cause us to crash, they'd have a mess."

"I see," the magician said. "I'll be right back."

A few moments later, he found Bartholomew and Kang hunched over a chess game in the bar, twin rifles resting against their chairs.

"Have you ever shot a rifle?" he asked the automat.

Kang lifted both hands, palms up. "Once I tried. I didn't hit anything."

Bartholomew looked up. "Do we have a plan?"

"Yes." The magician sat beside them. "I'm going to make the assumption that we not only want to repel an attack but that we want to stop them from following us and Prince Leo."

"We could toss Prince Leo off the train when we find the Russians," Bartholomew said.

Kang studied him, trying to determine if he was serious, then half-smiled and turned back to Celwyn. "Exactly what did you tell the Russians before we left Prague?"

The magician smiled. "In several taverns they are known to frequent, I let it be known that Prince Leo and the rubies would leave the city before noon today, traveling southeast toward Judenburg."

"So that they would have time to get ahead of us and attack." The big man moved his knight forward. "Check."

Kang frowned and moved his knight to face the white knight.

Celwyn crossed to the map, saying, "The Conductor tells me the two most likely spots for an attack are Zlin or somewhere near Murska Sobota." He pointed. "Or they might make an attempt in one of the villages we go through if we're going slowly enough."

The Professor regarded Celwyn, squinting as if he could read his mind.

"What do you have planned?"

The magician glanced at the door leading to the sleeping compartments.

"Would you retrieve the rubies from Prince Leo's room while the Professor distracts him, please?" he asked Bartholomew. "I will plant the idea in Miss Giovanna's thoughts to observe Ricardo while he is making lunch. She fancies herself a gourmet and will embrace the opportunity."

The big man nodded. "Where are the rubies?"

"They were in the false bottom of his jewelry case, but I moved them to the base of the lamp on the desk." Celwyn checked his watch. "We have about twenty minutes before Zlin, gentlemen." He leaned forward and said, "With your help, here is what I intend to do."

Celwyn could have removed the rubies without any help, but Kang and Bartholomew had complained of not being able to participate, and he was always happy to demonstrate his cooperation.

The view out the *Elizabeth's* windows brightened as the clouds dispersed, and the sun shone over apple orchards mile after mile. Like the scene had been staged just for them, a long, straight stretch of tracks opened up before the *Elizabeth*. In the distance, slivers of the Dřevnice River could be seen before the foothills of the Tatra Mountains.

From his position beside Conductor Smith, Celwyn brought up a pair of binoculars. Although for a long distance he couldn't see any buildings or other structures, far ahead, something metal had glinted in the sunlight. Seconds more and he verified what he suspected.

He tapped Conductor Smith on the shoulder. "Stop the train, please."

With their earlier conversation on his mind, Smith moved fast as he flipped switches and pulled levers. "A complete stop will take several miles," he shouted over the scream of the brakes.

"Do your best, Sir. I believe the track is blocked ahead," Celwyn called back as he sprinted out of the cab toward the rear. To conserve his energy, the magician would let the brakes do as much of the work as possible before intervening.

As planned, Kang met him on the platform before the sleeping car. The wind nearly took Celwyn's hat off, and the screeching of the *Elizabeth's* brakes became continual. They climbed the metal ladder on the side of the car and crawled onto the roof. While the wind gusts tried to push them over the side, they also brought the fresh scent of the forests.

"What do you see?"

"Debris… great quantities of it," Kang said as he lowered his binoculars. "Will we stop in time?"

"I will be sure that we do." Celwyn watched the tracks in the distance. More of the debris became visible, and only minutes remained before impact. He asked, "Bartholomew is at the dining room windows?"

"Yes." The Professor wiggled onto his belly and raised his rifle. "He is positioned behind the shutters as planned. All of the crew have instructions to remain at their stations."

Celwyn turned and swept a hand from the front of the train to the rear, causing the shrieking of the brakes to escalate as they neared the mound of debris. Several wagons had been piled on the tracks, full of whatever the villains could find. Sweat beaded on his forehead as the magician braced himself, pulling at the air until the *Elizabeth* slowed still further. A minute more and she rolled forward and stopped. Clouds of steam enveloped the train, and her engines hissed. When the steam cleared, more than two score men holding rifles became visible on both sides of the tracks. Kang still lay prone beside the magician with his rifle tucked under his chin.

A bear of a man stepped forward, a long knife hanging from his belt to his knee. He smiled, and even from a distance, Celwyn confirmed that this was the Russian with the beard and bad teeth

Prince Leo had described with a moderate degree of terror. After seeing the devil in his face, Celwyn could understand why the dwarf had been fearfully eluding him for months.

Judging from their clothes, the other men appeared to be a mix of city and country hooligans; nevertheless, their rifles all looked alike.

"Where is he?" The man with the beard called out in a deep Russian accent.

Kang shouted, "What do you want?"

"Мудак! Send out the dwarf. Tell him to give back what he stole."

From his position atop the railcar, Celwyn wiggled his fingers. Curses and screams erupted from the attackers as their hands flamed and they dropped their weapons. One of them tried to pick up his rifle only to bellow again. Their leader gazed at the top of the train.

"Show yourself! Or are you a coward?"

With a smile, the magician popped a peyote button in his mouth and jumped to the ground. As he approached the Russian, the other rogues backed up.

Celwyn pointed, and the wagons of rubble in front of the train broke apart and transformed into sheep, small and fat, *baahhing* loudly as they scattered into the brush beside the tracks. At least half of the attackers crossed themselves and ran. The bearded Russian barked an order, and the rest subsided.

The magician stared at the *Elizabeth*. In seconds, the train shimmered and turned from black to a brilliant red. "Highly appropriate, wouldn't you say?" Celwyn asked as he approached to within a few feet of the Russian and tossed the pouch of rubies in the air, and caught it again, the royal Romanov crest clearly visible. He threw it upward again, where it hung suspended, then opened, a cascade of rubies trickling to the ground.

A brilliant flash of light covered them just as a loud *pop* came from close behind Celwyn. When he turned, the Russian drew his knife and ran the magician through.

Celwyn cried out and clutched his side. A fusillade of shots rang out from the train as Conductor Smith leaped from the cab, blasting a wide area with his rifle.

Blood gushed through Celwyn's fingers, and as the darkness closed in, he heard feet running, Bartholomew roaring, and then Kang caught him as he fell.

Chapter 10

"INTO THE TRAIN WITH HIM!" KANG bellowed. "Careful! Do not drop him." The automat pressed firmly on Celwyn's side as Abe and Andy carried him inside. Bartholomew met them and transferred the magician to the sofa. The big man knelt beside him.

"Get the train moving! Get us out of here!" Bartholomew yelled. Shots peppered the side of the car. As he looked at the magician, he whispered, "Is he dead?"

Kang said, "No. But—" He found Ricardo in front of the crowd by the kitchen door. "Bring hot water." He kept pressure on Celwyn's wound until he spied Prince Leo. "Get my bag from my room. Everyone move!"

Ricardo whirled and entered the kitchen. Mary Giovanna edged closer.

"May I help?"

Kang's voice broke as he peeled away the magician's coat and blood-soaked shirt. "Yes, tear up some sheets. Hurry!" Celwyn groaned as Leo rushed back into the room. Kang grabbed the bag from him and dug inside it. Bartholomew continued to hold the magician's hand and gasped when he saw the wound gushing blood again.

"Good God!"

Kang heard the dwarf's reaction as he worked. "It is bad, but there is … someone who can … repair this." He found a vial of smelling salts and shoved them under Celwyn's nose.

"Come on, Jonas—" Kang shook his shoulder. "Wake up!" He lifted the magician's head. "Breathe, damn it!"

Fresh blood gushed from the wound. Mary Giovanna handed Kang the bandages. In seconds, they were soaked through. She handed him more. Kang told Bartholomew, "Press firmly against his side while I," he held more smelling salts under Celwyn's nose, "get him conscious."

"Damn you, Jonas! Wake up!" Kang shouted in his face.

The magician groaned. Blood dribbled out of his mouth, but he opened his eyes and coughed.

Bartholomew leaned into his face and told him, "Heal yourself, Jonas."

"Stop the bleeding first," Kang said. "Your right side."

Celwyn's nose twitched, and he expelled a long sigh. Another shudder came from deep within him.

"The blood—it has stopped," Bartholomew said. He still held the bandages against the magician.

Kang's voice shook. "Good, Jonas. Now heal the cut; it is very deep." He peeled away the top layer of bandages. "I'll help you."

Bartholomew's hands trembled as he took the bandages from Kang. Beyond him, Mary Giovanna hovered close, her expression unreadable.

"Jonas, you are my friend. You must live," Bartholomew implored him in a whisper.

In the tomb-like quiet of the room, the ticking of the wall clock sounded loud.

Kang felt the skin on Celwyn's side and studied the wound from inches away. In a moment, he murmured, "He has the liver together." A second more, and he leaned even closer. With a fingertip, he examined the hole in the magician's side. "Ah." Kang sat back and finally smiled at Bartholomew. To Celwyn, he said, "You are nearly there, my friend. Almost." Kang used forceps to hold the flesh in place as it began to change color. From the kitchen came murmurs and whispers.

Kang eyed Bartholomew, who said, "They don't need to see this."

By the time the big man had herded everyone out of the room, Celwyn breathed a bit better. His eyes remained closed.

The Professor ran a gloved finger over the wound. Although an angry red color and somewhat bloody around the edges, the hole was closed, and the skin as smooth as if it had never been cut open.

Bartholomew rejoined him by the sofa and touched the magician's hand.

"You keep scaring me, Jonas."

"He certainly does." Kang expelled a long breath. "Listen, please, Jonas. You need to rest and finish healing. We'll get you into your room, and one of us will stay with you." He received a nod from Bartholomew. "Don't even think of arguing with us."

Like the magician was made of glass, Bartholomew lifted him from the couch, and Kang hurried ahead to open the door to the sleeping car.

In a croak, Celwyn asked, "What happened ... to the Russian?"

"I shot him in the foot, sort of," Kang told him. "Then Bartholomew shot him between the eyes."

When Celwyn awoke, he didn't feel the usual motion of the train. The events of the afternoon rushed back to him, especially the image of the Russian's bloody blade as he fell to the ground. Through his cabin window, a collection of stars hung low overhead, twinkling to get his attention. He inhaled with relief; he had been afraid that he wouldn't see them again, at least from down here.

The magician ached like he hadn't in decades, possibly centuries. When he touched his side, he found a fresh bandage wrapped around his middle.

"Welcome back, Jonas." Kang spoke from the foot of the bed.

The magician regarded him through half-open eyes. By the door, a too- bright lamp glowed. He dimmed it without moving. Kang's mouth opened and closed, but he didn't say anything. It wasn't from surprise, but concern that he'd expelled effort on magic when the automat expected him to rest.

"I'm sorry I scared you, my friend," Celwyn said.

"I should expect it by now, you know." The automat studied him with a somber expression.

It took effort, but Celwyn lifted himself upright several inches then fell back again.

"Xiau, you saved me."

Kang shook his head. "I just assisted."

Celwyn smiled, then grimaced. "It hurts to laugh. We both know you and Bartholomew did more than that."

"No. It was just our turn to help."

Bartholomew entered the room, and when he heard Celwyn, relief flooded his face.

"I was just saying how thankful I am that you both were there," the magician told him.

With a scowl, the big man dropped into a nearby chair, clenching and unclenching his hands.

"I should have done more."

"No, you did as I asked. I should have made better plans." Celwyn found it hard to breathe. "What happened? I saw a flash of light."

Bartholomew's scowl changed to a growl. "It was what is called a flashbulb, for taking pictures. That porter, Stephen, snuck into the dining room, and then out the door behind you. The pop you heard was the bulb."

"We will talk more … tomorrow." Celwyn sighed, suddenly tired. "Where are we?"

Kang gazed out the window. "My guess is Trencin. When you wake up again, I'll know for sure." He reached out a hand to tap Celwyn's foot. "You are falling asleep, despite yourself."

"Sleep, Jonas," Bartholomew said. "We will be here."

Minutes or hours later, the magician's nightmares became unbearable. Celwyn opened his eyes to escape them: he never dwelled on the beautiful or terrifying things that he dreamt of and wasn't going to start now. Beauty was intransient, which made him sad. The other pointless; death was death.

The train's engines had just begun to rumble, and dawn pinked the edges of the sky. The *Elizabeth* sat next to a lake. Across its glassy surface, a wispy layer of fog hovered, and he heard a chorus of frogs harmonizing across the water. If he had felt better, he would have added some background flutes to the frog opera.

At the foot of the bed, Kang still slouched in the chair. Celwyn doubted the mechanical man slept. More likely, he had powered down, recharging himself from within. The magician wiggled a hand to remove the blanket from his bed and tuck it around Kang. The automat blinked at him.

"Since you didn't get up to do that, I won't scold you. Is it true that little instances of magic won't drain your energy?"

"Yes." Celwyn smiled at him. "I am much better."

"Don't even try to tell me you are back to normal." He raised his eyes heavenward and down again. "You almost died."

Celwyn tried to shrug and winced. "I agree, it will be a few days."

"At least."

"While I was dreaming, I tried to remember the last time I had been wounded as badly." Celwyn tapped a finger on his chin. "It was Nantes in 1685. An errant cannonball in the head."

"Really?? You consider yourself invincible." Kang glared. "That was highly dangerous." The train's wheels screeched as she began to roll forward, and soon they accelerated.

"Mostly, I am lucky. The more unpredictable my movements, the safer I am."

"Perhaps." The automat's mood changed, and he rubbed his hands together. "Do you want breakfast? I do."

"Soon. Tell me what else happened yesterday."

"Let me request breakfast first."

By the time Kang returned, Celwyn had verified that he had no other injuries and had unwrapped the bandage to see under it. The automat sat a tea tray on the table next to the bed.

"There is a bloodstained mess on the sofa you might want to clean up from here. I threw a blanket over it and told Ricardo we'd take care of it." Kang held up a hand. "Let me clarify: fix the sofa from here when you are up to it, please."

"I assure you, I am taking things slowly." Celwyn watched Kang pour. "I feel better just smelling that. You know, I'd miss Earl Grey very much if I died."

"You should take this seriously." Kang tried not to smile and poured a second cup before he sat down. "Stephen is confined to his quarters for now. I borrowed Andy from the Conductor and left him on the door with instructions to use force if Stephen tries to leave."

"Stephen's actions are not those of a porter."

"We'll keep him confined for a while." Kang nodded. "When Andy relieves Abe at the coal bin, they let Stephen out to use the facilities. During the night, we'll have other arrangements."

"Tell me about Stephen." The magician shifted in the bed, trying to get comfortable.

"At first, Bartholomew thought the man was in league with the Russians. But upon questioning, he discovered Stephen is a reporter through and through, no doubt at all."

Celwyn choked on the tea and coughed. Then cursed.

The door behind Kang opened, revealing a purple boat hat with a long ribbon and then Prince Leo's beak-like nose. The dwarf edged into the room in a matching velvet suit. Celwyn gaped and started to laugh. It hurt. "What the hell?"

Kang glowered at Prince Leo.

"Jonas, I wanted to say how sorry I am that you were hurt," the dwarf simpered.

"So am I," the magician replied. It wasn't entirely Prince Leo's fault. The theft of the royal rubies had started the whole thing, but Celwyn had been enjoying himself until he was knifed.

Prince Leo said, "I couldn't see too well from our window before the shooting started."

The *Elizabeth* blew her whistle and slowed as she entered a sizable town. Several streets away, the colorful flags of a bazaar fluttered in the breeze. Moments more, and a large stable of horses blocked their view. The train did not stop, passing by small businesses that lined the road before a tiny mosque. The *Elizabeth* blew her whistle again and began to pick up speed as she entered fields of greenery for as far as he could see.

Celwyn shifted on the bed, grimaced, and regarded Prince Leo, who licked his lips and said, "One of the crew said..."

"You mean the crew confined to the kitchen during the confrontation?" Kang inquired in a hard voice. "One of them caused this."

Prince Leo shot a glance at the automat. "Perhaps. Regardless of how I know, is it true you gave the rubies back to the Russians?"

"I don't know if they picked them up out of the dirt." Celwyn eyed him with growing annoyance.

"But Jonas..."

"You should be thanking me instead of whining at me. Combined with the magic display and the death of their leader, you shouldn't be pursued by them anymore."

Kang asked, "Would you prefer that we put you off the train at the next city we pass through? You could take the next train heading back to Prague and look for them."

Celwyn smiled at his friend. Always logical and sly. He stared at Kang's ears until they grew larger and developed into tigers' ears, tufted points and all. The magician's lips twitched. Like the automat said, he was so easily amused.

Prince Leo looked to see what Celwyn was smiling at and gasped. The little man knocked his chair back and stood.

"Leaving?" Celwyn asked with an even broader smile. It seemed Leo remembered the tiger from its earlier visit.

"Yes!" Prince Leo bolted from the room. Immediately, a clash of pottery came from in the hallway, along with a virulent Italian curse.

Ricardo backed into the room with the breakfast cart, and his expression said he'd like to throw Prince Leo off the train himself. When he saw the magician, his frown relaxed into a moue of concern.

"Sir? Are you well enough to eat?"

Celwyn pushed himself up in the bed, doing his best to hide the pain.

"I am starving. This is also my first breakfast you have prepared."

Although of average height, Ricardo had the wiry movements of a circus performer and the kind of energy that seemed to always be just under control. He placed a tray in front of the magician. "For this breakfast, I present many nations: Eggs Benedict, Black Forest ham, English muffins, and French strawberries." As he set another tray in front of Kang, the train hit a trestle at a good clip, and everything rattled. "I hope you enjoy your breakfast. I was very worried, Sir."

When Ricardo turned to leave, Celwyn said, "I hope to not worry you again, Ricardo. Tell me about Stephen, please."

With a frown, Ricardo faced him and said, "Things were very rushed before we left. I called on both references for him but should have done more."

Celwyn put a hand on his arm. "Please. I meant no criticism. I'm asking what you know."

Kang pulled another chair forward and urged their new chef to sit. It was at that point that Ricardo saw Kang's ears. Celwyn flipped a hand, reverting them to their usual appearance; entertainment was so transient at times. Ricardo directed another puzzled look at Kang, shook his head as if he had a fly up his nose, and sat on the edge of the seat.

"You can smoke if you like," Celwyn told him. The man did so incessantly and at the moment, probably wished for a cigarette.

"I will wait." Ricardo sighed with regret. "Stephen came to us from the usual staffing agency. Mrs. Thomas talked with him and sent him to me. He seemed clean, articulate, and eager to work."

The Professor said, "Bartholomew asked everyone to remain in the kitchen."

Celwyn had been eating and savoring while they talked. The béarnaise sauce had just the right amount of lemon juice. The magician chewed another bite with pleasure and then asked, "What happened after the train stopped?"

Ricardo shrugged. "I didn't see him leave the kitchen. There was much noise and confusion." He swallowed, looked at Kang and then the magician. "I heard the shots and came running."

"Don't worry, please. Your job is as chef, not combatant." Celwyn told him, "We'll question Stephen directly."

"Thank you." Ricardo stood. "I will send someone for your dishes in a while." His black eyes noted Celwyn's bandage. "I am so very glad that you are still with us."

Chapter 11

THE REST OF THE MORNING PASSED peacefully. Bartholomew relieved the automat at Celwyn's side and brought with him another tea tray and some news. While they talked, fields of flowers covered the landscape for as far as the eye could see, and in the distance, a sliver of a sapphire blue lake glimmered. Qing sat on the window ledge as fascinated as he could be. He emitted little chirps every time he saw a cow or horse.

"I have spoken with Conductor Smith. We are on schedule and will arrive in Uzhgorod by noon. Satu Mare this evening."

"Thank you." Celwyn poured and sighed with pleasure. "What did the crew see yesterday?"

Bartholomew patted a yawn. "Your block worked well for the kitchen itself. Most of the crew saw nothing, but they heard the shots and the yelling." With his pinky in the air, the big man sipped tea from a delicate porcelain cup, his hand much bigger than the cup. “They were concerned, but not alarmed … up to that point. Conductor Smith could see everything as planned and is a crack shot. He confronted the Russians. He single-handedly chased most of them off. Afterwards, he found a bullet hole in his hat. We’re lucky to still have him.”

Aware that Kang wasn’t there to contradict him, Celwyn said, “My injury will be healed soon. I’ll thank him in person.”

“Oh?” The big man’s brows rose in disbelief.

Time to change the subject. “Stephen is confined to his quarters?”

Bartholomew tiptoed to the door and jerked it open. Satisfied no one listened there, he came back and sat again.

“Yes. Confined and guarded.”

“Could you bring him here, please? I think we will learn enough, even if I have to invade his thoughts, to either accept he meant no harm or fling him off the train at the next stop.”

“I know which you would prefer.”

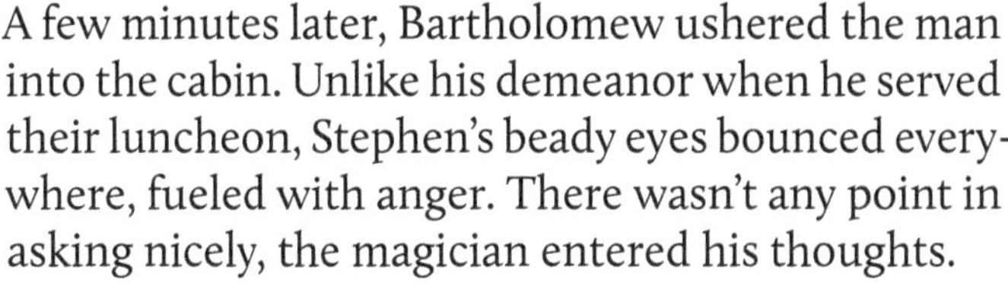

A few minutes later, Bartholomew ushered the man into the cabin. Unlike his demeanor when he served their luncheon, Stephen’s beady eyes bounced everywhere, fueled with anger. There wasn’t any point in asking nicely, the magician entered his thoughts.

“…they don’t know… rich bastards… wonder what’s in that trunk… black bastard is big…”

The magician had heard enough.

"Sit down."

Bartholomew pulled Stephen into the other chair at the foot of the bed, within punching or grabbing range.

"Tell us who you are working for," the magician asked in a quiet voice.

The man's smile held more satisfaction than humor, along with a large dose of confidence. He held up his hands, palms up. "I do not understand your request."

Bartholomew reached under the bed and retrieved what he'd brought in earlier: a heavy-looking black camera and flashbulb contraption. The magician would wager it cost a great deal of money that only a newspaper publisher could supply.

"I found this hidden in the storage car." The big man laid it on the bed.

They waited. Sweat broke out above the reporter's brow. He pursed his lips, glanced at the camera and then stared at it.

"We're searching your room at the moment." The magician scowled, his patience evaporating. "I almost died when you set off that flash, Sir. Shall we stop the train and pitch you out?"

A flush ran up Stephen's neck and suffused his face. "You can't do that!"

Celwyn kept his voice matter of fact. "We can. This is our *private* train."

Bartholomew asked, with the kind of friendliness that should send a shiver up the man's spine,

"What are we going to find in your room?" He placed a heavy hand on the porter's shoulder.

As he spoke, a shadow passed between the sun and the *Elizabeth*. In one stride, Bartholomew reached the window, opened it, and stuck his head out. When he turned around, his expression told them he had just seen something more fantastic than the bucolic landscape they traveled through.

Celwyn raised a brow and tried to see around him. "What is it?"

"A large red and blue balloon with a little grey-haired man in the basket below," Bartholomew murmured as he stared out the window. "It moved fast. Off to the south."

A moment later, the Professor arrived with two bulky notebooks and a smile that showed he had enjoyed his investigating task. He sat on Celwyn's trunk and announced, "Lunch is in a half hour." Kang handed one of the notebooks to Celwyn and the other to Bartholomew. "So, let's get this over with."

As they read, the reporter tried to get up, but Bartholomew laid a firm hand on his shoulder again. "Stay still, or I'll sit on you."

In the reporter's thoughts, Celwyn heard loud and clear, *Black bastard...*

The magician sent a personal cloud of frigid air over the reporter.

"You should apologize for that thought, Stephen."

He shivered violently and stared wide-eyed at Celwyn.

After a few more moments of reading the notebook, the magician asked, "Once again, who are you working for?"

Stephen looked away, toward the door.

"Let's open the camera," Bartholomew suggested, once again confirming the magician's opinion that his logic rivaled that of the automat.

"No! You'll expose the film."

"Exactly."

The magician picked up the camera.

"Alright! Mr. Herzog, publisher of the Česká Novina."

Bartholomew tapped the page he was reading, "I quote, 'It is true, Mr. Celwyn is a magician, but is he also a murderer? This reporter saw what he did that night at the Opera House, and it was murder.'" He looked down his nose at Stephen. "You can't murder a vampire, you idiot."

As Celwyn scanned more of the reporter's notes, his expression darkened.

"You have been following us around Prague for weeks. And spying on everyone at our home." If the magician had felt better, he would have boxed the man's ears. Instead, he settled for a green snake, no bigger than his little finger, with ruby-red eyes. He sent it over the man's shoe and up his pant leg.

Stephen's scream echoed in the cabin before turning into a series of shrieks.

"I suggest taking off your trousers," Bartholomew said.

The reporter balanced on one leg as he tore off his pants.

"You can return to your quarters, Stephen. We'll keep the notebooks and camera."

With a nod from Celwyn, Kang opened the door and stood back as the man ran out of the room, flinging curses.

Qing had watched the interview from atop the armoire, and when the snake fell to the floor, he dived and ascended again with his prize.

"He loves presents." Celwyn enjoyed seeing the bird hop up and down on top of the armoire.

"That will entertain him the rest of the day," Bartholomew murmured as he checked the window again for the balloon. "Xiau says you spoil him."

"Yes, he does." Kang reentered the room and sat at the foot of the bed.

"It's good that he has a new toy besides my jewelry." Bartholomew watched Qing toss the snake in the air and catch it again, then went back to reading the notes again. He tapped the top of the notebook. "This has weeks' worth of details about Tellyhouse, Annabelle, Zander, and Patrick. It even describes Mrs. Thomas's trips to the greengrocers."

Celwyn sighed, not with pain. Irritation made his voice low and dangerous. "What are we going to do about Stephen?"

"Back when I first met you, you would have just killed him," Kang observed.

Celwyn touched his side with a grimace. "I still might. Choices were simpler before I met you two and everyone at Tellyhouse."

"Of course, they were." Kang held up a finger and said, "Let's start with some facts: Stephen can expose us to the police in several cities." He held up another finger. "He probably won't give up pursuing us." The third finger went up. "The notoriety he would cause us would not be good."

"Nevertheless, he would need proof," the magician said.

Bartholomew closed the notebook and slapped his thigh with it. "If we keep his camera and notes, he would be less dangerous to us. At least for a while, until he reproduced what he could remember."

"That picture that he took was of Jonas dumping the rubies in the dirt."

The big man nearly smiled. "Poor Prince Leo. By now, the remaining ruffians would have retrieved them."

"A logical conclusion." Kang gazed through the window, deep in thought. "If so, the Russians are no longer a threat. The reporter's picture would be interesting, but it reveals no magic or crime." He pointed to the notebooks. "The threat to us is in his notes."

Celwyn lifted the cover of one of the notebooks and let it fall. "We can assume this publisher Herzog knows some of this information and is most likely waiting for more. The display at the Opera House was only four days ago."

"Yes, Stephen has probably sent some tidbits to his boss by telegraph," Bartholomew reasoned.

Silence settled over them as they thought; the only sound was the clanking from the train and the clicking of Qing's metallic feet as he hopped around with his prize.

"Should we keep Stephen close by or distance ourselves?" Celwyn finally asked.

Kang said, "I suggest that when we arrive in town, we offer him an opportunity to continue with us as a porter. Or tell him he can walk away without his notebooks and camera. If he stays, we watch him. He'd be subject to search at any time, and we would have to make sure he didn't share any information with others."

The train hit a patch of rough track, and everything bounced. Books fell off Celwyn's dresser. By the time it stopped, the conversation had resumed, and the magician gestured to put the books back in place.

"Do we assume he wouldn't start over?" Celwyn asked. "I can block what he sees and hears. We would eventually become very boring to him."

Bartholomew pursed his lips. "That has merit."

"Or we can shoot him," Kang added with a twinkle in his eye.

"And here I am, the violent part of this enterprise." Celwyn innocently blinked at him. "Meanwhile, how long will it be until we arrive in Tehran?"

"About a fortnight," the big man said.

Kang frowned. "We should unload Stephen before Tehran to make sure he doesn't know about Singapore."

They heard running in the hall, and the door burst open. The porter Jackson shouted, "Please come—the Conductor requests that you hurry!"

Bartholomew approached the bed to stand beside Kang.

"Either we help you, or you don't go."

"You don't have to carry me."

Kang held up a hand. "I would settle for Bartholomew supporting you, and we go slow with me, ready to catch you if you fall."

It took several minutes to maneuver down the hall, across the dining room, through the kitchen, storage, crew quarters, and eventually to the locomotive. By the time they arrived, Bartholomew carried Celwyn. He deposited the magician against the doorway of the cab.

Conductor Smith saw them and pointed.

"That damned thing has been dogging us for hours. If it lands on the tracks, we're in trouble."

"Interesting." Kang squinted out the window.

Conductor Smith said, "It is getting much closer."

The magician gazed out the front window. A few miles ahead, a large balloon hovered just above the fields next to the tracks. Conductor Smith growled, "He came down so low, he almost clipped the caboose a while ago, then sailed off again. It could have derailed the entire train. Thought you should know."

For as far as Celwyn could see, verdant farmland lay to the east and west. In the south, the foothills loomed, heralding a horizon of tall mountains and glimpses of glistening peaks.

"Mount Salov," Kang said.

"Thank you, Conductor." Celwyn held onto the door jamb to turn around. "Please keep us informed if things change."

Kang asked, "Is Satu Mare still far away?"

"We'll be there before sundown." Conductor Smith pulled back on a red handle, then pushed it forward again. As they picked up speed, the engine grew louder.

Kang regarded Celwyn, and he was not amused. "You look very pale, and you aren't hiding the pain very well."

"Come along, Jonas," Bartholomew said as he picked him up.

By late afternoon, the terrain changed to orchards. Hundreds of baskets full of peaches decorated mile after mile of country lanes. They saw carts overladen with grain stalks, and children helped harvest or played in the dirt. Every time the *Elizabeth* chugged around a curve, Celwyn peered out the window and gazed ahead of the train. Most of the time, he spied the giant red and blue balloon in the distance. Twice, the balloon soared until it drifted through the clouds. Celwyn squinted and then grinned malevolently. On two occasions, he'd seen the reflection of a spyglass from it.

Near sundown, the *Elizabeth* wound her way down from the foothills and entered a wide plain. As expected, the balloon hovered above the grassy fields in front of them. When the train drew near, the magician noticed the basket of the balloon tilting, then righting itself and dipping again. The wind caught the balloon, dragging it across the field toward a stand of trees. In the next moment, the balloon twisted and dropped farther before it struck the trees and caught fire.

Chapter 12

"THIS IS AS FAR AS YOU GO, JONAS." Bartholomew deposited him against the rail leading off the train. "We will handle this."

Andy and Abe followed the big man as they hurried across the field of grass toward the trees. Abe toted a rifle as he ran.

Kang came down the steps and handed Celwyn binoculars. "Three men. The fire is out, and the balloon is ripped badly. The men do not appear to be hurt."

As Celwyn adjusted the binoculars, he chuckled. "Bet old Jules is fit to be tied." Another thought occurred to him. "Or he crashed on purpose."

"You think it is Verne?"

"Certainly. They've been trailing us since we left Prague." He checked. "Ah, you are correct, they are unhurt. They're unloading their belongings now." The magician turned and started up the steps into the train. Slowly. The automat drew close, ready to catch him if he collapsed. "I'll inform Prince Leo and his daughter of Verne's arrival and..." The magician sighed, catching his breath, "and rearrange our quarters."

"Jonas, let me help you." Kang followed him inside and held on to his elbow. "Are you sure you are all right?"

"My magic will support me as well as you or Bartholomew could." Celwyn didn't tell him he desperately needed to rest. Xiau would only fuss.

Kang verified Celwyn entered the sleeping car, then whirled and headed toward the kitchen to fetch the porters.

Celwyn rapped on the first compartment door and leaned against the jamb. Prince Leo opened it, and over the top of his head, the magician could see a very interested Mary Giovanna peering out the window at the balloon.

"Should you be out of bed?" Prince Leo asked. His worry could be about the magician, or because he didn't want to be blamed if Celwyn fell.

"For another few minutes." The magician breathed deep. "Please gather your things together. We will be making some changes to our sleeping arrangements."

"But," Prince Leo grabbed the magician's sleeve, "what is going on?"

Mary Giovanna pointed out the window. "There are men coming toward the train. It looks like a big tent collapsed in those trees."

"A flying balloon crashed into the trees. Leo, let me know as soon as you've packed, please."

Twenty minutes later, Bartholomew arranged Celwyn on the sofa next to the bar, and grumbled, "I don't think you should be out of bed yet."

"I can rest here just as well."

"Bartholomew is right," Kang said as he watched Verne's helpers enter the train, deposit the last of the luggage, and then follow Ricardo toward the kitchen. They wore the coarse clothes of laborers.

Verne perched atop a pile of trunks in the middle of the room, looking the worse for wear with mud on his chin and his tie askew. Mary Giovanna had settled herself at the dining table with a book, and Prince Leo eyed the newcomer before waddling across the room to claim a chair by the bar.

From inside Celwyn's jacket, Qing pecked at a button, hoping to escape and inspect whoever had arrived.

"Ouch. All right." Celwyn opened his coat, and the bird inched his way out. He walked along the back of the sofa to the Professor, who rubbed his neck. Qing rubbed back. Then he saw Prince Leo.

"I remember that bird." The dwarf stared at him. "I don't like him."

Mary Giovanna put her book down, exposing a view of the gold-trimmed necklace she wore. Qing deserted Prince Leo and flew over to the table.

"Our guests are Prince Leo and his daughter Mary Giovanna." Celwyn asked Verne, "Have you met Bartholomew?"

The author studied Qing with wide eyes and nodded. "Yes, he introduced himself when he assisted us in decamping from the balloon."

After the pleasantries were exchanged, Celwyn asked, "What about those men we just saw?"

"Just men I hired for the trip."

The magician caught up on his breathing, without Kang noticing, and asked, "Why were you following us?"

"I wasn't. I was traveling to Beijing." Verne glanced at the floor and then up again. "The trip has been planned for several months." The author avoided his gaze and pretended interest in the pianoforte beside the bar.

Celwyn didn't have to enter his thoughts to know Verne was lying.

"Actually, I was racing this train. Until we crashed," Verne said with a modicum of confidence. "It was a test of what the balloon could do." He began bouncing his shoe against the trunk he sat on.

Bartholomew asked, "What happened?"

Verne shrugged as only a Frenchman could. "We drifted a little too close to the ground, then a gust of wind caught us and propelled us into the trees." His hand soared like a bird upward. While he talked, the magician shifted position on the sofa, trying to get comfortable. Kang fussed over him and tucked a blanket around his shoulders.

"Are you ill, Jonas?" Verne asked.

"No. Just an accident." Beyond Verne, Qing had taken up a position on the table directly in front of Mary Giovanna. They stared at each other, neither one blinking.

Verne asked the room, "Excuse me, but where are you traveling to?"

Bartholomew caught a nod from the magician and verified a matching nod from Kang. They'd tell him something, but not everything. The big man lowered his voice, not for others' ears. "To Tehran, and then Bengal." The train rumbled, getting ready for departure. "We can drop you, and your balloon crew, off in Satu Mare, in an hour or so. Once there, you can offer them funds for their return to Prague. Is that acceptable?"

"Yes, yes."

The ticking of the wall clock was the only thing heard as an uncomfortable silence descended on the room.

"Would you like to continue your journey with us?" Kang asked.

Verne faced him, relief filling his face. "Err, thank you. Yes, I would."

Celwyn turned toward the windows so that Verne wouldn't see his expression. He hadn't been sure before, but now he knew Verne had crashed the balloon purposely in order to join their party. *How interesting*, he thought.

The magician entered Verne's thoughts and found that the author was not going to Beijing: of all places, Verne intended to travel to Singapore also.

"Drat."

Kang asked, "What?"

"We'll discuss it later."

Bartholomew nodded and stood. "I'll ask Ricardo to feed Verne's crew before we drop them off."

"Please request that the porters help transport our new guest's luggage to his room, too." Kang studied the mound of trunks with narrowed eyes, probably wondering how the balloon could fly so high with that much weight.

As Bartholomew headed toward the front of the train, Celwyn said, "The cabin that Prince Leo and his daughter occupied has been restored to the original configuration. It is now three smaller compartments. Jules, you will occupy the one next to Bartholomew." Celwyn took several deep breaths. His side ached anew. Perhaps he wasn't ready yet for this much activity.

"Time to rest, Jonas." Kang helped the magician to his feet. "Now, I know why you look so pale."

The magician acquiesced, leaning against Kang as they moved toward the sleeper car.

"I'll have you know that I intend to sit at the table for dinner."

"Of course, you do. We'll need to talk about your wound first." As the automat steered the magician down the hall, he asked, "Is it healing internally?"

"I assume so," Celwyn answered but wondered if it was.

"Make sure."

"I will check," Celwyn said and entered his room. "By tomorrow, I will be better. Oh..." He remembered the tableau at the dining table.

Kang helped him onto the bed. "Yes?"

"You might want to retrieve Qing before he does something rather rude."

Chapter 13

When they pulled into the train station in Satu Mare an hour later, through his partly open window, Celwyn saw evidence of the Roman and Mongol influence everywhere. He spied minarets, church spires, a proliferation of pointed roofs, and women swathed in black shawls and burkas as they walked through the streets, hiding their faces behind mysterious veils.

The screeching of the *Elizabeth's* brakes intensified, and the magician lifted a finger, opening his window the rest of the way. He inhaled spices and a hint of rain. Voices speaking in Arabic, Deutsche, and Roma floated inside. A child yelled, "*Achtung*!" and then laughed, reminding him of Zander.

He brought pen and paper closer to the improvised desk in his lap. Time to write to the lad and add a few words of good news for Annabelle and Patrick: there would be no further threats from the Russians.

He didn't mention his injury and hoped not to receive pointed questions and advice if anyone else told them.

By the time the magician had finished his letters, the transport of coal onto the train had begun. Conductor Smith appeared a mite gruff as he supervised the transport, barking orders with a scowl painted across his face. Celwyn checked his pocket-watch. At the moment, Ricardo should be at the bazaar with a few porters, accompanied by Bartholomew, for security. Per the big man, they expected to order provisions, including ice and whatever they'd need until their next stop. Celwyn hoped they found something delectable for their dinner. A few minutes later, he spied Kang escorting Verne onto the crowded sidewalk and wondered where they were going. Conductor Smith must have been left behind as his babysitter.

The magician tested the skin under his bandage. It didn't feel overly warm anymore. He also could tell he was getting stronger as long as he took careful steps. A furtive movement outside caught his attention.

It appeared lock-picking must be one of Stephen's talents. The reporter scurried down the steps and away from the train.

Before he reached the thoroughfare, Celwyn turned him into a hamster and brought him across the yard and through his window by his tail. As Stephen hung in the air in front of him, the magician growled. "You're lucky I don't put a necklace on you and feed you to Qing."

For what seemed like hours, Celwyn kept himself entertained by looking out his cabin window. He found people to be quite interesting. Beyond the train yard, the sidewalks teemed with pedestrians and tourists ... and assorted people who would prey on both. By eight o'clock, the darkness of the evening seemed complete, only punctuated by occasional streetlights.

Not too long afterward, Kang and the big man arrived to escort the magician to dinner. Bartholomew ignored his protests that he could sit up and helped the magician to his feet. For most of the afternoon, Celwyn had been tortured by the scent of roast beef that perfumed the air. He also thought he detected the aroma of roasted potatoes, but couldn't be sure.

"I want to try to walk without magic, or your assistance, to the dining room." Resting this afternoon had done him a world of good; at least he could tell he was better, but it was best not to say anything to feed Kang's overprotectiveness. The magician steadied himself on Bartholomew's arm. "Before we go, since a discussion would be difficult with our guests present, could you ponder this question?" He had to pause and breathe deeply before he continued. "What are we going to do about the reporter Stephen?" He handed a cardboard box to Kang.

Both Kang and Bartholomew peeked inside the flap. The big man's eyes widened.

"His… his face looks the same … and his ears," Bartholomew whispered with a gulp. The big man's superstitious nature was legendary between the three of them.

Kang didn't say a word as he watched the magician catch up on his breathing.

"He tried to escape from the train after you went into town. If you will put him in his room, please? I'll add a magical lock on the door since a regular one doesn't appear adequate."

"Will he remain a rodent forever?" Bartholomew backed away from the box.

"Only for another few minutes," Celwyn assured him as the three of them walked down the hall toward the dining room. "Then, he'll be back to normal."

When Celwyn took his place at the table, Ludvik and Jackson were busy filling water glasses and ladling out a rich cream soup.

"This looks very good." The magician realized it felt wonderful to be out of his room and amid companionable activity. He celebrated by adjusting Jackson's paltry mustache, and it became a bushy line above his lip. A kit of pigeons could perch on it.

"Ricardo calls this turtle soup," Ludvik said. As he opened the wine, he did a double take upon seeing Jackson's mustache. Celwyn covered his amusement by drinking water.

As usual, Kang sat to the magician's right, wearing a blissful expression as he picked up his spoon. Across from Celwyn, Bartholomew occupied the chair that Annabelle used to sit in. To the magician's left, Mary Giovanna wore a neutral satin gown and severe frown. Perhaps it was for Prince Leo, who fairly glowed in a bilious yellow shirt. Verne sat between the automat and Bartholomew, still in the same gray suit from when he crashed his balloon. Judging from the smudges of dirt on the back of his jacket, he had tumbled out on his left side.

"Tell us about your balloon, please," Bartholomew asked the author.

"Balloons such as mine have been in use since the 1760s or so, yet they are still rare. The mechanics have improved, but wind gusts are always dangerous and unpredictable." His face brightened. "My book that featured a similar one, *Cinq Gemaines en Ballon,* was published about ten years ago."

"*Five Weeks in a Balloon*," Bartholomew translated.

"I have read that book, Mr. Verne." Mary Giovanna replaced her wine glass on the table and spoke slowly. "I enjoyed it very much. Phileas Fogg was a romantic figure in it."

The light of good humor in Verne's eyes faded, and he hesitated. "Thank you, my dear."

"How do you write with so much detail? Did you fly in a balloon over Africa before you wrote about it?" she asked.

"Yes." Verne's eyes shifted. "No."

Celwyn smiled. He would give something to know what all Jules had been up to. However, it was Kang who asked a most telling question.

"Mr. Verne, your books are filled with inventions and technology the world is still catching up to." He made sure he had the author's full attention when he asked, "Does it all exist? How do you know of it?"

Kang had telegraphed the question, and Verne was ready.

"It is all from my imagination." He tapped his head. "I have the imagination of a ten-year-old who has gone to school for many years."

Kang pursed his lips, holding in a remark, while Bartholomew continued to stare at the author with a moderate amount of speculation. Celwyn had a hunch they would discover the man's secrets. And soon.

Jackson arrived with their entrées. As he served them, the magician curled the tips of the porter's mustache on each side of his nose. Celwyn grinned into his napkin. Kang saw him and shook his head with a broad smile. "It is obvious you are feeling better, my friend."

It would be best to keep the conversation going. "How wonderful your accounts are, Jules," the magician said. "Most fanciful."

"Thank you." Verne nodded and began eating. "I must say, your chef is exceptionally talented. I love this sauce and fresh peas."

As he spoke, Celwyn observed something natural and something he usually considered a happy occurrence. But in this instance, he found it disturbing. As Mary Giovanna ate, she seemed unaware of a look of admiration from Bartholomew from across the table. As quick as it had occurred, it disappeared, leaving the magician with a sense of foreboding. With studied effort, Celwyn returned his attention to his plate. No. It was not his concern.

The conversation continued to the dessert course and the pouring of cups of rich coffee. The atmosphere around them had the jovial quality of good food, drink, and, for the mind, discussions of a wide diversity of interests. Celwyn felt tired but couldn't bring himself to leave the table yet.

From the doorway to the kitchen, Ricardo watched them, his eyes alive with pride. Celwyn tapped a spoon on his glass and said, "Lady, and gentlemen, allow me to introduce you to our chef." He gestured to Ricardo as the applause built.

"Chef Ricardo!"

Ricardo beamed with pleasure and embarrassment and escaped as soon as he could.

Kang put his napkin on the table and in a voice that brooked no argument, said, "Jonas needs to rest." He stood, as did Bartholomew.

"Please put a block on the door," Bartholomew asked the magician as they entered his room. "So we can talk in confidence."

When he'd done so, Celwyn climbed back in bed and leaned against a mountain of pillows. He added glasses and a whiskey bottle to the side table.

"I do feel better."

Kang studied him from under lowered brows. "You look somewhat better."

"I've had time to think while lying here." He poured and sent the drinks around.

"Thank you. We're listening," Bartholomew said.

"You'll remember we agreed that we should make haste on our journey to Singapore." The magician sipped. For some reason, the liquor didn't agree with the recent flavors from dinner. He added a tray of tea and poured again.

"You'll have to get rid of that tray before the porters see it. They'll realize they didn't bring any tea in here," Kang told him.

Celwyn nodded. "I will remember. To continue, our traveling plans haven't changed. With that in mind, I propose that we do our best not to come to the attention of the police, which means no reporters or other attention courtesy of Jules."

Bartholomew downed his whiskey. "Mr. Verne seems harmless enough."

"He is, but he gossips like a fishwife." Kang frowned. "I think Jonas is saying that we can't trust Verne."

"Correct."

"Hmm," Bartholomew sighed as he poured another drink. "If we leave the reporter behind here or in another city, he would be convinced there is a newsworthy reason he was left behind."

"True. He would be certain we are worth pursuing." Celwyn shifted, trying to get comfortable. "Another problem exists."

"Which is?" Kang asked as he folded a blanket over the magician's legs.

"Our stowaway reporter could be employed by Jules or by one of his publishing friends."

Kang threw up his hands. "Wonderful."

"I like Mr. Verne, but we must protect our plans." Bartholomew checked outside the window, seeing nothing amiss in the train yard from the dim light of the street torches.

Kang said, "Let's separate the problems for a moment. If we happen to misplace Mr. Verne before we get to Singapore, we can continue with our preparations and then head back to Prague. He wouldn't be able to find us to bother us."

"I like that," the big man said.

"Very logical," Celwyn agreed.

Kang poured another drink, and they toasted before lapsing into companionable silence.

After a moment, Celwyn said, "We can't keep Stephen locked up until Singapore."

"We could mail his camera and notebooks back to Prague and then tell him we did so." The automat tapped his chin with a finger. "But first, we really should read them thoroughly to see how damaging they are before we decide what to do with them."

Celwyn added a soft harpsichord melody to the room. The music flowed like a lazy river tumbling over rocks falling to another pool and undulating forward again. "I'll read them tonight."

"You know, we did not discuss Prince Leo and his daughter." Kang couldn't help a worried glance at Bartholomew.

The magician frowned. Kang must know of Bartholomew's fascination with the woman and was curious if it was returned. Again, Celwyn didn't consider it any of his own business. Not at all.

The automat said, "You should know that yesterday I discovered Mary Giovanna by the cabin where the reporter was confined. It appeared that she was talking to him through the door."

Bartholomew's frown deepened, but he didn't say anything.

"Was she wearing clothes?" the magician asked.

Kang rolled his eyes at Celwyn's attempt at humor. "A heavy coat and a man's hat."

"What did she do when she saw you?" the big man asked.

"She smiled at me, like 'wasn't it a nice day?' and walked away."

Chapter 14

At dawn, Celwyn made his way to the dining room without assistance. Perhaps he wouldn't be able to run from an enemy, but he could confront one with a bit of magical help.

How long had it been since he had allowed someone like that blasted Russian to surprise him like this? A while, probably since his visit to San Antonio, when an annoyed preacher climbed into the church bell tower and shot the magician's hat off. Although as drunk as he could be, the preacher later insisted he thought Celwyn was a spy for Santa Anna's army.

When Celwyn peeked in the kitchen, he discovered Jackson already at work and, of all things, operating the hand-cranked coffee grinder. He caused the porter to re-tie his shoe, and when he stood again, all the coffee had been ground.

"Good morning."

Jackson jumped.

"Could I have some Earl Grey, please?"

As Celwyn turned back to the dining room, he decided that today Jackson's mustache would be plucked and as dark, straight, and thin as a Frenchman's, just a fashionable sliver of hair on his upper lip.

The magician settled into a chair, and while he waited for his tea, he noticed the clues from the previous evening's activities scattered around him; the chess set remained on the dining room table, but the white queen lay on the floor under the bar. Someone was an unhappy chess player. Next to the game, a glass bowl full of cigar ash emitted an acrid odor. Underneath the bowl was a drawing of a balloon and the mechanics that flew it.

The sketch caused Celwyn to wonder. If Jules had already produced books of the overland train race and the balloon, what else did he have in mind? He obviously participated in activities that were only partially fiction, no matter his denials.

"Ah, thank you," he told the porter when his tea arrived. "We haven't had a chance to talk yet." As Jackson poured, he asked, "Tell me about yourself, please? You enjoy travel?"

"I have lived in Prague for a few years, and yes, I love to travel. Your train is a wonderful opportunity." The porter's mustache moved as he talked, and Celwyn decided this was a good style. Perhaps Jackson would thank him later for it. "I have worked on farms, in the city, but have yet to see the Orient."

The first stirrings of the train's departure began. A rumble and a vibration that started as a light foot massage progressed through the car and toward the caboose. As the sun rose, revealing the train yard, Celwyn spied other trains that had arrived during the night. The one next to them appeared to be empty, but to the right of it, a white-jacketed waiter paced outside an observation car, quarreling with a florid man in a long coat. The magician opened the window long enough to ascertain they were arguing over a woman. He shivered in the early morning cold and closed the window again.

"Should you be out of bed?" Kang stood behind him with folded arms and a skeptical look.

"Of course," Celwyn said.

"You do look sturdier," Kang remarked as he took the other chair. He poured from a fresh coffee service Jackson had just delivered. "Oh, my!" He pointed.

In the yard, the white-jacketed waiter had drawn a pistol and aimed it at the other man. Celwyn flipped a hand, sending the firearm flying high into the air. Both men hopped backward. To complete their fright, Celwyn blew the *Elizabeth's* whistle. They scattered like cats in the rain.

"You know that will perturb our conductor."

Celwyn flexed the fingers of both hands. "You don't want me to become 'rusty,' as the Americans say."

Kang sipped coffee and tried not to smile. "It is good to have you back, Jonas." Steam drifted by the window from the *Elizabeth's* engines as she prepared for departure. "I'm sure the passengers there," he gestured to the other train with several porters clustered at a door, "and ours, appreciate the wake-up call."

"Speaking of passengers," the magician said, "I read Stephen's notebooks last night."

Bartholomew entered the room in a hurry, blinking and tying his tie. "Is there a problem? I heard the whistle."

"Not yet." Celwyn poured him a cup of tea and resisted the urge to send the empty pot back to the kitchen. He settled for planting a compelling thought in Jackson and Ludvik's heads to check the tea service in the dining room. A few moments more, and they arrived with a fresh pot.

"Ludvik, thank you. You can assume we'll need more in another twenty minutes or so."

As Ludvik exited again, Kang told Bartholomew, "Jonas read the notebooks from the reporter."

Celwyn checked the doorway to the sleeping car. "I did. It was a struggle to stay awake while I read. The idiot included many details and plenty of speculation but no facts." That Stephen was responsible for Celwyn's wound did not endear him to the magician.

"Interesting," Kang commented as he gazed outside, watching the white-jacketed waiter as he returned and searched underneath the cars for his gun.

Celwyn sat back in his chair. "I recommend that we turn Stephen loose. I'll scare the devil out of him. We'll keep the camera and notebooks, so he doesn't use them."

"Do you think Mr. Verne is really in league with him?" Bartholomew asked with a glance at the hallway leading to the cabins.

Celwyn's voice took on a hard edge. "I'll have a chat with Jules about that later." He got to his feet and thought about Bartholomew's question all the way to the crew's quarters.

The low foothills before Chernivtsi appeared dry and ripe for a grass fire. Toward the east, Celwyn spied a settlement of a dozen or more buildings, surrounded by cattle pens. A bit closer to the tracks, a shepherd tended sheep in a greener area.

After consulting his watch, the magician sighed in disappointment, at least an hour until luncheon. Qing hopped closer and rubbed his chin. Celwyn rubbed back, admiring how the metal tips of the bird's feathers reflected the light from the windows. Qing blinked at him like a satisfied cat.

Bartholomew sat in the other chair reading a journal on education, and at the dining table, Prince Leo played checkers with Mary Giovanna. The magician closed the novel he'd been reading, *Victorian Ghost Stories of Brighton*, and shut his eyes. Inner thoughts in the room filtered to him like a playful swarm of butterflies.

"I wonder if she sees my trap… two jumps…"

"…I hope Zander doesn't forget me…."

"Poor Father… he has always underestimated me…"

Bartholomew said aloud, "Hmm. It says here that students learn better if I tell a joke before we start our lessons."

"I do not know any jokes ... except when Jonas insists he doesn't spoil Qing," Kang said without looking up from his book.

The door from the kitchen opened, and Stephen, the reporter, entered with a tray and a blank expression. He replenished the tea service, carefully avoiding Celwyn's gaze. During their earlier discussion, the magician may have frightened the man, but either way, the man agreed to leave them alone in exchange for his passage to Tehran. He would function as a porter, as originally agreed.

After the reporter left again, Kang asked, "So, what did you tell the others about Stephen's house arrest?"

"That he had something contagious."

With a cry of "Aha!" Mary Giovanna jumped her checkers across the board, laughing.

"That wasn't ladylike," Prince Leo protested.

"Of course not, since you lost." She glanced speculatively at Bartholomew as if she could guess his skill at checkers. "I wonder if anyone else would care to play."

Bartholomew regarded Prince Leo, who had vacated his chair and headed toward the sleeping car, calling back, "Good luck." As the dwarf passed through, Verne came into the room.

"Good morning, my friends!" The author joined Celwyn by the bar. "I have had a most productive morning at my desk. Jonas," he clapped the magician on the shoulder, "it is so good that you are better."

"I agree. It is fortunate that we were close by when your balloon crashed."

Beyond Verne, Kang's shoulders shook in silent amusement.

"Ah... absolutely." Verne made himself a cup of tea. "I must also thank you for the accommodations. They are conducive to my creative processes—"

The door opened from the kitchen to admit Stephen with an armload of table linens. He saw the author and froze, the linens spilling from his hands. As the reporter bent to pick them up, he stared at Verne.

"...my creative muse, too. I think ... my next book will be successful."

While Verne chattered, Stephen finished delivering the linens and retreated to the kitchen. Bartholomew raised an amused brow before continuing his checker game. Kang nodded at Celwyn.

"From where do you know Stephen?" Celwyn asked Verne in a voice that purred with certainty.

"Nowhere!"

Short of shaking the information out of him, there was a quicker way. Celwyn entered the man's thoughts like a warm knife into butter. "*Mon dieu... Why is he here? I must talk with Hertzel... I must know...* Why *is he here?*"

The magician would let the big man and Kang know the author's worry later. Things were not as bad as they thought; Verne hadn't invited the reporter.

Across the room, Bartholomew moved a checker forward, and Mary Giovanna pounced. She removed most of his checkers and placed a hand over his fingers, saying, "A delightful game. Thank you."

Celwyn noticed she gazed right into Bartholomew's eyes and that she left her hand over his long after etiquette dictated.

Kang noticed also. "The plot thickens. I just hope he has his wits about him."

The dishes and glassware clinked and wobbled as they crossed a trestle and rumbled onto a narrow covered bridge over a deep ravine. Seconds more, and they bounced back onto the tracks between fields of golden grain. A pair of crows flew high above, cawing.

"Salmon pâté. There is also chicken or marinated pork with capers, Sir," Ludvik said as he offered Verne the sandwich tray.

"Thank you, this looks lovely." The author made a selection. He looked at the others. "Where will we stop tonight?"

The tray moved to Kang, who said, "We cross the Staraya River this afternoon. Chernivtsi is our destination for this evening."

Celwyn had traversed the Staraya River about a hundred miles east of here during the Slovene Peasant Revolt. Between the shooting and lack of organization, it had not been enjoyable. He looked outside, seeing only the grassy fields waving in the wake of the train and the low mountains in the distance.

Prince Leo put cheer in his voice. “I hear that is a picturesque city of many cultures.”

“I hope to see some of the city,” Mary Giovanna said. “Perhaps you will accompany me?” She tilted her chin disarmingly at Bartholomew.

Nothing like putting him on the spot, the magician thought. Celwyn also determined that he would keep Mary where he could see her. “We will all go and stay together for safety’s sake.”

As Ludvik hovered with the sandwich platter, Kang took two. One pâté and one chicken. “Please let Ricardo know we will be dining in town this evening.”

Chapter 15

As THE MAGICIAN AND THE OTHERS strolled the shopping district of Chernivtsi, the sun began her descent for the night. Celwyn patted a pocket containing a new variety of Ceylon tea he had just purchased and again considered that it was much easier to transport than the parcel of books Kang had tucked under his arm. Bartholomew's purchase was not surprising, although it might prove tedious by the time they returned to Prague. His new book by Gordon, *Humor for Everyday Man,* promised several entertaining one-line jokes to make a young audience smile.

In front of their promenade, Prince Leo drew stares from other pedestrians. Like a well-fed, squat peacock, he flitted from storefront to storefront in a blue cape and knee-high orange boots. "This is wonderful! Just look at those rugs." A few blocks before, they had discovered that the dwarf enjoyed patronizing perfumeries, and Celwyn debated how much longer he must walk downwind of the man.

Mary Giovanna's fingertips rested on Bartholomew's proffered arm as they passed by a bakery and a store offering women's gloves. Neither proprietor seemed to interest her. In her other hand, she held a bouquet of yellow flowers that Bartholomew had purchased for her.

Verne asked, "We are dining early? Where are we dining?"

"The *La Barbacoa*." Kang walked on Verne's other side, glancing in all directions as if expecting trouble. "It was recommended by our conductor."

"Smith and the others are anxious for their night in town, too. That is why we're dining early." The magician stopped to point across the street. "There it is, the white building with the iron latticework."

Minutes later, they stood in the entrance foyer and waited for their table. Kang asked Celwyn, "Who is watching the reporter?"

"I assigned him to help Abe and Andy. After the coal is loaded, they will make sure he is entertained." Celwyn also made sure that the twins knew there was a reward in it for them for keeping Stephen under surveillance.

Their stroll back to the *Elizabeth* was leisurely and full of good food and wine. Although usually quiet, Mary Giovanna had regaled them with stories of her theatre work throughout the soup and well through the main course. She appeared much more animated than usual, unnaturally so. From what Celwyn heard, her stories seemed to be an edited version of the truth, perhaps for Bartholomew's ears, but nonetheless they displayed her love of performing, especially Sciantosa.

As they walked, Kang kept glancing at Celwyn until he finally asked, "Are you tiring?"

"A bit, perhaps." He gestured. "I can see the smokestacks of the *Elizabeth* in the distance."

"For god sakes, Jonas." Kang stomped into the street, waving his arm until a hire carriage stopped. He opened the door and motioned Celwyn inside as he told the others, "I am taking Jonas to the train; please enjoy the rest of your promenade."

Once settled inside, they pulled out their pipes from their coats.

"Where is Qing?"

Celwyn puffed. "My lavatory, probably destroying my cufflinks as we speak."

As he tamped tobacco into the bowl of his pipe, the Professor said, "At least he is entertained."

They smoked in companionable silence, listening to the rhythmic clopping of the horses' hooves and the shouts from the vendors they passed by. When they reached the train, Kang helped Celwyn to the steps and paid the driver.

Ricardo had been watching for their return from the dining room window. He met them at the door and guided Celwyn to one of the bar chairs. They conferred for a few minutes until the other crew members joined them.

"Please enjoy your evening out, gentlemen." Kang bowed.

From his pocket, the magician extracted a peyote button and popped it into his mouth. He chewed and watched Abe and Andy trotting across the train yard to the cobblestones, and some of his fatigue faded away. Conductor Smith followed, trailing cigar smoke and wearing a broad grin.

Ricardo herded Ludvik, Jackson, and Stephen ahead of him as they left the train yard. The crew sported their best coats and ties. The reporter also wore a resentful scowl that he aimed back at the train's dining room. Ricardo tugged on his arm, and they set off.

"Ricardo won't let him out of his sight," Kang said.

Another hire carriage entered the yard and approached the train. When Prince Leo and the rest of their party passed by the departing porters, Stephen seemed to stare a bit too long at them. The magician watched the crew until they disappeared into the mist of the night.

From the chair beside him, Kang observed, "Although we stop every night, the men appreciate a chance for frivolity in the bigger cities."

"And dancing." Celwyn smiled to himself, picturing Sully doing a jig and waving his pipe over his head.

"Ricardo will insist they return before too late."

"Not that I always think of my stomach, but I'm hoping for cinnamon rolls for breakfast."

In a flurry of good cheer, the rest of their party entered the dining room, shedding hats and coats.

When everyone had settled with a glass of whiskey, or wine, their evening began. Prince Leo's story about devious swans guarding the moat in front of one of the Queen's castles came first. Into a void in the conversation, Mary Giovanna looked Celwyn in the eye and asked a question that stopped all other talks.

"Is it true, Mr. Celwyn, that you can read our thoughts?"

Bartholomew had been about to sip his drink and instead sat it down again. Kang reared back to glower first at Mary Giovanna and then turned it on her father.

"Of course." Celwyn returned her stare evenly. Verne sat away from the others at the dining table, working in his notebook and out of earshot to a point. "May I assume you heard this from your father?"

"Yes." She glanced at Prince Leo, who looked ready to deny it.

Celwyn leaned back in his chair. "I do so only when our party is threatened or for other urgencies."

"Not for sport, then," she said with a twist to her lips and a dark light in her eyes.

The magician had a feeling that she baited him and perhaps even had a specific thought or challenge prepared in her mind for him to discover. He didn't like manipulation or control. He returned her stare and did not stroll into her thoughts.

"What else did you tell her, Leo?" Celwyn asked with the quiet tone of voice the dwarf was familiar with.

Prince Leo's evening ensemble did not go well with the flush that suffused his cheeks.

"Why nothing. Nothing!" His eyes pleaded with his daughter.

"Father," her expression dripped with disdain, "You forget how Mr. Celwyn greeted you when he found us on the train? I was there and saw—"

"Stop, Mary," Prince Leo's flush faded as a fine sheen of sweat replaced it. "You saw something that was a trick of light. That is all."

Into the awkward silence, the first tentative notes of a playful horn floated, cavorting in an upward spiral, and then rushing into the darkest minors. Verne had been blocked and continued to blissfully tap his lips with his pen and write in his notebook. The others hesitated, anticipating more.

The tiger returned, padding across the room in silence, making his entrance even more terrifying. He walked by the others and up to the dwarf, lying at his feet. The cat's eyes shone malevolently as he eyed Prince Leo. The cat licked his boot, and the dwarf squealed in his throat.

No one moved. The stench of the cat became overwhelming. It kept its eyes on Prince Leo. When Celwyn stretched, the cat did, also.

"Leo. As you know, occasionally the police become interested in my activities. That is inconvenient, wouldn't you say?"

The little man nodded, glancing at the magician and back to the tiger. A low growl escaped from its open mouth when the animal laid a heavy paw across both of Leo's boots. The dwarf squirmed, and sweat rolled down his face.

"So, when a reporter sneaks onto this train, it isn't too farfetched to assume our activities are of interest and would end up in the newspapers. Do you understand?"

"Y-y-yess, Jonas."

"It is desirable that you, and your daughter, do not talk about me, or any of our party, to Mr. Verne or Stephen. He is a journalist masquerading as one of our porters."

Mary Giovanna watched the tiger, who reclined no more than a few feet from her hand, with a kind of fascination that Celwyn couldn't interpret. When she saw her father's fear, her eyes danced with delight.

"I understand, as does my father." She giggled and turned to him. "Don't you?"

He nodded.

The lights dimmed and then brightened. The tiger had disappeared.

Prince Leo stood up on shaky legs.

"I say, something appears to be wrong with the lights." Verne looked up from his notebook. "I've done enough work for the night. Wouldn't it be wonderful if Jonas played the pianoforte for us?"

Chapter 16

THE NEXT MORNING DAWNED CLEAR, with a crisp fall breeze chasing itself across the city, through the spires, and around the tallest buildings. Celwyn patted Qing's back as he opened his coat for the bird to climb inside and snuggle in. Still aware of his injury, the magician took care as he headed up the hallway of the sleeper car, passing discordant snoring from Verne and Prince Leo's rooms. A light shone from under Mary Giovanna's door.

Jackson turned. He had just sat the tea tray on the bar as the magician entered the room.

"Good morning, Sir. We have Earl Grey, as usual, and a sampling of the new Ceylon you purchased."

"Thank you, I will try it first." He poured a cup and asked, "Do you know when the Conductor plans to depart? I don't hear the engine yet."

"No, I do not."

Jackson's mustache this morning had reverted back to its wispy form. Celwyn stared a moment until it appeared full and well-trimmed. Satisfied, he said, "We may need a quick trip into town for more of the Ceylon when the shops open."

"Yes, Sir."

The magician inhaled the steam from his cup. "Nice." As he took a sip, Jackson opened the shades on the windows. Celwyn happened to be watching as the porter froze, staggered backward, and then fainted dead away.

In one painful stride, Celwyn reached the window.

Just feet away, Stephen had been propped against a stunted tree with his legs splayed before him. A hatchet lay next to his severed hands, lying like misshapen trolls in the dry grass beside him. The slashes across his neck looked deep, and his sightless eyes were aimed straight at the *Elizabeth*.

Celwyn used magic to hide the scene from anyone passing by, whirled, and used more magic to propel himself down the hall of the sleeper car. He pounded on Bartholomew and Kang's doors. Kang opened his door first.

"Dead body—come on."

Bartholomew stepped into the hall, and Celwyn leaned on him as they followed Kang back up the hall until they reached the window overlooking the train yard.

The Professor cursed as he looked outside. "Should we hide the body and leave? Or stay and answer questions? And him?" Kang asked as he pointed to Jackson at their feet.

"I didn't do that," Celwyn said. "He just fainted." The magician dribbled water on the porter's face before transporting him back to the kitchen and erasing the memory of what he'd seen.

Bartholomew licked his lips. "I vote we leave with all possible haste."

"As do I," Kang agreed. "I'll ask the Conductor to do so."

The magician turned and, with a wave of his hand, wrapped the body in a tarp. For some reason, it reminded Celwyn of the wrapping and disposal of Talos on the *Zelda*. Too bad they weren't at sea as before; this would be an easier mess to clean up.

"I'll remove the body," Bartholomew offered without enthusiasm.

"I'll do it." In a moment, the body had disappeared. Celwyn stopped Kang with a hand on his arm. "Please ask the rest of the crew to gather here on your way up front. Don't say why. We'll talk with them. Tell Conductor Smith what occurred."

Ricardo couldn't have looked more miserable as he and the rest of the crew gathered at the dining table. Some appeared worse for wear from their late-night frivolities. The magician leaned forward with both hands on the table. Bartholomew and Kang stood on each side of him.

Celwyn turned to Abe and Andy. "I know you need to get back to the coal. Quickly: when you returned last evening, was there anyone loitering outside the train?"

Abe answered. "No. I had to carry Andy inside; he was so drunk." He gave his twin brother a shove, and the huge muscles of his shoulders rippled.

"I don't remember a thing," Andy said. "Why?"

"Last night, one of our porters, Stephen, was murdered," Kang said, gesturing outside. "And left out there. We do not wish to involve the police." He eyed them for hysteria and saw only confusion. "We wanted you to know. Please return to your stations. I've already spoken with Conductor Smith." As evidence, the *Elizabeth's* engines rumbled, vibrating the floor.

When the door closed behind the twins, Bartholomew turned to Ricardo and the remaining porters. "What time did you return last night?"

This early, roused from bed and told of a murder, Ludvik appeared paler and less substantial than usual, yet his eyes moved fast, haunted by something. "We came inside about two in the morning."

Bartholomew asked, "Was Stephen with you?" As he spoke, Prince Leo opened the door from the sleeping car, ushering Mary Giovanna ahead of him into the room.

Ludvik looked at Ricardo and said nothing.

Celwyn handed around cups of tea, insisting that the chef and porters take one. "Drink some. It will help you concentrate."

Ricardo studied his cup as if looking for an answer. "We tired of Stephen's complaining." He nodded at the others. “So, we left him in the pub and went to a different one. I am sorry.”

“There’s nothing to be sorry about, my friend.”

Analytical as always, Kang asked them, “Please, from the beginning, tell us what he said, or did, last night?”

“He was quiet until we got to the first cârciumă.” Jackson set his cup down without drinking from it. “We thought he was just happy to be out on the town after being sick.”

“When he finished his second beer, he started to complain. We told him to stop. He didn’t; we left.” Ludvik added a shrug as expressive as one of Verne’s.

Bartholomew asked, “What did he complain about?”

“You, Sirs.” Ricardo finished his tea, glanced at the magician, and put the cup back into the saucer. “He kept saying you had secrets.”

We certainly do, the magician thought. “His death will be another one.” He nodded at Ricardo. “Can you handle the work without him, or should we hire someone at our next stop?”

“I will let you know after breakfast.” Ricardo stood. To the others, he said, “Come along; we are behind schedule.”

Jackson still seemed a bit green around the gills, his usual efficiency long gone. It was Ludvik who told Celwyn, “I will be back with a fresh pot of tea.” He indicated Prince Leo and his daughter. “And coffee.”

Three hours later, they'd traveled far from the scene of the murder. While Kang concentrated on the maps, Bartholomew asked, "Do you think we will be suspected?" The train flew along the tracks, slowing only at populated areas where obstacles, such as cows or carts could become a problem. The air across the fields looked clear, and visibility was in their favor.

"Possibly not. I emptied his pockets before burying the body." The magician frowned, winced, and shifted position on the sofa. It was hell being wounded. "However, it wouldn't hurt for us to cross the border into the Soroca area before the police become curious about us."

Kang tapped the map under his elbow. "That will occur this afternoon. Rabnita is the first sizable city after that. At this pace, we should be there by dusk." Pastures flew by outside, the cattle staring at the train with moderate interest as they chewed.

Several minutes passed by before Celwyn spoke again.

"I wonder why Stephen was killed."

"I do, also," Bartholomew said. "And in such a blatant manner. Was it to call attention to us or because of something connected to him?"

Verne entered the room in one of his little gray suits. He represented the gray parrot, compared to Prince Leo, the most flamboyant tropical parrot. As always, Verne's mustache had been waxed and curled to perfection. The magician made a mental note to try that style on Jackson soon.

"Good morning, my friends! Another productive day at my desk with my favorite pen." The author stretched. "Where are we?"

Bartholomew brought him a cup of coffee. "Near Ocnita."

Verne thanked him and remained in the middle of the room for a moment, studying each of them before slowly settling into one of the club chairs. "Something has happened? So many serious faces."

Kang looked at Celwyn as if to say, 'he is your acquaintance, you tell him.'

The magician inhaled and spoke. "The reporter Stephen, the man who pretended to be our porter, is dead. He has been murdered."

Verne knocked over his coffee. Kang reached and threw him a bar towel.

As he wiped up the liquid, Verne sputtered, "Dead?"

"Yes. Mutilated and cut up." Kang didn't try to soften the news. "And placed next to our train."

The author paled. "Are you sure it was Stephen?"

"Quite. Each of his hands had been chopped off, and then he was stabbed." Celwyn didn't hold back the horrific nature of the crime: Verne needed to know that consequences sometimes followed indiscriminate gossiping.

Bartholomew leaned forward and in a voice as hard as steel, asked the author, "*Who is it*? Who is following us?"

Verne didn't say anything and peered into his coffee cup as if it would help him.

"Jules?" Celwyn demanded.

The author wet his lips and wiped the table again. "I do not know."

Celwyn blew a cold wind across the room. When Verne looked up to find the source, the magician's glare met him. "Who is it?" Unlike when he made a point with Prince Leo, the magician preferred not to use magic in front of Verne, it would only make him more curious. The magician waited.

"Phileas Fogg."

Bartholomew's brows rose in surprise. "The hero from your book?"

"Yes." Verne sipped coffee. "Phileas Fogg is real, the same as you and me. He wants money for his ideas that I used in the book." The author's eyes shifted. "I do not believe he would hurt anyone except me."

"Stephen said Herzog employed him to spy on us." The automat stared at Verne.

That surprised the author, and he blinked rapidly. "It could be. But Fogg could also have used Stephen." He opened his hands in supplication. "I do not know for certain but suspect it."

"Perhaps Fogg would attack Stephen if he blackmailed him or threatened him," Kang said. "What did the reporter know?"

Verne sat up and snapped, "I do not like being questioned like a criminal."

"We do not like being tricked," Celwyn retorted and narrowed his eyes. "Your balloon accident was not an accident."

"You can't prove that!"

"It is enough to know it."

Kang put a hand on Celwyn's arm. "Allow me." To Verne, he said, "Why are you here?"

The author shrugged again, this time seemingly just a shrug. "I must travel east."

It sounded true enough, and Verne met their eyes without wavering. The others exchanged a look. That would have to do for now.

The discussion between them did not affect Verne's appetite at luncheon. He declared the quiche a success and congratulated Ricardo during one of his trips to the table.

"Thank you, Sir." Their chef turned to Kang and asked, "Will you Sirs be dining on the train this evening?"

"Balti is big enough to have at least one inn with a restaurant. We will dine there and lessen the work for you today."

"Should we hire someone to replace Stephen?" Bartholomew asked.

Mary Giovanna put down her fork to listen to the conversation. Prince Leo did also.

"Yes. But it isn't urgent."

"We will check in town before our dinner. There may be someone anxious to travel." Celwyn asked, "Do you need anything else?"

"Whatever fresh fruit they have would be..."

"Consider it done," the magician told him.

Prince Leo continued to eat, enjoying a bite of the quiche just as the train hit rough tracks. The train lurched, and he grabbed his water glass.

Mary Giovanna was not as lucky. A bowl of stewed figs bounced into her lap. She gathered them with her bare fingers and flung the gooey mess into her plate.

"Excuse me." She batted away her father's hands when he tried to help her and stood.

The door to the sleeper car closed behind her as Kang retrieved the dish from the floor and handed it to Jackson. Prince Leo leaned closer to them and said, "Please be careful mentioning our destinations to Mary. Why are you going to Baghdad?"

"Classified," Kang replied.

Bartholomew smiled but hid it behind his napkin. The big man had never warmed up to their guest after he'd attached himself to them a few months ago. The danger he represented to Annabelle and Zander would not be easily forgiven.

Prince Leo looked ready to pursue the subject until Celwyn said, "I'm debating what to name my pet tiger. Do you have any suggestions?"

The dwarf's mouth snapped shut.

Verne looked from one to the other, trying to understand why the Professor and Bartholomew grinned like they'd just played a practical joke. He lifted his brows and then went back to eating.

"We need newspapers when we're out this evening." The automat nodded to himself, eyed the remains of the figs, and put his fork down.

Before addressing them again, Celwyn debated if he wanted dessert. Perhaps not. "Also, we need to look for some of that Ceylon tea too. Because of our hasty departure this morning, I wasn't able to obtain more of it." He regarded Verne. "If it is Phileas Fogg who pursues you, what does he look like? Not on the page, but in reality?"

Verne studied the magician from head to toe. "The cleanest description is the easiest." He seemed pleased with himself. "You and Fogg are identical in appearance, except his hair is not dark like yours. It is bright red."

Chapter 17

LATE THAT AFTERNOON, MARY Giovanna strolled down the main street of Balti in a fashionable dress and bustle, complete with parasol and hat. Her conservative colors seemed even more so compared to her father's, who had chosen a brilliant green suit with a gold walking stick. No wonder the Russians had been able to find the man.

Behind them, Celwyn kept pace with Verne, who chattered about his new book and the problems he had with some of his characters. The magician asked an occasional question to keep the conversation going, but his attention, as was Kang and Bartholomew's, centered on the pedestrians of the city. Had Phileas Fogg followed them here?

Celwyn buttoned his coat. The fall winds had returned, swirling through the trees and bringing the smell of smoke from household stoves and the nearby mill. In the near distance, he spied a tall white steeple surrounded by red and blue minarets and several brick buildings. Most of the street signs had been printed in Russian, with either a Serbian or Turkish version underneath. The magician gazed down several of the streets and studied the architecture. If he allowed himself to do so, he would be able to see the town as it was years ago. But not now; there were things weighing on his mind.

"How many more days until we reach Tehran?" Verne asked.

From beside him, Kang said, "Today is Tuesday. We may be there by Saturday. It depends upon the Maramura Mountains." As he spoke, a meandering melody reached them with an afterthought twang to it.

Soon they found the source as they approached a corner. Musicians sat on the sidewalk cross-legged with sitars in their laps, playing more for themselves than the pedestrians. Celwyn was sufficiently distracted by their situation to not participate, and he and the others waited for a large carriage to pass by before crossing the street. On the next block, pairs of men in dark elbisesi poured water on the cobblestones and swept the stones with brooms to push the manure away from foot traffic. Nothing could be done about the smell, and as usual, Kang wrinkled his nose.

Prince Leo stopped, open-mouthed, in front of a shop whose window had been filled with bolts of fabric. Velvets and satins predominated. As if he had just found the gates of heaven, the dwarf dropped his daughter's hand and stepped inside. Everyone else continued down the street.

"It seems like evening already," Bartholomew said. Clouds had obscured the setting sun, and there appeared to be very few streetlights this side of the avenue. In contrast, just ahead, the main district glowed with scores of torches and the noise and smell of much more traffic.

"There is a staffing agency across the street." Kang indicated an older brick building under a tattered brown awning.

"I'll go." Considering his recent injury, Celwyn moved as fast as he could across the avenue ahead of several horse-drawn carts. As he attained the opposite sidewalk, he noticed a young man, really little more than a boy, waiting outside the building. He had no coat and appeared cold and very alone.

Two men approached him.

In seconds, they'd knocked the lad's spectacles off, then his hat, which rolled into the mushy dung pile at the curb. One of the men shoved the boy to the ground, and the other lifted his foot to kick him. As discreetly as possible, considering Kang watched and would complain about the notoriety, the magician pelted the attackers with the manure. They yelled as more manure bombarded them. When the dung pile arose from the ground in the shape of a bear, they backed up. When it roared, the men screamed and ran. The dung quivered like a bowl of jelly, and then subsided back into the street again.

The entire episode happened so quickly few pedestrians witnessed the scene, and those that did quickly disappeared. Celwyn reached to help the young man up, but his eyes remained closed, so the magician opened a hand, and cold water splashed his face.

"Here, allow me to help you." Celwyn did so and handed over the lad's spectacles, which now had clean lenses. When he saw the boy's frantic look, he added, "I chased them away."

The lad had the physique and quick movements of someone who didn't eat on a regular basis.

"What is your name?"

The boy dug in the bag at his feet and produced a small tablet and chalk. After a few strokes of the chalk, he handed the tablet to Celwyn.

The magician sighed as he read the tablet: those ruffians had attacked a mute. He wished he had done more to them. "You write like you have been educated, Otto. Are you hoping for employment?" Celwyn pointed to the shop sign, *Arbeits*, above their heads.

Otto nodded.

"Are you willing to travel out of this city?"

As Celwyn conversed with the boy, Kang trotted up to them, leaving Verne with Bartholomew and Mary Giovanna. The magician noticed she wasted no time slipping her arm through the big man's. Or perhaps, she felt nervous because of the gloom of the street.

"Otto, this is my friend, Professor Kang." As they shook hands, Celwyn said, "He is looking for employment." The magician waved at Bartholomew, who escorted Verne and Mary Giovanna to join them on the curb. "This our guest, Miss Mary Giovanna, and our colleague and friend, Bartholomew. This gentleman is Mr. Verne." They exchanged acknowledgements, and then he added, "Otto is looking for employment and is willing to travel out of this city."

Mary Giovanna politely pretended to admire the shoes in the window of the shop next door while more silent questions flew between the three friends. After a moment, Bartholomew squatted until he was on eye level with Otto. "Would you be interested in working for us?"

When Otto left to retrieve his belongings, Celwyn tucked a packet of biscuits and apples into the pockets of a new coat without touching it. It was doubtful the boy would notice the coat for at least a few minutes. The magician watched him a moment more and then joined the others as they approached the *Gida Kaz* for dinner. Their new porter had agreed to gather his belongings and meet them at the train. Celwyn would make sure he had his dinner … and keep him alive.

When the automat asked how he explained the coat to Otto, the magician told him he hadn't. Before the automat could tease him more, Prince Leo came running up the cobblestones toting a large box, and they filed inside the restaurant.

In an aside, Kang told Bartholomew and Celwyn, "If Otto stays with us, we can take him along to Singapore and eventually to Prague. It is a more civilized city of many nationalities. I doubt we'll need three porters, but the lad might do better there."

"Or working at Tellyhouse?" Celwyn raised a brow at them.

"I've moved Stephen's belongings into the storage car," Ricardo said as he and Celwyn walked out of the kitchen a few hours later. "The bed has been made up for Otto, and I have added some of my clothes to his new quarters. He can roll up the cuffs as needed."

The magician reached for his coin purse, but Ricardo stopped him. "My idea, Sir. Do not insult me." They had reached the dining room. "I understand he cannot speak. No one from my crew will be rude to him, I can assure you."

Celwyn said, "Thank you, my friend." Through the windows, they watched Otto picking his way across the train yard. By the time he reached the train, Celwyn met him on the steps.

"Welcome. I hope you enjoy beef goulash. Ricardo has a plate ready for you. And there is some crusty bread."

The magician handed a whiskey to Bartholomew, joined him on the sofa, and crossed his legs. Things were quiet. Across the room, Prince Leo played checkers with Kang at the dining table. It neared midnight, and the shades had been drawn, making the room cozier. Both Verne and Mary Giovanna had retired for the night.

"I think Otto will work out fine." Bartholomew sniffed his glass and drank. "Tomorrow, I'll verify our itinerary with him to be sure he is ready for a long journey and instruct him on the need to keep the information away from our guests."

As he nodded and listened to the big man, the magician added a phonograph to the table next to the bar. The hand crank began to whirl, and the music of R.P. Chope played just loud enough to be heard while allowing them to continue a conversation. So beautiful. Celwyn held a baton and conducted until the piece ended.

He savored the taste of his last evening whiskey and wondered how much longer he could put off speaking with Bartholomew about Prince Leo's daughter. Xiau should take care of this, but they'd argued about it until he'd agreed to do it. He didn't look forward to the task. Bartholomew was as honest and innocent as could be and a ready victim for a wily woman.

Hell. After a long inward sigh, he said, "This isn't my business, my friend, but have you spoken enough with Mary Giovanna to determine her character?" When he saw the big man's face stiffen, Celwyn regretted the conversation even more but plowed ahead like a ship through stormy seas. "She seems a mite… unpredictable. At dinner, she appeared angry, especially at her father."

Bartholomew maintained his annoyed expression another moment, then nodded and relaxed.

"I saw that also." The big man tapped Celwyn's knee. "Do not distress yourself. She is a nice woman."

Celwyn took a deep breath. "You should know that before you displayed a personal interest in her, I asked the Professor to wire his contacts to learn more about her. We'll have answers by Tehran."

"I doubt there will be anything to learn." Bartholomew pursed his lips. "She has told me of Rome and Toulouse and her theatre work there." His eyes took on the glazed head-in-the-sand-in-love inward stare.

Wonderful, the magician thought. It had progressed further than he thought. He tried again.

"Just be careful with your heart, my friend."

The next morning dawned rainy and dreary. From his favorite chair in front of the windows, the magician sipped his morning tea and watched the day's first pedestrians on the far side of the train yard. Verne sat next to him, stirring sugar into his coffee.

"It is early, Jules," Celwyn said.

Verne dumped in more cream and sipped. "It is. Usually by now I have written two pages. But this morning?" He slapped the table, and Celwyn jumped. "Nothing! I cannot write!"

The magician poured more tea and wished for a quiet few moments to wake up. However, politeness dictated a conversation. "Does it seem like a well that has run dry? Or is something bothering you, interfering with your inspiration or concentration?"

Verne growled to himself, "Both."

Celwyn chuckled. "I never have that problem." When he wanted magic, the magic always responded. The only question unanswered was what form of magic he would settle upon.

The door to the kitchen opened, and Otto backed into the room carrying a tray. He had washed and appeared fed and rested. Celwyn welcomed him and said, "Otto, do you remember Mr. Verne?"

The porter nodded at the introduction, replaced the tea and coffee pots, and left again. Next to the teapot lay a piece of paper.

"Remember, Otto is mute. Do not be offended if he doesn't speak." The magician opened the paper. "He will write communications as needed."

> Dear Mr. Celwyn. Thank you for this position.
>
> I am grateful to you and the others.
>
> Otto.

As he read the note, the magician speculated about Otto's past, watching the pedestrians hurrying down the street outside. A few of them stopped and studied the *Elizabeth.* He cursed under his breath. That was just what they needed: more attention.

After several minutes, he said, "Jules, I am your host, and it is time you told me about your connection to Stephen. What does his murder have to do with you?"

The author eyed him from under bushy eyebrows and looked away. Minutes of uncomfortable silence went by. Celwyn began tapping his foot.

"Oh, all right. Phileas Fogg hired Stephen to join your train and write a big story. Fogg is a partner in several periodicals." He opened and closed his hands as if he could release his own duplicity. "In reality, the man was supposed to spy on me also." His voice trembled. "I fear what Fogg will do now."

In the train yard, the loading of coal onto the *Elizabeth* began. The delivery cart appeared full, and it would take a while for the transfer. Celwyn didn't mind: if it took long enough, he would have a breakfast that didn't jiggle and jerk while he tried to eat it.

"You confirm that Phileas Fogg is real? Not just a character?"

"Yes."

"When did you discover that he had followed you from Prague?"

Verne finished his coffee and sat the cup down again as he considered his reply.

"After I joined your party on this train."

"Go on." Celwyn looked at him with disgust. Verne was a guest, not part of their party.

Verne didn't note the magician's displeasure as he tried to pour more coffee, only succeeding in slopping part of it into his cup. "I am much more concerned about Phileas Fogg than I can say. I portrayed him as affable and adventurous in the manuscript. In reality, he is petty, vindictive, and dangerous."

"Once more: why is he following you?"

The author looked away, and his lips tightened. Just as Celwyn entered his thoughts, two things occurred simultaneously. Kang joined them at the table, and a man who matched the description of Phileas Fogg strolled across the train yard as big as day, heading straight toward the *Elizabeth.*

Chapter 18

VERNE'S EYES BULGED, AND HE GOT to his feet faster than Celwyn would have thought possible. The magician eased him back into his chair. "I will protect you."

As if the train had been public, and he'd just shown his ticket to a purser, Phileas Fogg climbed up the steps into the *Elizabeth.*

Then the magician received another surprise.

Professor Xiau Kang, mechanical man, mild-mannered doctor and scientist, jumped up again and walked right up to the intruder, tilting his head back to confront the much taller man. Celwyn smiled. Every day, Xiau continued to amaze him.

"Who are you, sir? This is a private train." With his hands on his hips, Kang's stance had a certain aggression and readiness about it.

Perhaps I won't be needed; Celwyn leaned back and studied the intruder.

Fogg's suit appeared to be of a fine cut, his hat expensive, and cuffs pressed just so. In Celwyn's estimation, the man stood at exactly his own height and breadth, handsome to a point, and his eyes as green as the magician's own. He supposed they looked a bit alike. When Fogg removed his hat, the expected red hair shone like a healthy spaniel who had just been brushed.

The man bowed. "Phileas Fogg. And you are?"

Bartholomew arrived in the room, saw the interloper, and advanced closer.

"That is Bartholomew of Juba, Sudan." Celwyn gestured. "This is Professor Kang, and I am Jonas Celwyn. But you already know that." He nodded at Verne. "You also know each other."

"Yes," Fogg said, "My business is with Mr. Verne." He addressed the author, "Could we step outside for a moment?"

Verne had scuttled behind the magician and leaned around him to peer at Fogg. He shook his head, fear dancing a jig in his eyes.

The magician rubbed his face and gazed longingly at his tea. Some of his mornings featured dead bodies and no tea; others, it was unnecessary drama and no tea. He was beginning to sense a deplorable pattern emerging.

"Let's all sit down."

Phileas Fogg hesitated.

"Or Bartholomew will remove you from our train." Celwyn turned to Otto as they settled at the table. "Please ask Ricardo to hold breakfast for a while." Otto nodded and retreated to the kitchen as fast as he could.

The look Bartholomew shot the intruder indicated he would enjoy tossing him into the mud outside, but he sat beside the magician and poured coffee while Kang covered Verne with a speculative and annoyed look. Then he transferred the assessment to the interloper. Several moments passed, the only sounds were the scraping and thumping noises from the loading of the coal. The task would complete soon.

The magician sighed. Either his breakfast would again bounce across the table, or they'd delay departure. He glared at Fogg. The man had settled into a seat next to Kang, as comfortable as could be, and picked up a cup.

"Before your arrival, Mr. Verne related how you had hired Stephen, a reporter, to infiltrate our train." Celwyn held onto as much control as he could muster, and not just because of this interruption. He smelled bacon, and his stomach rumbled in admiration. Another reminder of the disruption to his morning.

Bartholomew leaned forward, fixing Phileas Fogg with a stare. His ham-sized hands flexed. "He also mentioned that you promised the reporter a sensational story about us," he nodded at Verne, "and that you are pursuing Mr. Verne because of his book. You are expecting to be compensated."

If he hadn't been watching, Celwyn would have missed the slight shake of Fogg's head and then the ghost of a smile before the man said, "Yes, that is correct." Fogg addressed the author. "I wanted to inform you that I am dropping my suit for compensation." He drained his cup and stood.

Really? He invaded their train just for that? Celwyn entered Fogg's thoughts and heard too much self-congratulation on the man's performance to believe what he had said. Then came a few derogatory thoughts about Kang and opinions about Bartholomew's skin color. Celwyn's attempt at restraint evaporated.

Sometimes, quiet magical displays are the best. The magician sent a line of fire ants across the man's hand, up his sleeve, then down his tall collar. At first, Fogg pretended he didn't feel anything. Then he slapped his neck, and by the time he made it down the steps to the train yard, he was tearing off his tie and running.

As he watched Phileas Fogg's retreat, Bartholomew just smiled.

Later that morning, Celwyn brought a pad of paper and fistful of pencils to the kitchen and handed them to Otto. "For communicating to and from the crew."

Ludvik smiled as he folded a towel. "We have developed a system. Otto will wink for 'yes,' and shake his head for 'no.'" He pretended to sock Otto in the arm and received a playful push back.

The happiness on Otto's face made up for Celwyn's irritating morning.

The magician asked Ricardo, "What is for luncheon? It smells very good."

Their chef stopped chopping carrots long enough to say, "Pork tenderloin. Now, everyone except Jackson, get out of my kitchen. You have work to do."

"Verne is in his cabin writing," the automat told Celwyn while they watched the endless hilly terrain go by and inhaled the smell of the forests from the open window. Across the room, Bartholomew sat next to Mary Giovanna on the sofa, talking in low tones. As Kang watched them, he said, "We need to discuss our plans for when we arrive in Tehran next week."

"Tonight, we stay in Rostov?"

"Yes."

"There is no guarantee we can talk privately this evening. We need to talk now." Celwyn gazed at Mary Giovanna. "I think you will soon see Mary fleeing for the water closet in her room."

"Oh?" Kang asked with a brow up. "How long will she be gone?"

Celwyn pursed his lips. "Oh, as long as necessary while we talk."

As predicted, Mary Giovanna excused herself rather hurriedly and left the room. Bartholomew stared at the hallway door a moment and joined them at the table.

"We need to discuss Tehran ... and our guests," the automat told him.

Bartholomew nodded. "Prince Leo and his daughter will be leaving the train when we arrive there."

"How do you feel about that?" the magician asked.

Bartholomew didn't answer for a moment, but when he did, they had to listen closely because he spoke so low. "It has only been a year since my wife died. I cannot completely trust my judgement about personal matters."

Kang told him, "There is no hurry."

"But there is." Bartholomew opened his hands and sighed. "Mary wants me to remain with her and her father." He spared a look at the door to the sleeper car. "Prince Leo asked me not to tell her that we're heading east to Tehran."

Celwyn had expected something like this.

"I told her I would consider it, but I hadn't had a private moment to discuss it with you two." The big man sighed.

Taking the scenario further, Celwyn speculated on what Annabelle's opinion would be of Mary Giovanna. He had a hunch that Bartholomew had already considered what Annabelle would think; they were close friends. The magician had also witnessed Mary Giovanna's moods and considered them far beyond 'womanly problems.' A glimpse at Kang revealed his furrowed brow and lowered gaze.

Qing hopped off the windowsill, onto the bar and began pecking at a whiskey decanter. Of all the things the mechanical bird did, this was the loudest and most annoying.

Celwyn asked Bartholomew, "What do you want to do?"

"It would partly depend on how much assistance I could be to them, perhaps to help her and her father settle at a hotel."

"We could wait a few days in Tehran for you," Kang said. "Or we could continue to Singapore and pick you up on the way back."

The Professor's logic prevailed as usual. Celwyn regarded Bartholomew. "At this point, I do not anticipate any problems in Singapore, and either way would be fine."

"However, we'd prefer you were with us." Kang elbowed him. "I would miss our checker's games."

"Zander would be inconsolable if you did not return to Prague with us," Celwyn reminded him.

Bartholomew nearly smiled through his worry. "You know how to make things difficult, Jonas."

Ludvik arrived with more refreshments and the news that luncheon would be ready soon. After he left again, Kang said, "Let's speak of Mr. Verne before we're interrupted."

"This will be easier." Celwyn told them, "I like Jules but do not need him with us once we arrive in Singapore."

Kang said, "Agreed. Mr. Verne needs to disassociate himself from us long before then."

The train blew her whistle as they rounded a long curve, seconds more, and the *Elizabeth* chugged through a village so small that the train was longer than the row of brick houses.

"I do not trust that man, Fogg," the big man grumbled.

"Neither do we. How do we get rid of Mr. Verne? That should exorcise Fogg from our activities," the automat said.

"The simplest approach, perhaps? I scare him away." Celwyn rubbed his hands together. "If so, I am entertained, and our problem is solved."

Kang laughed. "No, you aren't recovered enough yet."

"What are Mr. Verne's plans?" Bartholomew remained serious. "Other than keeping ahead of Fogg?" Qing's pecking on the decanter grew louder. "Stop that!" Qing halted long enough to stare at him and then went back to pecking.

Celwyn frowned. "Unknown. No matter what, we need to get to Singapore before Jules ... or Fogg if he still pursues him."

"It is curious why he continues to follow Mr. Verne, is it not?" Kang asked.

Mary Giovanna opened the door from the sleeper car and started into the room. The magician wiggled his little finger, and she grabbed her stomach and rushed out again. Bartholomew hadn't spotted her, which was just as well.

"If we encourage Mr. Verne off the train when we first arrive in Tehran, he would still be able to travel on to Singapore before us on another train." Kang pulled at his lip and thought. "We'd run the risk of seeing him along the way or after we arrived there."

Ludvik entered the room pushing the cart loaded with their luncheon dishes.

"I'll go wash up," Celwyn said with an innocent batting of his eyes, "and check on Mary Giovanna to see if she is feeling well enough to join us."

Bartholomew dutifully kept his attention on the view outside but couldn't control the amusement dancing in his eyes.

Throughout lunch, Verne regaled the table with stories of his travels around the world.

"No matter where I have been, I always return to Amiens. France is my home." Verne savored a bite of salad. "Hmm. I love eggs on a salad."

"How odd." Mary Giovanna looked down her nose at the author. "I always found Paris dirty and the people horrid. Uneducated." She picked at her lettuce as if she suspected something to crawl out of it. "Their culture is devoid of imagination. They cannot recognize art." She wrinkled her nose at a spear of tomato. "In Italia, we have art and much more."

Verne reared up, ready to climb over the table. Prince Leo grabbed his arm and turned to his daughter, "Apologize, Mary."

"I tell the truth!"

Bartholomew looked as uncomfortable as only a besotted man could in the circumstances.

Prince Leo tried again, "Mary—"

She slapped him hard and stood, knocking over her chair.

Celwyn decided to let the woman's personality play out, a much better example, or deterrent, than any words he could offer Bartholomew. The big man should see all sides of what he was considering, and from what Kang had said, she had done something similar several times before when Bartholomew wasn't present.

"Giovanna—you must—"

"You are a poor excuse for a father. A disgrace!" She started across the room and whirled, coming back to flatten her hands on the table and glare at them. "It is your fault I am here," she ground out. "I should be on a stage now, not burrowing into obscurity in a desert hellhole!" Her voice had risen to a screech. She backhanded the water carafe, sending it flying off the table.

Celwyn had endured enough. He stared at Mary Giovanna; she grimaced and ran for her water closet.

"Look—" The magician pointed outside. When Verne dutifully did so, Celwyn cleaned up the mess the young woman had made. He said, "Let us have peace for the rest of our meal. Ricardo has done an excellent job with the roast pork."

"I agree." Kang chewed. "It is superb."

It appeared to be a toss-up who was more miserable: Bartholomew or Prince Leo? The big man looked like he wished he was back in Juba.

Prince Leo gazed at the door his daughter had fled through. "There is something wrong with her," he said, more to himself than the table. He turned to Celwyn and spoke so softly they almost couldn't hear him, "She frightens me."

After the luncheon dishes had been removed, Verne left to write in his room, and Celwyn steered Prince Leo over to the sofa, gesturing for Bartholomew and Kang to follow. The stretch of tracks they traveled along seemed particularly bumpy, and the green fields had been replaced by a rocky landscape of desolation. Occasionally, sprouts of green grew between the rocks, and a collection of scraggly trees decorated the hillsides, clutching at the inhospitable landscape.

The magician handed Prince Leo a cup of coffee and settled in the opposite chair. The others stood behind him.

"Tell us about your daughter, Leo," he urged in a gentle voice.

The *Elizabeth* started down a gradual incline. When she blew her whistle, the dwarf jumped, spilling his coffee. Celwyn sent him a towel from the bar and waited. When the man spoke, it was more to himself than those with him.

"She has always been different, peculiar if you will. Sometimes violent to other children." He sighed. "When she became an adult, her mother left her more than adequate funds. Yet, Mary loves the stage. She considers everyday living a performance."

"How so?" Bartholomew asked.

"You've seen some of it." Prince Leo shrugged. "She makes entrances, does everything she can to garner admiration. Sometimes it is shocking. Other times, she acts normally. Then at times, she is like what we saw a few minutes ago."

"Nudity is shocking," Kang commented.

Bartholomew made an effort to balance the facts. "There is nothing wrong with the stage."

"No, except it comes with criticism, and she cannot accept the criticism." The dwarf looked at them, one at a time, trying to help them understand. "She becomes erratic. Talks crazily."

Kang said, "Critics can be cruel."

A long train, loaded with bins of grain and traveling the other way on an adjacent track, roared by them. Everyone jumped. When it was quiet again, conversation resumed.

"She needs constant praise. Woe to anyone who impedes her career." Prince Leo shuddered.

"Isn't a trip to Tehran out of her way for her theatre work?" Celwyn asked.

"Well..." Prince Leo squirmed. "I may have told her we were boarding the *Royal Victoria* in Bagdad."

"That's south of Tehran—you lied to her." Celwyn's mouth opened. If he didn't feel sorry for the man, he would have had him up in the air and twirling. "Good grief!"

Bartholomew's brow furrowed. "We veer east, toward Sarab and eventually Tehran, very soon."

"I did not think it wise to correct Mary's assumption that we were going to Bagdad." The dwarf opened his hands, appealing to them.

"Why not?" Celwyn demanded.

"I didn't want to fight with her."

"Coward." The magician grumbled.

Bartholomew exhaled heavily. "Now, I understand. She was intent on a few weeks in Baghdad before the *Royal Victoria* came through and then on to Byzantium."

"Eventually, back to Rome, Seville, and Munich?" Kang asked.

The big man nodded. "Yes. She mentioned those cities and more. I didn't know what to say."

"And now, one of us needs to tell her we aren't traveling south to where she could pick up that train. She could take a train from Tehran to Bagdad, though, Correct?" Celwyn stared at the dwarf.

"Yes."

"She can't travel alone that distance," Bartholomew said.

Prince Leo said, "I know. I will escort her all the way to Rome if that is where she wants to go." He looked at the magician. "The Russians no longer pursue me because of Jonas."

A lamp sailed by Prince Leo's head and crashed into the bar.

"So! You *lied* to me!" Mary Giovanna screamed as she stalked toward them.

Kang murmured, "Oh, no."

Bright red color suffused the woman's face, and she had the frantic look of a rabid animal as she waved her arms at them.

Prince Leo stood and slipped behind his chair. "I was coming in to tell you as soon as we finished talking." He put out a hand. "Please, Mary. It will only be a few days from Tehran to Baghdad. Please."

When she seized a crystal ashtray, ready to let it fly, Celwyn removed it from her hand. It hovered in the air above her. She tried to grab it. "*Give that back to me*!"

"Miss, this is my train. Calm yourself." Celwyn's voice hardened. "*Now*."

"You think I am afraid of you?" She spun around and ran back into the sleeper car. "You will all regret this!!"

Ludvik had come through from the kitchen and saw the suspended ashtray and shattered lamp. He swiveled, retreating to the kitchen.

Chapter 19

After Prince Leo had been convinced to go comfort his daughter, Kang said, "At least we don't have to invent a reason to remove them when we reach Tehran."

"True." Celwyn poured tea and sniffed the air. "On a brighter note, I smell cookies baking."

Kang smiled briefly. "I smell them too, but it isn't enough of a distraction to forget what just happened."

"I agree." Bartholomew's face displayed the misery he felt. "I misjudged Mary."

"Love is blind," Celwyn said. "Or similar."

"Not yet, but it was nearly that way," the big man admitted.

"When the time comes, I would suggest that you are very careful in letting her know that your feelings have changed," Kang said.

"A modicum of caution is good," Celwyn agreed. If the subject wasn't so serious, Kang would have made a comment about the magician's lack of caution.

Outside the train, the landscape had become rocky, with larger boulders multiplying across the hills, heralding the beginning of the mountains. Celwyn opened the window without getting up, immediately smelling the high forests in the distance and noting how much colder the air had become. He closed the window again as Kang spoke.

"These rails are fairly new," he said as if it were he who could read thoughts now. "The Alborz Mountains reach 4,800 feet."

Celwyn nodded. "If necessary, I will help the *Elizabeth* when we reach the highest point of the crossing."

"I'm glad we're able to plan for a few minutes," Bartholomew said as he crossed to the large map on the wall. "We haven't had much of a chance because of your injury ... and because of the guests."

Kang joined him at the wall. "Over the next few days, we'll stop in either Sarab or Zanjan, depending on how well we do. After Tehran, Gorgan will be a stop just before the main part of the mountains. I hear it is a very nice town to visit."

"How many days will it be before we reach Gazipur?" the big man asked, tracing their path with a finger on the map.

Kang pursed his lips. "About ten days after we leave Tehran."

Otto arrived, balancing a large vase of flowers in his arms. Ludvik followed him with a dustpan.

Either Ludvik hadn't told him of the earlier incident, which Celwyn had cleaned up, or magic didn't frighten either of them. Ludvik stared at the spot where the other vase had crashed, saw nothing, and hid the dustpan behind his back.

"Otto has no family, true?" Bartholomew asked.

"I think so," Celwyn said. "It pains him to talk about it."

Bartholomew sighed all the way to his very large feet. "We appear to be a group without families. All I have left is an aunt in Juba. She is as strong as an ox and mean as a snake. She will outlive me." He brightened. "She still gathers all of the vegetables in her garden herself."

"As you know, I used to have a brother." Kang shuddered. "Thankfully, he is no more. It isn't nice to say, but I would not exist at the moment if he hadn't been disposed of by Jonas."

"Speaking of that, what happened to his power source?" Celwyn pointed to his chest and told Bartholomew, "It is the 'heart' of the automats."

Kang said, "I do not know. Didn't you throw it over the side? Either way, I'm glad I do not have to fear him anymore."

"What was he like when you were younger?" Bartholomew asked.

"Secretive and strange." Kang lifted his brows. "'Younger' is a relative term. I have always looked exactly like this."

Celwyn turned toward him. "Do you want some fashionable updates?"

"No!" Kang pretended outrage. "Now stop that. And leave my ears alone." He eyed the magician. "Did you have a family? Where were you born?"

"Trying to distract me? I was born in Edinburgh." Celwyn had told few people of that fact, but it seemed easy to tell Bartholomew and Kang until he heard Kang's reaction.

"A *Scotsman*?" Kang laughed. "I do not believe it."

Celwyn's chin went up. "It is so." He tried not to smile back at the automat.

The magician crossed his ankles, relaxing and closing his eyes. Remembering. A sad expression replaced his smile and then cleared. "I'm trying to recall the last time I talked of this and think it was soon after I met Suzanne. She was curious." His eyes remained closed as his hand opened, and a wavey image appeared to stand beside him. The transparent and beautiful young woman with flowing hair placed a hand on his shoulder. "We had taken a short journey to the coast near Inverurie. Near the olde homestead. My father had been lord over the fields for as far as you could see. My mother had inherited the land, mind you."

"You grew up there?" Bartholomew asked.

"Gryphon Hall had been in her family for years." Celwyn's eyes opened wide, accompanying a sour smile. "It was quite the scandal when she married my father; he was a widower with a young son. He was also an alchemist and as mysterious as you'd expect." The magician fell silent for a moment before continuing. "My father had a rather unsavory reputation, which his children inherited along with a striking resemblance to himself."

"How surprising," Kang commented with as much sarcasm as he could.

"Yes, we were examples of direct inheritance. Although as my brother grew older, he became quite individual both in appearance and, ah, some habits few others knew about." Celwyn laughed as he remembered. "During that time, and for many years, my father consulted with Borelli, the Queen's alchemist. In his early years at court, he hid his magic, but not from his children. As I grew older, I noticed that children of my age couldn't do what I could, and realized it was not always advisable to question odd things to anyone outside our family." He regarded his companions. "However, my half-brother could hide his talents better. He was supposedly wiser and exhibited different abilities."

"Fascinating," Kang murmured. "Such as?"

"While I can read thoughts, he cannot. Yet, some of his abilities were more powerful. He could perform magic at greater distances from where he appeared to be at any moment. Otherwise, in many ways, our magic is very much alike."

"Is he immortal also?" Bartholomew asked.

Celwyn shrugged. "Yes. I haven't seen him in well over three hundred years." He stroked the arm of the image of Suzanne, remembering her, and then dissolved the image. "He has a nasty disposition, probably inherited from his mother. The last I saw of him was in the courtyard of the Fotheringhay Castle in England." At Bartholomew's frown of confusion, he added, "The year was 1542. We sat in the audience, drunk as lords."

"Why?"

"To watch the beheading of Mary, Queen of Scots, of course."

Kang shook his head in disbelief.

"At the time, it was considered high entertainment. Only those with engraved invitations were allowed to attend." He thought more. "I think I still have mine somewhere."

"Like the Professor says, nothing is boring with you, Jonas." Bartholomew stood and stretched. "What was your brother's name?"

"Pelaez." The magician made a face. "That is the only name I've ever known for him. If he exists still, I wonder if I'd even recognize him."

The train hit a trestle square on, and when the vase of flowers would have fallen, the magician yawned and rescued it.

That night, it seemed as if they were in the presence of another woman when a demure and reserved Mary Giovanna joined them at the dinner table. Everyone stood until Kang had pushed her chair in. On her other side, Prince Leo tried to hide his trembling hand as he picked up his water glass and pointedly avoided looking at his daughter. Just as they began the meal, Verne arrived, full of apologies.

"My lambs, I am so sorry I am late. I was in the middle of a scene." He sat and snapped open his napkin. "However, my hero: he prevailed!"

The automat spooned soup. "Tell us about your writing process, please? How do you find your characters?"

"How do you decide upon their actions?" Bartholomew asked.

Verne tasted his soup, and a beam of satisfaction creased his face like a ray from the sun. "My characters find me. They materialize as the plot comes alive, and then they decide what will happen."

The Professor's raised eyebrows indicated his disbelief.

"I am serious. I do not sketch out the plots; they come to me as I write." Verne shrugged. "The characters evolve to match them. Each situation, every reaction. The emotions, they drive everything. They stir the plot like a whisk through eggs!"

The conversation continued through the roasted chicken, the buttered and parslied new potatoes, and on to fresh berries. Celwyn kept a discreet eye on Mary Giovanna. Although the conversation remained as light as the cream on the berries, she kept a white-knuckle grip on her fork, and her dark eyes pinned on her father, who still refused to look at her.

As they adjourned from the table, Celwyn told Prince Leo in an aside, "Keep your door locked at night until we reach Tehran."

"I will." The dwarf blinked at him while they stood at the windows and pretended interest in the rocks and trees they passed. His daughter remained on the other side of the room in conversation with Bartholomew, but her attention centered on her father. His voice shook a bit as he said, "This phase will pass. She is just confused."

"Are you sure?"

"She would never hurt me."

Celwyn made sure everyone could hear as he said, "It is already getting cooler outside. A good thing we travel before the snow."

"This land is so desolate, I wonder how people survived before modern times," the dwarf said.

Celwyn pointed out a pair of camels that didn't even raise their heads as the train chugged by less than a dozen feet from them. "Without them, nothing would have been possible." A moment more, and he added, "There is always danger, even in desolate places. Wild rivers rush down from the foothills during the storms. They could wash the *Elizabeth* right off the rails."

"Sometimes, danger is much closer," Prince Leo whispered with a furtive look over his shoulder that belied his earlier denial.

Chapter 20

TWO DAYS LATER, THE *ELIZABETH* arrived at the least occupied part of the train yard in Tehran as directed by the station master. At high noon, only two other trains had berthed there, but dozens of workers readied carts of produce and stacked bales of wool. The rest of the terminal yard teemed with passengers and vendors.

By arrangement, Ricardo and Jackson hopped off the train first and headed for the Grand Bazaar for a lunch out and supplies.

A flurry of activity on the *Elizabeth* kept the magician entertained as Mary Giovanna and her father prepared to decamp, constantly calling for Ludvik to find an errant boa, tie, or handkerchief. The porter was also prevailed upon to help transport their trunks into the dining room and then outside. As usual, Ludvik displayed a measure of calmness that the magician envied.

Bartholomew did his best to keep busy and out of Mary Giovanna's sight. At the moment, he remained in the train yard supervising the loading of coal. In front of him, the local laborers kept a steady pace as they shoveled. After a few minutes, the big man removed his jacket and rolled up his sleeves as the sun bore down directly overhead, making the light more intense in the dry air.

From the center of the city bells tolled, calling the faithful to prayer.

"There are Christians here, too?" Celwyn asked Kang.

"Yes, but the majority is Shi'a Islam." The Professor glanced out the window. "Uprisings from some of the other groups are common. There is nothing as intolerant as one religion to another."

"For the moment, though, they seem peaceful." The bells continued to echo musically.

Kang sat in front of a collection of maps spread across the dining table. The regular map table was full of other maps he hadn't finished with yet. He folded up one of them and tied string around it. "Can I assume that we're leaving early tomorrow morning?" On a larger map, he tapped a province with his pencil. "I wish we could travel at night."

Celwyn shook his head. "From what the Conductor tells me, serious travel will have to be always with daylight so that he can see the tracks. I could spend some energy lighting the tracks but not for the preciseness needed and the distance required for him to stop the train. Nor could I do it all night and protect us all day." He turned and put up his chin so they could see his profile. "I need to rest to look my best, you know."

Bartholomew had joined them, and he laughed.

Xiau didn't seem to notice. "I understand about the tracks." Kang's voice held a certain amount of resignation. "I miss Elizabeth greatly."

The door to the sleeping car opened, and Prince Leo entered in a flowing white robe. Celwyn blinked. Between the beard and the robe, he resembled a tiny but devious Moses.

The automat blurted, "Where did you get that?"

Prince Leo twirled and said, "Do you like it? I found it at our last stop." He advanced on the coffee service. "Luncheon will be in town?"

Celwyn noted with a bit of curiosity and relief that Leo did not seem as afraid today.

Kang said, "Yes, we will dine in town. You and your daughter are welcome to join us."

Prince Leo's carefree mood evaporated like raindrops on a hot sidewalk. "I will ask her. But, either way, I will have dinner with you later at the hotel."

"Which hotel?" Celwyn asked.

"The Markazi. It is well known."

The magician checked the door leading to the sleeping car. "Is she calmer today?"

Prince Leo licked his lips. "She is. I am pleased for as long as it lasts."

Among other subjects, the Professor read extensively about mental illnesses and the various forms of insanity. Celwyn had never asked his friend about the material he'd read; perhaps it was time to do so.

"As soon as she is on her way to Rome or Munich, she should be more complacent," Kang said with a frown at their guest.

"I hope so." Prince Leo didn't sound convinced.

Minutes of expectant silence went by; the internal creaking and clanging of the train their only company until the magician said, "When she joins us out here, we should allow her time to speak privately with Bartholomew."

A nervous tick started in Prince Leo's right eye. "Why?"

"I believe he does not wish to accompany her on her journey, and he needs to tell her so."

"Oh, my." Fresh anxiety bounced in the dwarf's eyes like frenzied balls in a pinball machine. His reaction justified Celwyn's foreboding about the impending conversation.

A half-hour later, Bartholomew again re-entered the train just as Mary Giovanna arrived from the sleeper car. Verne followed on her heels. The author spied Kang and Celwyn in a game of whist and trotted over to them. Kang put down his cards and stood.

"We're going outside to smoke before our trip into town," the automat said as Celwyn grabbed Verne's elbow and steered him toward the steps going down.

"But—I want coffee—"

Celwyn propelled him down the steps. "Soon."

They lit pipes and politely turned their backs on the train while observing the bustle of activity on Seraz Boulevard, a block away. Camels, horses, wagons, and carriages filled the road, seemingly at ease with their diverse needs and effects on each other. At the end of the street, a cluster of activity could be seen in front of a news agent's stall.

"It is easy to spot the Europeans," Kang said. "They are ill-dressed for this climate."

Celwyn buttoned his collar to keep Qing inside. "Like we are." He shivered a bit, even in the heat, as if an omen. "We are leaving tomorrow," he told the dwarf, "Which is soon enough for me."

Prince Leo nodded. "As expected." He pointed to his robe, which dragged through the dirt as he paced beside them. "I plan ahead. This is quite comfortable."

Shouting erupted from inside the train. Through the window, they saw Mary Giovanna fly at Bartholomew, screeching like a banshee. Being closest to the steps, Celwyn was first inside with Kang right behind him.

Bartholomew held the young woman at arm's length.

"Bastard!" she screamed. Her color was high, and saliva dripped from her mouth.

"Please, I mean—" Twin scratches bled down the big man's cheek.

Mary Giovanna shook off his hands and whirled to face the rest of them.

"It is your fault!" she spat at her father, who tried to hide behind Celwyn. "Yours, too!" she told the magician as she leaned over the dining table. With a hand, she swept the flower vase to the floor. The crash echoed in the stunned room.

What the young woman did next, Celwyn did not expect.

As she straightened again, her face contorted into a rictus smile that sent a shiver down the magician's spine. She curtsied to them in a sweeping, exaggerated manner, then cradled her arms as if she held dozens of roses, bowing and smiling to an imaginary audience at her feet. "Thank you, thank you!" Then she became still and began to tremble as she wept great sobbing sighs. When she raised her face again, she gestured to the back of an imaginary theatre and shouted, "Thank you! Thank you!"

Kang and the others watched in stunned silence.

Mary Giovanna knelt and picked up a shard of glass from the broken vase, playing with it and mumbling to herself. In a flash, her mood changed again as she laughed maniacally and drew it across her throat. Before she finished the slash, Celwyn stopped her hand, shaking the glass loose.

"Mary!" Prince Leo cried.

"Hold her hands," Celwyn told Kang and Bartholomew as he approached her. When they'd done so, he stopped the gushing blood staining her dress and closed the gash in her throat. She shook from head to foot, mumbling and moaning, her eyes closed. Gradually, she quieted and would have slid to the floor if Kang and Bartholomew hadn't eased her into a chair.

"Mary..." Prince Leo hovered close as if to provide comfort but was afraid to touch her.

When she raised her head again, her eyes had lost their madness. She focused as clearly and calmly as if she had been sitting at high tea with the Queen. Without any embarrassment or agitation, she regarded Kang and then Bartholomew, who each held one of her arms.

"I do not need to be restrained," she told them in a low voice. "I am fine."

With a nod from Celwyn, they released her and moved away quickly. Neither of them were fools.

Mary Giovanna patted the bald spot on top of Prince Leo's head.

"Father, let us talk no more of this. Only our future."

The dwarf appeared speechless like he couldn't decide if he was afraid for her ... or of her.

Celwyn watched the woman, his head tilted to the side as he decided what to do. She seemed composed, the picture of a prim Victorian young woman in lace and ribbons. Only the front of her blouse was soaked in blood.

After another moment, her father straightened, tentative relief painting his face.

"If Ludvik will call us a carriage and help load our luggage, we will be on our way after Mary changes her attire."

"That won't be necessary." With a nod, Celwyn removed the blood from her blouse and debated whether to keep the two of them on the train in case she became erratic again. Finally, he nodded his assent.

Verne came inside from the train yard, radiating his usual good cheer and an ability to ignore the tension in the room.

"Why the long faces? We are in a wonderful city. I can't wait to see all of it!"

"Whew!" Celwyn exclaimed minutes later and sat down. He blamed some of his exhaustion from expelling magic and the rest on his wound. Or it could be just a reaction to the scene they'd just witnessed.

The others joined him, and Bartholomew dabbed at his face while they watched Ludvik finish loading trunks, most of them likely filled with gaudy suits, into a carriage. Prince Leo handed his daughter inside the cab and scrambled in behind her. Through the window, he waved a farewell. His daughter did not, sitting ramrod straight, and continuing to stare ahead without blinking.

"She has circus eyes."

Bartholomew eyed the magician. "You are feeling poetic?"

"Perhaps lyrical. Her mind is a spinning Ferris wheel, going up, up, and spinning away." Celwyn stared at the farthest point where they had seen the departing carriage. "I hope she gets the help she needs before she does something rash."

"As do I." Bartholomew winced as he touched his face.

"You should put some tincture on those scratches," the Professor advised Bartholomew. "Ricardo has first aid supplies in the kitchen."

The big man nodded and inhaled deeply. "I'm glad that is over with, and we can go forward."

"To a wonderful falafel!" Verne agreed and rubbed his hands together. "Later, I am meeting friends at the palace."

Chapter 21

At the last minute, Celwyn decided to leave Qing behind. He made another green snake with insane red eyes, gave it to him, and hoped that was all he'd play with until they returned. Without Qing, there was no need for a coat, and the magician enjoyed the prospect of just wearing a vest and shirtsleeves. They would revel in the warm desert breezes for their outing.

As they descended the train steps, a hire carriage rolled up and drew level with the train. Ricardo and Jackson piled out and began unloading packages.

"More supplies will be delivered in the morning," Ricardo said, smiling broadly. "We found everything we needed and more. We will eat very well indeed." The porters transported the packages inside while Celwyn and the others traded places with them in the carriage.

"Who is on guard duty tonight? I assume the rest of the crew have their evening out planned?" Bartholomew asked as they drove away in a cloud of dust.

"Abe and Andy," the automat told him. "They are taking the next hire cab into town and will be back before we retire."

"A reminder, we're meeting Prince Leo for dinner at the Markazi later this evening," Celwyn said as he examined the scratches on Bartholomew's face. They looked like they hurt, so he fixed them. "I believe we'll have time to explore much of the Grand Bazaar first."

"It is miles long..." Bartholomew said. "There will be many tobacco sellers."

"Can you imagine how many book merchants there will be?" Kang marveled.

"At last, it is becoming cooler," Bartholomew said. They had spent part of the afternoon in the Hammam Baths. From beside the pools, attendants swept large leaves over tepid water to cool the patrons. Jars of cold cider and lager also provided respite from the heat.

As they emerged into the street, sundown covered the city. Celwyn yawned and inhaled the mysterious scents around them. Some smelled sweet, some pungent.

The sounds of the evening changed, becoming sharper and clearer. Instead of gas lamps, the streets had been lit with torches mounted above the roadway, and swaths of smoke from them invited the unwary into sinuous dark alleys that begged to be explored. Bartholomew pointed out suggestions of movement in the shadows: friend or foe? Kang voted for foe, while Bartholomew didn't commit himself but touched the pistol in his belt.

Their open carriage bumped along, led by twin Arabian horses sporting tall red feathers and a persnickety attitude. As they veered from side to side, their driver tapped their back with his crop. One horse showed his teeth, causing Celwyn to chuckle.

"Why is Mr. Verne not with us this evening?" Bartholomew asked.

"He said he was meeting friends at the palace." The magician frowned. "He'd better not mention us."

Kang kept a keen eye on the shops, the dubious characters in front of buildings, and other attractions they passed. He pointed. "Prince Leo has excellent taste. The Markazi Hotel is supposed to be one of the finest in the city. See? There are the lights from it up ahead."

Celwyn saw them too, and then the hotel. It stood three stories high, covered in a creamy yellow stucco that glowed in the semi-darkness. Grand arches, two dozen feet high, had been carved into the façade every few feet, and mature and languid palms framed the building on all sides. In the street, a long line of carriages and taxis competed for proximity.

"I hope Prince Leo is finished primping. They are supposed to meet us in the bar." Celwyn eyed

Bartholomew for signs of stress. "Are you prepared to see Mary Giovanna again so soon after her outburst?"

The big man squared his shoulders. "I will be fine."

After they alighted from their carriage, the crowd thickened around them as they approached a pair of footmen standing on each side of the grand entrance. They looked regal in flowing elbisesi, and ceremonial sabers hung from their sashes. Celwyn and the others tipped their hats, passed under the arches, and joined a queue. With one slow step at a time, they ascended a tall flight of stairs behind a large party, slowing as they neared the hotel's entrance doors. Jovial shouts in Deutsche and Farsi surrounded them.

Their tone changed to growls and displeasure as a slight man in a floppy hat shoved through the crowd on the landing and down the stairs, bumping hard into the Professor. Celwyn grabbed Kang's elbow just as he fell backwards. The man in the hat pushed his way down the rest of the stairs without looking up or apologizing, disappearing into the crowd below.

"Ruffian," Bartholomew called after him.

"Look at your sleeve." Celwyn pointed to a dark smear down Kang's arm.

A woman next to him shrieked.

"Blut!"

"Blut! There is blood!"

"Come on—" Celwyn had a hunch. A horrible one. He cursed and elbowed his way upward with the others close behind.

The magician sprinted to the front desk and, in a rapid-fire exchange, learned Prince Leo's room number. In seconds, they crossed the expanse of the great lobby to a central staircase that curled upward. As they flew up the stairs and down the hall, Bartholomew took the lead.

"Room 225!" Celwyn called, moving as best he could in his depleted condition.

When they arrived in front of Prince Leo's hotel room, Bartholomew knocked.

Nothing. Not a sound.

"Again—" Kang said.

This time, Bartholomew pounded hard on the door.

"Watch the hall," Celwyn said as he covered the handle with his body as if he had a key and unlocked the door. As they went in, laughter floated to them from a group of revelers coming up the hallway.

The automat closed the door behind them. They were at once bathed in the warm glow of the room's wall sconces, the light painting the velvet sofas and tapestries and highlighting the plush luxury along with the horror.

The body of Prince Leo lay in the middle of the floor. A large knife had been buried in his chest, and blood from a dozen cuts across his torso still dribbled to the floor. His sightless eyes stared at the cherubs cavorting across the ornate ceiling.

Kang whistled in shock.

"It is my fault; I should have gone with them." Bartholomew turned away, his lips so tight he didn't have any.

"No, she would have tried to kill you, too, my friend." Celwyn side-stepped into the bedrooms and then returned to stand over the dwarf. "Most of her things are gone."

The Professor examined the body. He held up the end of a short rope attached to the dwarf's wrist.

"That is how she was able to take her time with him," the magician said.

"He has been dead for a while. See there?" Kang pointed to Leo's stomach. "Some of the other wounds were inflicted post-mortem over a period of hours. Some bled profusely, some very little."

Bartholomew sat heavily on the sofa and put his head in his hands. When he looked up again, his eyes were dry and his lips grim.

"...I thought that was her passing by us on the entrance steps. I should have run after her."

"It was her. Dressed as a man," the automat said.

Celwyn nodded. "'Crazy Mary' indeed. I believe she wiped her bloody hand on the Professor on purpose. Her way of showing us her superiority ... and hate." He removed the blood from Kang's shirt as he stood up.

"Or to implicate us. We should get out of here, my friends." Bartholomew crossed to the door.

"On point as usual." Celwyn said, "And we should hurry. By now, she could have told the police to check this room to catch us here."

Within moments they again slipped down the stairs, and when they reached the center of the lobby, Kang stopped in his tracks. He turned around. "Concerning the probability of the police arriving, can you think of any reason we couldn't have dinner next door? And a stiff drink first to forget this by? The police won't look for us there."

"I'm starving." Bartholomew scratched his chin. "It won't change what occurred."

"Why not?" As they walked under an arch and down to the street, the implications of what they found settled on the magician. "We will toast Prince Leo. Eventually, avenge him, too. Leo vexed me at times, but I knew him for many years, and no one deserves to die like that."

They walked three abreast down the avenue, politely standing aside for the police as they arrived and rushed into the hotel.

"We will bring her to justice." Kang agreed with a hard glint in his eye.

At the first hint of dawn in the eastern sky, calls to prayer echoed throughout the city. Bells tolled, competing for a lost soul's piety. Closer to the train, a donkey brayed, another answered, and several more joined in. Even more interesting; on the sidewalk, when a beggar dressed in a long beard and rags herded a hefty pig by, he stared through the *Elizabeth's* dining room windows.

The magician closed his own cabin window, trapping the colder air inside. With luck, it would remain so until they reached the foothills and they began the climb through the much cooler mountains. After he finished dressing and talking to Qing, he headed down the hall to the dining room with the bird on his shoulder.

The Professor already sat at the map table under a bright lamp. In the low light, the charts he studied appeared intricate. Kang sighed at them and addressed Celwyn.

"I knew you wouldn't stay in bed and rest."

The magician smiled at him.

The automat pursed his lips in thought. "I liked Leo, also. We will miss him."

Celwyn dropped a yellow tie on the table. "I found this behind the bed in his room. We can remember him wearing it."

"Appropriate. I would like that."

"He would too," the magician said as he sat and poured, enjoying his first swallow of Earl Grey as much as he could. "What is worrying you about our proposed route?"

Kang stared. "How did you know I was worried?"

"Your left eye twitches."

"Fine. Yes, I'm worried." He pointed to the map. "From what I can discover and what Conductor Smith reports, we can't count on the tracks between Yasuj and Shiraz to be passable."

"How much of them are a problem?"

"Too much." Kang frowned. "Probably thirty miles, maybe more."

Bartholomew entered the room much slower than usual and sat as carefully as if he suspected his chair might crumble. He lay his head on the table and groaned.

"How did I get back to the train?"

"After we walked you out of the restaurant," Kang said, "Jonas had to use magic to get you into the carriage. He isn't strong enough yet to lift you."

"Correction, I'm not strong enough yet to carry you very far." The magician regarded the big man. "You drank more than I thought possible. Did it help you forget Mary? Or the murder?"

Bartholomew shook his head and winced. "I like your name for her. Crazy Mary. No, I won't forget her for a while." He looked at the teapot and made a face.

"I'll get you some strong coffee, my friend." Celwyn clapped him on the shoulder. As he left for the kitchen, the cart with their supplies trundled into the yard and up to the train. Beyond it, the beggar and the pig walked by again.

Chapter 22

When Celwyn returned carrying a coffee tray, Otto followed him with a fresh tea service. They found Bartholomew leaning over Kang's shoulder and studying the map. "Although I cannot focus well at the moment, I agree we have a problem."

The Professor tapped the map. "We can gamble and travel to the south, then connect with the route we used on the way to Prague."

Celwyn poured coffee, added several sugars, and handed the cup to Bartholomew.

"I like that plan, except we should avoid Pushkari, where I burned down Van Maskloc's house." Celwyn watched the train yard outside for a moment. "They may still wonder about Telly and Zander. Especially after we were seen with him that afternoon."

"Will they remember our train?" The big man asked. "We can hope it has been long enough. You could also disguise the color of it temporarily, Jonas."

Kang frowned and used a pencil to make a calculation. "Do we hurry or play it safe? Depending on the weather, going south adds about a day."

The others shrugged.

"I'll go chat with the Conductor." Kang shoved his chair under the table but still frowned at the map for a moment before trotting toward the kitchen.

"Please ask him to get us underway as quickly as possible. The heat will soon be intolerable," Bartholomew called as the automat hurried away.

Unspoken was the fact that it would be best that they leave before Prince Leo's murder investigation reached them.

A few minutes later, the noise at the front of the train increased as the engines started up. Kang came back, held up a hand, and kept going to the sleeping car. He returned carrying a handful of envelopes.

"Ludvik is going to help with shoveling the coal until we're further away from here." The automat grabbed a coffee cup and drained it. "While you napped yesterday, Jonas, I retrieved the telegraphed answers to our inquiry about Mary Giovanna." Kang distributed them. "My apologies, I just remembered them."

A minute later, Celwyn stood at the window and read his missive aloud.

> Dear Professor, we miss you at the University. Stop. Answer: A pair of

> murders occurred spring of 1859 in Paris. One a theatre critic, one an actor. Stop. The subject of your inquiry was suspected, but there wasn't enough evidence to press charges. She was later discovered sitting on one of the graves with a knife and basket of roses, laughing uncontrollably."

With a sigh, the magician again looked out the window. The beggar was gone, but the pig stood next to a post chewing dry grass without a care in the world. "I can't believe I missed the signs of depravity in that woman."

"You aren't the only one." Bartholomew frowned. "Mine," he held up another telegram, "is similar, reporting on her activities in Verona about four years ago. The report concludes that she is a very disturbed individual." He gazed heavenward. "How could I have been so naïve? And how did her father not know and keep away from her?"

Kang read his through and looked up. "My letter was sent from Marseilles and is a bit more troubling. Like you, I also wonder what her father would have done if he'd read these telegrams. Would he have allowed himself to be alone with her?"

> "Axel Parrier, son of a wealthy landowner, was found with his tongue cut out and butchered like a pig. He had been affianced to Miss Mary Giovanna, an actress. She was not

> suspected, but after she left town, a dress with copious amounts of blood was found on top of his grave, along with an engagement ring. Stop. The authorities are not sure it was hers. Evidence found of digging around the grave and indications that someone lay in the dirt next to the coffin...."

The magician also speculated about what Leo would have done if he knew. Everyone on the train had been in danger. Kang's voice came, just above a whisper. "Prince Leo died mid-afternoon yesterday. If I'd picked these up sooner, we might have saved him."

"I blame myself... for not doing more," Bartholomew said. "It is not your fault."

"Damn it. If anyone is at fault, it is mine; I should have monitored her thoughts when she started acting so oddly." The magician sighed, cursed again, and continued to wish he had done more.

Twelve days passed uneventfully as they traveled through hilly countryside, only interrupted by forests and the occasional dry stream. They blew through Pushkari, Van Maskolc's city, without stopping and kept the train windows shuttered.

When the *Elizabeth* turned east at Kota, Verne's spirits climbed. "We will arrive in Dhanbad soon, my friends."

They had just finished luncheon. Celwyn sat in front of the pianoforte, and Qing perched on his shoulder. Bartholomew put down the book he'd picked up but didn't respond, while Kang lowered the *Telegraph* with its sensational headlines. He asked the author, "What will you do when we reach Gazipur?"

"I was hoping to travel further south with you, but..." Verne exhaled and said, "... I will hire a carriage and continue by train onto Singapore, if not."

The magician hummed a few notes under his breath. Having Verne around felt suffocating at times. He wanted to let fly with magic and his music with it.

"How many more days?" he asked in a growl.

"Three," Kang replied with a knowing smile.

The magician grumbled in his throat. The Professor enjoyed watching him learn control. If Xiau wasn't correct about attracting undo attention, Celwyn wouldn't bother. He softly played a trill in A minor. The urge for music crept up his arms, leaving a trail of goosebumps. Qing nuzzled his ear. He played another scale. A bird who loves music should be humored.

"What will all of you do in Bengal?" the author asked.

The big man faced him. "Visit with friends, perhaps travel north, over to Beijing."

Celwyn noted that Bartholomew could prevaricate rather well, except for a tendency to laugh while he did so.

Verne's face displayed astonishment as if Bartholomew had said he would ski to Beijing. "Are there rail lines that go there?"

"We'll have to determine that before finalizing our plans," Kang told him.

"Hmmm." Verne eyed them with a modicum of speculation.

The magician's patience ended. As Verne reached for his book, Celwyn waved a hand, and heavy blinding snow fell on the barren landscape outside. Celwyn began to play the pianoforte with a touch so light it seemed as if the snowflakes fell on the keys. Thousands of twinkling red lights descended with the flakes, and as they covered the rocks of the foothills, the magician added an echoing soprano whose voice undulated within the snow and music. Beside them, a thin river twisted and turned as it accompanied the *Elizabeth* through a low valley.

The train bounced over a trestle onto a secondary set of tracks.

"Conductor Smith is very good at his job," Kang remarked as he caught Celwyn's eye and pointed at Verne.

"I've blocked what he can see and hear, go ahead."

Kang raised a sarcastic brow. "With the unusual weather outside, I assumed so. Have you any thoughts about how we'll avoid him on the way to Singapore?"

"What I have at the moment is more of a feeling than a concrete plan."

Celwyn ran a leisurely scale to the upper keys and rapidly brought it down into the lower clef. Above the oblivious Verne, dancers in kimonos twirled through bright colored flags, weaving across the room, over the furniture, and down again. Acrobats as tiny as a thumb tumbled out of the ceiling and bounded up again to sprint through the air above their heads, tossing crystal balls between them.

As a chorus of horns echoed, intertwining with the free-floating flags, the acrobats faded away, replaced by schools of fish in brilliant reds who swam through the air as if through water. Clouds of silvery trout hovered over the dining table as a tribute to Kang's fondness for the dish. The music sweetened and then tempered as the fish shimmered to nothing, replaced by thick greenery and the pungent scent of the jungle.

An assortment of dishes crashed into the music. Otto stood in the kitchen doorway, face pale and his eyes bulging behind their spectacles. As Celwyn hesitated on what to say, the porter stepped into the wavering tendrils of the jungle and reached a hand to touch one of them, but stopped when he saw a parrot with unnaturally bright eyes. It landed on his shoulder and fluffed its feathers, and a smile spread across Otto's face.

"Welcome to my world," Celwyn told him.

A few moments later, Kang said, "I'm glad you enjoyed yourself, Jonas. Please unblock Verne. We're pulling into Lalganj in a few minutes."

Bartholomew had observed Otto's smile as he picked up the broken pottery and left again. "Thank you, Jonas. I needed that respite and a reminder of beauty. Too bad the snowstorm stopped."

"You are most welcome." Celwyn turned to the automat. "You know, Otto might benefit from borrowing some of your texts. He seems to have an open and artistic mind."

"And nerves of steel." Kang stared at the kitchen door. "I had considered that. He has a basic education in writing and probably reading. But I doubt much more."

Rows of vegetation began replacing the rocky hills, and another train passed by them, heading west on the other tracks. As the train disappeared around a bend, its cars appeared ungainly with stack after stack of hay swaying against the wind. Minutes more and the *Elizabeth* decelerated past mud-block buildings that gradually increased in size and complexity.

The town of Lalganj arose before them, prosperous and busy.

While the *Elizabeth* coasted to a stop, Celwyn asked, "Before Verne returns from his room, please consider this; do you think Phileas Fogg is following us?" From their surprised reactions, Celwyn had his answer. "Perhaps we should tarry here a few days to be sure that he catches up to us?" He batted his eyes as innocently as he could.

A broad smile spread across Bartholomew's face.

"It is quite evident you are feeling better, Jonas," the Professor drawled as he stood and started to pace. "Your mind surprises me sometimes." He sent them both a quick look. "It is a quandary because, despite your desire for confrontation, Verne is afraid of the man."

"Ponder it more, please. If we made sure that Fogg found us here, he could keep Verne entertained while we slip away to Singapore." The magician drained his teacup and put it back on the tray, picturing the author like a grey bunny hopping from one hiding hole to another.

"The territory of Bengal is big," Bartholomew said. "Perhaps that is what Jonas is thinking." He laughed.

Kang laughed. "Both of your minds are alike in some respects."

The door from the sleeping car rattled. Celwyn wiggled a finger, jamming the lock. He regarded them expectantly.

"I need to analyze this more." The automat shook his head.

Bartholomew nodded. "I do, also."

Celwyn sighed and opened the door to the sleeping car.

"That door sticks." Verne trotted through and asked, "Are we dining in town this evening?"

As the author nattered on, Celwyn considered their situation. There was a third option: keep Verne with them. He was a nice fellow, and with him close by, they could be sure that he didn't talk to nefarious strangers, such as publishers and reporters.

Chapter 23

Conductor Smith puffed on his pipe until clouds of smoke hovered above his head while he paced and barked orders at the laborers unloading the coal cart. When they had finished, he pressed coins into each of their palms. From their surprise, the coins appeared to be unexpected. It neared five in the afternoon when the empty cart left the train yard, and more carts arrived bearing ice and water.

Bartholomew climbed back inside the train with Verne in his wake. Both carried parcels and wore satisfied looks. The big man tossed a package to Kang and another to the magician. He laid a larger one on the table next to the automat's elbow.

"Pastries and tea. My friends, you are so predictable."

"And happily, so. Thank you." Celwyn stuck his nose in the bag and inhaled. "If my protector," he nodded at Kang, "approves, next time I will go with you to the pastry shop."

"You looked tired, Jonas. Don't argue." Kang unwrapped his package and stacked blocks of wood on the dining table. "Very nice, thank you, Bartholomew." He examined one piece closely, running a nail down the grain. "I've never carved teak before."

"My muse is calling me. I must write. Excuse me." Verne headed toward the sleeping compartments. "However, I will certainly return for dinner."

After he closed the door behind him, Kang asked, "Does he know our dinner will be cold meats and fruit?"

"Or whatever else we can discover?" Bartholomew shook his head. "I'd wager he doesn't know that the crew, including Ricardo, went into town."

"He soon will." Celwyn poured tea and eyed Kang until the automat looked up and after seeing the smile the magician wore, a nervous tic started in his eye. When he seemed curious enough, the magician asked, "Do you remember the wooden toys you made for Zander and Telly?"

"Of course."

"They resembled birds, yet a little man sat in a small box atop the birds." Celwyn wiggled a brow at the automat, who tried to ignore him.

"The man waved at whoever was below." Bartholomew grinned. "And he looked like you."

Celwyn laughed. "Right down to the ears."

"That reminds me." Kang put the wood down with a glare at the magician. "Stop enhancing my ears, it scares the porters." After another moment, he looked at the other two again. "Why are you both staring at me and so amused? You are as subtle as bad fan dancers." Kang sorted wood and examined the grain in the light. They waited. He stopped his inspection and faced them. "Oh, all right. This must not be mentioned to anyone. Especially not to our loquacious guest."

Celwyn crossed his heart. "Absolutely."

"I concur." Excitement flared in Bartholomew's eyes.

Kang continued to fuss with the wood. "Hundreds of years ago, when the automats like myself were made, some of the necromancers, alchemists, and mystics did their best to blend the occult and sciences into the mechanical animals and men."

"Rebia, the bear of Hohenzollern Castle?" Celwyn speculated.

Kang nodded. "Some efforts were successful, such as the singing birds of Ceylon. I participated up to a point and benefited from the richness of ideas." He watched as Celwyn elevated a piece of wood, twirling it faster than they could see. "One of the forward thinkers, Urbano Tokar, worked with me on the possibilities of flight."

"Oh..." Bartholomew's eyes took on a glazed, inward look. "Oh, my goodness! Wind drafts, weights, engines..."

"Yes. I can see that you have heard of him."

"I studied him."

Kang rewrapped all the wood except one piece. "We were successful, but rampant superstition in many countries drove us to hide our work. Tokar took some of our projects to Mexico and then onto the jungles near the equator." He shrugged. "The Mayans were not shy. They embraced the flying machines."

"I wonder why?" Celwyn asked. "Usually, indigenous people are somewhat superstitious."

"I've read a book about their gods and how they were portrayed with wings and other features." Bartholomew played with the string from the package. "Were they based on the unearthly visitors?"

Kang didn't seem surprised at all at the question; in fact, he shrugged. But his eyes twinkled. "I have rare books about their culture and history ... if you'd like to see them. The wealthy Mayans even had wooden toys for their children that looked like the toys that I made."

While they talked, Celwyn produced a set of carving tools and placed them beside Kang's hand as he spoke. "It sounds fascinating. I had no idea." After Kang saw the tools, the magician continued, "What happened to Tokar?"

"The Spaniards killed him." Kang grasped the wood and began scraping the end of it. "A nice fellow. Such a waste of a great mind." The chips went flying. "When he died, his notes and papers were sent to me by one of our mutual friends."

"When was this?" Bartholomew asked.

Kang's expression continued to darken, and his aggression on the wood increased. "Ten years ago, when I first settled in San Francisco. Then it was stolen from my office at the University." He smiled without humor and ripped off a long strip of wood.

Celwyn guessed, "They didn't get everything, did they?"

Kang blew a big cloud of wood dust into the air, and the other two backed up. "No. Much of the information is still here." He tapped his head. "Some of it we'd never written down, the most important of which are the details about the propulsion factors."

Bartholomew regarded him with awe, as if he were a god. "I never knew."

Kang tilted his head at the wood like Qing does when he is curious about something.

"Could this be what Talos was really after on the *Zelda*?" Bartholomew speculated.

Celwyn sat back, amazement in his voice, "It certainly opens up all kinds of scenarios."

Kang growled and uttered a curse word the magician didn't know that Xiau knew.

"How worried should we be that someone is after this knowledge?" the big man asked.

Kang put more effort behind a cut, switched tools, and dug at the middle of the chunk of wood. "I really can't say. I'm only an academic trying to manage a temperamental magician who takes too many chances and has no common sense and get back to my wife." Chips went flying again. "That is enough to worry about."

Bartholomew tried not to laugh but failed. Celwyn rolled his eyes.

"Furthermore." The automat glared at nothing in particular. "In another thirty years or so, the danger and competition won't matter; the everyday scientists and warmongers will perfect the technology by then. Why bother with me?"

"Perhaps," Celwyn said. "However, we should be on guard in case someone is still after you."

"There is a bright side. At least it isn't a vampire or Jax," Bartholomew said.

The magician shook his head. "Yes, but remember? Jax escaped that night into the crowd."

"You certainly know how to bring a festive mood down, Jonas." The big man's face grew pensive.

Kang just glowered.

Celwyn asked, "Have either of you considered our earlier dilemma about what to do about Verne?"

"Somewhat. I do not have a definitive solution." The big man said, "Do you?"

"I am leaning toward keeping Verne with us."

"But Jonas—" Bartholomew's surprise showed in his raised voice.

The magician put a hand up. "Hear me out. I propose that if Phileas Fogg is trailing us, we let him frighten Verne thoroughly." He glanced at the train yard, seeing only the normal activity, the yard men, and passengers disembarking from carriages. "Then, I show Jules a worthy example of my magic and make sure that he knows the penalty of my displeasure."

Kang said, "Go on."

Celwyn peered at them over his steepled fingers. "I would promise him that if he complies, someday he can use me and you—if either of you agrees—as characters in one of his books."

"The story would preferably be set in a location far from us," Kang said.

For a long minute, Bartholomew rubbed a fist across the table and back again, thinking. "He would behave for that kind of pay-off."

"Or because he would fear to cross me." The magician agreed with an amused gleam in his eye.

Chapter 24

THE LANDSCAPE OF INDIA BECAME increasingly lush over the next few days, with long stretches of jungle and forests so dense Celwyn could only see a few feet into them as the *Elizabeth* chugged by. He found flashes of oranges, yellows, and brilliant blues from the orchids and exotic birds hidden in the branches and vines especially intriguing. The jungle represented an opportunity to study so many species. There was one person who would appreciate it even more than those on the train, and Celwyn wished Zander traveled with them.

As if the big man could also read minds, he verbalized the thought.

"Zander would have loved to have seen that leopard a few minutes ago." Bartholomew stretched to his full height and sat down again in front of the windows. "You realize, by the time we get home, he will be an accomplished artist."

"Oh?" Kang asked as he dealt cards for solitaire.

"Yes. I asked him to draw a picture for me every day until we return," Bartholomew said.

Celwyn eyed him. "Too bad we can't bring him the real thing."

The tiger that had sat next to Prince Leo's feet took shape, lying on its side, and stretching. With a yawn, it rolled onto its back and rocked onto its side again. This time, its black stripes had been enriched with slivers of sapphires. When the cat flexed its muscles, the jewels rolled across its flesh.

"Hence my remark about watching over a temperamental magician." Kang considered the animal. "What should we name him? Prince?"

Celwyn grew somber. "If I had been with Prince Leo, his daughter wouldn't have butchered him." They quieted and thought for a few moments. "We could—excuse me, *I* could have done better."

"Not necessarily." Kang shook his head.

"The signs were there," Celwyn said. "I should have kept him safe on the train until we had the responses to her background."

"He felt some responsibility over not being around Mary when she was younger, and he wouldn't have truly believed the danger..." the Professor shuddered, "...from his own child."

"You can't harbor all the guilt for his death, Jonas." Bartholomew clapped him on the shoulder and walked to the window and back. "Remember? I should have retrieved the messages as soon as we arrived in Tehran."

"And I should have made sure we read them sooner." Kang moved his foot further away from the tiger. "You can't blame yourself, Jonas."

The magician rubbed his face. "I still bear the main fault."

When the kitchen door opened, Otto backed in with the luncheon cart, and the big cat faded away.

Celwyn's guilt, however, lingered in his mind along with his memories of Leo.

Verne pushed back his chair from the dining table and joined Celwyn at the open window. As whiffs of humidity and greenery reached them, they gazed at the forest surrounding the train. Glimpses of the Bay of Bengal glimmered in the distance, and dozens of islands dotted the surface like freckles.

Verne asked, "When will we reach Chittagong?"

"Sunset is about seven tonight, and the *Elizabeth* will arrive a bit before then," Kang told him and went back to his maps.

The train slowed around a curve and slowed, rumbling across a bridge over a high gorge. Below them, a river plummeted over boulders, exploding in furious spray then rushing forward even faster before becoming a spectacular waterfall and dropping to another level below.

The *Elizabeth* coasted to a stop above the falls.

"I asked the Conductor to pause here a moment." Celwyn leaned forward to see the bottom of the falls.

"The view is incredible," Verne murmured. "I can't believe it. It is times like this I wish I could paint."

Much closer now, the enormity of the Bay of Bengal could be seen, glittering like a million jewels before the horizon. Along scores of miles to the west, a white beach framed the water and the swamps changed to forests ribboned with herds of deer. Fields of mangos and bananas bordered the jungle that seemed to swallow everything in front of it.

Celwyn sent Bartholomew a silent message and raised a brow at Kang, who raised one in return.

"Jules, we are prepared to take you with us beyond Chittagong."

Verne clapped his hands in delight. "Oh, Jonas! I am honored."

"There is a condition. Call it a price, if you will," Celwyn told him. "You must accede to my terms or our association will end. Abruptly."

"What conditions?" The author's enthusiasm deflated as if he was a balloon, and someone had poked a hole in his belly.

Celwyn made sure he had Verne's complete attention. "If you stay with us, you may not talk about us or consort with editors or publishers and tell them of us."

"No reporters either," Kang added.

"But—"

Bartholomew glared at him. "No one."

"Someday," Celwyn said, "with our permission, you may speak of us, or use us in your novels. But only with our permission."

Verne's eyes shifted. "I'll do my best. But I can't help it if I have acquaintances or what they hear."

Celwyn leaned down until they were at eye level. "Yes, you can. Do you wish to stay with us? Yes, or no?"

"Jonas—"

Celwyn inhaled and stood tall. He had bet Kang it would come to this. He should have wagered money on it.

From the air around them, a chorus of tenors and sopranos arose riding a river of tinkling bells. Deep and full, the French horns arrived, resonant with a melody of minor notes that ascended and descended as the air in the dining car grew cold and blue.

Verne's mouth fell open as he looked from side to side for the source.

The music grew louder, and the top of the train unfolded as if made of paper, revealing a world of infinite high clouds in a cerulean sky. Celwyn grasped Verne's hand, and they rose upward through the roof to hover above the train.

"J-J-Jonassss..." Verne clutched the magician's arm.

With his other hand, Celwyn gestured, bringing Kang and Bartholomew upward until they floated beside them.

"My heavens! The view is incredible. So clear," Kang called above the breeze whipping by them and the roar of the rushing river below.

Bartholomew's hands shook as he waved them through the air. Then he whirled, once, twice, and on the third turn managed, "Jonas ... it is frightening but wonderful!"

Verne screamed silently and watched the foam and mist rising from the river far below his feet.

Celwyn released Verne's other hand, and he fell a few feet and then rose again. The author's panic grew when he realized he couldn't see the magician anymore.

"Jonas!!" Verne wailed.

Celwyn appeared again and twirled him, bringing him close until they floated nose to nose.

The magician smiled and caused a halo of flames to encircle Verne's head that spread, enveloping them both. Verne squeaked and fainted. The magician replaced the flames with a light shower, reviving the author.

"Yes, Jules. Everything you heard about me is true." He patted the author's cheek. "I have a temper too, which I hope you never see."

"You should listen to him," Bartholomew suggested as he gazed downward to the falls and then across the bay.

As they talked, Kang turned to face the wind. He lay on his back, floating free as he spread his arms wide. His blissful expression displayed the kind of happiness Celwyn seldom saw in his friend.

But back to business.

"Do you accept our terms to stay with us?" he asked Verne.

When the author hesitated, Celwyn swung him forward over the yawning drop above the gorge. A second more, he brought him back.

"Yes! I agree!"

"No matter what you see?"

In a cloud, dozens of yellow birds as small as coins flew toward the author, peering closely into his eyes, fluttering around him and chattering in sharp voices as the music from inside the train grew louder.

"Yes! Yes! No matter what!"

After they once again relaxed inside the train, and the roof of the car appeared as if it had never opened to the sky, Verne stared at Celwyn for minutes before announcing in a querulous voice that he would spend the rest of the afternoon writing. Before he left, he requested a bottle of whiskey be sent to his room.

Once more, the *Elizabeth* traveled southeast at a good clip across the lowlands at sea level. Many miles away, the top of cream-colored buildings could be seen under the pointed spires of minarets.

"I'm so glad you enjoyed your entertainment this afternoon, Jonas."

With a glance at Bartholomew snoring on the sofa beside them, Celwyn asked, "Did you like the view?"

"You know I did," the automat answered and grew serious. "Even more, I want to see my wife, and I hope we have telegrams waiting for us in town."

"I do, also. I miss Zander, Annabelle, and Patrick too." He watched Otto heading toward them with the coffee and tea service. "Does he have any friends?" he asked in an aside.

"No."

Celwyn waited until Otto deposited the tray to address him. "This train will wait for us in Skudai. Are you satisfied to remain there until we get back from Singapore, and then journey back with us to Prague?"

Otto listened, looked at Kang, and then back to the magician. The happiness in his eyes told them what he couldn't say.

"Thank you. We had hoped you would agree."

When Otto had left, he asked Kang, "Can you picture him with Zander in the classroom at Tellyhouse?"

Kang thought a moment. "He has the intelligence and drive to become a scholar."

"I thought so, too."

Kang laughed. "For someone who thinks they are so impervious, you are a romantic do-gooder."

"Pfft. I am not."

The train hit a trestle square on, bouncing their teacups nearly out of their saucers. As Kang sopped the liquid off his trousers, buildings began to appear on both sides of the train.

The magician stood. "I'd best get ready for our outing." He gave Qing a little pat on the rear as he put him on the couch beside Bartholomew. "I'm sure Bartholomew will be awake soon."

Chapter 25

NEARLY TWO HOURS LATER, KANG held a fistful of telegrams and wore a broad smile as they climbed back into their carriage. Bartholomew entered after him with several new pouches of tobacco and passed them out. "Maduro, and Perique, and Thuoc Lau for me." He saw the telegraphs and asked, "Are all of those from your wife?"

"No." Kang shuffled the green telegraph slips, handed several of them to him and a few to the magician. "Those are the ones not from Elizabeth. Enjoy."

Their coach bounded along, hit a pothole, and steadied again. At the moment, they traveled on Farashgani, the main thoroughfare of the French Bazaar. On each street, the magician noted a large population of beggars and even more children in threadbare clothes. Most offered paper flowers for sale. He noticed their mothers standing behind them holding babies, the situation a stark reminder of the cruelty in the world. "It would be nice if we could help some of them before we leave the city."

Bartholomew said, "Perhaps tomorrow I can look into that before our departure. There must be churches here that need donations."

"We are scheduled to spend the night in Skudai before we take a coach to Singapore," Kang reminded them.

"Weren't the tracks supposed to be extended to Singapore years ago?" Bartholomew asked as he opened the map he'd brought along. There were more carriages here, and traffic slowed nearly to a crawl. The magician's stomach awoke with a growl as the smell of cooking fires reached them.

"Apparently not. It will mean hours in another bouncing coach for us soon."

Celwyn said, "We'll put the *Elizabeth* into storage in Skudai and pay the crew to stay with her if they wish to wait for our return trip." They passed a mosque where dozens of men huddled in front of the entrance. "Conductor Smith, Otto, and Ricardo are already confirmed and are willing to wait for us." He'd given Conductor Smith instructions to wire Annabelle for funds if it became necessary to bring the *Elizabeth* back without them. The magician always assumed things may not turn out as planned, and in the last year, that had certainly proved true.

Bartholomew read one of the telegrams. "This first message reports that Interpol had been looking for Mary Giovanna for a year but had trouble confirming a good description." He read more and sighed all the way to his enormous feet.

"What else does it say?" Celwyn asked.

"That she would appear in disguise as various people at events. It seems she is adept with costumes and makeup."

"That isn't good to hear." The magician recalled her different moods and probing looks during their time together. At the time, he had thought she was studying him and the others like actors do, but now it seemed like more if she wanted to impersonate them, she probably knew how they walked and talked. With a few adjustments, she would have made a passable Professor Kang.

Kang said, "We are nearly at our destination. What do the other messages say?"

"The next one states that Mary had a quiet childhood in Verona, but in her last year of school, a scandal occurred that no one will talk about."

The automat rolled his eyes. "Wonderful."

Celwyn opened the first of his allotted telegrams. It consisted of names, dates, and deaths.

> Sergei Pavivich, theatre critic. Died from blunt force wounds August 1862, Rome
>
> Monique Devoe, actress. Died from multiple stab wounds January 1863, Rome
>
> Emile Sesto, actor. Died from a fall down a flight of stairs, June 1863, Rome

Walter Bernard, reporter. Died from a slit throat, December 1864, Rome

"For those deaths, Mary Giovanna was questioned in each case but never arrested." Celwyn handed the list to Bartholomew, then opened the next message. He whistled.

"Aha! This one is short and terse. '*She is suspected of murder. Be careful.*'" As their coach pulled to a stop behind a dozen other carriages, Celwyn passed it to Kang and opened the remaining telegram. "The last one is from the reviews of her stage appearance in Paris. Shakespeare's King Lear. Well. She was probably not amused after seeing it." When he finished reading the telegram, he murmured to himself. "Interesting."

"What?"

"The review was written by Pavivich, the dead critic mentioned in the other telegram." Celwyn read more. "He was beaten to death with a piece of wood and stabbed repeatedly. It was as if his assailant was in a frenzy."

Verne had been quiet during the exchange of information and listened to the telegrams. Now he commented.

"A very distasteful outcome. I rather liked that young woman."

Their coach inched forward. Bartholomew pointed. "There is our restaurant."

A brightly lit establishment came into view with a line of well-dressed people crowded in front. Palms and abundant greenery framed the entrance, along with colorful awnings and flags.

"It is early for such a waiting line, is it not?" Kang asked. "The food must be excellent."

"We must bring Elizabeth here on the return trip." Celwyn sniffed the air, hoping for a tantalizing hint of what was to come.

Hours later, with everyone still jovial from beautifully prepared pheasant and champagne, their carriage rolled toward the train yard, its lanterns swinging from side to side, keeping time with the potholes and steps of the swaying horses. To everyone they passed by, Bartholomew sang an operatic song in his language.

Dusk threw long shadows across the street, over dog carts and donkeys, shading the pedestrians and vendors. Every light on the *Elizabeth* twinkled as they approached and pulled to a stop a few feet from the entrance.

Shouting erupted from inside the train. A tall red-haired man hurtled down the stairs with Jackson in close pursuit. Celwyn threw open the carriage door and gave chase. After a short time, he stumbled to a stop when he realized he'd lost his quarry in the crowd.

He caught up on his breathing as Jackson joined him, panting, "I'm sorry, Sir."

"Hell. At least we tried." Celwyn slapped their porter on his back. "If I hadn't eaten so much at dinner, I would have been faster." He didn't mention that his injury from the Russians might have slowed him down, but Kang undoubtedly would. As they walked back, detouring around a gaggle of Tibetan monks, he asked, "Did he take anything?"

"I don't know. I caught him going through the maps and papers in the dining room." Jackson's pencil-thin mustache drew together as he pursed his lips. "He stuffed something in his jacket before he ran."

"If Mr. Verne hadn't been between me and the carriage door, I would have given chase as well." Bartholomew finished paying the driver and turned to glare into the shadows between them and the parade of pedestrians on the avenue.

"Guards," the automat said.

With a nod, the magician told Jackson, "We will need to take turns at guard duty during the night. You and the others will still have your evening out. Please tell Conductor Smith that I want to leave at first light." At least they had achieved their goal of enticing their enemy out in the open.

"Damn Fogg," Verne grumbled.

The magician agreed but suspected that it wasn't Verne the intruder had been curious about. It had to be either Kang or the location of their eventual destination; their intruder hadn't been searching Verne's room, instead rifling through Kang's papers and their maps.

Phileas Fogg now knew a little more about both.

It had taken nearly all day to skirt the swamps and chug around the jungles to reach Skudai. The train yard had changed little in six months. Tonight, they would remain on the train and board the first land coach to Singapore in the morning.

"We're only four hours from the real Elizabeth," Kang said as they sat down to dinner. He unfurled his napkin with an extra flourish and smiled. "It has been a long journey, my friends, and I thank you for your company and assistance."

A seductive aroma of ginger, lemongrass, and spicy pork filled the air as Jackson served the soup. Celwyn inhaled. "Someone should make a cologne from this."

Bartholomew sniffed his bowl. "We wouldn't attract women that way, but perhaps an epicurean dog or two."

Verne sat quietly, sipping soup, deep in his thoughts. He couldn't help a furtive glance out the window at the pedestrians and where vendors called out to the unwary.

"Do not worry, Jules," Celwyn said. "I have a block on the train. Mr. Fogg cannot reach you in here."

The author's eyes skittered to him and then back to his soup.

"That is one of the benefits of your magic, Jonas. Thank you." His hand trembled as he tried to spoon soup. "It is very upsetting that he was on this train. Very." Apparently, there were worse things than floating hundreds of feet above a roaring river. Verne couldn't keep his spoon steady and dribbled soup down his shirt. As he blotted the spill, Celwyn addressed him.

"Fogg will not come near you while we are with you. You might consider hiring a personal guard in

Singapore if you fear the man so much. We plan to conduct our business quickly and return to Prague." Kang and Bartholomew had agreed that the author didn't need to know more.

Jackson arrived with the salad. As he dished it onto plates, he said, "Chef has made a new salad dressing for tonight and hopes that you will like it."

The automat dutifully tasted the salad. "Honey and anise? I pronounce it extraordinary. Please relay my compliments."

"Excellent," Bartholomew declared. "I love lemon, and what is this?" He held up a piece of what looked like a pale green fruit. "It is not sweet yet tastes very good."

Jackson said, "Avocado. I will let Ricardo know you are enjoying it."

As the door closed behind the porter, Bartholomew addressed the author, "May I ask where you are staying in Singapore?"

Verne studied his salad as if he didn't know what it was. "The Empress." His eye began to twitch. "I will look into hiring a full-time guard."

The Professor regarded him like he would a word puzzle in that it only would be a matter of time before he put the clues together. "Why Singapore?"

"No particular reason." His eyes dropped to his plate. "I just love the city and find it inspiring."

That is a long distance for inspiration, the magician thought. Before Verne could return the favor and ask them about their own plans, Celwyn said, "Please remember our agreement, Jules."

The author gulped his wine and peered at the magician over the rim.

"I made a promise that I will keep."

"Thank you."

Verne finished the glass and poured more. "How long will it take to reach Singapore tomorrow?"

"Four hours. We leave at nine in the morning." Bartholomew eyed Verne. "Singapore is on the tip of a peninsula. Didn't you ride the coach service north when you left Singapore to come to Prague?"

This time, not only did the author's eyes drop to his plate, but his index finger began tapping the table. "Err, no. I went another way."

Celwyn's interest grew. "Such as?"

Verne's chin went up. "Out of Beijing. Then west by train." He spied Jackson entering the room, pushing the cart holding their main course. "This looks very good." He rubbed his hands together.

Celwyn let it go. A frown from Kang and glower from Bartholomew displayed their own skepticism.

Chapter 26

LITTLE LIGHT PENETRATED THE clouds over Skudai the next morning.

Bartholomew left the flurry of activity by the locomotive, opting to rejoin Kang and Celwyn in the train yard in front of the dining room. Beside them, Jackson and Ludvik presided over a mountain of trunks as Otto backed down the stairs adding another to the collection. Most of their things would remain on the train. The pile of trunks belonged to Verne.

"Did the Conductor have any more questions?" Celwyn asked the big man as they waited and watched the road about 500 feet away. It lacked a few minutes before eight in the morning, and Celwyn itched to get going. He'd ordered a local carriage to take them to the coach yard and a cart for the luggage. Both appeared to be late.

Bartholomew said, "No. He confirmed your instructions. Two of the crew will remain on the

Elizabeth at all times, each of them guarding the entry doors. Otherwise, their time is their own. The crew and train will remain here for three weeks."

"Why three weeks?" Kang asked, stepping out of the way as their rented carriage finally clattered to a stop in front of them. "I do not understand."

Celwyn had put off worrying them as long as he could. "In case we are delayed … for whatever reason … I want the *Elizabeth* to travel back to Prague before the winter weather makes the trip impossible." The magician began picking up bags and handing them off to Jackson. "Conductor Smith has been given funds to pay and feed the crew and the information to contact Annabelle for more if he has to take the train back without us."

Bartholomew told them, "The fees for the train yard here are paid up also."

"I am leaving valuable books and other things here." Kang frowned.

"Your concern is also mine. I am leaving my pianoforte. But, as you've mentioned several times, we seem to attract trouble." Celwyn elbowed him. "Never fear; I plan ahead."

"There's more, isn't there, Jonas?" Bartholomew stared at the magician as he tossed a trunk onto the cart as if it were a cigarette butt. "It won't just be the police you and the Professor will be avoiding."

The magician checked before he answered; Verne had gone back inside the train. Still, he lowered his voice. "Jules is afraid of Phileas Fogg. Why? I think the man pursues us as much as he does Verne." As the loading of the cart continued, a horse-drawn cart raced by on the nearby road but didn't stop. "In case there is trouble in Singapore, I want this train, and those we employ, to be taken care of."

"I agree, but wonder." Bartholomew sent the magician a speculative look full of humor.

"Do you have any specific suspicions?" Kang asked.

As a light shower began to fall, Celwyn handed off another trunk to Jackson and answered the others.

"I don't, however, I track Verne's evasiveness for clues. The most recent one occurred last night. Remember he supposedly departed Beijing to travel to Prague? There are inconsistencies that make me suspicious."

Bartholomew finished loading the cart and thanked Ludvik. Off to the side, Otto stood at attention and near tears. The magician approached him.

"We're going to Singapore to pick up the Professor's wife. It will be just a few days." He patted him on the shoulder. "You will like her very much."

The lad nodded and showed his tablet to Celwyn. The magician read it and sighed. He hugged Otto and then held him at arm's length.

"Yes, where we are going could be dangerous. That is why I will not put you in danger." He pointed to the train. "You deserve security. This is your home until we get back. Ricardo, the Conductor, and the others will take care of you. If we're delayed, I want you to go to Prague with them and join our household there."

Otto blinked rapidly and nodded.

"I've already written to our friends there and our ward Zander. He is looking forward to your arrival."

Over Otto's shoulder, the magician saw Verne finally exiting the train, clutching a small bag. "We must go. Do not give up on us."

Celwyn was the last one into the carriage.

The magician sat back in the carriage seat, for the thousandth time wishing they made carriages with enough leg room for anyone over five feet tall. He also noted the lingering barnyard odor permeating the coach interior. Across from him, Verne held his bag to his chest as if it contained the crown jewels and kept his eyes on the streets they rattled through. Celwyn waved a hand, and a mountain of containers beside the road fell across the cobblestones behind them.

"That should discourage anyone following us." He asked the author, "What is in the bag, Jules?"

Bartholomew sat on Verne's left, and Kang faced him. He should be intimidated enough not to lie. The big man noted, "It must be valuable from the way you hold the bag so close."

Verne looked surprised. "What? Oh. Just my pens and ink. They are truly valuable. One was given to me by Victor Hugo." He unzipped the top of the bag, extracted several ornate fountain pens from inside, and passed them around. "They are sentimental to me also. I've used these pens ever since I began writing."

"Very nice." Celwyn handed the pen back to him. "I understand their value."

"We're running late," Kang commented. "When we get to the coach park, we will have to hurry to get everything transferred." He aimed a thumb at the rear of their own carriage. "You travel with more trunks than most women, Mr. Verne."

"Probably." The author sent a wistful look outside again. "I will lose hours of writing while we travel today."

It was at this point that the magician became convinced of a change in Verne.

"Why are you no longer nervous about Phileas Fogg?"

Verne shrugged with studied deception. "Like you said, he won't bother me."

Kang turned a highly suspicious look upon the author, and Celwyn agreed. What had happened? He entered the author's mind but only found thoughts of the plot of his book and Verne's fear that his protagonist would have to die.

With a final medley of bumps and jolts, the Skudai carriage arrived at the coach park in Singapore in the early afternoon.

The magician smiled as he remembered their colorful exit from the same yard six months ago. As if he could read his mind, the automat tapped Celwyn's knee and pointed at the same gates that the magician had closed and locked to impede their pursuers as they sped away north.

Celwyn said, "I wonder if the police still think of us."

"We'll soon know." Kang scanned the crowd waiting in front of the terminal. "There she is!"

Elizabeth Kang remained a most handsome woman. With her flame-red hair and high cheekbones, she stood out from the others as she searched the passengers alighting from the incoming coaches. Her elaborate hat bobbed as she fought her way forward.

Kang leapt out of the coach before it stopped rolling and enveloped his wife in his arms. Celwyn blinked away a tear. Long ago, he also assumed responsibility for their separation, and it felt good to see them so happy after all this time.

The magician, Verne, and the big man alighted from the coach as Elizabeth and Xiau approached them arm in arm.

"We meet again, Mr. Celwyn," Elizabeth said as he kissed her hand. She turned to Bartholomew and smiled. "You must be Bartholomew. Xiau has told me so much about you."

The big man also kissed her hand. "At last, we meet, Mrs. Kang. I am honored."

Verne stepped forward and bowed. "Jules Verne, at your service, Madam."

As they talked, another carriage pulled up, and porters began transferring Verne's luggage into it. The brass plate on the side of the carriage announced that it belonged to the Empress Hotel.

"Where is our coach?" Kang asked.

Celwyn pointed with his eyes at Verne.

"Good precaution." Bartholomew saw him and nodded.

The author turned back to them and said his goodbyes, with a handshake for each of them. His manner had the relaxed look of a man without a care in the world; he no longer worried about who might be in the crowd around him. Really? Celwyn entered the author's thoughts to find out why. After a moment he gave up: Verne's mind was still filled with plots, the danger to his hero, and nothing more. Not even lunch.

"*Au revoir*!" Verne waved and like an overfed grey rabbit, scampered away to board his coach.

An hour later, as they walked across a wide and ornate lobby, Celwyn said, "I love Raffles. A wonderful hotel."

Palm trees in painted pots lined the walls, and the heady scent of a hot house lemon tree taller than the big man greeted them. Gilded man-size mirrors decorated the walls, and the brass on every door had been shined so bright the magician could see his blurry reflection. The spicy atmosphere inside the hotel had a certain heaviness as if soon thunderstorms would reverberate above the chandeliers.

"Two adjacent suites, please," Kang requested of the desk clerk. "If possible, overlooking the bay?"

While the Professor checked them in, Celwyn sat on the trunks and caught up on his breathing. Damn Russians. It had been several weeks, and he still felt the effects of the sword in his side. To distract himself, he surveyed the lobby, including a variety of hats, from bowlers to turbans and several headdresses. Some of the clientele in the lobby displayed elaborate ensembles more suited to a museum. The best example stood in the middle of the enormous room: a stern-faced woman in a black evening gown stalking to and fro and wearing a crown. What he did not see was Phileas Fogg.

Bartholomew elbowed him. "Check the north door leading to the gardens."

Celwyn stood and stretched, scanning the area until he spied a heavily muscled, medium-sized man with a precise haircut under a small cap, and wearing a severe blue suit that reminded Celwyn of a navy uniform. The man stared at Kang and Elizabeth with a disquieting intenseness. When the stare moved to Bartholomew and himself, Celwyn returned it. The man whirled and disappeared into the gardens.

"Stay with the Professor..."

The magician sprinted after the dark blue suit, glimpsing him disappearing between rows of elephant ear ferns and into a forest of healthy roses. Two days ago, the magician would have had more trouble running at all. Celwyn increased his speed as he went, vaulting over the gate and onto the main street. A carriage sped by, with the man inside doing his best to hide in the darkened cab. Two more blue-suited men sat with him.

The magician cursed. When he re-entered the hotel through the main doors, he found his party beside the grand staircase. As he approached them, he caused Elizabeth's hat to become unpinned and threaten to fall.

"Oh, drat." She grabbed at the hat, pecked Kang's cheek, and headed for the powder room behind her. "I'll be right back."

Kang's expression displayed a certain amount of sarcasm. "What is it, Jonas? I suspect there was nothing wrong with her hat until just now."

Bartholomew drew close, so they could confer without eavesdroppers.

"It was the first thing I could think of. As we suspected, we are of interest to someone." Celwyn put a hand on Bartholomew's shoulder and told Kang, "Our friend spotted a man watching you. When he ran, I followed him."

"Oh, bloody hell!" The automat stamped his foot and glanced at the powder room door. "I had so hoped my reunion with Elizabeth would not spell danger."

"We should develop a way of communication between us. I can't keep knocking Elizabeth's hat off," Celwyn said.

Kang told him, "I will figure something out." Qing peeked out from Celwyn's collar and squawked at Kang. He rubbed the bird's head. "Do not worry, Qing. And leave Elizabeth's jewelry alone." As the Professor spoke, his wife rejoined them.

"Damn thing just fell off." She patted her hat. "Shall we go in to lunch? It is nearly two in the afternoon, and I am famished."

Chapter 27

OVER A LUNCHEON OF CLAMS, SALAD *Narcisse,* and broiled sole, Elizabeth asked Bartholomew many questions, causing him to smile and relax. She skillfully skirted the topic of Mary Giovanna, as well as his earlier tragedy at home in Sudan. Celwyn assumed she had been coached by Kang. During their journey, the automat had written to her every day, and the magician presumed almost everything had been related to Elizabeth. Except possibly the dangerous situations they encountered ... or his magic. He watched Elizabeth as she ate a spear of asparagus and speculated what her reaction to a ballerina on the ceiling would be. Between the big man, Kang, and himself, they had not yet decided what to tell her.

As they exited the restaurant, Kang and Elizabeth turned toward the grand staircase.

"While you two get caught up, Bartholomew and I will take a walk." Celwyn made sure Kang watched him as he spoke, "I requested that the desk clerk guarantee that you aren't disturbed." As Elizabeth started up the stairs, he added in a softer voice. "Two armed porters will be in the hallway between our suites. At night, I'll add more protection."

Celwyn and Bartholomew departed through the hotel's front doors. Each doorman touched his hat with a gloved hand, and the magician and the big man returned the courtesy. Feeling a bit weary, courtesy of the infernal Russians, Celwyn held on to the rail as they went down the stairs and onto the crowded sidewalk.

As they left the hotel behind, Bartholomew inhaled the fall air, shivered, and drew his coat closer. "Where are we going?"

Carriages, rickshaws, and bicycles clogged the street while vendors wearing strings of bananas beckoned to them, called out prices, and juggled melons. Bartholomew bought some of the fruit, and they walked on.

"No real destination. Just stretch our legs, give Xiau time alone with Elizabeth, and," the magician nodded toward the dense crowd around them, "perhaps attract the attention of whoever is watching us."

"I like that. We've been inactive too long." The big man rolled his shoulders and chuckled. "If we're lucky, we may also find a well-stocked tobacconist or tea proprietor."

They ambled on, and Celwyn said, "I have noticed, my friend, that you have an extraordinary ability to know when you are being watched."

"I do, usually." They passed a bakery, and both inhaled deeply. "Sometimes, the sensation is diminished if I am distracted." He checked behind them. "For some reason, I keep expecting to see Mary Giovanna."

The magician grimaced. "Humph. She should be well on her way back to Rome by now. I would like to think we are the last people she wants to see since we can identify her as Prince Leo's killer. She knows we can. By now, she probably regrets smearing his blood on Xiau."

"If she could have set the police after us, she would have."

"Agreed. She is angry with you and dislikes me."

"An understatement." At the corner, they stepped into the street. "She hates me."

A woman screamed as a four-horse coach bore down upon them at full speed. Celwyn threw the fruit in the air and shoved Bartholomew out of the way.

As he fell under the horses, the magician made himself small, no more than a foot long. He bounded upward again at normal size, twisting away just before the hooves came down on his face. Shots rang out, one hitting him in the shoulder.

Celwyn lurched away from the volley of bullets and grabbed the side handles of the carriage. With a foot on the running board, he let it carry him away from the shooting.

The coach did not slow as it raced around the corner, tilting up on two wheels. The magician dropped to the ground and rolled away across the street as the coach raced north. Bartholomew ran up to him and knelt, covering him with his jacket.

"You are wounded!"

The magician held his breath. "It isn't ... that bad... Your coat—keep me covered."

He sighed heavily and went through every curse word he knew silently.

Moments later, he groaned and handed Bartholomew the bullet. "What kind of bullet is that?"

"I haven't seen one like this before," the big man said as he twirled it between his fingers. "It is from a rifle, is all I know."

"I'm very grateful Qing is in my room."

"I am also," the big man said and stood, "No matter how much of a nuisance he is. Let's get you back to the hotel and have the Professor look at your shoulder."

As Bartholomew helped him up, the magician asked, "Who shot at me?"

"Unknown. I chased two men down an alley and lost them."

"Blue suits again?" Celwyn wobbled, and Bartholomew steadied him.

"Yes. How did you evade the horses? They didn't trample you?" With the magician leaning on Bartholomew, they walked slowly toward the hotel.

Celwyn increased his grip on the big man. "Let's rest a moment." He felt weaker with each step. "To answer your question, I made myself small, then the shooting started. I…" he breathed deeply, "am fortunate the bullet wasn't in the same place where the Russian stabbed me."

Minutes later, they started up the steps of the Raffles' entrance as Bartholomew said, "You look disheveled and bloody. You should clean up what my jacket doesn't cover."

"Done."

Bartholomew inspected him. "That will do. You still seem very pale."

"I lost a bit of blood … is all." They crossed the foyer with Bartholomew supporting him as if he had too much to drink. It took a while to ascend the steps to the next floor.

When Kang answered his door, he saw Bartholomew's expression and called over his shoulder, "I will be next door for a few minutes." They nodded to the porters on guard, and Kang took over, propping up the magician while Bartholomew unlocked their door.

"What happened?" The Professor asked as he steered Celwyn to the sofa and began examining his shoulder.

Bartholomew brought him some water and a towel while Qing flew above them, squawking. He circled Celwyn until finally landing beside him and waiting to be petted.

"A carriage tried to run us down. Then someone shot at Jonas while he was under the horses. He cleaned up most of the blood and dirt before we got here."

"I assume they got away, or you'd still be out there chasing them." Kang held Celwyn's shirt open. "I see a bruise, it looks like it came from a hoof."

"It could have … been worse," Celwyn panted.

Kang said, "Does it hurt?"

It took the magician a moment to catch his breath. "My shoulder hurts where I took the bullet out."

"I see where it was removed. You know, you're so good at that, it looks like a doctor removed it."

Celwyn leaned back on the mound of pillows on the sofa. "What are you going to tell Elizabeth?" He tried to see his shoulder but could only see part of the wound. "She needs to be on guard but not frightened."

"We have the armed porters in the hall." The Professor grimaced. "I really didn't want to tell her about why we might need them."

As Kang peeled off Celwyn's bloody shirt, Bartholomew returned with another shirt. He cringed when he saw the deep bruising on the magician's back.

"That doesn't hurt?"

"Some. Thank you." Celwyn took the shirt from Bartholomew. "I must remember to check with the tailors here. I seem to be running low."

"Pfft! This is not about tailors!" Kang nearly shouted. "I leave you two alone for a half hour, and you are in trouble." The automat wiped off the magician's shoulder like he shaved wood when carving: rather violently. "I should have gone with you."

"I need to heal myself, Xiau." Celwyn lay on his other side on the sofa. "I am fortunate Bartholomew was with me." He closed his eyes. "This is about you. It seems like our enemies wanted to remove both of us—we're just the big dogs protecting you."

When Celwyn awoke again, Elizabeth and Bartholomew sat next to him playing chess. As the setting sun shone through the suite's window, Kang regarded Celwyn from the foot of the sofa.

"Don't get up," the automat told him.

Elizabeth faced him. "You and Xiau seem to attract danger, Mr. Celwyn."

Sometimes, the magician found himself speechless. Her expression appeared to be half-annoyed and half-amused like she tolerated his and Kang's foibles.

"I would be honored if you would call me Jonas. Xiau does."

She nodded. "All right, Jonas. And now Bartholomew is involved in your dangerous activities."

"She came over to get me and saw you from the doorway," Kang explained. "There was no turning her away after that."

"I am most willingly involved, Madam," Bartholomew assured her and moved his pawn forward.

Elizabeth played with a captured bishop while regarding the three of them as she would errant schoolboys. "I am beginning to understand the frustration in some of Annabelle's letters."

The men exchanged silent expressive glances.

Elizabeth tapped her husband on the shoulder. "I want to know what is going on, dear. Completely. Annabelle said it took you months to confide in her." She pinned Kang with a stern look. "That is not acceptable."

Celwyn started to laugh at his expression, but it hurt, so he stopped.

Bartholomew asked with his innocent expression, "How much of our adventures do you know about?"

"All about the madman Van Maskolc and the vampires, to begin with."

Kang choked on the tea he had been sipping. "You know about that?"

Elizabeth's smile had a level of postponed annoyance in it. "Yes. Annabelle also said something about a 'Jax.'"

"Oh." The automat studied the toe of his shoe as if it were the most interesting thing in the world.

"It seems you are well-informed, Mrs. Kang," Celwyn said, still enjoying Kang's discomfort.

"You may call me Elizabeth." She turned. To Bartholomew, she said, "You also, please."

The automat started pacing, always a sign of stress. He glanced at his wife, as pretty as a picture in an elegant lace dress and seeming quite calm with the subject matter.

"I do not like you being in danger," Elizabeth told him as she removed Bartholomew's bishop. "However, I understand."

Celwyn felt better and hitched up his pillows without touching them, enjoying the automat's reaction when Elizabeth's eyes widened, but she didn't say a word.

Kang did. "Must you?"

"I suspect there are many things you haven't told me." She shot a quick glance at her husband.

The Professor stopped beside her chair and kissed the top of her head. She covered his hand with her own.

"Annabelle wrote to me of how all of you protected her and Zander."

"He is a very lucky young man," Bartholomew said. "Your husband and Jonas rescued him, and Telly." His eyes brimmed with tears and the memory.

"You also played a big part, my friend," Kang corrected him and crossed to the bell pull. "We're going to need more whiskey. And tea."

Hours later, Elizabeth had been told of their earlier adventures, except some of the details of the finale at the Opera House. She asked many questions and made some comments about Jax that included a few colorful words in Mandarin Celwyn hadn't heard before. At one point, she looked puzzled.

"How could—"

Kang held up a hand. "I think the easiest way to explain would be a demonstration. But, let us finish the story first."

By the time Bartholomew had related the last stages of the rail trip to Singapore and the attack earlier in the afternoon, Elizabeth had switched from tea to whiskey.

"So, we do not know how Verne is connected to the attack today, do we?" she asked.

"No." The automat once again sat next to Celwyn's feet, keeping an eye on the magician.

"The men in the alley were already running when I gave chase." Bartholomew frowned as he inched his remaining bishop forward. "They wore naval uniforms. The last I saw of them, they disappeared toward the harbor."

Kang said, "Which lends itself toward the supposition they are sailors." He regarded the magician down his nose. "Who have you antagonized in a navy?"

"Me?" Celwyn tried to sound outraged. "No one. More likely, it is you."

"You two," Elizabeth said fondly.

Bartholomew extended a long leg and regarded them. "This doesn't appear to have anything to do with Phileas Fogg or Verne. That would narrow down the objective to one of us." He knocked over one of the captured pawns. "It was only after we got Jonas settled that I found a bullet hole in my pant leg. They missed."

"Oh, no!" When Elizabeth turned to him, the automat patted her hand and said, "It is not you they want." Kang frowned. "She was here in Singapore all this time and was not attacked."

"Perhaps our enemy is afraid of water buffalos." Celwyn offered her a smile. "I hope your mother's garden is flourishing."

She turned red as a rose and demanded, "*How* do you know about those damn water buffalos?"

"Do I have your permission?" the magician asked Xiau. "It will make things easier if she knows."

Kang threw up his hands. "Go ahead."

"What are you talking about?"

Celwyn winced and turned on his side. "You probably remember that after we arrived in this city that a large, and rather nasty, police lieutenant visited your mother's house. Once there, Lieutenant Dooney threatened to arrest your husband."

Her tone sounded grim. "I remember. He was extraordinarily obnoxious."

"I agree," Celwyn said. "So, I was just as obnoxious."

He opened his hand, and on the coffee table between them, a mist thickened and then cleared, revealing a yard-long replica of her mother's garden. A tiny copy of Elizabeth, her mother, the nurse, and Kang stood inside the roofless house, gazing out at the garden. The chorus of French horns once again began to play as the braying from the herd of water buffalos harmonized. Into the ruckus waddled Lieutenant Dooney, followed by the other officers.

"You see, Elizabeth, I am a magician."

Her mouth was open. No words came out.

Bartholomew squinted at the display. "I am sorry I missed this encounter. My, my Jonas. The buffalos' faces look just like the Lieutenant's."

"Don't they, though?"

Elizabeth spoke slowly as if she only had so many words to spend. "I wondered for a long time what happened that day." She watched the garden scene as once again Lieutenant Dooney slipped and fell on his backside in the manure and mud. "You were there? Why?"

"I did not wish to intrude more than necessary, madam."

"But..." Her eyes were as wide as they would go. "The... the..." She started to laugh. "You are a very real magician, Jonas. The three of you must have some amusing times together."

Her husband rolled his eyes. "Amusing may not be the proper word."

"Exciting times, too," Bartholomew said.

Celwyn swept a hand, and on the wall beside them, the distant image of the *Elizabeth* hurtling down Mt. Kilar appeared. Snow as high as the train's smokestacks rose on each side of her. As before, the debris from the avalanche came into view below.

The image of the train's interior became clear, revealing Celwyn and the conductor standing inside the cab. The magician's hands rose, and sweat poured off his face as the train lifted off the tracks, soaring into the air and over the debris threatening to derail them. Once again, the bottom of the caboose trailed through the snow as it sailed by overhead. A cold breeze blew across the room and fluttered the hair on Elizabeth's brow.

Kang put his arm around his wife and, with a finger, closed her open mouth again. "Jonas would have made sure you didn't see this at the time."

"I was there." Bartholomew's hand tremored as he hid his king behind his rook. "It was a very ... intense few moments, madam."

"Why did you get hurt today?" she stammered and looked at the magician. "With that kind of power, can't you avoid danger?"

Celwyn shrugged, and the image on the wall faded away. "Most of the time, I can do so. Someone shooting at me from ambush is an exception. I have other talents that we won't discuss now." He saw Bartholomew snicker, and Kang eyed his wife warily as Celwyn continued, "They help me anticipate bad situations. But above all, I have to know about the danger ahead of time."

"This afternoon's encounter was orchestrated and came from two directions: the horses to distract us and then the fusillade from the rifles." Bartholomew shook his head in disgust.

The Professor continued to hold Elizabeth's hand. "Our enemies undoubtedly know we're registered in this hotel." He kissed her forehead. "We'll stay together, and you won't leave without taking one of us with you," he looked at her pleadingly. "Please."

"As you wish." She patted his cheek with a mischievous smile. "I hope that all of you enjoy shopping. I must find a wedding present for Annabelle and her betrothed."

Kang finally breathed again. "Elizabeth has agreed to return to Prague with us."

"Congratulations, my friend." Celwyn turned to Elizabeth. "You will be welcomed by the love birds, who expect you to help with the details of the wedding."

"I look forward to it and to Zander." She placed her queen in front of Bartholomew and stood. "It is nearly eight in the evening, and I suggest we have dinner sent up."

"And let Jonas rest." Kang once again directed a worried look at the magician, one that he didn't try to hide.

Chapter 28

> "The Sea does not belong to despots. Upon its surface, men can still exercise fight, tear one another to pieces, and be carried away with terrestrial horros. But at their feet below its level their reign ceases, their influence is quenched, and the power disappears."
>
> —Jules Verne

AFTER BREAKFAST THE NEXT morning, the Kangs strolled arm in arm out of the hotel, and down the steps to the street. Celwyn and Bartholomew already waiting to the side of the entrance behind the greenery and watching.

"Did you leave that bird in your room?"

"No. As Xiau says, I spoil him." Celwyn nodded toward the street. "If you are correct in that we are being observed, by now, our enemy should be aware that the Professor and Elizabeth have left the hotel."

"I agree." A hard glint shone in the big man's eye. "I don't like using them as bait, but this has to be resolved." He eyed Celwyn. "You know, you really aren't strong enough for combat after yesterday. Xiau says so."

"Nonsense. I'll use magic to keep up with you, my friend."

"We can't let them get too far in front of us," Celwyn said as they neared the outside doors. Thirty feet away on the sidewalk, Kang shaded his eyes and pretended to decide which direction to walk.

Bartholomew grabbed Celwyn's arm and pulled him back. "Across the street."

"Ah." The magician could just spot the back of a navy uniform behind a flower cart. "There is probably more than the one there." He pointed as a second navy man walked up the street, swiftly gaining on the Kangs.

The big man took the lead as they streaked down the entry stairs and ran. Celwyn grimaced. Already his shoulder throbbed.

As the Professor steered his wife around a crowd fascinated by a juggler, another navy man crossed the street from the north, dodging coaches and horse-drawn carts. So quick, it had to have been rehearsed; both men reached the Kangs at the same time. One of them shoved the automat to the ground while the other scooped Elizabeth into his arms. A third man bundled Elizabeth into a carriage as the other man kicked Kang down again.

Celwyn swept a hand, and the men went tumbling. But as he turned to the carriage, one of them leaned out the window and started shooting at Bartholomew. The big man dived behind another cart. By the time Celwyn had removed the gun, the other man had landed on top of Kang, holding him down with a pistol to his head.

Celwyn growled and sent both shooters flying through the air, slamming them into nearby buildings.

"*Elizabeth*!" Kang shouted.

"There!" Bartholomew pointed to the speeding carriage racing east through the next intersection.

"To the docks!" Kang yelled as they piled into a nearby coach to the consternation of a flustered dowager already seated inside it. While the automat shoved coins and terse instructions at the driver, Celwyn did his best to charm the elderly woman in between catching his breath.

Moments later, they arrived at the docks in a hail of gravel. Their horses reared and then subsided as Bartholomew tossed the driver more coins. Kang jumped out, frantically running from side to side before vaulting to the top of a shipping container to scan the area.

"Thank you, madam." Celwyn kissed the dowager's hand through the window and bowed before joining the others as they ran toward the collection of carriages parked before the ships.

Like a trained acrobat, Kang scaled another stack of containers.

"Nothing!" He leapt down and bolted to their left and back. "*Where is she*?"

Celwyn used magic to climb the nearest tree and expand the search area. At the southern tip of the peninsula, furthest from the docks, he saw one of the navy men trotting away from them, disappearing under more trees.

"Come on!" He sprang to the ground and pointed.

They sprinted for half a mile or more to where they'd seen the navy man. Celwyn's breathing became labored. The farther they went, they passed fewer people and buildings until there was nothing in front of them but a rocky shore and the water. A rutted path led to a promontory. At the far end of it sat the carriage that had abducted Elizabeth. They were alone here. As the clouds above them receded, swaths of sunlight painted the water below. It glimmered as brilliantly as the gods intended.

The further they went, Celwyn fell behind the others, his injured shoulder throbbing. He waved Bartholomew ahead to keep up with Kang, and each of his steps became a supreme endeavor, each magical effort even more. Yet, somehow the magician knew he had to reserve his energy for what they might find.

Celwyn closed the distance in time to see a pair of navy men carrying a tarp-wrapped bundle on their shoulders, presumably Elizabeth, to the far side of the promontory. When Kang and Bartholomew drew closer, one of the men turned and fired over their heads. The magician stopped running long enough to send twin rifles to Kang and Bartholomew.

Bartholomew returned fire, careful to not aim at the bundle.

With a final burst of magic, Celwyn reached the top of the rocks in time to see that Kang and Bartholomew had descended to the other side. They minced their way across a floating pier, following the navy men and trading shots. Celwyn only half saw them as with a shiver of premonition, he stared at a long black cylinder, nearly a dozen times wider than a carriage and almost a city block long, that floated underneath the pier. The navy men handed Elizabeth through an opening on top of the thing. More navy men pointed guns at Kang and Bartholomew. Words were exchanged, and they lowered their weapons, surrendering to the navy men as the bundle disappeared inside.

Celwyn summoned the last of his strength and jumped over the rocks and onto the sand, just in time to see the sailors shove Kang and Bartholomew down the opening behind Elizabeth. When Kang dropped his rifle on top of the cylinder, a metallic clang rang in the air.

The magician loped across the pier as the last navy man entered the top of the cylinder. When the lid at the other end clicked shut, Celwyn leaped on top and unlocked it without touching it. Seconds more, it closed again when he tried to open it and a low whirring noise came from under him as waves of water sloshed over the top of the metal hull. The machine began to move forward and descend.

"No, you don't—" Celwyn cursed and flattened himself on top, holding on as he encased himself in an airtight glass cage. Water climbed up the sides of the glass. He drilled a nice hole through the structure underneath his chin, and a rush of fresh air blew over him. With a blink of his eye, a collection of more holes appeared further down, and he spied a satisfying line of bubbles trailing behind the craft in the water. There should be a noticeable leak inside the infernal contraption.

A moment more, and the monstrosity ascended a few feet upward to the surface. It stopped moving, and seawater sloughed off it as the hatch in front of him opened again. Celwyn couldn't see anyone but soon heard a very familiar voice.

"Jonas, there is a pistol in my back. Your presence is requested inside ... after you close the holes you made." Someone must have jabbed him with the gun. Bartholomew yelped and said, "Please."

A minute later, the magician peaked inside the hatch and then climbed down a metal staircase as a navy man as big as Bartholomew backed him up with a handgun nestled in his neck. Between the two of them, they nearly filled a narrow passage framed in metallic walls and bathed in eerie blue light and deep shadows.

When the magician reached the bottom of the staircase, another pistol pressed against his side, exactly where the Russian's blade had gone through. With a wince, Celwyn allowed it, wanting to know more of what, or who, resided inside this tin tub and where in the hell Elizabeth and the Professor had gone. From all directions, he heard jabbering thoughts in as many languages. As his captors walked him forward, they followed behind Bartholomew, and Celwyn caught up on his breathing.

They passed a half dozen closed metal doors, and the magician still didn't see either of the Kangs. The vibration underneath their feet increased, although the low humming noise did not. Bartholomew's captor shoved him through a door. Celwyn couldn't stand the situation any longer.

He had recovered some of his energy and wits and began to suspect their chances of escape lessened with each moment. The magician dissolved the gun pressing against his side, and in a blink of an eye, his escort was no longer standing. Then he peeked inside the door they'd pushed the big man through and stopped dead still. It was rare that Celwyn was astounded, and at the moment, he was speechless.

Kang stood off to the side, holding a ruffled but healthy-looking Elizabeth in his arms. Two guns were trained on them. A foot away, more guns covered Bartholomew head to toe. All of which the magician could deal with, but it was the scene beyond them that he found so impossible as to be believed.

For nearly the width of the room, scores of silvery fish swam beyond a glass wall. Pieces of plants and fluffy shells floated by. In front of the aquatic show, Phileas Fogg sat at a checkerboard across from Jules Verne. The author turned to blink at them but didn't say a word.

A deep voice came, seeming to emanate from inside the walls.

"Stand down, Mr. Celwyn, or my men will shoot."

I don't think so, Celwyn thought. He turned and flexed his hand. The vibration under their feet lessened and then stopped. Phileas Fogg's head jerked up as a loud gong began frantically chiming, and the instant quieting of the vibration under them seemed more ominous for what it represented. The magician stared at the guards on each side of Bartholomew until they dropped to the floor. The men next to the Kangs fell at the same time. The big man picked up two of their guns and stuck one in his belt. He handed the other to the Professor, and they waited.

The magician approached the wall of glass. The flotsam and fish still went by, only now it appeared the contraption they were inside of drifted as it gradually sank. He pivoted.

From the hallway, a man dressed in a black uniform entered the room and approached Celwyn.

"What have you done to my ship, Mr. Celwyn?"

The magician regarded him. Medium-sized, he had dark hair and skin, either from the sun or heritage, and his eyes had that other-worldly silver sheen that reminded Celwyn of a feral cat. The man emitted a dangerous anger as he returned the magician's assessment.

Celwyn turned fully around and removed all the navy men from the room. Not through the exit, they just dissolved. From the other side of the door, tentative pounding began. Celwyn's nose twitched, and after a few more noises, an eerie form of silence enveloped them again. Near the aquatic window, a faint bubbling noise from outside the glass filled the room before clouds of effervescences bounced against the glass. The fluctuations were caused by Celwyn as he brought the ship to the surface again. In the near hushed stillness, the magician imagined he heard the inhabitants in the room breathing.

The magician strode toward the man, who still presented a stance of offense, not defense, despite the magician's display of power. Celwyn's voice shook with a high level of anger he could barely contain.

"First, your men run me over, then shoot me. Then you attack Mrs. Kang." He flicked a hand, and a sizzling bolt of lightning streaked above the man's head and exploded into the wall by the door. "Then, you trick us into this 'ship' as you call it."

"Rather clever plan, was it not?" Fogg said with a smirk.

"No. Not at all." Kang's cold fury equaled Celwyn's. "What is going on?"

The dark-skinned man paused, seeming to check his anger. "This is the *Nautilus*," he spread his hands open. "She represents a new era at sea where ships sail below the surface." The man spoke in a deep voice laced with an accent Celwyn couldn't place.

For some reason, Celwyn glanced at Verne. He saw no surprise there: the author seemed to know all about the *Nautilus*. The magician assumed the entire world would read about it someday.

Kang settled Elizabeth into a chair, turned, and approached the tableau in the middle of the room.

"Source of power?"

Celwyn couldn't believe that his friend thought mechanics were important now.

"Special batteries."

"Speed?" Kang asked in a matter-of-fact tone.

Then the magician understood: Kang was trying to diffuse his anger. Celwyn glared but understood: Elizabeth's safety came first. He made a supreme effort to control his rage.

"Forty knots. Sometimes more "

Kang nodded and retreated to stand beside his wife again. He implored Celwyn with his eyes. The magician breathed deeply and cursed again. Violence with Elizabeth this close was not a good idea. Then the magician smiled a smile that others have found it best to be wary of: there were other ways of dealing with this affront.

"At the moment, I have wrapped your rudder to where it won't turn. You can't steer. I've disabled your engine." Celwyn relieved some of his ire by showering the room in brilliant stars as he glowered at the man before him. "Apologize, Sir, or worse will befall your *Nautilus*."

Verne jumped to his feet and rushed to the magician, tugging on his arm.

"Please, Jonas. Sit down. Let us talk."

Bartholomew growled at him. "So, you can explain what you and Mr. Fogg are doing here?" He scowled. "You are no longer afraid of him."

The author wet his lips as the man in black marched to one of the sofas and sat. When Verne spied Kang urging Elizabeth to do the same, he followed. At the magician's nod, Bartholomew joined them.

Fogg stood and stretched, and a whiff of his disgusting cigar reached them. The man sauntered to the sofa to sit beside the man in the black uniform. He patted an insolent yawn. Celwyn noted that Fogg had positioned himself where he could watch the magician as he paced in front of the aquatic show a few feet away.

After another moment, Celwyn stopped pacing, and the last of the stars faded away.

"Well, sir?" He couldn't control the anger in his voice and didn't want to.

"I am Captain Nemo." The man stood and offered his hand to the magician. "I apologize that your party was endangered." His face held no expression.

Celwyn hesitated and then shook the man's hand. In doing so, he entered his mind, falling into a storm of violent and disturbing images. Swaths of color painted raging sea battles as cannons roared and bucked under bilious clouds of smoke on throngs of ships. Screams from dying men echoed in a cacophony as their ships sank. Images of barren fields replaced the ships. Row after row of bodies lay in the dirt, shrouded in white sheets, a telltale sign of the plague. Celwyn backed out, disturbed at the intensity of Nemo's thoughts.

Captain Nemo hadn't let go of his hand. Celwyn removed it, strode to the glass window, and on the way back, released the rudder of the ship. The engines must have started again as the vibration under their feet came again, and the echoing gongs gradually stopped.

"Please do not take us any farther away from Singapore. I only released your ship so that she would not continue to sink without my help." He gestured. "The rudder is also released."

The ship appeared stationary, yet she moved forward just perceptively. Larger, dark shapes could be seen in the far reaches of the water and up-close tangles of sinuous seaweed undulated in the current. Through it, dozens of bulbous yellow fish swam.

Captain Nemo said, "Again, my apology for the attack. We wanted Professor Kang to accompany us, and this method seemed the most expedient way of getting him here."

"Why?" Bartholomew demanded and rubbed his clenched fists up and down his knees.

"To show him a scientific exhibit," the Captain told him. "And we thought that the *Nautilus* would pique his curiosity."

The Professor couldn't believe it. "You thought I would accede to your wishes after you man-handled my *wife*?"

With a telling glance at Phileas Fogg, Captain Nemo said, "It was suggested as leverage, yes. Mr. Fogg reported that your stay in Singapore would be a short one, so we acted."

Celwyn's anger returned. They had been manipulated and then trapped. He barked at Verne, "What the *hell* are you doing here?"

"And sitting with the man you were so afraid of?" Bartholomew demanded.

Verne squirmed like his underwear itched. "You remember I said that Mr. Fogg appeared in my book."

"Yes." Celwyn leaned against the sofa the Kangs sat on, tired and wishing he could sit down instead of being on alert in case the mood of the room changed.

"There will also be a book about the *Nautilus*."

"Ah. So, everything unreal is based on something real?" The big man raised his brows.

Verne shrugged. "Something like that."

"And our question?" Bartholomew asked.

"Mr. Fogg did pursue me, but we spoke before I reached Singapore. We resolved our problem, and he escorted me aboard the *Nautilus*." Verne shot a quick look at Captain Nemo and received a nod. "He and the Captain are partners, and I am beholden to the Captain."

Phileas Fogg cleared his throat. "I have a financial interest in this ship and other projects." He clapped Verne hard on the shoulder. The author winced. "Jules and I have come to an understanding." Fogg glanced at Kang, and then Celwyn. "It was never about money, although I led him to believe so."

The magician watched the exchange, gauging the undercurrents between Captain Nemo and the other two men. He'd wager Nemo did not like Fogg.

"Why did you want Professor Kang on this ship?" Celwyn asked Captain Nemo. "We will not allow you to spirit him away." As he spoke, a disheveled Elizabeth grasped her husband's hand and held on. The look of determination in her eye said she was still game, kidnapping or not.

"I realize that now." Captain Nemo smoothed the creases in his uniform and straightened his cuffs. "That was a miscalculation." He crossed to an enormous globe, much bigger than the one on the *Elizabeth*, and spun it until Singapore lay on top. "There is an island in the middle of the Bay of Bengal, about four hours from here. Once on the island, we request that Professor Kang observe one of our 'projects,' as Mr. Fogg puts it." He regarded Celwyn. "I can have you and your party back in Singapore within a day or two."

The tension in the room rose. Bartholomew leaned forward, on alert. Kang's eyes narrowed as he looked from Verne to each of the other two men. Then he stood, bringing Elizabeth to her feet as well.

"We need to confer. Privately."

Captain Nemo left the sofa without ceremony and turned. "I understand." Fogg joined him, and they headed for the door.

"You too, Jules," Celwyn growled.

"But Jonas—"

"No. You have forfeited our trust for now. I do not know what part you have in this yet." He glared. "Did you know they would kidnap Elizabeth? Just go."

When the door closed behind them, the magician staggered and then sat. The automat reached his side and studied Celwyn with a frown before attempting to look at the bandage on his shoulder.

"I believe it is past noon, and I need tea," the magician told him.

Kang tried not to roll his eyes and succeeded. "You need to rest. And your shoulder is bleeding again."

Celwyn stopped the bleeding. "Fixed. I just need to sit ... a moment." He opened his hand, and a tea service, a bottle of whiskey, and a plate of sandwiches appeared. Elizabeth gasped. The others helped themselves without hesitation. After the automat had poured and passed cups around, he sat back and held Elizabeth's hand.

"Well. This is an interesting situation." Bartholomew chewed. "Good ham."

"Indeed." Celwyn sipped tea and sighed, at last resting. He noted details of the room he'd been too busy to see before. In front of the glass wall lay tables of books bordered by a full library. The texts appeared to be of medical, geographical, and architectural subjects. The examples from Edward Kelley and Galileo looked like originals, and the amount of astronomy texts seemed to be extensive, as much as the tomes on the occult and alchemy. Kang followed his perusal, and his mouth dropped open when he saw John Dee's 1576 *General and Rare Memorials Pertayning to the Perfect Arte of Navigation.*

Displays of artifacts covered every surface, some of them lighted by directed wall sconces or behind small cards of identification. Bartholomew picked up an elephant's tusk and examined the card.

"Early 1500's Marnya excavation. It smells old." Bartholomew sniffed it. "Reminds me of a dirty cave."

"This ship, the very premise of it, is fantastic," the Professor murmured as he stared out the glass at a fat black fish with opaque eyes and red gills. "It is an unbelievable scientific opportunity."

Elizabeth threw him a worried look and then sent a beseeching one to Celwyn.

"Perhaps even more of an opportunity that we realize," Celwyn said, aware of Mrs. Kang's concern and the responsibility he had to both of them and to Bartholomew. "However, there is common sense."

Kang eyed him thoughtfully, thinking without commenting.

"Tea can soothe any situation." Bartholomew set his cup down carefully.

"You are beginning to sound like Jonas. But for now, I fear for my wife's safety. What are we going to do?" the Professor asked.

"I know I do not trust Mr. Fogg," the big man said. "At all. And the Captain has the miasma of something unsettling about him."

Elizabeth said, "I agree."

"A big part of this decision is our security and the ability to leave when we want to." Bartholomew pointed through the glass to the abyss of water. "In a sense, we're prisoners." His big neck swiveled, and he posed a question to Celwyn, "I assume you can control this ship at will?"

"I can, and Captain Nemo is aware of it. But only if I am not controlled by the threat of danger to one of you." He growled to himself. "I do not trust Nemo."

The automat said, "Logically, he will try to neutralize you."

With a sigh, Elizabeth put down her tea. "If I may? I suggest we stay together." She gestured at the corner of the room. "There is a water closet there. We could all stay in this room."

"That would be very helpful." Bartholomew gazed around them. "Jonas could provide food and drink as needed."

"And blankets." Kang regarded the sofas they sat on. "These would do as beds. And two of us always awake and on guard."

It appeared they'd formed a plan.

"I need rest now." The magician felt even more tired because the moment's tension had eased.

"You look like it," the automat told him.

A knock sounded, and Captain Nemo preceded Verne into the room.

Kang and the others exchanged a swift look that said, *We were listened to.*

Celwyn inserted himself in front of the others and faced Captain Nemo.

"Professor Kang would be honored to view your 'project.' We prefer to remain here until that occurs."

Captain Nemo smiled without humor. "For your safety, as you perceive it."

"Yes," Kang told him.

Nemo pivoted on his heel with military precision.

"Enjoy my study, as my guests." He started for the door. "We will arrive at the Nicobar Islands soon."

"Jules, feel free to remain," Celwyn purred. "We have questions for you."

Chapter 29

TO DEMONSTRATE HIS PRIORITIES, Verne demurely sat in front of the tray of sandwiches and filled a plate. "There is only fish, or sea vegetable-based food, aboard the *Nautilus*." He bit into a sandwich. "This ham is very tasty. Where did you get it?"

Celwyn watched him without favor. Kang read his expression and put a hand on the magician's arm. "Don't scare him, please. Elizabeth doesn't need the stress of it."

The magician frowned. "Fine. I bow to your common sense."

"Tell us why you are here, Mr. Verne," Bartholomew asked. "Money is not the only incentive, is it?"

Verne dotted his lips with a napkin and patted a burp. Elizabeth poured tea, and Kang passed it across the table. Their methods to extract information were a bit different from the magician's.

"For all of my books, my imagination is mixed with the truth or the various phenomena I have encountered." He sipped and selected another sandwich. "It lends details and richness to a novel that is extraordinary. The book about the *Nautilus* will be released in a few years. The Captain has requested I wait until then."

"With all of that said, why are you here now?" Elizabeth inquired in a sweet voice.

Celwyn appreciated the logic that seemed to run in the Kang family.

"Captain Nemo and I have an arrangement." Verne shrugged and chewed. "When he wants me here, I am here."

A spherical-shaped fish bumped the glass beside them. They watched it wiggle away into the deep water.

"What is Phileas Fogg's function in this 'project'?" Celwyn asked.

"Ask Captain Nemo. I do not really know." Verne drank his tea and eyed the remaining sandwiches on the plate. "I have never been to the Nicobar Islands."

"For your safety, Jules, it is best you remain outside this room and in Fogg and Nemo's good graces. You aren't in mine right now." Celwyn studied the vents and other openings. "I have disabled his ability to listen to us here, but I do not intend to do anything else unless necessary."

Kang murmured, "Thank you. I was going to suggest that." He faced Verne. "If you do as Jonas has suggested, you can't be put in danger as a ploy to control us."

The author shook his head. "I doubt Captain Nemo would do that. He is a good man." He got to his feet, eyed the remaining sandwiches, and patted his stomach with satisfaction. "However, I must get back to my writing." Verne bowed to Elizabeth. "I am sorry for your ordeal, Madam, and am pleased that you were not harmed."

"Really." She eyed his retreating back. "I wonder how much he knew."

For several minutes Bartholomew selected items that made noise when they fell, such as tables of lamps and artifacts, and barricaded the door with them.

"They won't sneak in, and this will give Jonas time to wake up."

As he stretched out on the sofa, Celwyn positioned himself to see out the aquatic window. It only took a minute to discover that floating under the sea is an extraordinary place for beautiful dreams. A cascade of bubbles rushed through the dark green water like a river. In contrast, the light in front of the *Nautilus* illuminated a broad swath of the area ahead of them.

"Don't let me sleep too long, please," the magician requested, feeling tiredness overtake him like an unseen hand extinguished a long row of internal lights one by one.

"Never fear." Kang said, "We won't be able to tolerate your snoring that long."

"Flummery and balderdash," Celwyn mumbled as his eyes closed.

Kang, Elizabeth, and Bartholomew moved chairs as far from the sofa as they could and settled in front of the chess set.

As they watched the magician sleep, Elizabeth asked in a low voice, "Are you worried about him?"

"I normally wouldn't be, but..." Kang twirled a white knight between his fingers, "he wasn't in any condition to run more than a mile to get here."

The big man glanced at Celwyn. "It takes a great deal out of him to perform magic. Thankfully, he had the foresight to conserve what energy he did have until he got here."

"You worry about him," Elizabeth said.

"Yes, he's had two serious wounds in the last few weeks." Bartholomew shot the patient a glance.

"We need to let Jonas heal as much as possible and do what we can for ourselves," Kang said, and Bartholomew nodded in agreement. "We have another couple of hours until he wakes." The Professor eyed his wife, "Do you want to rest also? The other sofa is available."

She squeezed his hand. "No, I'm too anxious from my little adventure this morning." She made a face as she pushed at her hair. "I really fancied that hat I lost."

"I will buy you several more of them. With even more elaborate feathers."

"You are correct, dear. You will." Elizabeth's smile was fond. "Can we talk about our predicament?"

"It is not ideal." Bartholomew sighed.

"My love, stay as close as possible to us, either on this ship or wherever we go, please." Kang's look begged Elizabeth.

Bartholomew patted the revolver in his waistband and sniffed the air. "Jonas will protect us, and your husband and I will also fight as needed. Do you smell that?"

"Yes," the automat answered. "It is part of the air circulation system of the ship."

"I don't like it much."

A long tone sounded from the other end of the ship, and a gong sounded faintly. They exchanged puzzled glances. "How odd," the big man said. "Ah, I feel the ship turning."

"It seems like it." Elizabeth nodded. After another moment, she asked, "Explain Jonas' magic, please?"

Kang popped up and strode to the windows and back, seeing nothing in front of them. "To your question, Jonas' magic is sometimes temporary; sometimes it lasts a long time. If he is angry, it becomes violent and unpredictable."

"Nemo was lucky all Jonas did was send a lightning bolt above his head and tie up the rudder," the big man said.

The automat watched Celwyn sleep. "He has exhibited much more control since I have known him. I nag him about it."

Elizabeth poked him in the ribs. "Oh, you do?"

"Jonas also has a big heart," Bartholomew told her. "He tries to hide it. Have you heard the story of how we met?"

While they talked, Kang explored the books in Nemo's library. He pulled Johannes Trithemius's *Steganographia* off the top shelf and caressed the cover. He'd only heard a rumor this existed. He also spied an older Mayan codex that had long been thought lost to history. The automat blinked at the treasure before him, wishing he could spend months wallowing in these tomes. He brought the codex back to the table as Elizabeth and Bartholomew began another game of chess, while in the background, Celwyn snored as if a butterfly tickled his nose.

Chapter 30

"What is there unreasonable in admitting the Intervention of a supernatural power in the most ordinary circumstances of life?"

—Jules Verne

IT LACKED A FEW MINUTES BEFORE three in the afternoon when Celwyn awoke and found the others sitting close by. Outside the glass, the seawater had lightened to the color of emeralds, and the bubbles increased. Celwyn strode to the windows, noting the engines of the *Nautilus* vibrated at a moderate rate. He wished their train could operate so quietly. Someday, perhaps, it would.

"Are you rested?" Kang asked.

"Yes." The magician studied the water and leaned close to the glass to gaze above the ship. "We're traveling near the surface. The wind is creating waves above us."

Again, they felt the ship turning, and the bubbles increased as she descended at a sharp angle. All of a sudden, the water turned black. Elizabeth gulped.

The *Nautilus* had entered a tunnel. Only feet away, a jagged rock wall with glittering veins running through it like an erratic metallic river stayed with them. Inside the *Nautilus*, all the lights came on.

"That is a dandy trick." Celwyn pointed at the wall sconces.

"Yes, it is," Kang agreed as they watched the tunnel for clues and held their breath.

The walls seemed to narrow. Would the ship scrape the side of the tunnel? Celwyn's nerves felt alive. He clapped Bartholomew on the shoulder.

"Any guesses as to what is ahead?"

"No." A fine sheen of perspiration shone on the big man's forehead, and he wet his lips. "You should know, I have a rather mild case of claustrophobia that I ... haven't mentioned before."

Kang told him, "It should be over soon, my friend. There—"

The engines slowed, and the color of the water grew darker as a knock sounded at the door behind them.

Celwyn turned, and with a flick of his hand—Bartholomew's blockade reverted to the shelves and tables. The chairs became upright. He stepped in front of the others as the door opened.

Phileas Fogg entered, followed by more sailors and Captain Nemo. Two men in expensive city suits stood behind Fogg.

The magician noted Fogg had come in first, perhaps as Nemo's version of a royal taste tester to interpret the degree of Celwyn's displeasure. He regarded the two men and asked, "Who are these men?"

"My associates," Fogg said.

"Look!" Elizabeth pointed.

As the *Nautilus* slowed, the ship left the tunnel, propelled forward in water so black, it didn't look like water as much as a sea of ink. Above them, faint streaks of sunlight patterned the surface, becoming more defined as the *Nautilus* ascended through more bubbles.

Captain Nemo approached them from across the room, standing off to the right by the bookshelves.

"I see you provided your own refreshments, Mr. Celwyn." He touched one of the cups with a fingertip. "I have never spent the time to study magic."

Studying is only part of it, Celwyn thought. He felt his anger return: no one treats his friends in this manner. In the next moment, the cup shimmered, and changed into a salivating wolf no more than five inches high. It barked flames as it lunged at Captain Nemo, and he retreated several feet.

Fogg turned and saw that his men no longer stood behind him. He eyed Celwyn but said nothing.

"Your abduction of Mrs. Kang has not been forgotten or forgiven," the magician told them with heat. With a glare, Celwyn wrapped Nemo in the embrace of a thick python that wound itself around his legs, curling upward. Immediately, the man's face turned red when the snake began to squeeze. Fogg ran across the room toward the exit. Celwyn froze the bastard mid-stride.

The magician eyed Captain Nemo and grated, "If I wanted to, I could elevate this ship, although not for more than a few minutes at the moment. Why? Because I'm still healing from when your men *shot* me." He flipped a hand, and the snake dissolved. Nemo bent double, gasping, and holding his sides.

Celwyn leaned into his face.

"Do *not* antagonize me." He felt Kang's hand on his arm and shook it off. "All right."

"Captain," Kang said, "why are we here? What is your project?"

Captain Nemo wheezed and pointed at Fogg. "Allow him ... to speak."

Beyond the window, amid the murkiness of the water, they could see tall shadows in front of towering black walls, then more deep shadows. From above, ribbons of light streamed downward, reflecting across the water. The *Nautilus* floated in a large lake.

Celwyn stared, and Fogg finished the step he had started to take. He pulled at his vest while he collected himself, faced them, and cleared his throat.

"Please." He gestured at Captain Nemo. "There is no need for violence." He bowed to Elizabeth. "Please accept our apologies for this morning."

When Elizabeth would have spoken, Kang stamped his foot and told Fogg, "An apology isn't enough for your effrontery! That was ungentlemanly of you and uncalled for!"

Celwyn noted he wasn't the only one simmering with a good dose of anger.

Bartholomew's eyes blazed. "As was shooting at us the day before. Why?"

"Sir, we would prefer to show you our project." Fogg glanced at Captain Nemo. "We are losing daylight."

"I suggest we finish our apologies later ... if that is acceptable." Captain Nemo started to bow and thought better of the idea. "It will soon be dark."

"Will Mr. Verne be with us?" the automat asked.

Captain Nemo and Phileas Fogg exchanged another telling look. This 'project' must be important on several levels.

"But of course," Captain Nemo said.

As they ascended the metal staircase to the surface, Elizabeth was positioned between Bartholomew and Kang, with Celwyn bringing up the rear. At each stage of their exit, Bartholomew went first to verify the danger while Celwyn ensured they weren't attacked from behind. In the magician's opinion, Kang represented the true target of their party, and Elizabeth, the most vulnerable.

They gathered on top of the submarine, and the scope of the amphitheater surrounding the ship became much more apparent. Its circumference measured a good quarter mile, and the interior walls rose at least as tall as a five-story building. Like enormous stone soldiers, the forest of stalagmites flanked the lake, and the massive opening above them appeared big enough to drive a train through. All around the opening, like small satellites orbiting a sun, a dozen or more holes let in streams of light above long stretches of the obsidian sand that led to the water.

It neared four in the afternoon, and as Fogg had noted, the sun had begun to wane. They filed onto a short wooden pier and waited for Nemo and Fogg.

"Oh my—" Bartholomew pointed into the depths of the pool under their feet. A suggestion of something enormous moved in the murky water. Kang leaned over the pier to observe and backed away again.

After Fogg had emerged to stand behind Captain Nemo, Celwyn stared at the hatch and locked it with a loud click.

"I wouldn't feel comfortable if more of your crew accompanied us," the magician told them. "I'm sure you understand."

Captain Nemo's face darkened. Again, Celwyn assumed whatever they wanted from Kang was of supreme importance for Nemo to bow to this.

"We need to hurry." Fogg turned to the others. "Please allow us to lead the way." He gestured at the large gap between the man-size rocks fifty feet away. "The jungle begins right there, and we have a short walk through it."

One by one, they entered the lush greenery where the air felt like the dank inside of a fishbowl as they dodged puddles, ducked under dripping vines, and pushed through thick foliage. Unseen animals skittered under the brush before them. The jungle blocked most of the sunlight overhead as Bartholomew led them forward in a crouch, his gun drawn. Kang held his pistol in one hand and Elizabeth's hand in the other, steadying her across the uneven ground. No conversation passed between them. Despite the tension floating around them, Celwyn enjoyed the spicy scent of jasmine and other flowers he couldn't name; it had been years since he had hiked through jungle.

After a while, the canopies of the trees thinned out, and the vegetation disappeared when they attained a short rise and looked down.

The jungle had been cleared for a long distance in each direction, exposing an unusually flat surface covered in gravel. All rocks and tree roots had been removed.

To their right sat a large replica of the toy that Kang had carved for Zander and Telly. The magician felt a fission of excitement race through him. Like the toy, this very much resembled a squat bird with a wooden box on top of its nose. In length, it appeared to be as long as a small boat.

"My heavens!" Bartholomew exclaimed.

Kang's mouth fell open, but no words came out. Celwyn turned so that he could observe their hosts.

"Do you recognize it, Professor Kang?" Fogg asked with an unreadable expression.

For several moments Kang just stared and then started forward with Elizabeth. Bartholomew followed, pivoting to be sure of their hosts' positions. Trust between them did not exist, no matter the distracting phenomena.

After a short walk across the gravel, they arrived beside the replica. Now that they stood this close, the magician observed that it had been made of wood that had been well-sanded and shaped. At the front end, a ring of long wooden blades had been attached to the nose of the apparatus.

Captain Nemo stopped beside the contraption and patted it.

"You can see why we needed light so that you could see what we've created." He looked at the sky. "We only have a few minutes before we must return to the ship."

"Lanterns? I could—" Celwyn asked.

Captain Nemo shook his head. "Lanterns we have, but after dusk, we'd become attractive to the animals in the jungle. Regretfully, it is best we go back shortly."

Kang checked with Bartholomew, who nodded and stepped forward to stand beside Elizabeth.

As he circled the craft, the Professor still didn't say a word, carefully examining the balloon-like wheels, the blades in front, and something mechanical at the tail end that Celwyn didn't recognize. Like he'd done it a thousand times, Kang climbed into the wooden box on top.

"Professor Kang, we will return tomorrow, if that is acceptable?" Captain Nemo pointed upward. "There are clouds coming in, and our light is leaving us even faster."

All the way back to the amphitheater of stalagmites, both Bartholomew and the automat remained silent, seeming in a stupor after seeing the craft. Celwyn had a different reaction: he would rather see more of Nemo's ship. He elevated himself a few feet and found the entrance into the cave hard to spot, yet even under the gloom of dusk, he had no trouble recognizing the entire amphitheater as a hollowed-out volcano.

"Captain, did we enter the island through a lava tube?" Celwyn asked as they navigated through the last of the jungle. Several more of Nemo's crew stood off to the side next to a large hut, and torches had been lit to provide a path to the pier and the submarine. Dozens of storage bins lay beyond the hut.

"Yes, there are several. But only one is big enough for my ship. This island is also one of our regular stops, Mr. Celwyn." Captain Nemo turned to his crew. "Quickly, before it gets any darker, please cover the craft. I saw that tiger again." They saluted, grabbed rifles, and marched outside.

As he walked down the pier toward the *Nautilus,* the Professor still appeared dazed and distracted, afloat in a blissful state of scientific euphoria. Bartholomew led the way in front of him and Elizabeth, with Captain Nemo next and the magician bringing up the rear of their parade as they crossed the pier. Celwyn verified Phileas Fogg remained far enough away from them, standing outside the entrance to the jungle and smoking a foul-smelling cigarette.

When they reached the submarine, Kang turned to speak. Elizabeth continued forward. She tripped on one of the boards and fell face-first into the water.

Without hesitation, Captain Nemo dove in after her. Celwyn didn't hesitate either and, in a flurry of water, brought them both upward and onto the boards. The back of something enormous, slick, and shiny surfaced right behind them, sloshing a wave of water across the pier before it sank into the depths again.

Celwyn swept a hand over Elizabeth and Captain Nemo, drying them. Phileas Fogg came running up the pier and stopped dead still as he watched their transformation.

Kang bounded forward and gathered Elizabeth into his arms.

The magician leaned on his knees and exhaled in relief. That was an unexpected close call.

"Thank you for your bravery, sir," Celwyn told Nemo after the shock subsided. The magician noted the Captain's surprise as he shook his hand. "My apologies for earlier."

This close, Celwyn got a good look into the man's eyes. Curious, he entered Nemo's mind, again finding the maelstrom of bloody images and violence. However, this time he felt the man's deep empathy and sadness. The ugliness of the world had seemingly left its mark on him. On a hunch,

Celwyn asked without speaking, *Was it Fogg's idea to shoot at us and kidnap Elizabeth?*

Captain Nemo's face contorted, and he backed up a step. He raised his brows at the magician. "I see what I heard is true. Yes, to your question. I was assured there would be no injuries."

The magician nodded and asked silently, *What does Fogg hold over you?*

Nemo checked to see if the man was far enough away not to hear. "Money. The flying machine is my dream, and he funds it. And partially other activities of this ship."

The Kangs approached them. "Thank you, from both of us," the Professor told Celwyn and Captain Nemo. He held Elizabeth close, as if she would dissolve if he didn't keep her near.

"Xiau." She wiggled. "I have trouble breathing when you hold me so tightly."

Captain Nemo inspected his uniform, and a ghost of a smile crossed his lips. "No wrinkles." He picked up his hat from where it had fallen. "As it is, it is I who owe you, Mr. Celwyn, for getting us out of the water before the Mizuchi reached us."

"That is what the Japanese call a water dragon, correct?" Kang asked. Captain Nemo nodded.

Celwyn lowered his voice, "I'm afraid I couldn't restore Mrs. Kang's hair to its original style."

Elizabeth raised her head from Kang's chest. "I heard that. I can imagine what it looks like." She appeared pale, and her eyes shone brightly. "Jonas, and Captain Nemo, you performed a very chivalrous act just now. Thank you."

"You are most welcome, Madam." Nemo bowed, hopped onto the hull, and stood beside the hatch. "We have prepared sleeping quarters for all of you. Once there, you will find toiletries and a change of clothes."

Chapter 31

A SHORT TIME LATER, CELWYN AND the others relaxed in front of the aquatic window in Captain Nemo's study. Verne had joined them, as uncharacteristically quiet as an eavesdropping mouse.

With a pointed look at his wife, Kang told her, "I want one of those," indicating the man-sized globe next to them. "I believe it is only a few months until Christmas."

"Of course you do, dear." She still fussed with her hair and had been since they regrouped a few minutes ago.

Bartholomew glanced at Verne. "I suspect he wants to know what the Professor thinks of that apparatus in the field."

Celwyn nodded, but his attention centered on Fogg as he mixed drinks at the bar. The magician watched him to be sure the man mixed nothing into them. This evening Fogg wore a green velvet coat with brass buttons that the magician envied. The coat reminded him of a mechanical bird who liked to snuggle and chew his collars and who had been wiggling and doing his best to escape for the last hour. Celwyn opened his coat and let Qing out. In seconds, the bird sat on a table beside the aquatic window, making little squeaking noises and pecking at the tiny fish swimming by.

As Captain Nemo entered the room, Fogg ferried the drinks to the sofas. The magician locked the door behind him as a precaution. Although the Captain had become less of a threat, he did not trust Fogg not to corrupt the crew or bring in his own men.

Captain Nemo sat next to Verne, with Fogg on his other side, as they faced the Kangs and Bartholomew. Celwyn paced behind them. Through the glass, he saw that the water had darkened wholly as the night became complete.

"Very smooth," Bartholomew commented as he sipped.

Captain Nemo said, "It is made in Manila at my direction."

Riding a metallic scent, fresh air blew into the room from the vents near the ceiling. To Celwyn, it smelled clean but made him want to sneeze. The sconces had been turned up, bathing the room in a warm light. The magician could imagine sitting here and relaxing for hours with the mystery of the sea just outside the window. Preferably with a flamboyant electrical storm raging across the water.

"Dinner will be served soon," Captain Nemo said. "I look forward to acting as your host." He eyed Celwyn. "It is the least I can do after the less than auspicious beginning to our relationship."

Celwyn nodded an acknowledgement and popped a peyote button in his mouth. He chewed as he watched Verne's anxious eyes and noted the man's nervous hands clenching and unclenching.

Fogg addressed Kang, "Professor, what did you think of the flying machine?"

"Why do you ask?" Kang stared at him. Captain Nemo, he had forgiven, but not Fogg.

The magician had never seen Kang so angry. Minutes ago, when he'd told Xiau of his silent questions and Nemo's answers, Kang had glared at Fogg's back. Now, he looked ready to throttle him.

Celwyn asked Captain Nemo, "Are the crew under your control or," he pointed to Fogg, "his?" Bartholomew's brows went up, and he put a hand over his mouth to hide a smile.

Captain Nemo's eyes narrowed, and his annoyance wasn't with Celwyn.

"Mine. Completely."

Kang took the thread the magician had started and ran with it. "What is the arrangement between the two of you?" he asked the man who'd endangered his wife.

Phileas Fogg leaned back, balancing his glass on his knee. "There is nothing like a direct approach with an impertinent question." He played with the tips of his curled mustaches.

Celwyn regarded him. "You terrorized Mr. Verne and stole from us in Baghdad."

Fogg yawned in a slow, affected manner. "I wanted to keep an eye on Jules. If he was afraid, that was not my concern."

Celwyn doubted it. Verne had served as Fogg's excuse to surveil Kang.

"What did you take from our train?" the magician asked.

Bartholomew knew Celwyn's tones of voice and set his glass down as the tension in the room rose.

The Professor sipped and waited while Captain Nemo studied each of them, more in curiosity than alarm.

"Without answers, Mr. Fogg, you no longer have our cooperation." The magician faced him. "We will go back to Singapore as soon as possible."

In one fluid movement, Phileas Fogg stood and produced a revolver. He aimed it at Elizabeth.

"I think not."

Celwyn had wanted to confirm Fogg's character and didn't need any more of a demonstration. "You are an idiot, sir."

"Phileas, that is not necessary." Captain Nemo started to get up.

Fogg, still aiming at Elizabeth's face, said, "So pretty. It will be a shame if I—"

Celwyn lifted his chin, and the revolver spun into the air slowly, twirling, until it lowered to Fogg, the barrel inches from his lips.

"Open your mouth, Mr. Fogg," Celwyn said.

The man grabbed for the gun and screamed as his hand flamed. In the silence of the room, a loud click sounded as Celwyn cocked the revolver. Sweat poured off Fogg's face.

Nemo addressed Kang, "He provides financing for this and other projects. I did not agree to hurt any of you."

Celwyn tapped Fogg's lips with the gun. "What do you want, Mr. Fogg?"

A gong sounded deep within the *Nautilus* and the lights dimmed slightly.

Captain Nemo faced Celwyn. "Please, let us put away this distastefulness for now? Dinner is ready."

The Captain's private dining room barely held the five of them, a round table, and a glass-fronted buffet. After a pointed suggestion from Celwyn, Fogg elected to dine in his room. Verne noted the tension and decided to skip the gathering to write.

A centerpiece of orchids from the jungle graced the table, providing bright color against the gray and blue of the walls and uniforms. A smaller round glass window took up most of the wall at the head of the table. Through it, the water seemed as black as night, and every so often a piece of flotsam would float by, fluffy and odd-looking. Below the *Nautilus,* something agitated the water, sending up long chains of bubbles.

"According to the local islanders, the Mizuchi resides in this lake. I doubt it is a dragon; instead, most likely an abnormally large species of whale shark crossed with something unknown," Captain Nemo said. "Today, we almost met it intimately."

Elizabeth shivered and asked, "Is this a salt-water lake?"

"Yes. It has been here for hundreds of years." Captain Nemo grew pensive. "The Mizuchi may have been here that long, too. It eats anything that should be unlucky enough to swim in here from the sea, and it has become enormous. It can't swim out again."

"I'm so very glad that it was not you it had for its dinner, Madam." Celwyn shuddered at the thought of how close the thing had come. "You have had a very stressful day."

The Captain poured wine, making eye contact with the magician.

"Again, I thank you, Mr. Celwyn, for your quick assistance."

Elizabeth added, "We may not have made it out in time, otherwise."

"It was a pleasure to assist you both." Celwyn raised his glass. "It has indeed been an exhilarating day."

One of the crew arrived with a tray of oysters. Bartholomew's nose twitched.

"Is there something wrong?" Nemo beckoned one of the crew forward.

"These appear to be uncooked," the big man said.

Without hesitation, Captain Nemo asked the crewman, "Could you also bring some of the fresh shrimp? Grilled with that caper sauce, please?"

Another crewman refilled their water glasses as the others sampled the oysters.

"Excellent," Kang commented.

The shrimp arrived before the soup and received comments of admiration. When platters of baked fish and vegetables appeared, Captain Nemo said, "Professor, I need your expertise and have a different approach than Mr. Fogg."

"Such as exquisite food and drink?" Kang asked.

Elizabeth dabbed her lips with her napkin. "Thank you for your hospitality, Captain. You may not be aware of it, but my husband and I were separated for many months and are anxious to travel to Prague." She buttered a roll. "How long is our presence requested?"

Once more, the magician was reminded of the value and presence of the fairer sex in a delicate situation. She imparted information, a point of view, and politeness in very short order.

"Not long. Tomorrow, I am hoping your husband will examine what you saw today." He looked at Kang. "And, if possible, give us an opinion of the viability of it, or tell us what is wrong with it."

"Excuse me but," Elizabeth asked, "what is it?"

The automat touched her hand and bestowed upon her what he thought was a virtuous smile. "It appears to be a replica of what we called a flying machine. Throughout the world, there are various inventors and scientists who are just beginning to engineer and build these machines."

Bartholomew's eyes couldn't get any bigger. "To fly through the *air*?" Sweat beaded across his forehead like a garland.

Celwyn noted that the big man no longer found the craft an amusing tidbit to tease Kang with.

"Yes," Kang told him, and they all saw the big man pale further.

"The other inventors are far behind what we have accomplished, by many years," Captain Nemo informed them as solemnly as if they had been in church. "This is my dream, Sirs and Madam."

Celwyn ate slowly, enjoying the flavors and trying to guess the possibilities behind the discussion of the flying project. Xiau looked ready to drop his fork and rush back into the jungle to see the thing again.

"I saw these flying machines many years ago in the Mayan jungle. I never rode in one," Kang told them as he thanked the crewman who poured more wine and then discreetly left again. He chewed and said, "I made notes and wrote theories as to how the machines would fly. There were also Tokar's notes he made before he died."

"You did not build a flying machine?" Captain Nemo frowned. "I heard that you had."

Bartholomew sat back with a disgusted frown. "So, this is why Fogg pursued the Professor."

Captain Nemo cut into his fish. "Yes. Mr. Fogg did think so and hoped you would help us." He looked at the automat. "May I ask who built the flying machine you saw?"

Kang's eyes dropped to his plate. After a moment he spoke, measuring his words as carefully as if he walked over a volcano, barefoot.

"I attended a military parade in 1483. It was summer in Tikal in the central Americas." The automat's eyes closed as he remembered. "The exhibition was held in front of a long stretch of jungle that had been cleared by slaves."

Captain Nemo said, "That was a very long time ago." He eyed Kang with speculation before continuing. "Once again, what I had heard over the years has proved to be true. First, Mr. Celwyn's … ah … attributes, and now your impressive longevity."

"Yes, I've lived for a long time." Kang tapped his chest, and they heard the resounding clunk. "I am mechanical."

"And brave," Bartholomew added.

"And extraordinarily intelligent and stubborn," Celwyn said.

Kang laughed. "You forget 'tolerant,' my friends."

"Let us talk of the parade again, if you please?" Captain Nemo's lips twitched in suppressed amusement. He regarded them all with interest, especially the Professor.

"As you wish," Kang said. "It was an extremely warm and clear day. All of a sudden, something blocked out the sun. The crowd became excited. Then came five flying machines across the top of the mountains. They circled the exhibition at a low altitude just above the troops." His gaze turned inward. "I can still hear the hum of their engines. In moments, they were gone again."

Nemo's eyes shone with excitement. Elizabeth's open-mouthed reaction indicated her husband had never told her the story. Celwyn hid a smirk: the automat would probably get an earful later about sharing with his beloved.

Kang said, "Over the next few months, I saw them two more times. Once, on the ground, and again from a distance."

Elizabeth asked, "What did they look like?"

"Similar to what we saw this afternoon." Kang pursed his lips. "The box where the man sits and steers the plane appeared smaller and flatter, so as not to block the wind."

Bartholomew said, "Which would allow the craft to fly faster." At the magician's glance of surprise, he added, "I studied mechanical engineering at university."

"Exactly," the automat said to the big man with an elevated speculative brow.

Captain Nemo drank his wine, seeming mesmerized by what he heard.

Kang shrugged. "I examined how they were built but didn't design them."

"Who did?" Celwyn asked.

For the first time since the magician had met Professor Xiau Kang, his friend shut him out.

"I cannot reveal that." Kang's lips compressed. However, the magician caught the wistful look in Kang's eyes; he would eventually tell him.

Dessert had been placed in front of them, but no one made a move to eat it. Captain Nemo stared at the automat like he wished he could climb inside his mind. Celwyn could have told him it wasn't possible since he'd tried, and failed, back on the *Zelda*.

After a moment, the Captain said, "I would be very appreciative if you would look at our effort in detail. When you asked Mr. Fogg what he took from your train, I believe it was some of your notes. They will be returned to you."

"Thank you."

"What is the purpose of these flying machines?" Bartholomew asked. "I can't imagine anyone brave enough to get in one."

Captain Nemo said, "Some say they will be for pleasure or commerce." His eyes took on a faraway glimmer. "I want to build one that will explore the farthest points on earth … and beyond."

"It sounds complicated but interesting," Elizabeth said.

"Others speculate that the machines will be used for war." Kang's frown showed he'd worried about this before.

Silence enveloped the table as each of them digested Kang's statement. Celwyn's original opinion of Captain Nemo had pegged him as having a warlike nature. Now, he wasn't as sure. He had no evidence other than the armor on the *Nautilus* and the scenes playing through the man's myriad of thoughts. The magician recalled the initial picture he'd seen in Nemo's mind of the submarine ramming a ship until it sank. It could be part of the man's imagination. If it were real, it did not bode well for their continued association.

Bartholomew said, "Whoever was able to make a reliable flying machine would become very wealthy, no matter the purpose it was put to."

Their host paused and then said, "Or the purpose could be one of utmost importance." He stood and bowed to Elizabeth. "Please excuse me. I will leave all of you to your own pursuits this evening. Thank you, Madam, for a most pleasant meal."

As they again entered the study, Bartholomew asked Celwyn, "Did you notice the pipe organ in the corner?"

"Is that a hint, my friend?" Celwyn smiled.

The automat and Elizabeth settled on the sofa with books and fond looks. Kang's earlier anxiousness had dissipated, and he appeared to be immersed in the romance of his marriage, alluring science forgotten for the moment.

Celwyn sat at the pipe organ, admiring the intricate carving on its wooden legs. The artistry continued across the top of the instrument, where care had been taken to depict elaborate details of cherubs, devils, and well-endowed sea maidens. Qing sat on the magician's shoulder and snuggled.

As he touched the keys, the magician felt a fission of energy from within the organ. *Interesting*, he thought. Celwyn had encountered several instruments over the years that included more than strings, brass, and metal: some contained spells, and others something much deeper. He waited a moment and began a light romantic melody, just a soft, quiet serenade. The tremor of energy subsided as if it, too, listened.

Kang elevated a brow and smiled while Bartholomew kept time with a raised finger as he crossed to the bookshelves and removed texts for engineering, biology, and air currents. When the big man spread them across the table in front of the aquatic window, to Celwyn's unscientific eye, they represented the basis of Captain Nemo's flying machine. While the magician played, Bartholomew's frown of concentration and intense interest in the books grew. Without stopping the music, the magician added a notebook and pen beside the big man's hand. Bartholomew stopped chewing on his lip and picked up the pen. After several notes, he stared at the paper before turning a surprised look on Celwyn.

An hour passed peacefully before Verne entered the room, poured two whiskies, and crossed to the chess set. Celwyn finished a trailing melody and joined him. Perhaps the author's thoughts would prove fruitful.

"You may have the white pieces, Jules," Celwyn said with a studiously blank expression.

Chapter 32

ONCE EVERYONE ARRIVED IN THE study the next morning, Celwyn told them, "One mystery is solved; Jules owes Phileas Fogg a great deal of money also. Not because of using the man in his books. There is also Verne's son who has gambling debts."

"How did you discover this?" Elizabeth asked as they sipped tea.

Kang controlled his smile at Celwyn and patted her hand. Marital teasing flew between them regularly, yet it did not distract Mrs. Kang's displeasure when she discovered anything they had not seen fit to tell her. "Mr. Verne will join us here at any moment. It is best if I explain later. After breakfast." Celwyn made sure Kang knew he owed him something for this minor rescue. The magician appreciated the attempt to prevent embarrassing questions, but eventually, his wife would have to be told of Celwyn's ability to read thoughts. "I mention it as background, so we can be sure of our position. Would he sacrifice us to Phileas Fogg?"

"Perhaps." Bartholomew's eyes cleared to alertness as he thought and sipped coffee. "Or will Mr. Verne wish to go back to Prague with us to get away from Mr. Fogg?"

"It is possible." The magician shrugged. "But as of this moment, I can't be sure of his motives."

"Or those of Captain Nemo," Kang commented. "Although, I am coming around to the conclusion Captain is a man of honor and that, if possible, he would remove Fogg from our sight."

"Perhaps he could dump Fogg on a coral reef surrounded by hungry sharks?"

With amusement, Bartholomew envisioned what Celwyn had pictured and said, "I've watched the crew. They rarely speak, and they worship Captain Nemo."

Celwyn glanced at the door. "Anything else?"

"The crew ignores Fogg completely," Bartholomew said. "We've seen those two men that he has on board. They aren't part of the crew."

For a long moment, Celwyn rubbed his chin and thought.

"So, if we can trust Captain Nemo, then we can trust his crew."

"Possibly," Kang said. He turned to Elizabeth. "Have you noticed anything else, my dear?"

"The crew avoids me like I'm a leper, as they should after what happened yesterday. Otherwise, I never hear them speak." She sat her cup down. "Unless they are serving our meals, I don't even see them."

Bartholomew said, "Same here." He, too, checked the door. "My verdict on Captain Nemo is changing; he has character. And he is dangerous." He added, "Xiau, he respects you very much, so I doubt he would hurt Elizabeth under any circumstances."

"What about me?" Celwyn asked with an exaggerated blinking of his eyes.

Bartholomew laughed. "I imagine he'd like to feed you to that snake you introduced him to, but at the same time, he recognizes we are all," he opened his hands, "a party of one."

Celwyn considered what he'd heard. "I understand him somewhat and have explored some of his—" He glanced at Elizabeth, "history. He is very complicated, and he wouldn't hurt me. Fogg, however, would shoot me in an instant." The magician pointed at the table between them, and a new tea service appeared. Steam rose from the stem of the pot, curling into the air. "Shall I pour?"

Kang saw Elizabeth controlling her surprise, unable to do more than shake her head to decline the tea. He said, "For our excursion today, our main focus will be examining the craft, not worrying about an attack."

"As long as Fogg is under surveillance." Celwyn handed Bartholomew a cup.

Everyone nodded in agreement. Kang rubbed his hands together. "This is good news. I am very curious and want to get going."

The magician felt the same. He glanced again at the door, wondering what a traditional breakfast aboard a submarine would consist of.

A warm rain pattered the jungle as they walked single file out of the volcano and across the lush landscape toward the clearing. When a thin black snake slithered over Celwyn's boot, he walked on, wishing he could have saved it for Qing. All around them, birds called or squawked, and he had to keep his collar buttoned to keep Qing inside. There was no telling what he would do with a feathered friend. Or foe, for that matter.

This time, Fogg led the way across the gravel to the craft. Kang walked a few paces behind him and began asking a series of questions about the engine and steering.

When they reached the flying machine, Bartholomew also had questions as he crawled underneath the belly of the thing to inspect the rudder and cables. Beyond Elizabeth and Celwyn, Captain Nemo stood off to the side, his posture at military attention, wearing an unreadable expression.

Kang climbed inside the cockpit, causing Elizabeth to grip Celwyn's arm. "Must he do that?"

Celwyn patted her hand. "I'm watching. He won't fall." The magician gazed at the far end of the clearing and noticed a half dozen of Nemo's crew waiting there. Some of them held red flags. Celwyn glanced at Elizabeth and hoped she hadn't seen them: climbing inside the craft was one thing, flying away in it another. Seconds more and he had made a folding chair for her, facing away from the end of the field and urged her into it.

Over the next few hours, Kang, assisted by Bartholomew, disassembled much of the engine. While Bartholomew reattached the parts, Kang made notes and moved on to the instrument panel. When they began testing dials and gauges, Bartholomew stood tall enough that he could reach inside the engine while Kang sat before the controls. At one point, the big man moved to the rear by the rudder and called out degrees of change as Kang manipulated the levers. He added more notes, and then he and Bartholomew conferred.

Throughout it all, Fogg remained a short distance away on the north side of the craft. Elizabeth grew tired of waiting, and her skirts swished as she paced beside the magician with a furrowed brow.

The rain returned and in seconds become a deluge. Several of the crew began covering the contraption with tarps. Elizabeth held an umbrella, and Captain Nemo provided several more as they retreated to the trees under the thick canopy of the jungle. The miasma of wet earth and animals enveloped them as a million insects blossomed into the air.

Captain Nemo said, "The rain is a daily occurrence that will last for several hours. Shall we?" He turned and led the way back through the jungle.

Once inside the volcanic amphitheater, they paused to admire a view few people would ever see. From the dozen or more fissures in the volcano's ceiling four hundred feet above them, rain fell in a crystalline veil through the light, cascading into the lake.

Celwyn inhaled, and dozens of harps arose, playing in staccato as their notes fell with the rain and echoed between the drops.

Captain Nemo listened for several moments before he nodded at the magician. "I was only twenty years old when I found this place," he spread his hands, "and stood here for a very long time thinking how fortunate I was."

"It is so beautiful," Elizabeth whispered.

"Thank you for allowing us to see it also," Celwyn told him, and as the music faded away, they walked toward the pier. Fogg had already trotted away from them and disappeared inside the *Nautilus.* Celwyn noted the width of the pier and construction.

"Captain, if I may," the magician gestured, and a sturdy iron rail framed the pier end to end. "To assist us and avoid any tumbles."

Nemo studied the rail and said, "It is appreciated. How long will it last?"

"Until we leave. However, if your crew chooses to enhance it, then it would last for quite a long time."

Elizabeth and Kang walked across the pier with Kang's hand on her elbow. Bartholomew stayed close behind them. Each of them touched the guardrail and glanced at Celwyn.

Captain Nemo bowed. "After you, Sir."

Celwyn could admit to a tiny thread of trepidation having Nemo behind him, rail or no rail, as they boarded the submarine.

After divesting themselves of raingear, everyone gathered in the study. Verne already sat at the chess table with his notebook and an expectant expression painted across his face. He displayed his impatience by tugging on his pointed beard.

Celwyn produced a tea service, wanting his own Earl Grey, and not in the mood for something unknown or exotic. He poured a cup for Elizabeth and himself while the others patronized the whiskey bottles. As they settled on the sofas, Fogg joined them, standing off to the side. Anticipation of the discussion of the flying machine electrified the air.

"Well, Professor?" Fogg asked. "What do you think?"

"Perhaps you should also be asking that question of Bartholomew. Did you know he has a university degree in engineering?"

"No, I did not." Nemo bestowed a speculative look upon the big man that lasted until the Professor began speaking.

"Your design needs work. It will fly, but not with efficiency and not without unacceptable risk."

"It isn't stable," Bartholomew summarized.

Captain Nemo frowned at the glass in front of him and sighed. "I was afraid of this."

The automat finished his drink, and Celwyn sent the bottle over to him. While Nemo didn't appear to notice it, Fogg narrowed his eyes at Kang more in jealousy than admiration. *Was it about the flying machine or more?*

As he poured, Kang continued, "I cannot say that my opinion is the only one you would need. There may be others who know more. Are you familiar with the anatomy of birds? Of how they glide, soar, and turn?"

Celwyn opened his coat, and Qing hopped onto the table. He began to strut around with his talons making a distinct metal tapping noise. The magician said, "This is Qing." The bird's glossy feathers looked as if he had been dipped in an inkwell.

Fogg goggled. "*What is that*?"

The magician wagered that the bird knew he was being admired. His eyes glittered first at Nemo and then the wall of glass. He'd grown fond of the fish and flew the short distance to them. As he settled on the ledge, ready to peck at the window, he twisted his head one way and then the other, preening at his reflection. He hopped onto the table with Verne, and when he opened his wings, the metallic tips of his feathers clinked against the glass like a chime. The author inched his notebook away from the bird's foot and covered the shiny barrel of his fountain pen.

Although Celwyn wanted to ignore Fogg, politeness dictated a response.

"He is a mechanical bird."

Kang told Fogg, not without a measure of pleasure, "He bites, too."

Captain Nemo's eyes twinkled, probably as close as he got to a smile. He asked the Professor, "Concerning the craft? What do you recommend?"

"Bartholomew and I need to confer. But in general, a complete redesign from the chassis to the size of the engine is required." Kang said, "The wing flaps are of special concern. Correct?" he asked Bartholomew.

"I'm familiar with building something mechanical on land, and what you are attempting is similar in some ways." The big man crossed his ankles. "A pilot can't control the pitch and yaw very well with what you have at the moment." He shuddered. "If some foolhardy person felt compelled to go up in the thing, it might not come down as they expect, or at least not at an angle to successfully land. It would also be vulnerable to even the most benign wind gusts."

Fogg said, "Talk about the engine, please."

Kang stared at him a moment, long enough to remind the man he was still not happy about what he'd done to Elizabeth. "To know what to do requires more research." The automat arose and brought Elizabeth to her feet. "I'd like to wash up before luncheon."

As they left the room, Celwyn stood next to the Captain. "Sir, we have finished our agreement and respectfully request to be taken back to Singapore. We appreciate your hospitality." He bowed and shook Nemo's hand. "I do not have much practice with apologies. Please excuse my temper yesterday."

"I understand and accept my part in the less than auspicious beginning of our association." Nemo directed a stare at Fogg while saying, "You will be able to sleep in your hotel tonight."

Chapter 33

"The Sea, it is an immense desert where man is never lonely, for he feels life stirring on all sides."

—Jules Verne

"THIS SOUP IS EXTRAORDINARY," Bartholomew said as he spooned more of it.

From his position next to him, Celwyn agreed. "I detect subtle hints of nutmeg, pepper, and something I cannot identify. Very nice."

The *Nautilus* kitchen staff had set up their mid-day repast in the study to accommodate all of them, including Verne and Phileas Fogg. The author had said little after making notes throughout their discussion of the flying machine. From his repeated sighs, he too appeared disheartened by the results of the inspection, but not as much as Captain Nemo and Fogg.

Qing sat on the table in front of the aquatic window, entertaining himself with pecks at the small fish that wiggled by. The submarine remained in the volcanic lake, pending departure at the end of their meal. When one of the fish kissed the glass, the bird backed up until the fish scurried away. Celwyn wiggled his fingers in the reflection, and Qing squawked.

"Your companion is an interesting addition to your party," Captain Nemo said.

Kang glanced at Qing. "Jonas spoils him."

"I suggest that you watch your jewelry around him," Elizabeth said.

Fogg nodded at Captain Nemo, who cleared his throat, saying, "Thank you for your report on the craft."

With a broad smile, Celwyn caught on to their interaction, even without monitoring their thoughts. He had a hunch as to what Nemo was about to say.

"Mr. Fogg and I are disappointed in what you reported but understand that we have work to do." He turned to Bartholomew on his left. "We have conferred, and we have a proposition for you."

Kang and Bartholomew exchanged a quick knowing look. They also had been expecting something of this sort. Celwyn wondered if they'd put a wager on it.

"We would like to offer you a large purse of money to stay with us and help redesign our flying machine." Nemo held up a hand. "We know this is sudden, and we're prepared to accommodate your schedule. Your assistance can be for a limited time if need be." He faced Celwyn. "I understand the rest of your party is traveling back to Prague. I propose that we bring Mr. Bartholomew back to you on the *Nautilus*."

It was Celwyn and the automat's turn to exchange a look. Kang asked, "To Byzantium? It would be the closest waterway to Prague if approached from this direction."

"We could take our train there to pick him up," the magician said.

"Or I could take a scheduled train from there to Prague." Bartholomew's smile reflected in his eyes. "Your project appeals to my sense of wonder, Captain. It is fascinating."

"You sound like a scientist as much as an engineer, my friend." Kang slapped him on the back.

Celwyn cleared his throat. "You are forgetting something, gentlemen."

Bartholomew's face fell. "Annabelle and Patrick's wedding."

Elizabeth resolved the quandary. "I will convince them to wait until January." She addressed Captain Nemo. "Will that do?"

"Yes, of course, Madam." Captain Nemo assured her. "Perhaps Mr. Bartholomew can return again at a later date, if convenient."

Verne beamed like he'd just won a literature prize or a knighthood. "I am so happy that this has been decided." He strutted to the bar. "We need champagne to celebrate."

A massive jolt shook the *Nautilus,* sending the dishes and diners to the floor. Qing screeched and flew to Celwyn. As he got back to his feet, the magician saw a tentacle twice as wide as a man slide across the glass and disappear below. Like a new volcano had burst upward from under them, another, even more violent, blow rocked the ship from underneath.

"Lower the armor!" Captain Nemo barked into the intercom and ran out of the room. The magician added as strong a block as he could across the glass and ran out the door after Nemo. Qing rode on his shoulder, screeching in his ear. When they reached the rear of the ship, they tumbled into the control room as a third blow shook the vessel. Celwyn scrambled to his feet.

Bartholomew arrived behind him and whispered, "Oh, my God—"

Along the south wall, a wide crack near the bottom of the bridge's glass wall gushed water. Celwyn raised a hand over it, and the water stopped flowing through the crack. Nemo and his crew stopped mid-stride to stare and then scrambled again because of what they saw.

Outside the aquatic window, only feet away, the lights from the ship illuminated a giant octopus locked in a mortal embrace with the Mizuchi. Scaly and black as the night and so large that the enormity of the creature couldn't be seen. The Mizuchi's teeth had to be longer than a horse. Rows of them were embedded in the side of the octopus as it twisted and squirmed to get away. Each time the monsters rolled, they slammed into the submarine.

"Close the armor! Quickly!" Nemo shouted.

"Sir—" Celwyn brought his hands together, bringing the armor over the window, the action like a huge interlocking eyelid closed, the grinding of the metal together audible to them all. Fogg arrived in time to see it, shoving through the crew to stand with them.

As the magician plugged a new seam gushing water, Nemo barked more orders, and the crew ran in all directions.

The magician grabbed his arm. “I can stop this, but I need to know how deep the lake is.”

“Unknown. But very deep.”

“That will have to do.” Celwyn swiveled, facing the starboard side of the ship where the monsters battled, and began flexing his hands so fast they blurred. Qing returned to his shoulder and then hid inside his collar.

Before the crew could move again, a tremendous blow struck the ship, and she nearly keeled over, sending everything to the deck. As the magician pulled himself upright again, he shouted, “I need to see out there!” He had to see exactly where the combatants were without exposing the window.

Nemo took his arm and led him to the center of the bridge and to a pair of brass tubes that reached to the ceiling. “Adjust it here.” He showed him how the knobs turned. “Like this.” He adjusted one of the tubes as Celwyn put his eye to the opening of the other.

The *Nautilus* swung wildly to starboard. The magician held on to the tube and didn’t end up on the floor again. The ship shuddered as it smashed into the obsidian wall of the lake. When the beasts came into view, the monster still held onto the octopus as they thrashed from side to side, very close to the ship. The magician measured the distance.

"In the next few minutes, expect your monster to dive. It will become very warm in here, Captain."

Again, the magician repeatedly flexed his hands so fast they couldn't be seen. He exhaled and concentrated as the water outside lightened, became extraordinarily clear, and *steamed*. The monsters rolled away from the ship and then back against it. Celwyn tried once more, his hands moving even faster, heating the air inside the ship too. The water bubbled and roiled as if in a massive cauldron. This time, the Mizuchi released the octopus. The monster rotated toward the *Nautilus* and stared at the ship with its enormous black eye as if it could see Celwyn inside. Then it turned and drifted downward through the boiling water. The octopus thrashed several more times and followed, fading into the murkiness below, leaking clouds of ink from its wounds.

The magician exhaled and leaned his forehead against the brass pipe.

"They're gone," Nemo said, the wonder evident in his voice as he looked through the tube. "You did something impossible, Sir."

Celwyn wiped the sweat off his face. Nemo and the others did the same. Beyond him, one of the crew shouted and gestured—another section of glass flowed with water where it met the floor. The magician stared at the fracture until it glazed over. "That is fixed internally, not externally. I would keep an eye on it." Celwyn staggered back a step.

Bartholomew reached him in one stride and with a glare at Fogg said, "I'm sorry, but he still hasn't recovered from being shot. Come along, Jonas." His voice brooked no argument as the big man scooped Celwyn into his arms and started out of the room. Qing flew behind them, cawing as loud as he could.

Captain Nemo reached the exit first, trotted up the corridor and cleared the crew out of the way. "In here," he backed into the study and helped Bartholomew prop the magician against the pillows.

The Captain bent over until he was on eye-level with Celwyn, and said, "Thank you, Mr. Celwyn, for myself and my crew."

"You are most welcome, Captain."

"Rest, Jonas, I insist," Bartholomew said and turned to the Professor. "No wounds."

Kang glared through the worry that clouded his eyes.

Chapter 34

AS HE LEANED AROUND THE BIG man, the automat studied Celwyn, who lay unmoving and pale. He pulled Bartholomew aside. "What happened?"

"It was that Mizuchi who nearly ate Elizabeth and Nemo and a giant octopus fighting." The big man shook his head. "I don't know what all Jonas did to save the ship, but he made the water in this lake boil. Literally, boil. Then the monsters dived down, away from us. It all took a great deal out of him." He lowered his voice. "And it is more than his exhaustion now. I'm worried about Jonas."

The Professor nodded. "This condition is not related to his magic."

A big tear formed in Bartholomew's eye and slid down his cheek.

Kang frowned, not voicing what the big man feared. "Where did Nemo go?"

"While you were fussing over Jonas, he left again for the control room," Elizabeth said as she joined them. "What are you two whispering about?" She pointed with her eyes at Celwyn. "I think he can hear you."

Celwyn raised himself up on an elbow. "That is correct."

Kang made a face at the magician and asked Bartholomew, "You are sure he is not hurt?" At the big man's nod, Kang requested, "Make him rest. I will be right back."

He hurried out of the room and down the hall, nearly running into Captain Nemo as he left the bridge. "Could we confer for a moment?" They flattened against a wall to let a pair of crewmen by. "In private, please?"

Nemo bowed. "A minute is all I have." They entered a well-appointed chamber just big enough for a table, chairs, and desk. Every inch of the walls had been covered in maps, and more stacks of charts had been piled on every surface. A vintage sextant was used as a paperweight.

"Do you know what Mr. Celwyn did for us just now?" The Captain sat and gestured to one of the velvet chairs.

"Enough of it." Kang sank into a chair as he stared at a most interesting map of the Aegean Sea. He had to resist trying to read the fine print next to Crete, where it looked like a deep trench led westward.

"It was unbelievable. He saved the *Nautilus*. The Mizuchi and an enormous octopus battled until Mr. Celwyn drove them away. Then he repaired the breaches in the hull. If he hadn't, we would be dead by now."

Kang couldn't help a smile. "You should know; he probably enjoyed every minute of it."

"Possibly. I am very thankful he was here." Nemo relaxed in his chair. "On another matter, once again, I must thank you for looking at the craft this morning."

It gave Kang great pleasure to be surrounded by maps. Elizabeth called it her husband's version of a child's reaction to a candy shop. Most of the parchments had been detailed by hand and, considering the bottles of Billings ink and pens nearby, very likely by Captain Nemo himself. The chart nearest to him appeared quite old.

Underwater shelves had been represented, and exact depths noted as the shelves continued to other maps. Minute details of the composition of the soil and rocks lined the margins, sometimes with drawings of mystical sea life. Intricate skulls floated in the waves where dangers to ships lurked above and below the surface. Detailed representations of the North Sea, and the Pacific Ocean, on linen, had been hung along another wall. Kang marveled at the depictions of huge ranges of underwater mountains. This wasn't just a listing of distances; this cataloged the vast waterways of the world and the pathways and channels leading all over the earth.

Kang's eyes widened—even more interesting were maps of underground rivers, some of them quite wide and hundreds of miles long, while others connected continents. He'd suspected their existence! The ancient people of forgotten lands probably traveled some of them. The Professor realized his mouth hung open in wonder and didn't care.

"Those are underground rivers and seas… have you taken the *Nautilus* through them?" Kang pointed at one after another. "Heavens! That is a volcanic tube under the Bering Strait…"

"Yes, some of them." Nemo used a pencil to point as he talked about a river underneath the pyramids that entered the Mediterranean by Alexandria and other rivers Kang had never heard of. He indicated the islands west of Japan. "We haven't any detailed maps from here yet."

The automat sat in stunned silence, overwhelmed by what he saw.

"Soon, we will. As time goes by, it becomes much more difficult for my ship to avoid detection and obstacles, so I must keep track of what I have discovered, and of course, have a path of escape I may need to use most urgently." Nemo shrugged and showed Kang another map. "Many of the underground rivers are not recorded, except a few of the ancient ones." He stared at the automat. "It makes one wonder how they descended below the surface and were able to travel along the waterways. For instance, what would the air quality be like?"

"I wonder also." The enormity of what they spoke about would entertain the automat for weeks.

"We are very cautious: the *Nautilus* could become entombed under hundreds of feet of rock, and we would eventually suffocate."

Kang sighed: everything in this room seemed wondrous. He sat still in his chair, absorbing the magnificent possibilities, and then returned to why he asked for an audience. He had to face the situation.

"I could lose hours in here, but it is my turn to request your assistance, Captain." Kang ran a finger from Limerick to Galway on the map under his hand. "I have heard stories over the years of a man who can heal ... unusual ... people who would normally die. His abilities are beyond a normal physician, beyond normal diseases." He looked Captain Nemo in the eye. "I heard that the man is a descendant of the demi-god Heka. Or possibly Gaia."

"It is said that it takes a demi-god to save an immortal, no matter his bloodline or lineage."

"I agree." Kang heard in his own voice the desperation he felt. "I'm not sure if Jonas knows his lineage, more less if he believes in his mortality."

Captain Nemo waited.

"The man is known as Thales." At least Kang hoped this was true.

"Then it is the same person I had heard of. Long before the Thales of Greece. This more ancient one was last seen in the Altai Mountains. Once before, I had wanted to reach him myself to—" Nemo's voice caught, and his eyes hooded over. "Let us just say that I was too late."

The Professor waited a moment. "I'm very sorry."

Captain Nemo sat straighter and asked, "I assume that Mr. Celwyn knows of this healer? And that he knows he is sick?"

"He has never mentioned the healer. But he does know he is sick, although he will not admit it." Kang inhaled deeply. "I believe that he is dying. Whatever is wrong is progressing slowly. For now."

"It isn't the sword wound or the gunshot?"

The automat shook his head. "There are complications that he can't heal himself, and he normally would be able to." Kang felt a kind of sadness and defeat he couldn't shake or understand.

"I owe you and Mr. Celwyn a debt and will do what I can to find Thales. When we meet again in Byzantium, I hope to have an answer for you."

Kang reached for a pen, dipped it in ink, and wrote. "This is our address in Prague where messages can be sent. Your help is much appreciated, Sir."

"Perhaps one day you will tell me who flew the flying machine that day in the Mayan jungle." A gong sounded, and the vibration in the submarine increased. "We are on our way to Singapore."

"I will tell you now," Kang winked as he blew on the ink to dry it, "if I may count on your discretion."

Chapter 35

THROUGH A HEAVY BANK OF CIRRUS clouds, the sun began to set and the hatch opened on the *Nautilus.* Bartholomew emerged first, handing Elizabeth out and steadying her against the swell that rocked the ship. After Kang and Celwyn joined them, they started across the platform to the rocks and sand under the promontory. In the distance, dozens of tall-masted ships swayed at anchor before the Singapore dockside.

Instead of expecting Elizabeth to climb to the top of the promontory, they skirted the rocks to the other side.

"It is quite a way to the road leading to the city," Kang said. "Jonas, could you make a bench under these trees for Elizabeth to wait under? And keep her company, please." He kissed her cheek. "We'll be right back with a carriage."

Bartholomew bowed to Elizabeth and confided, "We also want to discuss air-flow ratios of the flying machine. We will hurry back, I promise."

As they walked away, Celwyn called out to Kang, "Subtle, my friend. You just expect me to rest and not exert myself."

Xiau laughed as he and Bartholomew began jogging toward the road.

Elizabeth spied the bench the magician had added, sat, smoothed her skirts, and addressed him. "Is your gunshot wound healing?"

Celwyn settled beside her and watched the submarine drift under the surface and propel itself into the deeper water. "I understand they will attend to business close by and be ready when Bartholomew returns." A light breeze ruffled the surface of the water. "The gunshot wound, yes, it is healing. The sword wound? That seems a bit slower to heal." He tapped his side. "It is nearer my lung, I believe. When we ran here a few days ago from the road," he indicated the point Bartholomew and Kang had reached in the distance, "I had trouble breathing. But it is somewhat better now."

"How long ago did the sword attack occur?"

"About six weeks."

Elizabeth nodded with a glint in her eye. "Xiau didn't tell me of the attack. I heard you all talking about it, and I'm waiting."

Oh my. Celwyn decided a change in subject was in order. The automat should be here to absorb her annoyance, not have it spread over an adorable magician. He had his own irritations with a temperamental mechanical bird shredding his collar inside his coat. "Shall we discuss Annabelle and Patrick's wedding first?"

Hours later, the Kangs arrived, arm in arm, in the Raffles Hotel dining room. Celwyn and Bartholomew stood until Elizabeth was seated.

"Thank you, it is nice to dress for dinner again." She straightened the sleeves of her satin gown.

"Your hair is... is... looks very well..." Celwyn searched for a word. "Arranged."

Kang laughed. "If you were married, Jonas, you would say that daily, as a good husband should, not just when your wife is subjected to a dunking."

"Two hours with the hotel hairdresser did wonders," Elizabeth told her husband. "Thank you for reminding me of our recent adventure. I need a new blue hat."

The automat didn't say a word.

After Bartholomew put his napkin in his lap, he picked up the wine menu. "The last few days certainly were an adventure." The wistful look in his eyes confirmed that the big man was not only smitten by the flying machine but that he wouldn't sleep again until he had immersed himself in it to the utmost.

The automat accepted a menu, and before opening it, said, "We will be in constant communication as you go along until you no longer need me."

The big man laughed. "I know so little. I will never stop asking for your insight."

"From what Xiau tells me, you have an innate scientific sense: and will soon be an accomplished scientist." With a measured and serious expression, Celwyn said, "I see they have fresh octopus on the menu."

"Jonas!" Elizabeth exclaimed. "After what happened today—"

Kang giggled. "That was an enormous one, too. I wager it could feed the whole city."

"Would that depend on how it was cooked, wouldn't you say?" Celwyn asked. "I hear it is tough if overcooked."

Bartholomew saw Elizabeth's expression, suppressed his contribution to the joking, and told her, "I am so very glad our adventure did not turn out as badly as it started."

"I am also, but it reminds me." Celwyn turned to the big man. "Phileas Fogg will most likely turn on you as soon as you are no longer of use to him."

"I know. Therefore, I will be on guard." Bartholomew tapped a spot on the wine menu. "I vote for the red Tustane."

"And enlist Captain Nemo to guarantee your safety," Kang advised. "I spoke with him while Jonas was resting, and he understands our concern."

"I have faith that Captain Nemo will return Bartholomew to us safe and sound." Elizabeth put her menu on the table. "The baked chicken with marsala sauce, please."

"That reminds me," Celwyn said, "we should send a message to Ricardo and Captain Smith to restock the train. We will be heading north to them in a few days."

When the wine arrived, the automat held his glass high and said, "To Zander." He told Bartholomew, "I will give him the lessons you have prepared."

"And the jokes, and explain that I will not be gone too long?"

Celwyn tried to picture the automat telling a joke. With a few colorful enhancements, it could be an entertaining experience.

"Of course." Kang looked at Elizabeth and said, "I think my lovely wife will distract him, too."

"I understand Zander is an exceptional student," she said.

"We believe that Otto would benefit from an education also. He is a young man we brought with us on the way here," Kang looked to the others and received confirming nods.

Bartholomew's eyes lit up. "I look forward to teaching them both about the flying machine."

Celwyn accepted another glass of wine from the waiter and did not mention his suspicions that the flying machine would become a source of danger to them. Probably soon.

Chapter 36

As Kang and Bartholomew stood in the doorway of the Regency Hat Shop at noon the next day, Elizabeth called out to them, "One hour, please. And meet us back at the hotel for luncheon." In the armchair beside her, the one usually dedicated to unlucky husbands, Celwyn reclined and glowered at Kang from under lowered brows. He was being left behind because the automat thought him too ill to join the foray into the bohemian quarter.

"Don't sigh like that, please, Jonas," Elizabeth said. "I will be quick, and we can be enjoying a tea service in the hotel garden in a few minutes. It is just next door." From under a creation of ivory feathers and blue ribbons, she admired her profile. "You make an excellent companion and protector."

With a rather wicked smile, Kang waved as he and the big man let the shop door close behind them and scampered away.

The northern district of Singapore was known for a large population of donkeys, rug dealers, opium dens, and tourists. As they started down the first street, Kang decided it should also be known for the squid, chicken, shrimp, and papayas cooked right next to the cobblestones. The smell from the smoke did a great deal to disguise the odor from the donkeys.

"Jonas wonders what we talk about when we go off like this." Bartholomew grinned as they side-stepped a large, florid man who had decorated himself head to toe in bells and cymbals. The man blocked the path of an overdressed English woman. He shook himself violently until she covered her ears and handed him a coin.

"Novel approach to busking," Kang said. "As for Jonas, I think he is just plain nosy. And he thinks he isn't." With companionable chuckles, the two kept walking.

They passed a gaggle of vendors arguing in front of rows of baskets that towered above Bartholomew. Then came the sudden sweet aroma of pastries and fragrance of coffee that nearly stopped them in their tracks. A broad smile spread across the big man's face as they gazed at more than a dozen petite tables crowding the sidewalk, nearly every one of them filled. Beyond a short stucco wall, more tables in a courtyard surrounded a shaded central fountain. Kang stopped in front of the courtyard, hesitating.

Bartholomew had made up his mind. "We can have just one and still have luncheon with the others. Do you see that éclair over there?" He pointed to the nearest table on the other side of the low wall.

"Elizabeth will smell it on my breath. Or spot minute crumbs on my coat. She is very observant." Kang half-laughed and tried to be virtuous. "We really should keep moving if we want to see the bookstore and other shops before they come looking for us."

Bartholomew took a few steps into the courtyard. "You know, the bookstore is supposed to be close by, just on the next street over."

"Ha. You remember we shouldn't leave Jonas alone too long." The Professor contradicted his words and edged forward, as if tied to a string, to the tables in the corner behind the stone fountain—where any passerby, such as Elizabeth or Jonas, would be less likely to discover them. Just as he reached the tables, he stopped mid-stride. Silvery fish cascaded out the fountain top from the mouth of a cherub and into a pool of water below. The fish had snouts. Bartholomew saw them too and whirled to approach the fountain again.

"Is Jonas here?" Kang scanned the courtyard. "And playing with us?"

"I only see people eating excellent-looking pastries and talking." Bartholomew turned back to watch the fish wiggling in the water. Tiny bubbles erupted out of the fish snouts and floated to the surface. "Those are pig faces. It is decidedly odd."

"And magical." Kang nodded and wondered if anyone besides them could see the fish faces. "We should leave." Kang stared at the fish. "Not all magicians are as benign as Jonas."

With a smile, Bartholomew snorted. "I wouldn't call him benign, but I understand your concern."

They had turned, ready to depart, when a voice as cold as yesterday's corpse reached them.

"Join me, gentlemen."

The hair on Kang's neck quivered, and he pivoted. A blond man, as pale as an albino, and strong of face, regarded them with sleepy eyes. He appeared to be of medium age and height and dressed in a pristine white suit with a blood-red carnation in his lapel. Manicured nails and several bejeweled rings adorned his hands. He poured two cups of coffee from the decanter on the table.

Bartholomew looked at Kang, who raised a brow as if to say, "*We'll always wonder if we do not investigate.*" The automat pulled out rickety metal chairs from a neighboring table and placed them several feet away from the albino, leaving them free to run if necessary. As the automat sat, he glanced at the water: the fish no longer swam there at all.

Kang hesitated, then stared. He was certain there had only been the coffee service on the table a moment ago. Now, he saw a platter of delectable pastries, which did not make him hungry; instead, they increased his apprehension. Bartholomew must have seen the delectable addition, too. The big man licked his lips, but not because of the baklava.

All of a sudden, the fountain bubbled much louder behind them. Kang didn't want to look but couldn't help it.

Replicas of flying machines no bigger than his hand swam through the water, dipping and then soaring up a few inches and down again, propellers turning, tail flaps up. In each of the cockpits, tiny, faceless men, like the ones Kang had described from the Mayan jungle, waved at them.

Although both the automat and Bartholomew were used to what Celwyn did, Bartholomew let out a squeal and started to rise.

"Please, sit down." The stranger extended a hand. "I had hoped you would enjoy my personal style of entertainment. Is it accurate?"

The man's sepulchral voice chilled Kang. However, over the centuries, he'd run into fearful things before. "What do you want?"

The albino nodded, and his smile seemed as disconcerting to Kang as what bobbed in the fountain. "Excuse my manners. I am Felix Ratzel, gentlemen." He waited for a response and then went on, "I'm assuming you are Professor Kang and Bartholomew."

The big man still hadn't resumed his seat. "Answer the Professor's question."

If the man's voice had been unnerving, Ratzel's laugh sounded much worse.

All around them, the café seemed to fade away. The colors, movements, and sounds died to a fuzzy gray, as if under a filmy blanket. The albino's eyes shone through it. Something told Kang not to look directly into his eyes, and he prayed Bartholomew wouldn't either.

"I have heard that you knew about a flying machine, Professor. Is that true?" In the chair where the albino had been sat a taller, wiry, dark-haired man calmly sipping coffee.

Kang lurched to his feet and grasped Bartholomew's arm, pulling him along with him and sprinting away. He would have bet they wouldn't attain the sidewalk without being stopped, but soon they again dodged confused tourists in their shirts of gaudy and decidedly normal colors.

By the time Bartholomew and Kang arrived for luncheon, Celwyn had inhaled his second cup of tea. When he saw his friends' expressions, he waited until the Professor deposited a kiss on Elizabeth's cheek, admired her new hat, and pulled out a chair.

"What happened?" he asked. Both of them appeared jumpy.

The big man put Celwyn's new tobacco in front of him, "Dokha blend." He shrugged. "I'm not sure. But it appears you aren't the only magician in town."

Celwyn raised a brow at Kang.

"I hate to upset my wife, but I'm learning that not sharing information upsets her more." With his frown deep and voice low, he said, "We ran into someone who knew about us and the flying machine and wanted to know more about it." He described the albino and the scene full of sly magic.

Bartholomew furnished a description of the stranger's final appearance. "I did not feel afraid, as much as uneasy. Yet, I'm not sure why."

"Ratzel is not a name I recognize or your short description either." The magician glanced around them involuntarily. "Like you reported, nothing actually happened. Let us enjoy the garden here and our excellent company instead of worrying." Elizabeth nodded in approval. Kang eyed him with enough suspicion to where Celwyn turned away to study the collection of tea roses behind them.

"How many other immortal magicians are there?" Elizabeth asked.

The automat's eyes widened.

"Don't be so secretive, Xiau," she told him. "I would really like to know."

Celwyn slid into the gap while Kang tried to find a way to dodge the subject. "Your husband worries about you encountering dangerous forces, and yet he also knows you will be better prepared if you know what to expect." He eyed the Professor. "Correct?"

Kang glared and nodded.

"To answer your question, I do not know. The only other immortal magicians I knew were my father and brother. I had heard of others." Celwyn hoped that would satisfy Elizabeth's curiosity. He had other things to worry about and was not in a mood for nightmarish reminiscing.

Nothing about the encounter with Ratzel sounded familiar, yet as they had described it, a cold hand of premonition had wiggled its way up the magician's spine. Until he knew more, Celwyn wasn't ready to share this omen. Especially since he couldn't describe what scared him about it.

Chapter 37

TWO MORNINGS LATER, JUST AFTER dawn, the hotel porters loaded their trunks into an oversize horse-drawn cart that would follow the northbound coach for their return to Skudai. All around them, a low shelf of fog covered the areca trees, the white spires of nearby churches, and the squat brick buildings surrounding the coach yard.

"The fog is trapping the odorous smells from the manure," Kang said as he and the magician waited at the rear of the coach.

Celwyn raised a hand. "Would you prefer a field of roses? I can—"

"I'm sure you could." The Professor turned to gesture at the coach. "Even without taking Bartholomew's trunks with us, Elizabeth has managed to enhance our total number of trunks greatly."

Bartholomew stood off to the side, scanning the street. As the last trunks were loaded, Celwyn spotted what the big man had been looking for. With a loud clatter of hooves across the cobblestones, a second carriage arrived. Verne climbed out of it with alacrity, perhaps worried they would leave without him, and the driver started unloading his luggage.

The magician had wondered if the author would really go back with them. Before they left the *Nautilus,* Celwyn had agreed to Verne's request for transport to Prague. He did enjoy his company to a point, and Fogg wouldn't be a problem anymore since his attention would be on his pet flying machine.

Another porter loaded Bartholomew's bags into Verne's carriage, and as Kang watched the switch, he directed a frown at Celwyn. "We have a few moments until he takes that coach back to the harbor. I hope we're doing the right thing concerning our friend."

"It is an opportunity, and he wants to be with the *Nautilus.*" Celwyn asked, "I can see your worry. What else is wrong, my friend?"

"What?" The automat's distraction deepened. "Oh, nothing. Excuse me." He moved a few feet away to where Verne stood.

The Professor must have forgotten that Celwyn could read lips quite well, a talent he'd developed as a child. After walking off to the side, the magician studied them and speculated why Kang asked the author if there were any messages from Captain Nemo. He shrugged; he would eventually get it out of Kang.

With many tears and hugs, they said goodbye to Bartholomew.

"Be well, and be cautious," Celwyn said as he embraced him. Because he trusted Nemo, the magician had no fears for the big man. But he would miss him.

Bartholomew kissed Elizabeth's hand and bowed. "I will return. You and I must have a rematch at the chess board."

"Yes, we will." She smiled and hugged him.

Kang stared at the big man from under lowered brows. "Do not hesitate to ask questions; I will reply the same day I receive any. Take notes as you go. You have our itinerary, and we'll be checking for telegrams at every stop. We will not necessarily be traveling at speed. There are times we'll hold over a day or so along the way." He shook the big man's hand. "Above all, don't trust Fogg."

"I won't!" Bartholomew waved, and the coach's springs creaked as he climbed inside.

They arrived at the train terminal in Skudai just after noon. At the most northern point of the terminal yard, the *Royal Victoria* pulled out, leaving behind a noisy crowd of well-wishers as the train headed west. Celwyn considered that departure must be the most popular of the week; the train yard teamed with passengers newly arrived, some in too much of a hurry to shop, making the vendors even more aggressive to capture their attention. Several stray dogs ran through the crowd, one with a dead rat in its mouth. Kang turned Elizabeth around so she wouldn't see it.

Jackson and the other porters greeted them with another hired carriage and oversized cart. "Sirs and madam." He stood at attention with military correctness. Beside him, Otto smiled and pushed a mess of lanky black hair off his forehead. He shook their hands, not wanting to let go of them.

The porters looked expectantly at Elizabeth.

Kang stepped up. "This is Mrs. Elizabeth Randall Kang, my wife." She shook their hands as he continued, "Our porters, Jackson, Otto, and Ludvik."

Jackson gazed at the crowd behind them. "If I may ask, where is Mr. Bartholomew?"

"He is staying in Singapore for a few months." Celwyn indicated the author a few feet away as he fussed with his tie. "Mr. Verne has rejoined our party for the journey west."

As their luggage was unloaded and a baby breeze freshened, the automat made a face. "The odor from the manure is getting worse. I will be glad to be back on our train."

"It is only five minutes away on the other side of the terminal," Celwyn assured him.

Elizabeth threaded an arm through her husband's. "I look forward to our journey."

"Let us hope it is uneventful." The magician gazed around the yard. "No Russians here, and Phileas Fogg stays on the *Nautilus*."

"No Crazy Mary, either." Kang shuddered.

"Who is that?" Elizabeth asked with a raised brow.

Celwyn sighed. "Mary Giovanna."

When they reached the storage side of the train yard, Kang guided his wife around dock men, cracks in the sidewalk, errant dogs, crates, and other obstacles.

"Why can't I see where we're going?" She wore her husband's handkerchief as a blindfold over an expectant smile.

The automat steered her away from a mud puddle. "You'll know soon. I want it to be a surprise."

"Why?"

Celwyn led the way, circling the coal cart and onto the front of the train. Every inch of the *Elizabeth* had been polished until the brass shone and windows sparkled. Even from a distance, the gilded lettering on the nose of the locomotive gleamed in the afternoon sun.

Kang positioned Elizabeth in front of the engine. To the right, Conductor Smith, and his helpers, Abe and Andy, stood at attention. The blindfold was removed.

"Mrs. Elizabeth Kang, meet the *Elizabeth*."

She gasped. "Oh my!" Elizabeth touched the side of the train. "Just look at her!"

"Naming her was a present from Jonas," Kang said with a rough voice and a fond glance at the magician. "It is a testament to our friendship."

Celwyn heard his voice catch as he said, "Let's go aboard."

With the introductions, Elizabeth shook the Conductor's hand and those of the crew. The automat helped Elizabeth up the steps and into the cab. They passed through each car, and when they reached the kitchen, Ricardo greeted them in a clean apron and hat.

He bowed with pride. As he kissed Elizabeth's hand, he said, "*Incantato.*" Although he tried to make light of his next words, the relief in his voice came through clearly and showed in his eyes. "I am so happy you have returned. Where is Mr. Bartholomew?"

"He is staying in Singapore for a few months," Kang told him. "He rejoins us in January."

Ricardo frowned and picked up a towel. "Let us hope so. We have lunch nearly ready. Please send Otto back here as soon as the luggage is inside. If we're lucky, we'll have the dishes on the table before the train departs.

"It smells heavenly," Elizabeth said as Kang ushered her out of the kitchen and into the dining room.

The engines rumbled, coming to life as the magician inhaled the familiar scents of the train and sighed with contentment as he sank into his favorite chair. Kang poured tea, watching Elizabeth explore the room and hear their stories behind each artifact and decoration.

Ludvik and Otto emerged from the sleeping car and stopped long enough for Ludvik to bow and say, "The last of the trunks are aboard. Welcome back."

"Thank you, both. Is Mr. Verne in his room?" Celwyn asked.

Otto nodded emphatically and headed for the kitchen.

"Please let Conductor Smith know we're ready when he is," the automat said.

After Elizabeth left them to freshen up in their cabin, they passed a companionable few minutes in silence but couldn't help glances at the table where the cutlery had been sat out. "She won't be too long." Although he intended to assure Celwyn, it sounded like the automat assured himself.

Verne arrived with a book and an interested look directed at the dining room table. True to Kang's prediction, Elizabeth returned a few minutes later.

"When I was putting away my bag, I noticed you reconfigured the sleeping chambers again," Kang told Celwyn as they settled at the dining room table. He eyed his wife, "We will need the extra room for all of Elizabeth's things."

She blushed and reminded him, "We still haven't bought my new blue hat. The one I purchased the other day was white."

"There are several large cities along the way to Prague," Celwyn told her. He looked at the empty chair across the table and sighed. "I miss Bartholomew already."

Kang nodded. "I agree, but I respect that he wants to participate in something new and exciting."

"Please excuse my husband," Elizabeth said. "He thinks logically instead of with his emotions sometimes." She kissed his cheek.

Verne said, "Mr. Bartholomew will be very busy and happy." He looked Celwyn in the eye. "The Captain will ensure his safety."

"He damn well better," the magician said.

Otto entered the room from the kitchen carrying a tray, and Jackson followed behind him, bearing the soup cauldron.

Celwyn tapped a spoon on his water goblet. "Attention, please. I have a prediction."

Kang watched him. "Yes?"

"I predict that Ricardo will do everything in his power to provide a culinary celebration of our return."

Verne stayed with them as they left the table, pouring a whiskey and planting himself in the bar chair next to the globe.

From his position at the windows, Kang regarded the author. "Are you still working on your book about Prague Castle?"

"That is why I am returning there, yes."

Elizabeth asked, "Do you have family in Prague, Mr. Verne?"

"No," Verne told her. "My wife is in Amiens in northern France. She is expecting me this spring."

"Perhaps you will travel there on the *Nautilus* after she brings Bartholomew back to us."

Verne stared at her a moment and nodded. "A very good idea."

The magician appreciated the way Mrs. Elizabeth Kang's mind worked almost as much as he enjoyed Kang's surprise when he heard her express something he didn't know she knew.

"I would love to attend a ball at the Castle in Prague." Elizabeth emitted a wistful sigh before she looked at Kang. "It has been a very long time since we danced."

Without a word, the magician arose and crossed to the pianoforte. He feigned tossing back coattails from a tuxedo and sat down.

As he started to play, the *Elizabeth* rumbled away from civilization, entering the jungle that brought warm, humid air laced with a sharp and earthy animal tang into the room. The train began a slow climb as the music grew around them, floating and intricate as if telling a story. Celwyn sent Elizabeth a silent suggestion that her husband would love to dance. She shook her head slightly, as if a gnat had flown into her hair, and took her husband's hand.

The Kangs walked to the open area in front of the windows as the tinkling music rose in volume and tempo. Kang whirled Elizabeth around the floor, her feet as nimble as if she danced above it. The atmosphere became dreamy and light as the afternoon rain pattered the windows, and the air grew heavy. Verne leaned back, listening with a beatific smile. Across the room, Otto opened the kitchen door, mesmerized and listening to something the magician suspected he had never heard before.

As Elizabeth glided, her melodic laugh reached them, then her smile. The music segued into a grand march supported by a chorus of unseen horns. As the music soared, it reached a crescendo, and Kang and Elizabeth danced several feet above the floor. Minutes more, the melody ended, and they drifted back to the floor. Into the silence that followed, Celwyn enjoyed how much pleasure the music brought Kang as he gazed at his wife. Like atmospheric applause, the rain began an energetic staccato on the train's roof.

"Bravo, Jonas! Bravo!" Verne stood. "I must go write after that. The mood is upon me."

The door to the kitchen closed, but not before Celwyn caught the glance of longing Otto sent the pianoforte. Perhaps the lad would care to learn more than what he would find in Kang's books, Celwyn mused as he watched the rain for a moment. For the first time in weeks, he realized that his side did not hurt as much as it had. Good. *Damn Russians.*

The automat released his wife from where they stood, wrapped in each other's arms. "That was wonderful," she told him and then thanked the magician. She turned toward the sleeping car. "I need to unpack, Xiau. I want a bath in that enormous tub."

As she left them, the automat drew up a chair under the maps. "I hate unpacking."

"With Bartholomew gone, who will you play checkers with?" Celwyn asked.

"Well," Kang pursed his lips. "I'll have to wait until we see Zander. Elizabeth dislikes the game as much as you do." He eyed the magician. "She didn't notice we were off the floor during our dance. I would have let you explain that to her."

"I know you would have."

"You look much better today."

"I feel better. Is that why you wanted to talk with Captain Nemo earlier?"

"Pffft." Kang rolled his eyes. "You listened to his thoughts?"

The magician shrugged. "Several times and heard snippets of what is on his mind. Who is Thales? Why do you want Captain Nemo to find him?" He met Kang's stern expression with a stubborn one of his own. "I have no scruples to spying if it concerns me."

"You could trust me."

Celwyn laughed. "I do. And can assume you are worried about me."

The *Elizabeth* hit a trestle and then chugged around a curve and over the gorge where Celwyn had dangled Verne a week ago. The automat looked out the window a moment. "This is still a beautiful view of Bengal Bay. Did you know there are hundreds of islands in it?"

"I do. You are stalling." Celwyn sat and poured tea. "Are you going to tell me?"

"I imagine these are the situations where you wish you could read my mind, too." After a moment, Kang sighed. "I suppose I will have to tell you."

"Correct."

"It will cost you. First, tell me the status of the sword wound from the Russian."

Celwyn compressed his lips. Kang was as stubborn as an ox. Or worse, because of his excellent memory.

"Jonas?"

"What do you suspect?" Celwyn poured tea and handed Kang a cup. "And what does Captain Nemo have to do with it?"

Kang laughed and sat next to him. "We're asking each other questions instead of answering."

"Of course."

"So, tell me."

The magician threw up his hands. "Recently, I have been tiring more so than the situation warrants. It started around the time the Russian stabbed me."

Kang studied him. "Pain?"

"The stab wound is still healing. The bullet wound is better." He clapped his friend on the shoulder. "There is nothing to fear."

Kang continued to eye him and not smile.

"I am correct that it isn't serious." The magician stretched, touching the toes of his boots together. "As long as I've lived, it is to be expected that I would slow down eventually."

"How long is that?"

"December 31, 1352." Celwyn had told few people of that date, but it seemed easy to tell Kang. Until he heard his reaction.

"You are younger than me?" Kang laughed. "I do not believe it."

Celwyn's chin went up. "It is so." He tried not to smile back at Kang. "Regardless, please do not worry, I have no ailments, and I enjoy my tea and peyote. I am happy."

"You have me by about a hundred years," Kang said. "I had guessed more. Where were you made?"

Kang thought a moment. "I was told I was made in Prussia. But I think it was the Hunan Mountains of China."

"Is that where the Thales is that you asked Captain Nemo to find? Don't glare at me. Why is he looking for him?"

Celwyn realized he must have hit something sensitive when the automat popped up and started pacing. After three turns to the dining room table and back, he spoke.

"I do not accept that this is your advanced age. I am worried." He glowered at the magician. "My inner voice tells me it is more."

Celwyn glared back. "Why is this Thales involved?"

Kang sat and signaled for whiskey.

The magician poured.

"Because I want him to be. I've heard that Thales has been around since before the Greeks. Mind you, this is not the early astronomer called Thales."

"All right. What else?"

"It is rumored that the Thales we seek is able to repair the mortal wounds, or whatever ails immortals that no one else can heal. In the shadowy corners of the world, he is barely more than a wisp of memory, of myth. Yet, the rumors persist that he exists."

"And you decided who better than Captain Nemo to find him."

The Professor downed his drink. "Yes. This healer is said to be mysterious and capricious. Which fits with the ancient description of a demi-god who can save an immortal descendent. The same lineage, so to speak."

"The subject is fascinating. But this Thales is probably not needed." The magician stretched again and yawned to emphasize that his condition wasn't serious.

"Damn it, Jonas!" Kang threw his glass across the room. "I am worried! You look ... not well."

Celwyn swallowed what he had planned to say. He'd never seen his friend so angry. Or worried, which caused him pause.

"I am going to be fine," the magician assured him with as much conviction as he could. "If it gets worse, I will tell you."

"Each time you notice *any* change, you will tell me."

Celwyn said in a very good imitation of Elizabeth, "Yes, dear." In his own voice, he said, "Now, I have a request."

"Oh? You do?" Kang's tone did not sound amused.

Celwyn leaned forward, clearly entertained and not hiding it. "Who flew in those planes in the Mayan jungle? You said it wasn't the Mayans."

"For pity's sake, Jonas."

"Tell me, or I'll tell Elizabeth about—" He caught the automat's expression. "Yes, I would. I do not wish to scare her but—"

"Fine." Kang crossed the room and picked up the remnants of the glass. "It would be best, however, if no one else ever hears of this, Elizabeth and Verne included." He sat again. "Especially Verne. Elizabeth would just worry about me."

"I understand." Celwyn asked, "Was it other scientists?"

The Professor hesitated. "No, I believe the pilots were what the Mayans called the Ancient Ones. Not from Greek mythology, or perhaps not directly."

"What do you mean?"

Kang blinked at him. "Not of this earth."

At that moment, Otto arrived with a replacement tea service. If he saw the pieces of the broken cup on the tray, he didn't react. He did offer them both a shy smile before withdrawing. Celwyn poured a fresh cup. Slowly.

"The timing of our refreshments gave me a chance to absorb what you said." The magician thought a moment more. "It seems far-fetched, by the way. But now I understand why you don't want the others to know."

"Exactly. We never saw them close up or the flying machines either, except once, much later, and then only briefly. The propellers of their crafts rotated very fast, so their engines must have been extraordinary." Kang's eyes shone with the excitement of the event, re-lived even centuries later. "The pilots were hunched over the instrument panels. They looked hairless and pale, like tadpoles. And their uniforms seemed to shimmer under the sun. No one in that hemisphere wore clothes like that."

"Their faces?"

Kang blinked and thought. "I'm not sure. From what I remember, their faces were flat, no noses."

Celwyn whistled.

"They flew by you, and then?"

"They went back over the mountains." Kang's thoughts turned inward, and he whispered, "When I looked at them, I felt afraid. Very afraid, but I can't tell you why."

"My goodness," Celwyn exclaimed. "No wonder you didn't want others to know."

Kang nodded. "Now, let's talk about you."

The magician laughed. "Must we?"

"I need your promise to be careful and to let me take the lead in our defense until Bartholomew is back."

His friend looked so earnest, Celwyn agreed. He could always help by using magic and explaining himself later.

"You sure you don't want me to tell your wife about the time you were pushed off the ship in Singapore?"

Chapter 38

THE *ELIZABETH* TRAVELED THROUGH endless fields of wheat throughout the afternoon. It reminded the magician of a peaceful but supremely boring journey he had taken through Nebraska before he arrived in San Francisco.

Celwyn put down his book, *History of Prague*, and regarded Verne sitting in the other bar chair furiously writing in his notebook. Across the room, Kang perched at the map table, making marks on a new map.

"It took us almost a week to get to Bengal, and when we arrive in Punjab this afternoon, it would have been another week." Celwyn commented, "I do love this train, but I am anxious to be back in Prague."

"We are also."

Celwyn asked, "How many more days until we reach Tehran?"

"I expected you to ask." Kang checked the map and said, "Probably four, depending on the weather."

The magician traversed the room to stand over his shoulder. "To confirm, we're traveling this southern route," he pointed, "to avoid the snow in the higher mountains that we encountered on our first trip to Prague?"

"Where are you going with this, Jonas?" Kang eyed him.

With a sigh, the magician took the other chair. "Should we avoid Tehran? Is there another route to the west with reliable rails from this point?"

After a moment, Kang nodded. "I see. You are concerned that the police in Tehran would likely blame us for Prince Leo's death."

"It would be prudent to consider the possibility," Celwyn said. "Although I could toss any policeman out of our way, they would only wire ahead to other police headquarters. Even those in Prague."

"So, logically, we should take this threat on directly and be done with it." Kang thought more. "We could continue to Tehran and then go to the police and confront any accusations. However," he rubbed his chin, "We do not have Bartholomew with us, which may—"

"Complicate proving our innocence."

"Exactly. There is also circumstantial evidence of your violence against Prince Leo that his daughter could have used to inflame their suspicion."

"Many of my acquaintances experience violence."

Kang rolled his eyes. "I'm sure they do."

"Where is Elizabeth?" Celwyn asked. It wouldn't do to upset her needlessly.

"She is napping at the moment."

Proving he was listening to them, Verne called out from his seat at the bar, "I personally know of the threat of violence." He shuddered. "I'm afraid of heights, Jonas."

"Stop befriending reporters and sending us spies, then," Celwyn retorted.

Kang patted the air and said, "To get back to our problem, the question could be resolved by skipping Tehran all together. We could time our stops for coal and supplies to occur in other cities. If necessary, you can supplement the coal."

Celwyn rubbed his chin and thought. He really wanted to get back to Zander, Annabelle, and Patrick. He had a feeling Ricardo did, also. "We wouldn't know if we were under suspicion until we felt the breath of the law upon our necks in Tehran or in any city, including Prague."

Kang nodded. "As a compromise, we could arrive in Tehran at night, and discreetly inquire. How does that sound?"

After a moment, the magician agreed. "The best option, I believe." To Verne, he said, "Jules, it will be very important that we can trust your discretion. Perhaps it would be best if you remain on the train once we reach Tehran."

A few minutes later, the author left them to write in his cabin, and Celwyn remained at the map table. He waited until the Professor had made another mark before saying, "I have an idea."

With a bit of suspicion and even more wariness in his voice, Kang asked, "You do?"

The magician verified no one was at the kitchen door or coming through from the cabins into the room. "Yes. Do you agree Phileas Fogg is a nuisance and danger?"

"Of course."

"And that Bartholomew would be safer if he wasn't on the ship with him?"

The automat nodded, and the suspicion in his eyes faded, replaced with an optimistic gleam. When he rubbed his face, a wide streak of pencil lead decorated his chin and cheek. The magician grinned and added to the mark. Soon, the automat sported penciled curled whiskers like an inquisitive cat. Satisfied, he described what he thought might be a very good idea.

"The only reason Captain Nemo tolerates, and initially bowed down to Fogg, is that Fogg provides the funding for Nemo's dream, the flying machine." Celwyn remembered his initial anger at Nemo, which he eventually transferred to Fogg. "I have a proposal."

"Does it involve removing Fogg by force?" Kang asked with enthusiasm; he hadn't forgotten when Fogg endangered his wife. Celwyn noted the automat displayed selective enforcement of his ban against violence and favored Kang with a sardonic look before continuing.

"Of a sort. I propose that you and I fund the flying machine, replacing Fogg. Nemo can either keep us with him in the enterprise or buy us out later. It would also be safer for Bartholomew and Nemo not to have to guard against the bastard's greed."

"Oh—" The automat's mouth stayed open, and he leaned back in his chair. "Oh, my." His smile started slowly and spread. "I do enjoy your devious mind at times, Jonas."

"As I do yours."

Kang said, "We could transfer the money when we arrive in Prague."

"Would it be appropriate if we both wrote a letter to Nemo to tell him of a sudden infusion into his bank account?" Celwyn rooted around in the drawer of the table and produced paper.

"Yes, it would. How did you find Nemo's bank account number?"

Celwyn dipped the pen in ink and began a salutation to the Captain. "Do you really want to know?"

"Probably not. Though, we should tell him in the note to not mention this to Fogg. Suggest Nemo wait until the man poses no threat to Bartholomew, the rest of them, or the ship." Kang tapped the paper Celwyn wrote on. "You forgot a comma there."

"I'm sure I did. And yes, that is a good suggestion. We'll also have to discreetly inquire as to how much it would take to pay off Fogg completely and guarantee he left Nemo and the flying machine behind.

Or, we could just send a respectable amount to be sure that occurs."

Celwyn slid the paper across the table to him. "Please finish our letter. With commas."

"Pfft—" Kang rolled his eyes and started writing.

Chapter 39

LIKE THE GODS HAD POURED RICH golden orange light across the land, sunset came swiftly, blanketing the foothills that heralded Tehran. From their seats in front of the windows, Kang, Elizabeth, and Celwyn enjoyed the show of colors. They had been ready for their arrival for hours.

"How are Conductor Smith and the crew taking the news that we won't be here long?" Elizabeth asked. "And that we must be discreet?"

"I assured them we would stop for two days of rest and relaxation at Qazvin. They were satisfied," Celwyn said.

Kang looked up from his book long enough to comment.

"The Conductor reports that he can find us an inconspicuous berth for the *Elizabeth* tonight—if we provide enough rials with which to bribe the train officials." On the other side of the tracks, they began to pass clusters of mudbrick buildings and occasional pens of donkeys and goats. As each mile went by, the gloom of dusk deepened along with his frown. "I understand why Conductor Smith dislikes traveling at night, even with the light from in front of the locomotive."

Elizabeth put down her embroidery and stared out the window. "We aren't going too fast, so we should be fine until we get into town." She smiled at her husband and Celwyn to relay her reassurance. "Do you two want to tell me what we're really doing in town tonight? I saw you whispering earlier."

Celwyn raised a brow at the Professor. They'd agreed that Elizabeth would be an excellent subterfuge, accompanying Kang. The mechanical man was not seen with a woman initially, and her appearance would be striking and distracting. Celwyn planned to be close by, but not actually with them, since that was how they were seen during their last fateful visit. He would also be in disguise. Perhaps his hair would be an elegant white, slicked down, with matching whiskers.

Kang picked up his wife's hand. "You recall how Prince Leo was murdered in Tehran." He pointed to the city lights ahead of them. "We want to be sure the police do not blame us now or later."

"It is just a quick fact-finding mission before we dine," Celwyn told her.

When they'd talked, Kang had agreed that all they needed to do was get near enough to the policeman in charge to have Celwyn enter his thoughts, which the magician would manipulate, if needed. Kang related this to Elizabeth.

"From little things I've heard, I suspected as much about you, Jonas." Elizabeth eyed him. "I assume, as a gentleman, you will not be invading my privacy."

"You have my word."

Kang inserted as fast as he could, "And mine."

She frowned, wrinkling a beautiful brow. "Wouldn't it be less suspicious if I asked the policeman some questions? As Prince Leo's sister?"

Kang's eyes blinked as fast, like hummingbird's wings, and he sputtered, "Yes, but —"

Elizabeth pointed her embroidery scissors at him. "Do not fuss, dear. You would be there to protect me."

Celwyn enjoyed their exchange, observing the fondness waring with the fears and finally saying, "I like the plan as you have stated it, Madam. I ask that you keep in constant awareness of me, just as Xiau does." Kang nodded with vigor. "There are times when I will know of thoughts and intentions around us and will signal you of physical threats."

"And then?"

"I may wish for you to follow mine or your husband's directions quickly and without debate."

"Our safety depends upon it." Kang reached for her hand again and held on. "You are not used to imminent danger." He brought her fingers to his lips and kissed them. "I do not want you hurt."

"Madam, our directions may not appear logical, but they will be necessary."

Elizabeth cast anxious glances at each of them and took a deep breath before saying, "I am beginning to understand why you fall into some of the situations you do." She pursed her lips. "I agree that this is our best approach."

"I do, also," Celwyn told them.

Kang shot him a pained look and made his voice stronger. "We shall be beside you at all times."

"All right then." The magician stood and patted him on the shoulder. "Conductor Smith will have the coal loaded as soon as we arrive. We can leave any time thereafter if things become—shall we say, urgent and unfriendly."

A light rain accompanied them as they exited the train and neared the boulevard next to the train yard. With a few descriptive remarks about donkey manure from the automat, they approached a none-too-clean hire carriage. Before Elizabeth boarded, Celwyn wiggled a finger, and the interior became much more sanitary.

In Kurdish, Kang asked their driver to take them to the edge of the international district. The Grand Bazaar closed at sundown, and the dark alleyways surrounding it would not be safe. They had agreed to arrive on foot at the police station so that their taxi driver couldn't be traced back to the train.

The army's police force might not know of the *Elizabeth* and would hopefully look elsewhere for them. Both Kang and Elizabeth kept watch as they drove away from the trainyard, and Celwyn could have sworn he saw the same pig wandering around the gate that they'd last seen weeks ago. When he looked again, there was no pig there at all. Odd. A wisp of a memory tickled him and then disappeared as Elizabeth spoke.

"I'll be glad when this evening is over."

"I will be, also," the magician said.

Kang reared back and laughed. "No, you won't, Jonas. You like intrigue."

Celwyn just smiled and straightened his cuffs. Qing had not been amused when he'd had to return one of the magician's cufflinks.

A sliver of dusk could still be seen on the western horizon as they alit from the coach and walked eastward three abreast, with Elizabeth in the middle. The idea that Celwyn would march along at a distance to hide their identities had been abandoned. The magician was proud of his disguise, and as he stepped around an old man and his dog, he winked and continued to play with the waxed tips of his newly made mustache. Its fluffiness and size rivaled the Conductor's, and Celwyn rather liked it. At Elizabeth's request, he'd removed the charcoal one he'd drawn on her husband in favor of one made of neatly trimmed hair.

They continued on. When she noted some of the more disreputable men in front of closed shops and others waiting between darkened buildings, Elizabeth's grip on Kang's arm tightened. Celwyn had placed a block around them: there would be protection, even if unseen.

"The city maps indicate that police headquarters are just ahead." The Professor wrinkled his nose and cursed in gutter Arabic as they detoured around something pungent and indescribable.

Elizabeth's chin jerked up, and she looked at him. "Xiau, I had no idea you spoke that language."

Kang blinked at her. "We have never discussed your opinion of falafel either."

Celwyn controlled an urge to spit. That was one of the few things he refused to eat.

As they drew level with a woman holding a baby wrapped in a shawl, they slowed long enough to study her. She appeared dazed, unaware of the other pedestrians or the discordant noise around her. The eyes of a second child leaning against her leg stayed with Celwyn long after they'd passed down the street.

The magician said, "That little one appeared enormously sad."

"I wonder why." Elizabeth looked back over her shoulder. "I saw a full market bag. They seemed prosperous enough to provide food and essentials."

Celwyn pivoted. The woman and child had disappeared as if they'd never been there. Something about the encounter did not sit well with him, and the hair on his arms quivered.

"I agree." He bowed them forward. "Here we are."

The scent from the city's wood fires lays in a heavy haze around them as they gazed at the Muqr Charta police headquarters, which took up the entire block. On the right side of the building, pens holding at least a score of horses abutted the building. Then came a row of two-person carriages and dozens of bicycles that outnumbered the horses next to them. They watched the smoke rise from vents in the tile roof and disappear into the murky rain.

"A busy place," Kang observed as they ascended the stairs passing twin guards and entered the building. Slivers of mysterious light glowed from the only windows, the light not bright enough to be welcoming.

Inside, dozens of policemen filled an enormous room where the odors of tobacco, heavy cologne, and unwashed bodies competed. Celwyn voted for the first to kill the others and lit his pipe. Kang followed suit. On the other side of the dingy tile floor lay a series of tables next to a wide iron cage wedged into the corner. Inside it, a collection of men sat or slept on the floor. They watched Elizabeth's every move as their party approached the first of a dozen tables. Kang's expression showed he regretted agreeing to bring Elizabeth here.

"Good evening," Celwyn said in a loud voice. "We would like to see the officer in charge of the murder of Prince Leo Cardinale. It occurred several weeks ago."

The policeman seated behind the table narrowed his eyes and didn't answer immediately. The magician noticed the dirt under his nails looked thick enough to plant roses, yet his uniform had been thoroughly cleaned and pressed.

"What do you want him for?" he asked in Kurdish.

In that language, the automat said, "Do you speak English? Deutsche or French? My associates do not speak Kurdish. We wish to ask some questions of whoever is in charge." He indicated Elizabeth. "This is the victim's sister, Mrs. Parrish." Elizabeth nodded at the man, chin up.

"You won't tell me what this is about?" he asked in heavily accented Deutsche.

At this point, Celwyn would have just bounced him across the room until he complied. Kang chose butter instead.

"We will be pleased to share that information ... if the officer agrees that it is proper to do so."

The policeman turned his head and cursed under his breath in Turkish, probably assuming the others couldn't translate. He stalked away down a hall and disappeared into the last office.

Chapter 40

"IT HAS BEEN MORE THAN FIVE MINutes since he left." Elizabeth leaned forward to peer down the corridor. "Why is it taking so long?"

"I have no idea," Celwyn said. "But—ah, there he is. Waving us to him."

They entered a small office containing three wooden chairs and a battered desk groaning under towering amounts of paper. A corpulent man in an overly decorated uniform relaxed behind it in a swivel chair that squeaked. He did not get up as etiquette dictated, especially in the presence of a woman such as Elizabeth, instead continuing to tap his pipe into an ashtray.

"Wait outside the door, Dakhbash." The man fluttered a hand at their escort, who exited with a glower at Kang. After the door slammed, he said, "I am Captain Drury." He inspected Elizabeth a bit too long. Kang tensed. Celwyn, for once, was the one to lay a calming hand on his arm. The man's gaze moved to the magician and lingered even longer. "Please introduce yourselves."

His accent sounded moderately thick, the denseness like curdled milk, while his words were flies bravely swimming through it. Even so, Celwyn had no problem hearing the veiled suspicion in his voice and reading it on his face.

Kang caught Celwyn's reaction and spoke. "This is Mrs. Parrish, Prince Leo Cardinale's sister. I am Mr. Tiag of Manilla. And this," he indicated the magician, "is my solicitor, Mr. Trent. Mrs. Parrish wishes to know about her brother's death."

"And where you are in the investigation," Celwyn told him.

Kang kicked the magician and said, "Anything you can tell us is appreciated."

Elizabeth dabbed at her eyes with her handkerchief and said with a moan that grew in volume, "My poor, poor, dear brother."

The magician heard her, yet an overpowering sense of guilt had again enveloped him. He still felt responsible for Prince Leo, knowing he should have done more for him.

Captain Drury's oily beard reached his chest. It surrounded eyes that displayed the quickness of a squirrel hunting nuts but with the intelligence of an alligator.

As planned, Elizabeth cried into her handkerchief.

"Your brother was murdered. Brutally." The man stared at Celwyn. "Do I know you, Sir?"

"I doubt it."

Elizabeth cried louder.

"I have been Mr. Tiag's solicitor for years," Celwyn said, "and this is my first visit to your city."

Captain Drury's gaze lingered a long moment more before he shrugged. "We have been investigating." He read aloud from a page that he removed from under hundreds of sheets on his desk. "'The victim's daughter has disappeared, as have the three gentlemen who asked for his hotel room and visited that room.'" He switched the stare to Kang. "It is where his body was found."

"Is that all?" Elizabeth wailed. "Oh, Leo, Leo, Leo!"

From the man's expression, he wished Kang would shush her. Elizabeth grasped the automat's arm and buried her face in his shoulder as she bemoaned the tragedy.

"A young man visited us a few days after the murder." Drury raised his voice over the wailing. "He said he had seen the three men I mentioned and provided their descriptions. One was a tall, muscular black man."

"Do you know where the black man is at the moment?" Kang asked.

"No." He consulted his report. "However, the young man gave their names as Jonas Celwyn, a Professor Kang, and Bartholomew."

Mary Giovanna has been very helpful to the police, Celwyn thought.

Kang's pencil-thin mustache twitched as he quizzed the man. "Do you not find it odd the young man could precisely name three people who only asked for a room number?"

Captain Drury hesitated. "Perhaps. But I never turn away information." He eyed them. "If it weren't for your white hair, Mr. Trent, you would resemble the description of one of the men."

As a distraction, Celwyn laughed as he entered the man's mind and checked the level of his suspicion. While there, he added another thought: the helpful young man was really Prince Leo's missing daughter, sought for another suspicious death, and one who wears men's clothes on a regular basis. He also gave Drury a strong urge to visit the lavatory.

Captain Drury frowned and wiggled in his seat. He itched his ear with a sausage-size finger. "I suppose, however, that there could be other suspects."

On cue, Elizabeth spoke up. "Where *is* my niece, Mary Giovanna? She was traveling with him."

Celwyn hid a smile. Elizabeth had proved to be as intuitive and logical as Kang.

"She checked into the hotel with him, but we were unable to find her after the murder." Captain Drury got to his feet. "She is very lucky she was not killed also." He handed a card to Kang. "If you should hear from her, please let us know. A telegram would reach us."

Elizabeth stood also, and Kang and Celwyn followed suit.

"Thank you for your time." Elizabeth snuffled and dabbed at her eyes. "Oh, Leo, my poor, poor brother!"

A half-hour later, they were ushered to a table in the *Homayoon Restaurant* beside a simple Moorish fountain decorated with exquisitely painted tiles. The water bubbled in a quiet ambiance. Celwyn noticed Kang sending the water a furtive glance and then a sigh of relief.

The clientele of the restaurant included well-fed German businessmen, pale Nordic tourists, and Malay families dressed in white. Ferns and palms lined the white walls, and a sitar player in a pristine robe serenaded them from an alcove in the corner. The magician decided the prominent scent around them was of roasted peppers mixed with fragrant jasmine.

"Very nice choice for our dining venue, Xiau." Celwyn put his napkin in his lap, and said, "I believe we will enjoy our repast greatly this evening." He liked Tehran, to a point, and would enjoy staying longer in the city if they could; perhaps next time. With the police suspicions aroused, it would be best to decamp as planned.

"I do, also," Elizabeth said. "It smells heavenly." She sniffed the air. "The cook seems to favor garlic and spices." She turned to her husband. "I hope it isn't too spicy."

The Professor nodded. "I agree. We will be careful. Possibly the 'halloumi'?" As he studied the menu, he said, "That was a most successful visit to the police headquarters. We know more than before."

"Hmm. Halloumi is supposed to be a good cheese dish." The magician couldn't decide what to order. The Dolmeh had mint, and Tahdig sounded interesting. The skewers of chicken that the locals called 'Joojeh' used one of his favorite spices; saffron. "It was so helpful of Crazy Mary to throw suspicion upon us." His face brightened. "I returned the favor. Silently."

Elizabeth's mouth dropped open as Kang laughed. "Oh, you did. Excellent."

They placed their order, and the conversation resumed.

"At least we know it isn't too serious of an investigation. There were at least twenty files on top of the one he quoted to us." The magician spied the waiter approaching with a basket of flatbread. "Did you notice all of the case files on his desk? They wouldn't be sitting there if they'd been solved."

"Yes." Elizabeth sipped water. "But if you glance to the entrance behind you, you'll notice our friend with the dirty fingernails hiding under the palm fronds."

The magician looked and controlled his temper; it wouldn't do to make the police even more interested.

"Wonderful. That nosy corporal." Kang told Celwyn, "If you dispose of him, it will only make them more curious."

Celwyn turned back with a growl. "We didn't completely fool them."

"I concur." The automat sighed. "I had so hoped for an uneventful dinner."

The magician selected a pistachio from a bowl full of various nuts and cracked it open. "The policeman isn't here to arrest us, or he would have done so already." He pursed his lips. "He is just following us; therefore, we can finish our dinner in peace."

"I trust your conclusion." Kang said, "It would be a shame to waste this excellent vintage." He held the bottle of wine the waiter had presented him with up to the light. "I had no idea they grew grapes in South Africa."

When they left the *Homayoon*, Drury's corporal did not appear to be lurking anywhere on the street. Celwyn checked each doorway and stepped onto the cobblestones to verify no one hid behind the cart across the street.

"We can't afford to lead him back to the train." Kang flagged down a carriage. "Can we?" His mood had not been improved by an excellent dinner.

A team of four lively horses came to a stop, throwing up puddles, causing everyone at the curb to back up. Celwyn again checked the area. This time he found the corporal lurking in the crowd of pedestrians next to a newsstand.

The magician leaned down and said in Kang's ear, "The corporal is still here. Please ask the driver to take us to the best English pub in town." He nodded to their driver as they climbed into the hawdi.

In seconds, they drove away, their offer of double the fare guaranteeing the speed of their departure. Five blocks away, their coach stopped at the curb. The automat paid off the driver, adding a large tip, and requested he leave as soon as possible. As Celwyn trotted to one of the smaller hire coaches across the street, the Kangs followed him. Once inside one of them, they saw their original cab reverse direction in a wide arc and speed away. It drove away so fast it teetered on two wheels. For several minutes, the three of them sat in the smaller cab with the curtains closed as Celwyn peeked outside.

"That must have been a generous tip. Enough for the driver to buy his own cab."

Kang nodded. "It was."

As expected, a few seconds later, another carriage pulled up in front of the pub. Drury's watchdog argued with his driver, threw up his hands, and rushed inside with a hail of curses and gestures in his wake.

"I do not believe the corporal believes in tipping." Celwyn tapped on the glass between them and their driver. "We can leave now."

Once back on the *Elizabeth*, they settled into chairs as Kang said, "We should close the curtains, in case the corporal tracks us here."

The magician did so with a lazy wave of his hand.

"Considering what you gave that last coachman, it is highly unlikely." Elizabeth patted her hair in place. "I could use a whiskey, please."

"Pardon my manners." Celwyn poured and sent one to her without getting up. A second one reached Kang a moment later as Jackson arrived with a tea service. The porter studiously pretended he didn't see anything. After he'd been thanked and left again, Celwyn inhaled the steam from a fine cup of leaves and a successful evening.

"I noticed you haven't adjusted Jackson's mustache lately." Kang jumped as the phonograph next to the sofa began to play a light tinkling baroque propelled by an unseen hand at the hand crank.

Celwyn shrugged. "I ran out of different styles to try."

At Elizabeth's raised brow, Kang said, "You don't want to know; it only encourages him."

"Nonsense, I suggest not listening to your husband, Madam. I am innocent." The magician blinked guilelessly at the automat, and Elizabeth smiled as Celwyn continued. "Back to the present. At the moment, Ricardo and Otto are out hunting for a few supplies. That reminds me..." Celwyn stood again. "Conductor Smith will need to know to leave at first light."

He passed through the kitchen and the crew quarters, eventually reaching the locomotive where he found the Conductor and delivered his request. On the return trip, he checked the coal level and water tanks. The magician studied a few of the distances and wondered if he could devise an automatic loading of coal into the ovens as they traveled. One where he didn't have to constantly provide magic to make it work, perhaps one propelled by the fuel itself as it burned. *Ha!* He would tell Xiau about the idea to remind him that Celwyn did other things than worry the automat or play pranks for entertainment.

Those antics reminded him of someone. He stopped by his room and retrieved Qing, who brought along a cufflink. Bird entertainment. When they arrived in the dining room, he discovered Verne had joined them. Elizabeth shuffled cards, and they prepared to play whist.

"I wish I had gone with you into town." The author pouted.

Celwyn sat across from him and asked, "Did Ricardo feed you?"

"Yes, an excellent steak." Verne's face cleared. "Next time, I shall go with you."

Kang picked up a hefty book from atop the bar. "Gessner's, *Historia animalium.*" He looked at Celwyn with the kind of surprise that said he doubted the magician could read. "When did you get this?"

"In Singapore. A present for Zander."

Elizabeth frowned. "I normally understand the purpose of presents, but this, I do not understand."

"It is a 2,500-page encyclopedia of animals. It was published around 1558 and contains quadrupeds, amphibians, birds, and fishes." Kang answered, still staring at Celwyn. "I had no idea you'd heard of this."

"I hadn't. But the shopkeeper recommended it for a budding artist to learn how to draw animals in detail."

"Ah." Elizabeth nodded.

Kang put the book back, returned to the table, and picked up his cards. He regarded Verne. "The only thing you missed tonight was an uncomfortable meeting with a police captain who had eaten an excessive amount of garlic."

"Also, we discovered Mary Giovanna had told the police to suspect us of the murder." Elizabeth frowned as she sorted the cards in her hand.

"Oh." Verne's expression changed. "Perhaps it was best that I remained here."

They heard a voice and steps, and then Ricardo and Otto entered the train, each carrying a package.

"Only carrots and onions," Ricardo reported. "But we'll get more tomorrow."

"Where did you find vegetables? The bazaar was closed," Kang asked.

"The larger restaurants sometimes sell things this time of night if they bought too much during the day."

"Your meals are always excellent." Celwyn wondered if their discoveries meant a delectable Shepherd's pie tomorrow.

Ricardo bowed and motioned Otto to follow him out.

"Shall we discuss Disraeli, or the Russians taking a position in Kabul?" Verne asked.

"I vote that you take the fourth position for whist." Celwyn crossed to the door, staring through the glass before locking it and drawing the shade. He lowered the volume of the phonograph without a glance. "We cannot chance the music attracting the attention of the police. Of course, Disraeli can be dissected at the same time."

At the first hint of dawn through his shutters, Celwyn arose and dressed. All night, he'd slept badly, hearing noises but not quite waking up. Qing rode on his shoulder as he entered the dining room.

The magician froze. Two of the door panels were kicked in.

With a curse and flick of his wrist, every light in the car came on.

Slivers of wood covered the floor where the door had been forced open. Worse, a trail of smeared blood led from there to the sofa. Even from across the room, the magician had no trouble seeing every detail of the butchered body of Ludvik. He had been propped against the pillows and a whiskey glass placed in his hands, the intent to depict a macabre cocktail hour.

Celwyn whirled and, in seconds, rapped on Kang's cabin door. Since the automat did not sleep, he answered before Celwyn finished knocking.

"Come." The magician led the way back up the hall and across the room until they stood in front of the body. The magician shook with rage, and the first row of bar glasses shattered. "If you will get the Conductor up and the train moving—I'll take care of this."

Kang paused only long enough for a quick look at Ludvik's wounds before turning toward the kitchen. He ran by Ricardo coming through toward them.

Celwyn waved him in. Ricardo stopped a few feet from the body, and his eyes bulged.

"W… w… why?" His voice rose.

The magician placed a hand on his shoulder. "I do not know."

Ricardo swallowed several times before saying, "He wasn't in his room when I went to bed last night."

Celwyn told him, "Give me five minutes, and send in all of the crew." After another glass shattered, the magician controlled his anger and lowered his voice. "I am sorry this has happened. He was a nice young man."

"But why? Who would *do* this?" Ricardo wailed and wrung his hands.

Celwyn inhaled. "I think it was our guest, Miss Giovanna. We're certain she killed her father, and because of this," he gestured at the sofa, "I'm convinced she also murdered the reporter Stephen on our journey out here."

Ricardo backed away from the body, crossing himself, and reciting an incantation under his breath. The magician watched him stumble toward the kitchen and called, "Again, please wait five minutes, and bring the crew here, including the Conductor."

When the door had closed again, Celwyn swept a hand across the room, dressing Ludvik in a fine suit and tightly binding him in a tarp. Outside the train, a deep hole appeared, and soon the body was inside it. When the dirt was back in place, it appeared to have never been disturbed, and the grisly contents covered. The magician congratulated himself; everything happened so fast that the few pedestrians across the tracks didn't even look up.

Celwyn had just turned back to regard the mess on the sofa when the kitchen door opened, and the crew staggered in, blinking under the bright lights. Some walked as carefully as if the floor had been covered in eggshells and didn't want to break any of them. Confusion warred with fear on their faces.

Standing shoulder to shoulder, Kang and Celwyn faced them.

"Gentlemen, I am sorry to report that Ludvik's body was found about ten minutes ago. He was murdered, most likely by the young woman who was with us the first few weeks of our journey. Mary Giovanna." After hearing their gasps, the magician told them, "I buried him outside."

"Why? How?" Abe sputtered.

"We do not know why, but it appears that she broke in that door and drug the body across to the sofa." The automat's anger showed in his voice. "She is a disturbed individual, and we think she also killed Stephen a few weeks ago."

"A *woman*?" Andy asked. The crew stood in a ring around the sofa, some able to look at the mess, some not.

"Yes," Celwyn said.

"But she was so nice!" Jackson read Otto's tablet to them. Others nodded, not wanting to believe what they heard.

"She killed her father, Prince Leo, here in Tehran a few weeks ago," Kang said. "Then she implicated Bartholomew, Mr. Celwyn, and me."

Conductor Smith's face turned dark. "I have had some experience with false accusations. Ludvik was a fine young man. May he rest in peace." He faced his crew. "We have work to do. Come along, boys."

His exit set everyone in motion. That was one of the things Celwyn admired about him.

Ricardo eyed the bloody sofa and started to speak, but the Professor said kindly, "We will clean up here. Please, go start your day. We will take care of it."

"But Sir—"

"Please start your day and leave this to us."

Celwyn stared at the entryway leading off the train until the debris disappeared, as did the damage. A shiny new lock and handle appeared. Ricardo saw the change and ran back into the kitchen so fast the door almost hit him.

The automat stood over the sofa, measuring the bloodstains with his eyes. "I think she stabbed him and brought him here while he was still alive. Perhaps unconscious or tricked into thinking she would help him." He chewed on his lip. "Then she gutted him."

Celwyn made a face of distaste. "Are you finished looking at this?"

"Nearly." He bent low over the bloodstains again. "I think she alternates between calculating actions and manic ones." He backed off. "Go ahead."

Celwyn swept a hand, and the blood disappeared. "I'll verify that there is nothing else Crazy Mary left behind outside."

"Such as a knife?"

"Yes."

Chapter 41

An hour later, Otto served breakfast in a very subdued manner. Gone were his quick, shy smiles, and as he poured coffee, his hand shook so badly he slopped more coffee into the saucer than the cup.

"Please." Celwyn stopped him. "What happened is horrible, but as you can see, we're miles from Tehran, and whoever killed Ludvik isn't on our train." Celwyn had checked every car while the *Elizabeth* traveled at speed, flattening fields of grass as she flew by. The magician looked him in the eye. "I won't let anything happen to you. We will post guards on the train."

The lad nodded and exhaled.

"When we stop at night, if we ask you to stay on the train, it is for your safety," Kang reminded him.

Another nod.

"All right. Please let the others in the kitchen know, too," the Professor said.

With alarm filling her voice, Elizabeth put down her cup and demanded, "What are you two talking about?"

Kang turned to Verne and then to his wife. "You were still asleep when ... we had an incident. I was planning to wait until after breakfast to tell you."

"Tell me now." Elizabeth's lips trembled.

Kang touched her cheek. "I'm sorry, but one of the porters, Ludvik, was murdered and left inside this car last night after we went to bed. We're convinced it is Leo's daughter, Mary Giovanna, who did it."

Otto retreated to the kitchen, watching them over his shoulder with a furrowed brow.

"No!" Elizabeth exclaimed.

"I'm sorry, my dear." Kang patted her hand.

While Elizabeth's eyes couldn't get any wider, Verne calmly cocked his head and seemed to analyze the news.

"I liked Ludvik. How did it happen?"

"She smashed her way through the dining room door and left his body on the sofa." Elizabeth's gulp reminded Celwyn that she might not be as hardened to violence as the others. He gentled his voice, "I have completely cleaned everything, Madam. If you prefer, I can replace the sofa—"

"No, no. It is all right," she protested. "It is just shocking..." She eyed the sofa with enough uneasiness that the magician would have to replace it. Another color or style would help restore her equanimity.

"Where is the body?" Verne asked.

Kang shot him a disgusted look. Just as Elizabeth looked calmer, he had to be uncouth. "Buried back in Tehran," the automat told him.

"Interesting. Did she murder him in response to your visit with the police yesterday?" the author asked.

Kang glared. Elizabeth saw him and said, "It is all right, dear. I must confess that I am curious, too."

Celwyn shrugged. "It could be."

"Do you wonder how she got to Ludvik?" Verne asked.

The automat thought about it. "She could have stood outside the crew's quarters and got his attention from the windows without anyone else seeing her. It would have been easy for her. Like Bartholomew, I think he admired her."

"I see. You just said you will have guards on the train," Verne said.

"Yes, I did," Celwyn faced him. "And you will be expected to take a shift each night until we reach Prague. We'll issue you a pistol."

"*Me*?" the author's voice rose.

Kang didn't sound sorry as he said, "Yes. We'll be short a porter. Even though Jonas will use magic for most of it, when he is resting, we need to augment our security."

Verne seemed ready to object and then thought better of it after he spied the magician's expression.

A short time later, Ricardo removed the empty breakfast dishes wearing a frown contrary to his normally carefree mien. "I'll bring the tea service out in a few minutes."

Celwyn stopped his hand as he reached for another plate.

"Are you all right, Ricardo?"

"No!" It came out louder than usual. "I am angry. I heard from Otto that you will guard the train. That is comforting. It is appreciated. But ... why did that woman kill Ludvik and the other boy? *Why*? Will we die, too? Mio Dio!"

Celwyn pulled him into Bartholomew's empty chair. "She is mentally disturbed. She is *pazzo*. Our best strategy is to get far away from her. That is what we're doing." He pointed out the window where outbuildings in the distance whizzed by. "We're traveling fast."

"We should be in Qazvin by nightfall," Kang told him. "It is more than a hundred miles from Tehran."

Ricardo's eyes seemed a little less frantic.

"You are our responsibility, Ricardo. We will protect you." Celwyn told him, "What you can do is make sure the crew stays on the train when we ask them to. When in town, they must stay together."

"I understand." He got to his feet and began gathering dishes. "I need to get back to the kitchen." Before he left, he tried to lighten the atmosphere. "You know, we are nearly out of paprika. There had better be some in Qazvin."

Celwyn did smile. "We will find some there."

"I hate to ask, and we do not want to make things worse for you, but do you need to replace Ludvik before we reach Prague?" Kang inquired.

Their chef shrugged. "How long until we arrive there?"

Kang told him, "About two to three weeks, depending on the weather."

"Then we will be fine. If I may say so, you are all very self-contained as long as I keep the water boiling for tea!"

As the afternoon waned, from his position in a chair by the globe, the Professor said, "The population of Qazvin is larger than Zanjan."

Verne had remained in his room to write while Elizabeth kept them company, sitting on the new sofa with her embroidery. To Celwyn, everything seemed calm as he alternately read or studied the terrain through the windows. Occasionally, he would enjoy discovering little things outside he hadn't noticed before. A mosque here, a river there. After another half hour, the magician shifted in his seat, uncomfortable and not knowing exactly why, until he thought more.

Everything appeared too damned normal. He touched his side. The pain felt less, yet he didn't feel completely recovered, as if something unseen was pulling him downward. When he looked up, he found Kang's graveyard gaze upon him, that said, "*I know you are very ill.*"

Several miles went by before Kang broke the solemnity and cloud of unease that hung in the air.

"When we reach our destination tonight, we must send a telegraph to Annabelle to let her know of our probable arrival date." He put on a brave smile that couldn't hide his worry. "Zander will be most excited at the news."

The magician felt guilty knowing his condition upset Kang, so he made his voice cheerful. "We could find him more presents in Qazvin, too. It may not help though, Bartholomew's absence will not be well received."

"Of course, it won't. You can tell him."

Celwyn rolled his eyes. "Oh, so that is how it is."

"Excuse me, but we still need to shop for my new hat," Elizabeth reminded them.

Qing left his perch on the windowsill to walk across the sofa and sit on her knee. He eyed her embroidery needle.

"You don't want this." She handed him a yellow button from her sewing basket. He held it in the tip of his beak as he twisted his head to the side, and then hopped back on the windowsill.

As Celwyn watched him, and then Elizabeth and Kang, he felt a certain measure of normalcy. But his unease did not lessen. It grew.

Chapter 42

A FORTNIGHT LATER, THE *ELIZABETH* rounded the top of Mount Kladno overlooking Prague and began her descent to the city below.

Everyone had spent the morning packing their trunks. Verne's good humor infected each of them, even Ricardo, who had seemed the most affected by the murder of Ludvik.

Otto helped bring the author's trunks into the dining room, and for the first time in days, he grinned at what Verne was saying. Earlier, Elizabeth had listened to one of the author's stories and laughed. Celwyn had to admit that Verne had a certain charm, but he also had other habits.

As he watched the preparations for their arrival, the magician felt a sense of relief that over the last few weeks, no one else had been murdered, and there seemed to be no evidence that the *Elizabeth* was of concern to the police in any of the cities they had stopped in. He and the automat had garnered more attention from the kandora sellers than from the constabulary.

Verne stood at the windows, hanging on to the sill as the descending train rounded another curve. "There are the turrets of Prague Castle!" he cried.

The magician gazed over Verne's shoulder and saw the castle, then the spires of the minarets, and finally St. Vitus Cathedral. Fluffy clouds blocked some sun, but the gilt decorating the cathedral's cornices still gleamed through the filtered light.

"What will you do once we reach the city, Mr. Verne?" Elizabeth asked from her position on the sofa. Kang sat beside her, content, yet his eyes danced with the excitement of their arrival.

"What? Oh, I will write."

"You plan to stay in Prague until your book is complete?" Celwyn asked.

"Yes." Verne sniffed the air. "I can still smell that omelet from our luncheon. You know, I will miss Ricardo's cooking very much."

Celwyn regarded him a moment, then sent cold air over the author until he shivered and turned around. The magician said, "Please remember our agreement. Do not speak of us or our activities. Do not publish anything about us."

Verne glanced at Kang. "But Jonas—"

"You promised. Is your word worthless?"

"Under duress." Verne straightened his vest, checked Celwyn's expression, and then sighed. "Nevertheless, I will honor your wishes."

"Thank you."

The Professor tugged on the magician's sleeve. "I imagine Zander is already at the train yard, and Patrick is trying to keep him calm."

"You always know how to cheer me up, my friend." Celwyn checked the coins in his pocket. "Do we want to place a wager on how much taller he is?"

"One inch."

Celwyn tapped his lips and said, "Two."

"You do recall that I haven't met Zander yet," Elizabeth said.

Kang drew her close. "He will love you as I do."

As they left the outskirts of Prague behind and entered the older district, Celwyn watched the increasing number of buildings and trees. "Annabelle's Captain Patrick is an upstanding man. He will be leaving the Queen's army soon." He turned to the Kangs. "I have put a block on what Verne can hear. Madam, have you been told of Patrick's connection to me? And of the vampires we encountered a few months ago?"

Elizabeth lay her embroidery in her lap. "Annabelle told me some of it." She regarded her husband with a half-smile. "Is there something I should know?"

Kang sent the magician a resigned look. "Patrick's sister was engaged to Jonas. A vampire killed her, and when Patrick tried to avenge her death, one of them made him a vampire, too, partially. That would be the notorious Mrs. Karras, who followed us here."

"The same one that Jonas pushed off the *Royal Victoria* train?"

"Tossed is more accurate." Kang sent the magician an exasperated look. "Patrick has none of their taste for blood and lives normally, except he doesn't age."

"He is also stronger than a normal man," Celwyn said.

"I see," Elizabeth said. "I am sorry for your loss, Jonas. And for Patrick's."

"Thank you, Madam."

"Annabelle is quite smitten with Patrick, and I believe they'll be very happy. One problem we must face—" Kang hesitated with a glance at Celwyn, "is that Zander has become attached to all of us, Bartholomew included, and there are indications Patrick would like to be his father."

"Complications." Elizabeth ran a nail up and down the sofa arm as she thought. "Does Zander treat Annabelle like a mother?"

"I think so, do you?" Kang asked Celwyn.

"Yes." Celwyn thought for a moment. "But, because of the conditions in which we found him, he is also very much attached to the rest of us, too." The magician remembered holding the boy as he cried and cried the night Telly died. Then he recalled Van Maskolc. "As you know, we rescued him from a terrible situation."

"I do. I have noticed your fondness for Otto, also." She gazed at the kitchen door. "Have either of you decided what will happen to him when we arrive? I don't think he can survive on his own."

Kang looked at Celwyn, and the magician raised a quizzical brow at Kang. "Err, no, we hadn't planned ... anything yet."

"Men never do."

Kang held her hand and shrugged the sheepish shrug of one realizing he needed his partner's wisdom.

"Otto lived in India for several years before the war there. Ricardo tells me that before that, the lad's family home in Bavaria was bombed." Celwyn frowned. He felt so sorry for him. *Was that when he became mute?*

"We haven't considered Ricardo's position either." Kang raised both brows in question.

Celwyn left the windows and leaned over the back of the sofa. "I've given some of this a bit of thought. Because we will journey again in two months to Byzantium, I will offer Conductor Smith his salary and board in the hopes he will stay on with us. There may be duties at Tellyhouse that Edward could organize with him."

Kang nodded. "I like that."

"Tellyhouse sounds very big," Elizabeth said as she watched Verne frowning and staring out the window.

"It is, and it can accommodate a large staff as needed," Celwyn said. "If all of the train staff wishes to stay with us, I believe we can find a way to keep them busy and happy."

Elizabeth regarded them with a stern look. "Of course, we can. From what Annabelle has described and what I see here, I imagine our opinion of the number of staff needed to run a manor is not the same as yours."

"Our housekeeper, Mrs. Thomas, would agree with you, my dear."

"And Otto?" she asked. "Any ideas?"

They looked at each other, then Kang said, "We will confer."

Chapter 43

"LOOK! THERE THEY ARE!" KANG pointed.

The *Elizabeth* coasted to a stop in Prague's Praha station amid clouds of hissing steam. Patrick and Annabelle stood to one side and held onto each of Zander's hands to keep him from running onto the tracks. The screech of the train's brakes had barely stopped before they heard Zander yelling. Behind them, Mrs. Thomas looked over their shoulders at the train with her arms crossed and a serious expression on her broad face. Next to her, Edward's smile radiated happiness and relief.

With a hitch in his voice, Celwyn said, "I missed them all very much." While he waited for the train to settle, he chuckled. "My, my. Look how much taller Zander is."

"Oh, pfft. You must have cheated." Kang handed him a coin and guided Elizabeth down the stairs and to the ground.

As Celwyn trailed them, he inhaled the scents of the city and realized how glad he was to be on firm land again. Prague was as beautiful a city as she was old.

With a whoop, Zander tackled Kang, knocking them both down. Elizabeth started to laugh as she saw the boy's happiness, and her husband's. Then Annabelle embraced her, and Celwyn shook Patrick's hand. Zander ran to him, hugged him, and kissed his cheek. Then he saw Elizabeth. The magician introduced them, and Zander bowed gravely.

Verne stepped off the train and joined Celwyn to await his introductions. The magician wiped a tear away before saying, "May I present Annabelle Pearse Edmunds and her fiancée, Captain Patrick Swayne. This is the renowned author, Mr. Jules Verne." Celwyn continued the introductions as Mrs. Thomas and Edward stepped forward.

"May I present Mrs. Polly Thomas, our housekeeper, and this is Mr. Edward Murphy. He is our coachman and responsible for our security." Celwyn could have listed many other titles, but Edward embarrassed easily and blushed just as readily.

During the introductions, Zander insisted on holding Elizabeth's hand, and Celwyn's. He stared at the train. "Where is Bartholomew? *Where is he*?"

Kang bent down to his level, along with Celwyn.

"Bartholomew will return in January. That is only two months away," Celwyn told him.

"Is he hurt?" The boy's voice rose, and tears dribbled down his face.

"No." Kang hugged him. "He misses you very much."

"Why isn't he *here*?"

Celwyn told him, "He was asked to work on something." He ruffled the boy's hair. "You will get to go with us to pick him up in Byzantium."

"I know where that is! It was my lesson from last week!"

Celwyn sent Annabelle a nod of thanks over the boy's head. In an earlier telegram, he had requested that lesson and was pleased to see Annabelle had made it occur. It would help Zander to know the location of his friend, even if he didn't understand why the big man was missing.

Kang told Zander, "Never fear, I have lessons for you from Bartholomew."

The boy smiled and turned to the magician. "I missed you, Uncle Celwyn."

The magician lifted him up. "You are always missed by us, young man." Through the window of the *Elizabeth,* Celwyn spied Ricardo and his minions preparing to decamp from the train. He put Zander down. "Come, let's meet the rest of the crew."

They greeted Ricardo, Otto, and Jackson as they stepped off the train. Edward reached them at the same time, and while he shook Ricardo's hand and slapped him on the back, Zander gazed at Otto, who in return offered a tentative smile. Zander appeared captivated.

Celwyn said, "Already a bond: orphan to orphan."

Kang studied them. "It is certainly fascinating. Worth researching."

As they rejoined the others, another train pulled in beside them, quivered, and subsided. Annabelle had to raise her voice over the noise. "Where will you be staying in Prague, Mr. Verne?"

"The Marlborough. It is a wonderful hotel." He glanced at the Tellyhouse carriage and a second coach behind it, along with two more carts and horses. With a brow up in inquiry, he regarded Kang and Celwyn. "Is it possible for you to drop me off at my hotel?"

Kang consulted with the magician. "It will take several trips to unload the train. I acquired many more books."

"And my pianoforte. Yes, Jules, we can accommodate you."

From where she stood under the dining room windows, Mrs. Thomas watched Edward supervising the dispersal of their trunks onto the carts and carriages. She raised her voice to a level that could be heard across the city and to the top of St. Vitus Church, "Best get a move on, Sirs and Mams. Mr. Sully is preparing luncheon. And it will be ready within the hour." She clapped her hands. "*Move faster*, please."

"Sully?" Kang and Celwyn traded stricken expressions as they walked up to her.

Mrs. Thomas frowned and said, "I didn't have time to telegraph you. Chef Lucien quit us the day before yesterday. We have endured Mr. Sully's creations since then." She couldn't help a shudder. "I haven't started to look for a replacement yet, what with preparing for your arrival."

Kang exhaled and exchanged a look with Celwyn, who sighed with relief. "With your approval, we have a solution," he said just as Ricardo exited the train. "Ricardo is more than qualified to become the Tellyhouse chef."

Off to the side, Otto and Zander still regarded each other solemnly like silent diminutive soldiers, and then Otto handed Zander his tablet. He read it and nodded with a big grin.

Mrs. Thomas's attention was not on Ricardo but on the boys. She glanced at them and said, "I think we could try Riccardo in that position." She stared. "If I may, who is that young man with Master Zander?"

"Otto is an orphan," Kang told her. "He is also mute, and he functioned as one of our porters on our journey here." He motioned Edward closer and continued, "We are proposing that Otto," he pointed the lad out, "help Edward in the stables part-time, and participate with Zander in his schooling the rest of the day."

Mrs. Thomas' lips were set, but she didn't say anything. Personnel decisions were her purview, and she took the responsibility seriously. Not to mention the obligation she felt to keep the social classes separate and the inhabitants of Tellyhouse in society's good graces despite what her employers dreamt up.

"Seems like a nice lad. How old is he?" Edward asked, "Why does he have that tablet?"

"He says he is fifteen years old, just a few years older than Zander." Celwyn saw Edward's puzzled expression. "He cannot speak and uses the tablet to communicate."

As Elizabeth joined them again, Kang explained. "We think he is younger than he says and estimate his schooling is on the same level as Zander's. More importantly, he could use our protection."

"It is also important that Zander has a friend close to his own age." Celwyn nodded at the boys, and they waved back at him.

Without hesitation, Edward said, "I'll get him settled with us at the stables."

"He seems like a nice young man," Mrs. Thomas allowed. She watched him a moment more. "Edward, I'll make room for him at the house." She looked at the automat and then Celwyn. "With Miss Annabelle's approval, I will make the other arrangements, too, including moving Ricardo into the chef's quarters. They're larger."

"We trust your judgement, Mrs. Thomas," the Professor assured her.

"The place is not fully staffed at the moment. And with all of you here, I'll need the help." She turned, and her bellow rivaled the roar of the train that had earlier pulled in beside them. "Everyone into the carriages! *Now*!"

Kang chuckled. "We're home."

"We sure are," Celwyn murmured as they hurried Elizabeth to the main carriage, enjoying her open-mouthed reaction to Mrs. Thomas.

After they settled inside, Kang confided to his wife, "Mrs. Thomas takes no prisoners, but you'll get used to her."

Annabelle and Patrick wore broad smiles as they climbed inside and sat across from the Kangs.

"We probably should have prepared you for our housekeeper, but you'll grow to appreciate her soon," Annabelle said as she grasped Elizabeth's hand and hugged her. "I'm so glad you are here." Her blond curls bounced as she greeted them and turned a shy smile on Patrick. "We're anxious to get on with the wedding."

Patrick kissed her cheek. "Yes, we are, and want to hear all about your adventures, too." He included Celwyn and Kang in the last part of what he said.

Zander perched on Celwyn's lap, hugged him, and then sat back with all the seriousness a small boy could muster. "I'm happy you are all home," he said in careful English, "but I want Bartholomew home, too."

Elizabeth, Kang, and the magician exchanged a glance. Celwyn told him, "When we are done with luncheon, we'll explain more of what will happen. It will be soon."

Zander looked at Verne. Celwyn introduced them.

"Pleased to meet you," Zander said. "I met a new friend too. He cannot talk, but we will have fun!"

Kang leaned back, his arm around his wife, and a satisfied expression painted across his face. Elizabeth rested her head on his shoulder, and a moment later began a gentle snore as their carriage traveled down Strahovski Street toward the Marlborough. From beside her, Verne's eyes twinkled in amusement.

Zander pointed out the window at a white pony pulling a small cart of flowers. "There is a pony you could buy me, Uncle Celwyn."

"*Handle that*," Kang mouthed at Celwyn without Zander seeing him.

The magician ignored the automat and told the boy, "Someday, perhaps." He addressed the others, "On another subject ... because we can anticipate the inedible creations from Sully that await us at Tellyhouse; perhaps we should dine at the hotel too."

Annabelle tapped his knee with her fan. "Nonsense. It isn't that bad."

"Yes, it is," Patrick spoke up. "Do you want to guess what he put in the pancakes this morning?"

Hours later, luncheon had ended, and as they settled in the Tellyhouse parlor, Kang reached for his pipe. He froze when he spied Mrs. Thomas' eye on him, as well as Annabelle's, and pretended to scratch his side. Celwyn saw him, snickered, and turned to face the picture window. Rows of red and white roses lined the walk leading to the street. The carriage still sat there; Edward hadn't taken it to the stables, most likely expecting a summons to retrieve an item or two in town.

While he listened to the conversation behind him, the magician allowed Qing to escape from his coat and murmured, "Please behave. It is our first day at home." The bird turned a diamond gaze on him and hopped onto the windowsill to watch the birds outside.

"...missed you so much," Annabelle told them. "Zander especially."

Kang said, "I have an important question: do you think Ricardo will be cooking our dinner?" He pointed toward the dining room. "I don't know *what* was in the sauce on the trout just now. I love trout too much to suffer that again."

Elizabeth gave him a gentle shove. "It wasn't that bad."

"I hate to admit it, but it was." Annabelle patted her stomach.

Celwyn turned to them. "I am happy to announce that Ricardo has embraced his new role as chef of Tellyhouse and intends on making our dinner. He has drafted Jackson as one of his helpers. Sully is relieved to be returning to his duties as footman."

Mrs. Thomas pushed the coffee cart into the room. "If I may, recently Harrison joined us as our other footman and Greta as a scullery maid. The cleaning crew still do not sleep in, per your request, Sirs." Her tone indicated she didn't approve of the later arrangement.

"Who else is new, Mrs. Thomas?" the magician asked. Considering the nefarious activities of the inhabitants of Tellyhouse and their enemies, they probably had a rather high staff turnover.

She frowned as she poured and handed a cup to Annabelle. "We just lost our head gardener to the Rosens down the street. And last week both of our groomsmen and yardman left for the war in Egypt. Do you think those men from the train—?"

"Yes," Celwyn said. "Conductor Smith has said he has always maintained his own garden and will stay at least until January when we journey to Byzantium." He looked at Kang. "I don't know about Abe and Andy, do you?"

"No."

Mrs. Thomas said, "I'll speak to them after they get settled in. If you should change your mind about having a live-in cleaning staff, I still have room to board them." On her way out, she caught sight of Qing, snorted, and crossed herself. "I see that damn bird is back."

Chapter 44

"THIS COOKIE TASTES ... STRANGE." Patrick made a face. "Sometimes, Sully's cookies are edible, sometimes not," he informed Elizabeth and put the offending residue into his napkin. He sipped coffee to chase away the remaining taste. "At least he can't hurt this."

Kang raised a speculative brow at them. "I wonder if romance will blossom between Mrs. Thomas and Sully now that Chef Lucien is out of the way? I am willing to make a wager."

"Xiau!" Elizabeth exclaimed. "Don't gossip about the staff!"

"Put me down for saying Sully will try." Annabelle smiled. "It's all right. He comes to us to ask how to woo her." She laughed a bit maliciously. "I refer him to Patrick."

"Yes, she certainly does." Patrick maintained a serious expression, but his lips twitched. "My money is on Sully, too."

Celwyn smiled with them. He regarded the love-birds. "During luncheon, when we discussed the trip to Byzantium to pick up Bartholomew, you said you do not mind postponing your ceremony until after then. Are you sure?"

"It is only for two more months," Patrick said.

Annabelle told Elizabeth, "We can use the time to finalize the details, including my dress."

Zander had been sitting as quiet as a worried mouse between Annabelle and Patrick, listening to each word, perhaps to confirm they were all back with him. He grinned often and appeared much more confident than the first time Celwyn met him.

"I am not wearing a tie to the wedding," the boy announced. His bottom lip protruded with finality.

"You do not have to," Patrick told him. "But I bought you a tie just like the one I am going to wear."

Annabelle confided to Zander. "A tie makes you more handsome."

The boy looked at Celwyn.

"It is up to you," the magician told him as Edward arrived at the door.

"Everything has been transferred from the train, Sirs and Madams. Will there be anything else?"

"Have you eaten luncheon?" the magician asked.

"Not yet, Sir."

"Beware of the sauce on the fish that Sully prepared. And after you dine, please talk with the crew from the train and help them settle in." Celwyn said. "Especially Otto."

Edward nodded. "I plan to. If I may say so, it is good to have you all home again."

"And to see you again, Edward. I understand things were quiet while we were away."

With a telltale glance at Elizabeth, and tug on his luxuriant mustache, Edward replied, "Yes. Our arrangement with Francesca still stands. When I bring her the fee each week, it is a very interesting experience." He blushed.

The Professor laughed somewhat nervously, as did the magician. Elizabeth lowered her brows at them until the magician explained. "Bartholomew used to complain of it, too. When he returns home in January, he might want to assume that duty again if Edward is worried about his virtue."

"Sometimes I am." Edward's blush grew even redder.

Elizabeth turned the look on her husband.

"Allow me," Annabelle said in a low voice while Patrick followed Zander through the open arch into the parlor and to the checkers board. "Francesca is a witch and the head of Prague's very large and bawdy coven. To ensure our safety, we pay her to keep several spells over Tellyhouse."

With a check to verify Zander couldn't hear them from the parlor, Elizabeth gasped, "Witches? Against vampires?"

"Yes." Celwyn nodded. "And other things."

"Oh, I see." She bestowed an unamused and speculative look on her husband, "I have the feeling things were a great deal more dangerous a few months ago than you told me."

Kang seemed to shrink like a rat trapped in a hole. He looked at Celwyn, then Annabelle, for help.

The magician verified that Zander had his back to them as he and Patrick set up the checkerboard. A distraction might help the situation before Xiau landed in the doghouse out back. He put his finger to his lips, made sure Patrick saw the warning, and then opened his hand.

In the center of the room, a thin mist of green formed above the floor, then cleared, revealing a scene only a few inches high. Snow-capped mountains surrounded a city in the valley below. The drawbridge of the fairy tale castle of Prague had been raised.

Inside the courtyard, a wedding party gathered. Bartholomew stood out, easily recognizable, even down to his red cummerbund. Beside him, the Kangs held hands amid the legions of flowers and fountains. Knights in suits of armor lined the procession as Celwyn led Annabelle through the gardens toward Patrick, who waited patiently, resplendent in full military uniform.

In the windows of the castle, the faces of the royal family could be seen, and below them, a flower girl released a flock of miniature doves. While everyone watched the scene, the magician added a chorus of strings, the sound as light as the clouds hovering above the ceremony.

"There's Zander," Kang whispered, trying not to laugh. "He is wearing a tie."

"Do you see it? Your dress looks lovely," Elizabeth told Annabelle, awe filling her voice. "The lace is exquisite."

A restrained brace of horns heralded the bride's arrival at the altar, and the music segued into the wedding march. Over her veil, Annabelle wore a tiara that twinkled in the sunlight carpeting the parlor floor. As she walked toward the officiates and Patrick, a quartet of fairies, their wings beating so fast they seemed a blur, hung above them, scattering tiny flower petals into the air amid cascading stars.

Qing hopped off the windowsill and waddled into the scene on the floor. The metal webbing of his feet contrasted in a surreal way with the tiny wedding figures.

"Patrick, you may want to come here for a moment," Annabelle called. After he had done so, the magician swept a hand to dissolve the scene.

That should be distracting enough, the magician thought. Kang could thank him later.

As Patrick resumed his game of checkers, Zander chattered about how much fun they would have the next day. Elizabeth eyed Kang long enough to let him know she wasn't fooled by the distraction and turned to Annabelle. "We haven't had a chance to talk yet, and I want to hear what you've been up to."

Annabelle beamed. "I have so much to tell you." They rose.

From beside the checkerboard, Zander saw them and looked at Patrick. "May I be excused, please?"

"Certainly, we will finish this later."

Zander reached the two women and clasped both their hands as they crossed the hall and started up the stairs. "I have things to show you too, Miss Elizabeth."

"No spiders, young man," Annabelle warned him.

"No spiders."

Patrick rejoined the others in front of the picture window. "Zander has been practicing his drawing. I think he wants Elizabeth to see his portfolio."

"He was doing well, even before we left. Don't let me forget I have a book of animals for him." Celwyn poured more tea and inhaled the steam. In the street outside, a coach went by, its window curtains drawn. The sight reminded him of the cat-and-mouse games they'd played with their pursuers when they first arrived in Prague.

"Yes, he is," Patrick agreed. "On a different front, I should tell you how grateful we are that you returned safely: Zander needs the variety of lessons you can provide." He shrugged. "I can give lessons on field strategy, but little more."

"And bravery," Celwyn inserted.

Kang said, "And eventually, how to shoot and use weapons."

"Eventually. Annabelle has been teaching most of the lessons, and now she will be able to concentrate on the wedding." Patrick tugged on his lip and frowned.

"You look pensive," Kang told him.

"Does it show?" He ran a hand through his pale hair. "Apparently so." He hesitated. "I wanted to give you time to settle in, but—what the hell." He walked to the doorway and back. "That vampire, Mrs. Karras, attempted to speak to Annabelle a few days ago."

Celwyn's temper flared, and the crystals on the chandelier above them shook.

Patrick noticed his reaction and rushed into the story with his hand up. "There was no actual contact. Edward saw the woman, too. We were waiting in the coach in front of the dressmakers on Farni Street and jumped out of it to help just as Annabelle turned to get away from her."

"Then what happened?" the automat asked.

"Mrs. Karras saw us. She snarled and said we would see her again." Patrick sighed. "Then she kicked Edward hard enough to knock him down and ran. When the vampire disappeared into the crowd, I stayed with Annabelle. She was hysterical."

Celwyn cursed, and the chandelier swung as violently as if they'd just experienced an earthquake; he should have killed Mrs. Karras months ago.

"Do you remember when we first met her, what she told us?" he asked.

"Yes." The Professor looked out the window and back. "She said she wanted Annabelle. She called her a 'morsel.'"

Celwyn growled. "We need to find Mrs. Karras." He started to rise, but Kang blocked him.

"No." The automat turned to Patrick. "Jonas was wounded twice on our journey. It would be prudent if either you or I went with him in pursuit of Mrs. Karras."

"I am not afraid of her," Patrick told them and threw his shoulders back. "I am still very fit."

"You have retained your bronzed complexion from Punjab, too," Celwyn said with a smile as he edged around Kang. "Don't tell Annabelle I said so, but she appears a mite ghostly compared to you."

"Jonas!" Kang rolled his eyes and faced Patrick. "The last time I saw you confront Mrs. Karras, she stood on your chest, and you couldn't breathe."

"I know, but..."

"Really, this is unnecessary." Celwyn patted the air. "I can handle a vampire."

"Normally, yes, you can." Kang herded the magician away from the door. "You know I am right. If Bartholomew were here, he'd insist one or both of us go, also."

The magician sat back down and picked up his tea. "Indeed, he would." Celwyn subsided. For now.

"Let us stay in tonight," Patrick said. "Both Annabelle and Elizabeth would be highly annoyed if we left the house on your first night back, especially if they found out why."

Celwyn and the Professor exchanged a look of agreement.

"Not to mention that Zander will be very interested in where you are until Bartholomew is back," Patrick told them. "You two will again be a big part of his day, not just his lessons."

"All right, all right," Celwyn conceded. "But when anyone leaves the house, they will need extra protection." He stood up again. "I will confer with Edward about it."

Chapter 45

Annabelle held open the door to her parlor. Elizabeth entered and exclaimed, "My, what a beautiful room! I love the soft blues and greens." As she crossed to the windows overlooking the backyard, she admired the antique buffet and tables. "Silk is my favorite." She fingered the drapes.

"Mine, too." As Annabelle gestured to the matching sofas in front of the window, she pulled on a braided rope to summon the upstairs maid. "I hope you'll be just as comfortable in the suite above us. It is quite large, and I had your husband's collection of books moved to the tower room so that you'll have a free hand in making the rooms your own."

The maid arrived, red-cheeked, round-faced, and cap askew atop a mess of curls. She curtsied at Annabelle and bestowed a second curtsy on Elizabeth. "My name is Flossie, Mam."

"Pleased to meet you. I am Mrs. Elizabeth Kang."

Annabelle said, "We would love some tea, please, but do not rush."

After a nod that caused her cap to nearly fall off, Flossy gave them another curtsy and bustled out. As Annabelle watched her, she said, "I got so used to doing without a maid while we traveled here, I still usually do most things myself." She grinned at Elizabeth. "It scandalizes Mrs. Thomas' society sensibilities."

"I'm the same way. I like to be busy." Elizabeth sighed. "And I am so happy to be off that damn train." Her hat tilted as she imitated swaying from side to side in the rail car.

Annabelle laughed. "Everything will settle down now that everyone is here." She lowered her voice and checked the door. "I have a secret."

Elizabeth glanced at the door too and leaned forward, "Do tell."

"While the Professor, Bartholomew, and Uncle Celwyn were enjoying themselves on the way to Singapore, I did something I'd been wanting to do."

"What?"

"You know that I have funds?" Annabelle asked, with a twinkle in her eye worthy of Qing when he misbehaved.

"Yes?"

"I am wealthy. Indecently so."

Elizabeth beamed, enjoying the confidence. "Jonas said something about that it made you rather bold and increased your hat purchases."

"It is true." Annabelle looked at the door again and whispered, "Bold I am. I bought this house from the lessee."

"Wonderful!"

"We will be able to do whatever we want here, and I want a flower garden that I plant myself!"

Elizabeth clapped her hands. "This is delightful news. But why is it a secret?"

"Because I didn't ask anyone, such as my betrothed. And women usually aren't allowed to make such a large purchase without permission from someone. Except, in my case, I paid the price in full. So, other than a few sputters and blushes, it is done." She frowned. "Normally, as a group, we usually confer on big decisions. Of course, when it is about danger, then the men try to keep me in the dark."

"I understand that more than you know."

Annabelle nodded with a spark of irritation lighting her eyes. "In this case, I am certain that Bartholomew, Uncle Celwyn, or your husband would have tried to pay for it. It is time I paid for something." She smiled like a shrewd horse trader and then shrugged. "They will eventually find out and approve—I put the title in all of our names."

"What a lovely idea. I know they'll be pleased." Elizabeth smiled. "I wouldn't mind planting an herb garden myself."

Flossie arrived with a tray and tripped on the threshold. The china rattled, but nothing spilled as she continued into the room. "'Scuse me, ma'am." She set the tray on the table and jumped again as Zander came in on the run, nearly knocking her over.

"Apologize, please." Annabelle eyed him with a pointed look.

The boy balanced a large folder in his arms but managed to bow and say, "I am very sorry."

Flossy ruffled his curls and departed, again tripping over the threshold.

"What do you have there, Master Zander?" Elizabeth asked him.

"My drawings!" He laid them on the table between the women.

As they began to admire the artwork, Elizabeth asked, "What will Patrick do now that he is out of the army?"

"Ah," Annabelle lowered her voice. "It isn't set in stone yet, but he is leaning toward politics. He has some serious ideas and opinions on the city's future." She laughed, thought about it, and laughed more. "How we'll keep the assortment of enemies that Uncle Celwyn, and your husband, attract quiet during an election will be interesting and," she grinned, "completely their problem."

Chapter 46

THE NEXT DAY DAWNED RAINY AND cold, flooding the magician's bedroom with weak light like he had woken inside a dream.

"Such a contrast to Tehran," Celwyn told Qing as they stood in front of his bureau, and he tied his tie. "Today, we have several things to do, and I don't think Mrs. Thomas is in a mood for you, so," he tapped his shoulder, and the mechanical bird hopped up, "You will go with us."

Zander waited for him at the foot of the stairs, wide awake and dressed in mismatched clothes.

Celwyn was pleased to see him. As he straightened the boy's tie, he said, "It is nice to be home."

"I am very happy you came back." Zander smiled wide. "The Professor says he has lesson plans from Bartholomew for me, too." As they walked down the hall to the parlor, the banging of pots and pans, along with excitable voices, filtered to them from the kitchen. The boy leaned close to whisper, "I think we're having kippers for breakfast."

They settled on the sofa, and within a few minutes, Jackson brought in the coffee and tea services. A freshly shaven Patrick arrived right behind him. "Good morning, good morning."

"You are chipper this early," Celwyn said. "I think I'm still getting used to not being jostled from the train."

"I'm always up early," Patrick said. "Until we're married, my room is next to Annabelle's. My beloved snores like an army horse, and I can hear every snort." He poured coffee and added several spoons of sugar. "You haven't said much about your adventures on your trip."

Celwyn caught his eye and indicated Zander, who had opened a book with a big yawn. "We had a wonderful, uneventful journey."

Patrick winked. "That is nice. What is on the agenda today?"

"The Professor wants to visit his favorite bookstore. I need to visit the tea shop."

"Are books and tea all you expect to find?" He glanced at the boy. "I will be happy to accompany you."

Celwyn shook his head no and didn't mention he would feel better if one of them stayed behind to guard the house, instead asking, "By chance, has a package labeled *Archeology Specimens. Do not open.* arrived?" His supply of peyote needed immediate replenishment.

"Not that I remember. Mrs. Thomas would know."

The magician nodded and regarded Patrick. "Have you met Francesca and her coven?"

Patrick's eyes widened, half in fear, half with curiosity. "I have heard about her from Edward and Bartholomew. I don't think a man who is betrothed would discourage their boldness."

"Agreed. However, the information about your encounter with Mrs. Karras a few days ago might be of interest to them." This was the best the magician could do with little ears close by. "Francesca will want to avenge her daughter's death."

Patrick nodded. "If I were to visit, it would be best if I had a chaperone."

"That might be one of our errands today; we'll see." Celwyn shrugged. "Tell me about the other events here, please?"

Patrick pursed his lips and glanced at Zander before speaking quietly. "In the middle of the night, I found an intruder trying to get in the side door by the kitchen. My bedroom is directly above. This occurred about two weeks ago, before the incident with Mrs. Karras."

Zander looked up and said, "I heard Captain Patrick yelling, so I ran downstairs to scare off the burglar." He went back to reading his book as if a midnight intruder breaking into their home was an everyday occurrence.

The magician inhaled and held it until he could control his annoyance: this wasn't good. "He can't hear us anymore. Go ahead," Celwyn told Patrick.

"Thank you. It appeared the protection spell from the witches worked very well. The door was not damaged."

"What did the burglar look like?" Celwyn had a suspicion he wouldn't like the answer.

Patrick shot a glance at the top of Zander's head. "Exactly like the unwanted visitors that night at the Opera House."

Vampires, Celwyn deduced. He measured his voice. "After luncheon, the Professor and I will pay a visit to Francesca after all. Edward will drive us, and it would be best if you remained here." He saw Patrick's expression and added, "Mrs. Thomas is formidable, but Edward will be with us, the women would be unprotected, and ultimately you are more than capable of defending our castle if needed. Once Bartholomew returns, we'll again divide up the protection duties."

Patrick nodded and said, "I should be here to play with Zander, too." His expression belied his words, displaying a measure of seriousness, not playfulness. The magician suspected he itched to confront Mrs. Karras again. Celwyn understood: who wouldn't?

As Edward jiggled the reins and the carriage pulled away from Tellyhouse, the rain increased. Celwyn watched the clouds above them for a moment and asked, "What did Elizabeth say when you told her where we were going?" A robust breeze buffeted the cab, amused at the question.

"Stop smirking." Kang pretended to glare but couldn't. "Just what you would think. Annabelle had already told her all the lascivious details about Francesca and the coven. My wife is not happy and wanted to come with us. Stop laughing. I almost didn't get away."

Celwyn tried to look sympathetic.

Then Kang's face changed as realization dawned. "Ah ha! That is what you wanted. To go without me!"

"Would I do such a thing?" The magician chuckled. "Regardless, I think it best to visit the coven as early in the afternoon as possible, while some of them are still sleeping from their nighttime revelry. With Edward driving us, we will be able to make a quick getaway if needed. He brought his firearm."

"That certainly saves having to excessively bribe unwilling carriage drivers."

Their coach hit a puddle as big as the carriage sending tall sprays of water behind them like an aquatic peacock tail. Edward kept the horses moving at a good clip, probably so they wouldn't see more of the standing water and balk.

They continued down Konevova Street and turned toward the darker, more bohemian part of the city. Even during the middle of the day, it seemed gloomier because of the tall buildings crowding the avenue. On several corners, groups of men smoked under the eaves of century-old structures and stared long and hard at them as they drove by.

"When we visited the witches before, I thought our carriage driver's reluctance to venture onto this street was because of the reputation of the coven."

The Professor studied the neighborhood as they pulled to the curb. "Now, I am not as sure."

During the day, Francesca's house seemed just as impressive as at night with a full moon behind it. Three stories high and painted a brilliant blue, it leaned to the right with its dozens of darkened windows, looking very much like eyes watching the unwary.

They descended from the coach to the street. "Edward, please keep your firearm handy." Kang opened his umbrella and attained the walkway behind Celwyn, calling back, "There are stories of 'unusual' animals and entities in this area, not just about the witches."

"We will be about a half hour." Celwyn maintained a serious face. "Of course, we will send your regards to the witches."

Edward grunted, tipped his hat over his eyes, and settled his short rifle across his lap. "I'm sure they will regret missing an opportunity to become more familiar with me."

The magician chuckled as they passed by the strange-looking statues with black marks still lining the walkway to the house. In daylight, they reminded him of primitive soldiers, diminutive and somewhat phallic-like. All around them, a thick layer of silence covered everything as they climbed onto the porch.

While Celwyn knocked, Kang surveyed the street. "I can't see any pedestrians or signs that anyone lives in the other houses here. Can you?"

"No," Celwyn said, "but a curtain just moved in the window of that white house to the right. Francesca's domicile is well-monitored."

"As it should be, considering the inhabitants." Kang knocked. "This time, I stay with you. Don't leave me. Like I said, Elizabeth would not be amused if she smells another woman on me." The automat knocked again.

"I won't. Francesca will know you are here anyhow."

A very sleepy and annoyed witch answered the door. She stood as tall as she was round. From under a fringe of black hair, she squinted at them like they might be selling bibles. Beyond her ample rear, a dozen or more women slumbered so soundly they didn't even twitch when Qing stuck his head out of Celwyn's coat and squawked. It must have been a memorable night of debauchery. One of the witches slept with her head inside the band's tuba, while another lay face-first across the piano keys.

"Good afternoon. We're here to see Francesca. We will show ourselves upstairs." Celwyn walked around her. Kang followed so closely that he almost trod on his heel. The fat witch remained in the doorway, still holding the door open. It slammed as Celwyn stepped over a comatose old man wrapped in a purple robe, blocking the bottom of the staircase. Just as Kang went by, the man grabbed the automat's ankle and sat up.

"Who are you?" he croaked.

While Kang disengaged his leg and scampered up the staircase, the magician leaned over the rail, noting the nicotine-stained skeletal fingers and odor of hemp that wafted from the man in unseen clouds. His eyes had a murky appearance as if they did not have irises. Celwyn caught Kang's attention and mouthed the word "blind." Xiau nodded.

"We're here to see Francesca," Celwyn said and started up the next flight. They had nearly made it to the top when the man spoke again.

"Magician."

Celwyn froze and turned.

The man in the robe got to his feet slowly, as thin as a wraith, and toothless. Celwyn stared and shook his head. To Kang he said, "I do not recognize the voice, let us continue."

"You should be dead by now, Magician."

A dagger sailed by Celwyn's ear and embedded itself into the wall behind them. Another blade flew toward them, and Celwyn stopped it inches from the automat's metallic chest. The magician whirled and threw a large net over the old man. As he struggled to free himself, Celwyn told the automat, "Hurry!"

They ran up the remaining stairs to the third floor, and Celwyn didn't bother to knock on Francesca's door. He just opened it and propelled Kang inside in front of him, locking the door behind them.

Across the room, Francesca sat behind her desk like a queen on her throne, looking put upon and interrupted. Nothing had changed since the magician had last been here: her white-gold hair still curled like a meringue dessert, ascending in layers high atop her head and the long swan-like neck that graced her shoulders. The same black eyes snapped at Celwyn with irritation.

"What do you and your tin man want?" She tapped a be-ringed finger on the papers in front of her. "I'm busy."

Celwyn ushered Xiau to the other guest chair and sat down. He crossed his legs, at ease and not in a hurry.

"Good afternoon, Francesca. This is Professor Kang." He nodded toward the stairs. "Who is the old man who just tried to kill us?"

She smiled what Celwyn considered her malevolent but entertained smile. He had known her long enough to see many of her moods and the consequences. "You'll have to be more specific. Many people want you dead."

Celwyn said, "Purple robe, blind, shaved head. Will that do?"

Francesca's brows rose in puzzlement. "It could be McQueen." She shrugged. "Get out. I'm busy."

Kang said in an aside, "We need to get this over with before Elizabeth comes looking for me."

"I can imagine." Celwyn turned to the witch. "We arrived back in Prague yesterday."

"I know."

Celwyn didn't ask how. "And we're very appreciative of the spells you have been maintaining on Tellyhouse." He noticed the paperwork on the witch's desk had increased since his last visit. Hopefully, she didn't throw her fountain pen at him this time. "We're here for more of your services."

"Well, you should have said so sooner," Francesca retorted as she crossed to the bar in the corner and brought back a bottle of wine and glasses. "How can I help you?"

"You remember Mrs. Karras?"

Francesca's avarice-fueled smile vanished, and she cursed. "That vampire will fry in hell for killing my daughter." She cursed again and uncorked the wine. "Have you found her?"

Kang said, "She found us." He watched as she poured. "She sent one of her men to our house. Tellyhouse."

"Your spell held. There was no entry," Celwyn assured her.

Francesca no longer listened, instead, she stared at the framed picture on her desk. After a long moment, she downed her wine and said, "I loved my daughter. Those vampires killed her to get to you, Jonas. Bastard." A tear slid downward, leaving a trail through the powder on her cheek.

Celwyn would normally dread facing a grief-stricken mother—and he even more regretted speaking with a dangerous witch in mourning. However, Tellyhouse again faced dangers and needed her help. "I know, and I am grateful that you do not blame me. I want to avenge Christina as much as you do." He swallowed several times as Francesca's emotion infected him also. "I believe ... that I was falling in love with her."

Francesca poured another glass, once again, for herself. "Damn vampires." She drank the wine and growled, "What do you suggest? I haven't been able to find that Karras woman." From the floor below came a few toots of a horn and a guitar twanged as the resident band came to life.

"I've been thinking about it. We will use me as bait." Celwyn made sure he had solid contact with her eyes. "I will let you have the kill."

"Damn right you will," she said and raised the bottle to her lips. "Is that it? What else did you want?"

"A few more of your witches as added protection for my household staff. If anyone leaves Tellyhouse on errands, have the witches close enough to protect them," the magician said. "There will also be other instances where they will be needed."

Francesca sat again, leaned back in her chair, and regarded them down her nose. "That handsome man Bartholomew did not return with you."

"No, he did not," Kang said.

"I understand you also had a series of deaths on your journey. Not from vampires." She stared at Celwyn. "Who did you irritate now?" Qing stuck his head out of the magician's coat and quivered with excitement as she picked up her gold fountain pen and played with it.

"Yes, we had several murders." Kang studied her. "It is amazing how much you've discovered in a short time."

Francesca raised a penciled brow and gazed back at them.

"To continue," Celwyn said, "I haven't figured out how we will trap Mrs. Karras and her followers, but we will let you know."

Francesca's eyes grew harder until they resembled pebbles. Or rabbit droppings. "You'll tell me when you are close. We've spotted them several times, but they are quick, as you know."

Celwyn told her, "I do. Again, I am sorry for your loss."

Qing finished his escape and hopped onto the witch's desk. He strutted around her inkwell and approached her hand.

"I am very fond of Qing, Francesca."

It could be the bird had no idea of how dangerous the situation was or didn't care. He eyed the witch, took another step closer, and then pecked at one of her rings. Celwyn scooped him up and slipped him back inside his coat. "What is your fee for the extra help and enhancing the spell on Tellyhouse?"

She said through her teeth, "Next time, Bird." When she stood, her mood changed, and the magician didn't like her smile. "Nothing extravagant."

"What is it?"

The witch leaned over her desk, treating them to a view of her cleavage. "I want an invitation to Miss Annabelle's wedding." She laughed at their surprise as she crossed the room and held the door open. "The old man downstairs has been suitably distracted, but I'd hurry if I were you."

Chapter 47

DUSK SET UNDER A HEAVY CLOUD bank, blurring the glory of the Tellyhouse rose garden. Celwyn stood in front of the parlor window, missing Bartholomew and marveling at Francesca's network of spies. Kang had speculated upon it all the way home, but he'd mainly concentrated on the identity of the old man in the purple robe. Celwyn told him he knew of no one named McQueen who wanted to kill him.

Kang said, "That man, blind or not, used our voices to locate us when he threw the knives."

Before Celwyn could reply, Elizabeth arrived with her embroidery and Zander. She sat beside her husband and asked, "Did you have a good afternoon?"

"Yes, dear. We had time for school, too. It was Otto's first mathematics class. According to Zander, his new friend enjoyed the classroom very much."

From beside him, Zander said, “As a reward for our hard work, we should visit the zoo. Otto will like it.”

That suggestion fit with Celwyn’s plan. Being visible throughout the city would attract the vampires. Mrs. Karras wasn’t shy.

“We will take a day off from school,” he told the boy as the Lenskirsch clock in the dining room started chiming. Celwyn loved that clock and admired its intricate details. It must have taken scores of hours to build. With an assessing eye on Xiau, he bet the insides of the automat looked similar.

“Don’t you have class starting right now?” Outside Tellyhouse, the rain began, and any hope the magician had of a splendid sunset evaporated.

“Yes! Excuse me, please.” Zander ran out of the room.

“Tomorrow, we will visit the zoo after breakfast, and of course, have lunch in town.” Celwyn started for the door. “I’ll let Ricardo know.”

“Ha. Just an excuse to sniff around and see what is for dinner,” Kang called after him.

Celwyn turned Kang’s nose a bright blue before he left the room. It would fade in a few minutes, hopefully after Elizabeth saw it and enjoyed it. None of his magic could be more than superficial with an automat, but he could decorate him. When the magician entered the kitchen, he inhaled the aroma of warm bread and spied Ricardo fluttering between steaming pots and holding an upraised spoon like a culinary Merlin with his wand.

"It smells divine in here," Celwyn said, bowing a greeting to Jenny, the young woman in an apron and a collection of freckles who stood off to the side inspecting turnips. "What are we having?"

"Baked turkey, and for dessert, a sweet soufflé," Ricardo replied as he stirred a pot. "We need to make another trip to the market very soon."

The other scullery maid, Gretta, with her cheery smile and dimples, leaned over a table peeling potatoes.

"If you can trust us, we would be happy to fulfill a list for you tomorrow. We're planning an outing to the marketplace. We won't be here for luncheon." Zander would not be happy when they postponed the zoo. Thankfully, it was Xiau's turn to deliver bad news. The magician selected a carrot. "Perhaps you could leave us a cold supper and let the staff have the entire day off to themselves tomorrow."

"They would enjoy that." Ricardo checked the door leading to the hall. "But Mrs. Thomas may object."

"I will speak with her. I want everyone to have more than one day off if possible." Celwyn chewed. "I also have a request."

"Anything, Sir." Ricardo handed Celwyn a spoon.

As he tasted the soup, the magician murmured, "Heavenly." He hated to spoil the mood, but it had to be done. "We are again beset by disgruntled vampires. When the staff leaves the house, it is best that they do so in pairs." He savored the spoonful he'd just swallowed. "My congratulations, a very nice combination of flavors." He saw Ricardo bite his lip and hurried to add, "We hope to shortly rid ourselves of the vermin permanently."

Ricardo glanced at the door that led to the household office and asked with a nervous glint in his eye, "Does Mrs. Thomas know of the vampires? I haven't heard her talk of them."

"Err, no." The magician thought a moment, beginning to wonder if their chef was more afraid of Mrs. Thomas than the vampires. "I will tell her it is an insane criminal who escaped from the Azyl Sieber asylum. I drove by there the other day; it may be more believable for her." He returned the spoon to Ricardo, and his stomach growled in disappointment. "The plan is to instill vigilance without terrifying everyone."

"I understand."

The magician avoided the creak on the right side of the thirteenth stair step and approached the open door of the classroom. Neither Zander nor Annabelle noticed him, but Otto did, and his eyes lit up.

"'Jumping' is a verb." Annabelle tapped the blackboard with a wooden stick. In chalk, she had written the word in both English and Deutsch.

"What is 'jumping?'" Zander asked. From beside him, Otto wrote on his tablet. Zander leaned close enough to read it and said, "Oh, I see."

"It looks like Uncle Celwyn is here early for our geography lesson." Annabelle rubbed her temples. To Otto, she said, "Bartholomew usually does this lesson, but Uncle Celwyn volunteered until everything is back to normal." She patted them both on the head and hurried out.

"I did not volunteer as much as be persuaded by the others," the magician murmured to himself as he took Annabelle's place at the desk. In front of him, the boys traded kicks from under their desks. As he watched them, the situation with Mrs. Karras weighed on his mind.

"Today, we will learn defense instead of geography."

On the chalkboard, he wrote:

RUN.
FIGHT.
TALK.

"If you are in danger, which do you choose?"

They looked at each other. Otto wrote, "*Run.*"

"Yes," Celwyn said, "but it depends on the situation. Sometimes you must fight. Sometimes you can talk your way out of a bad spot. However, it is better not to be in a bad position in the first place."

"Like falling in a lake?" Zander asked.

"Yes or walking down a dark alley. What else?"

They discussed dangerous situations until Celwyn asked Zander, "Do you remember the genie-man?"

Zander instantly sobered as if all the lights had been turned off in his world. "I remember Telly." He turned to Otto. "She died. The genie-man made her die."

Otto signaled his sympathy with big dark eyes.

"The friends of the genie man are back. They are dangerous," Celwyn told them.

The boys blinked and exchanged wary glances.

"So, let's figure out what they look like and what you'll do if you see one of them. Does that sound good?"

Zander said, "Yes!"

A half-hour later, Mrs. Thomas arrived red-faced and out of breath at the classroom door. She goggled when she saw the boys wrestling on the carpet, with Celwyn sitting cross-legged beside them, offering advice.

"Kick as hard as you can. You want to get away from whoever has you." Celwyn leaned closer to them. "Who should you be afraid of?"

"Bad ... men," Zander panted as he rolled away from Otto and into the desk.

"Exactly. But it could be anyone who means you harm—"

"Mr. Celwyn!" Mrs. Thomas stamped her foot. "We're hearing terrible noises coming from this room."

Celwyn turned around. "My apologies." He got to his feet. The boys scooted around a highly unamused housekeeper. With a bow of apology, the magician led the way to the door, "We'll move class to the tower." He hooked a finger at the boys. "Come along."

Chapter 48

By the time they set off the next morning, the sun had not appeared, preferring to hide behind banks of high clouds. Zander had insisted that Otto accompany them, and Edward approved since the horses would be out all day pulling the carriage. Kang and Celwyn had agreed that they would have made the suggestion, if Zander hadn't.

Across from the magician, Elizabeth and Annabelle sat together, discussing the merits of ivory or white satin for the bows around the wedding flowers. Zander wrinkled his nose and pointed out the toy store as they clattered across cobblestones and onto Plzenska Street. They drew closer to the market and bazaar, and more carriages filled the street.

"I wish Xiau had wanted to go with us," Elizabeth complained, "instead of working on his papers."

"I concur. Patrick didn't want to go with us either." Annabelle asked Celwyn, "What all is on our list from Ricardo? I hope it includes a good ham."

Celwyn extracted the list from his pocket and deduced Qing had been chewing on it. The bird saw Elizabeth and squawked a greeting.

"He has always liked me," she confided to the magician. "Nonetheless, I agree with Xiau that you spoil him."

"He just needs entertainment." Celwyn smiled. "But to our business, the boys have brought along a wagon for our purchases at the bazaar." He looked over the list. "I'm not so sure we'll find everything, but we can try. Yes, I see ham on the list."

As they walked along the first row of the market's vendors, Elizabeth and Annabelle made faces and informed Celwyn that the produce could be better. Before they left the house, Kang had mentioned that the third aisle of merchants had a reputation for better quality. Celwyn led the way to the third row, the boys and wagon trailing close behind and the women bringing up the rear.

The magician had spotted several of Francesca's witches on the fringe of the crowd, there one minute and gone the next. Some of them had a unique appearance, such as the extraordinarily tall one, quite bald and wearing large hoop earrings and a flower necklace. Most of the other witches blended into the flock of shoppers as easily as another house frau.

Celwyn had made his own arrangements just in case the witches were not enough to keep everyone safe while he was kept busy by the vampires. Annabelle and the others in their party were unaware that instead of staying home, Kang had taken a hired carriage and followed them at a discreet distance as they shopped. If the vampires dared approach them, between the witches and other precautions, they would be surprised. If nothing happened, then they would have at least helped Ricardo with his supplies.

When they reached the bins of apples, Annabelle stood between Celwyn and Elizabeth, making selections.

"Are you going to continue the wrestling lessons with Zander and Otto?" Annabelle asked as she moved to another apple vendor.

"Yes." Celwyn accepted his change and said, "They need to be alert to danger and survive an attack. When we found Otto, he didn't know what to do when a pack of ruffians attacked him. He appeared very frightened."

"I understand. Look at them," Annabelle said. The boys giggled and whispered together. "Otto may be five years older, but he is still as much a child as Zander."

Celwyn watched them for several moments. "Almost like a brother, wouldn't you say?"

Annabelle's face lit up. "I know what you are thinking." She observed the boys as they led Elizabeth toward the fresh greens. "They play like brothers and could easily become brothers."

Elizabeth heard them and lowered her voice. "It is a splendid idea; Zander needs someone his own size to grow up with and to talk to, and Otto needs a family to show him love."

An hour later, they'd reached the end of the bazaar and began to backtrack against the crowd toward the carriage park. Otto towed the wagon full of their purchases while Zander pushed it from behind. While they walked, Annabelle held Ricardo's list under her nose and read it with a frown.

"The butcher will be next. I really hate going there," she sighed.

Celwyn didn't have to ask why; they both remembered from only a few months ago how Telly reacted to the bloody carcasses in the shop window on the day she died. "I don't blame you."

Just ahead, the boys slowed to allow a family to pass in front of them. Celwyn tapped Zander on the shoulder, "When you two are tired, I will pull the wagon."

Otto heard him and shook his head.

Celwyn bowed. "Carry on."

Annabelle elbowed him. "Look how happy Zander is."

The magician turned to see if he could spy Kang through the throng of shoppers around them but couldn't. They had agreed that if their trap proved unsuccessful, Kang would return to Tellyhouse after the bazaar. No need to unduly alarm Annabelle or Elizabeth.

As they neared the end of the aisle, from one side, a thin man in a dark coat, high boots, and a large hat walked directly toward Zander and Otto. Celwyn's sense of danger escalated, and he closed the few steps between them, inserting himself in front of the boys and wagon.

Enough of the weak sunlight glinted on the knife to warn him. The man feinted to the left and grabbed Zander, lifting him off his feet. Celwyn dissolved the knife just as Otto jumped on the man's back. His big hat went flying as they fell on top of Zander, and so did Otto. Annabelle screamed.

The magician flung the man off Zander and cursed as the attacker whirled and kicked Celwyn in his side, in the sword wound that hadn't yet healed. He grabbed the man, but instead of a fist, nails raked his face. The magician cursed as he found himself looking into Mary Giovanna's crazed eyes. She swung Zander into Celwyn hard. The boy cried out as the magician caught him.

"You will all *die*!" she screamed and ran into the crowd. In the next second, and contrary to how he usually handled attacks, Celwyn decided not to follow her—he couldn't leave the boys crying, afraid, and hurt. The magician knelt beside them.

Kang arrived as Elizabeth and Annabelle did, sliding to a stop between the boys and gathering them to him. "Are you all right?"

Otto shook his head, shaking like a leaf in the wind. Zander showed him a torn and bloody sleeve. "It doesn't hurt!" His lip trembled.

Celwyn heard him and cursed again. "To the carriage. Now..." He grabbed the wagon handle and gestured to the women. "After you."

The automat held each of the boys' hands as they followed Annabelle and Elizabeth to the carriage. The women fretted over Otto and Zander's arm as they climbed inside. Celwyn motioned Edward closer to inform him of the reappearance of Mary Giovanna and noted Edward's dark frown as he tossed their packages into the jump seat behind the cab. When he finished, Edward walked around the carriage with his pistol at his side, staring at the crowd, before climbing into the driver's seat.

The magician held Kang's arm so he wouldn't follow Otto into the carriage.

"What did you see?" he asked.

Kang rubbed his face hard. "I saw that woman as she moved purposely toward you. I ran..." he growled a choice word, "to you. But I was too late."

"Well, we certainly were successful in flushing out our enemy. Just not the one we expected." Celwyn studied the crowd. "And with consequences." He wondered how far away Mary had run.

"Why didn't you chase her?" Kang asked.

"I was worried about the boys more," Celwyn said.

"You have changed."

The magician said nothing. His side ached from where she kicked him. He covered the pain so the automat wouldn't notice.

Elizabeth tapped the glass. Kang held up a hand and told Celwyn, "Go on."

"Crazy Mary followed us here, but *why*?" The magician's anger caused the nearby awning to fly upward violently. "She must have been on the next train north out of Tehran after murdering Ludvik."

Annabelle leaned out of the carriage. "Professor! Uncle Celwyn—we need to go back to the house."

"I have numbed Zander's arm until you patch him up." Celwyn nodded at her, and she withdrew again.

"Thank you." The automat cast a worried look inside the carriage. "The attack shows Mary has no conscience. She tried to hurt a child! What's more, Otto looked just as terrified. Although he acquitted himself very bravely." Kang kicked the carriage tire, cursed, and kicked it again. "Bloody hell! Come on."

They climbed into the carriage. Annabelle still fussed over Zander's arm. As he settled next to Otto, Celwyn hugged him and said, "You both did very well. You were brave. We'll have another wrestling lesson this afternoon."

He noticed instead of fear in Otto's eyes, the boy seemed angry. As if he might have recognized Crazy Mary from her time on the train? Or something simpler ... angry because she had attacked his new friend, Zander?

Twenty minutes later, they rode past the long rows of roses and up the driveway to Tellyhouse.

When Mrs. Thomas heard of the attack, she handed what remained of Ricardo's list to Sully and sent him out. Everyone waited in the parlor until she stomped back inside with a forbidding look on her face and her hands on her hips.

"I put Abe on the front door until Mr. Sully returns." She glared at all of them, no favorites.

"That poor boy! I don't know what is going on, but I don't like it. Not at all."

Qing chose that moment to fly off the armoire straight at her.

She bellowed, "*Stop that*!"

Qing detoured across the room to Celwyn and burrowed into his coat.

Annabelle started to laugh and thought better of it, putting a hand in front of her face.

"Mrs. Thomas…" Elizabeth began.

The housekeeper advanced into the room, the floor vibrating with her every step. She said to Zander, "Come with me, young man. You are going to rest." The boy looked ready to object but followed her out of the room as Qing emerged far enough out of the magician's collar to squawk at her.

Celwyn did laugh, but quietly. Kang tried not to but couldn't help it, giggling into Celwyn's shoulder.

"You two!" Elizabeth exclaimed. "Do you know how hard it is to find someone of Mrs. Thomas' caliber to run a household? No, you don't."

Celwyn tamped the air with both hands, trying to calm her. "We apologize."

"Where is Otto?" Annabelle asked.

"He is upstairs studying in the classroom," Patrick said.

"I didn't bring it up because I didn't want to frighten Zander, but exactly what happened out there?" Patrick asked from his position in front of the windows. He'd been monitoring the street ever since they arrived. "It was a very uneventful day here."

Kang said, "Prince Leo's daughter, Mary Giovanna, has arrived in Prague. She attacked Zander."

"No, it was a man that we saw," Elizabeth objected as she sat on the sofa beside Annabelle.

"You were farther away." Celwyn held up a hand. "Mary Giovanna likes to dress in men's clothes … when she wears clothes at all."

Annabelle's mouth dropped open, as did Elizabeth's. Patrick's brow went up, and he controlled his relief, glad he didn't have to explain this time.

The magician checked the hallway for listeners and returned. "As you know from our letters, Prince Leo and his daughter traveled with us part of the way to Singapore."

Annabelle favored the whiskey bottle with a longing look while Elizabeth bestowed a speculative gaze on the Professor. The magician sent Annabelle a glass and watched the automat squirm as he realized what Celwyn intended to do. "We haven't found a good time to tell you about this, and we wanted to deal with it without upsetting you or disrupting your wedding plans."

Kang cleared his throat. "About a week after we left Prague, one of our porters was murdered."

"Oh, no!" Annabelle exclaimed.

The automat raised his voice. "There is more. When we reached Tehran, Prince Leo was also murdered in a similar way." He looked at the magician and carried on. "It was Mary Giovanna, his daughter. We'd witnessed her erratic behavior before the murders, and after she dispatched her father, we received enough information from our telegraphed inquiries to confirm her murderous activities."

Annabelle appeared speechless. She mouthed, "*His daughter?*" Meanwhile, Patrick joined her and held her hand. She turned a look on him, and he tried a supportive smile, probably assuming he would receive an earful later about sharing information with his betrothed.

"Mary deliberately smeared Prince Leo's blood on the Professor as she escaped. Then she tried to set the police after us for the killing." The magician moved back to his chair and decided he couldn't wait for the staff; in seconds, he had produced a tea service. Explanations were, by definition, tedious, and tea would most definitely help. "Yes, yes. I'll get rid of the teacups as soon as we're done." He poured. "Mrs. Thomas will never know."

"Yes, she will." Kang continued the story, "On the way back to Prague, we discovered Mary Giovanna had remained in Tehran: and the night we arrived there, she murdered Ludvik. He was another one of our porters."

"Why?" Annabelle demanded as she grabbed Patrick's arm again and held on.

"She has a history of suspicious murders in her wake." The automat fished in his pocket, produced a folded telegram, and handed it to her. "We had wired for information about her background, but as I said, we didn't get the information until after Prince Leo was butchered. Or," he sighed, "I should say we didn't read the information until then. There is more. A complication."

The Professor sent Celwyn a look that said it was his turn.

"Fine." With a sigh, the magician said, "Bartholomew was falling in love with the woman. When he came to his senses, she attacked him. He was not badly hurt."

"Thank God." Elizabeth burst out, "And now, she is after *a little boy*?"

"Mary Giovanna is unbalanced. She is out for vengeance against us, mainly Jonas, Bartholomew, and me," Kang said. "We can't predict what she will do."

"Tea?" Celwyn asked them as he poured a second cup. If everyone drank a cup of tea, all discussions would be civilized, no matter the subject. "I have dispatched Edward to visit Francesca. His mission is to see if the witches who were supposed to watch over us this morning saw anything."

An anxious and fearful silence descended over the room.

Patrick said, "I understand that you did not want to disrupt our happy time with these unpleasant occurrences."

"Humph." Annabelle released her fiancé's arm. "And not tell us *anything*." Elizabeth nodded her agreement with the observation.

"I am just as guilty." Kang appealed to them, "I couldn't live with myself if something happened to you."

Elizabeth said, "I understand, but we are stronger than we look."

"Yes, we are." Annabelle slapped the table in front of her.

The automat seemed a bit taken aback, so Celwyn finished what he was probably going to say. "We have also been augmenting the safety of those we love." Too late, he saw the slight shake of Kang's head.

"With the witches?" Annabelle asked.

Kang sighed. "Yes."

"They are probably dangerous, too." Elizabeth frowned but didn't direct it to her husband.

Celwyn sipped his tea. "Usually, they are. However, I have a long history with Francesca, who heads the coven, and she wants revenge for her daughter."

"For what?" Elizabeth asked.

Patrick said, "The same vampires killed her daughter Christina in front of the Opera House just before the Professor and Jonas left for Singapore to retrieve you. The vampires thought Jonas and Christina were close." He eyed Celwyn. "I'm surprised you don't receive a discount price from Francesca for multiple spells."

"I am also," the magician said. "To go on, if any of the staff leaves this house, one of the witches is assigned to protect that person."

"And now, we also must contend with Mary Giovanna," Kang said.

"Crazy Mary, indeed," Annabelle murmured and picked up Patrick's hand again.

"You have no idea." Kang sat up straighter. "If you and Elizabeth wish to hear more, we'll tell you all about what she has done. Most of it is highly unladylike. However, I am beyond trying to protect your sensibilities at the risk of your ire."

Elizabeth kissed his cheek.

Patrick said, "I feel sorry for Zander and Otto. It must have been frightening for them today."

"It was," Elizabeth said. "Did you see how Otto tried to defend Zander? He didn't hesitate."

Annabelle nodded. "They both have been enjoying their 'wrestling' class, as you call it."

"It gives them confidence." Patrick turned back for another look out the window. "And emboldens them."

"Otto enjoys being with us here." Elizabeth raised a knowing brow at Kang and Celwyn.

The two exchanged a silent question, and then the Professor said, "Since the subject has come up, Jonas and I have a proposal for all of you. We know Bartholomew would agree." He crossed to the hallway and checked for any small listeners. "We want to bring Otto into our family."

"Zander needs a brother." Annabelle's face lit up. "I've pondered this, too."

Elizabeth felt their eyes on her and smiled. "There are many reasons to do so." She regarded each of them in turn. "I wonder if we all thought of this at the same time."

"I am in." The relief in Patrick's voice mirrored their thoughts. "The events today show us that Otto needs us. He is a fine upstanding lad."

"Yes, and brave. He is also a very good student and loves to learn." With a glance at the coffee pot, Kang relaxed beside his wife again.

Celwyn poured a cup and floated it to him. "Someday, he will make something of himself, especially with the education we can give him." He sat back in his chair, pleased to hear their reactions. The magician never would have dreamed he could find so much pleasure in the company of the automat and everyone else, and for a moment, wallowed in the new, and very strange sense of family. He doubted society would understand this family and didn't care. All that was missing was Bartholomew.

Annabelle said, "I say we adopt Uncle Celwyn's proposal. Otto is a sweet lad who needs us. He can sleep in Zander's room, so we know where they both are when they get up to shenanigans."

"Is that an American word?" Patrick asked with a smile.

"Yes. Boys are always up to shenanigans," Annabelle told him.

"Then it is settled." The magician announced with a twist of his mustache, "I had so much confidence in your decision, I had already sent the news to Bartholomew in my last letter."

"Oh, you did?" Annabelle fixed him with a mock glare. "What isn't settled is for you, Bartholomew, and the Professor to keep secrets from us just to protect us." She shook her finger at him.

Kang laughed. Soon they all were, and Annabelle laughed with them.

A short time later, Kang, Patrick, and the magician sat at the kitchen table a few feet from the enormous stove Ricardo now called his own. Wisps of smoked brisket swirled around them as Celwyn made a selection from the tea canister, and the Professor nudged a plate of Ricardo's cookies closer. Each time he reached for one, the magician edged the plate back again.

"Thank you for taking time to talk with us," the automat told Ricardo, Mrs. Thomas, and Edward, who had been the last to arrive.

"How was your visit with Francesca?" Celwyn asked Edward. "Did they see the attack?"

Edward smoothed his tie as he glanced at Mrs. Thomas, telegraphing his nervousness around the table. "I escaped with my virtue again." More soberly, he added, "She reports that the witches she assigned to watch over us today have disappeared. The rest of them saw nothing. Francesca is extremely angry..." he swallowed, "at you, Sirs."

"Is she looking for them?" Patrick asked.

"Yes."

Celwyn could imagine Francesca's reaction and felt some responsibility. He frowned, thinking about what Crazy Mary would do, only half-hearing the outraged noises coming from Mrs. Thomas. They escalated to sounding like an outraged mouse stuck in a hole. He couldn't picture Mary capturing one of the witches, but she might kill one of them on impulse or as part of a plan. It had to be Mrs. Karras and her vampires picking the witches off.

"*Witches*?" Mrs. Thomas' voice rose like the squeal of a balloon releasing air. She didn't just disapprove; she didn't believe it.

"Yes, Madam." Kang glowered at Celwyn and pulled the cookie plate to himself. He nibbled a cookie and brushed the crumbs from his shirt.

Edward spoke up before the housekeeper did. "They will continue to protect us when we leave this house. I will do so also." He told Mrs. Thomas, "I'm a crack shot and rarely miss."

Mrs. Thomas demanded, "Protect us from what? And *why* are you talking to witches?"

Edward looked at Celwyn, who attempted charm with as disarming a smile as he had in store.

"Mrs. Thomas, therefore, we are meeting here now to explain that we have enemies." He glanced at Kang, who selected another cookie and bit into it with the satisfaction of knowing the magician had drawn the short straw to explain to Mrs. Thomas. Celwyn had resisted cheating on their wagers up to now, but that might change. He continued, "The Professor and I have asked the local coven to protect us. They are doing so. You haven't noticed they are there, and you won't in the future."

"That is ghastly. Witches! Why can't he..." she aimed a thumb at Edward, "just shoot whoever is bothering you?"

Celwyn kept his best, most persuasive expression in place. "Because sometimes bullets aren't good enough."

"*Excuse me*?" Mrs. Thomas shouted. The windows rattled. She regarded him like she would a butcher offering her day-old fish. Then her expression changed to one of horror. She crossed herself and started to rise. "I don't like this..."

"If it keeps Zander, Miss Annabelle, and everyone safe, you would," Patrick pointed out.

"I would." She sank down again.

Kang said, "We just ask that you do not allow anyone onto the property that you don't know and to be careful."

The housekeeper drew herself up. "No one would dare to bother me."

Celwyn could well believe it. He wouldn't want to be around if Mrs. Thomas became seriously annoyed. He caused the cookie nearest to Kang to inch across the plate.

"Our last piece of business is much more pleasant." Kang snagged the cookie and popped it into his mouth. "We would like to bring Otto into our family. Zander needs a brother, and Otto needs us."

"Ah." Edward nodded with satisfaction. "That is good news."

"We need more cookies," Ricardo announced when he saw the empty cookie plate. While Kang sheepishly shook his head, their chef filled the plate and said, "I had a feeling this would come to pass with Otto. It is very nice to hear."

"He would sleep in Zander's room and go to all of the classes with him," the magician told them.

"To that wrestling class?" Mrs. Thomas crossed her arms over her chest and frowned. "He's going to break his glasses."

"It is all part of their education," Kang said. "Today, what they already learned gave them confidence when confronted with danger."

"I suppose that it is necessary," she grumbled. "But it is not gentlemanly."

"We are proposing that Otto still helps with the horses and that Zander does, also." Celwyn brought the replenished cookie plate closer. He made a selection. Only one, though—dinner would soon be upon them, and he didn't have a receptacle to stuff cookies into like the automat.

Mrs. Thomas gaped. "The *horses*? A proper young man does not ..."

"A young man needs to work and have chores," Celwyn said.

Patrick felt brave enough to say, "I agree, as does Annabelle."

The housekeeper's bottom lip protruded, and she huffed, "It will be the talk of the neighborhood. There are many families in society here."

Celwyn laughed. "If that is the only scandalous attention we receive, we are doing very well, indeed."

"You have no idea. Sir." Mrs. Thomas looked from one to another of them and stood. "All right. I will make the arrangements."

"We appreciate your support and advice," Kang said as he picked crumbs off the cookie plate.

"As you should." She marched to the door and turned. "Again, it is a very ... interesting experience working for you, Sirs." She rolled her eyes. "I certainly cannot say it is boring." She called back after she passed through, "Not at all."

Chapter 49

"I NEED A DRINK," CELWYN ANNOUNCED as they reentered the parlor. Patrick rejoined Annabelle on the sofa and gazed at her as only the love-struck can. Across from them, Elizabeth stared out the window, the embroidery in her lap forgotten.

Celwyn selected a glass from the bar. "Anyone else?"

After receiving a few nods, he sent several glasses across the room and sat beside Annabelle. "Am I forgiven yet?"

She tried not to smile and finally hugged him. "Yes, but I have a comment."

Celwyn sipped and waited. He also thought fast—had he done something he shouldn't have or been caught at something he was thinking of doing? He stopped short of entering her thoughts; she seemed very determined.

"You don't look well." She narrowed her eyes at him. "Why?"

The magician cringed inwardly. "We, uh… forgot to mention…"

Elizabeth saw his discomfort and raised a brow at her husband as if to say, "*Clean up your own mess.*"

The Professor tried. "We were attacked on our journey, and Jonas was hurt. Twice." He saw Annabelle's expression building to an eruption and quickly said, "We have told Patrick, but…"

Annabelle reared back, glowered at Patrick, and then transferred it to the others.

"We didn't want to cause worry…" Patrick began sheepishly.

"Save it, dear," Annabelle growled. "I need a cigarette."

Celwyn made his voice as matter-of-fact as possible. "I received a sword wound from the Russians here," he indicated his left side, "who were after Prince Leo and his stolen rubies."

"And the second injury?" she demanded.

"In Singapore, Captain Nemo's men shot me in the shoulder. At Phileas Fogg's suggestion, mind you." The magician finished his glass and set it down. "The wounds have healed. End of story." It pained him to lie, as much as the wound pained him now, but it wouldn't do to worry the inhabitants of Tellyhouse.

Annabelle asked, "Why did they shoot you?" She transferred a stare to Kang.

Elizabeth's voice held the sarcastic martyrdom Kang used at times. "After dinner, I'll tell you of all of their adventures and the ones that occurred before

I joined the party." She looked at her husband, then Patrick, and finally back to Annabelle. "I thought you'd been brought up to date, but I will make sure that you are." She sent a tolerant look around the room. "After all, someone has to do so."

"Thank you." Annabelle turned to Celwyn. "If this happened over a month ago, why do you look so tired and sickly?"

Kang said, "He is still healing, despite what he says. Plus, today, Crazy Mary kicked him in the side, and I bet right in the wound."

As he spoke, Mrs. Thomas ushered a bewildered-looking Otto into the room. Zander bounded in after them, dodging imaginary obstacles along the way.

"Sit down, please." Annabelle pointed to the chairs in front of the windows. Qing chose that moment to fly off the armoire and circle above them as fast as he could.

Mrs. Thomas glared, said, "I don't see *anything*," and marched out again.

Zander watched their bemused expressions for a moment, then said, "I see Qing! He is our pet."

Celwyn controlled his enjoyment of the moment and asked Zander about his injury from the morning's attack. Ever since they returned home, he had berated himself: he should have been more vigilant. Even more, he regretted not going after Mary after the attack. Although he wouldn't tell the automat, he didn't feel normal, and he hesitated.

"It doesn't hurt." Zander displayed his arm. "When can I take the plaster off?"

"Tomorrow," Annabelle told him. "And you can't get it wet during your bath tonight."

The boy started kicking the chair leg. "All right."

"'All right' what?" Kang asked.

Zander sat up. "All right, ma'am."

Elizabeth said, "Much better. We have good news."

Otto clutched his tablet to his chest and wetted his lips as he watched the exchange.

"Otto," Patrick smiled at him. "We would like you to join our family and be a friend and brother to Zander. Would you like that?"

Otto's eyes watered behind his spectacles. As his first tear fell, he nodded.

"I have a brother!" Zander whooped and started running in circles around the parlor.

Qing landed on Celwyn's shoulder. The magician stroked the bird's back as he said, "We are very fond of you, Otto."

"This is wonderful." Elizabeth patted Otto's shoulder.

Otto wrote on his tablet and handed it to her.

"He asks about the horses." She handed the tablet back. "Both you and Zander will have chores in the stables."

Otto smiled as widely as Zander.

Zander said, "I love horses."

"I sure hope so." Patrick grinned.

Otto wiped his eyes.

Annabelle said, "You'll sleep in Zander's room; it is quite large. And you will have many classes."

"Do you have a favorite subject?" Patrick asked Otto.

The lad wrote fast. Celwyn looked at the result. "Science."

Kang slapped his thigh. "I thought so!"

"As long as I am not drafted to teach mathematics, I will help," Celwyn assured them. "I have a long letter ready for Bartholomew and a telegraph confirming the news."

"Where do you send it?" Patrick asked.

Kang said, "Bartholomew retrieves his messages from Singapore general delivery every week."

Otto handed his tablet to Celwyn again.

Celwyn patted his shoulder. "Yes, we are sure. We want you to be happy here. Study hard, and we will send you to university to learn more and become anything you want to be."

"What is 'university'?" Zander asked.

Otto scribbled fast and handed him the tablet.

Zander scratched his head. "More school. Is it hard?"

"It won't be by the time you are older." Kang stood. "I need to work on your lesson plans." He turned at the door. "Be assured, I will be down for dinner."

"I'm surprised, after all of those cookies." The magician grinned at him, and Elizabeth's eyes widened.

Annabelle addressed the boys, "Tomorrow, we'll order new clothes for you, Otto, and clothes for Zander's new chores at the stables." She pinned them with a look. "All boots will be left in the tack room."

When Otto and Zander started upstairs to organize their room, Celwyn added a minimum of shirts, vests, and trousers to their closet for Otto. Annabelle liked to make decisions about clothing, and he'd learned not to get in the way of that activity.

The magician leaned back and observed the estate grounds through the picture window. The afternoon had grown cold as a strong wind blew through the trees, scattering gold and orange leaves everywhere. Celwyn felt a measure of relief that for this winter, and the ones in the future, Otto would be attired for the weather and sleep in a warm bed. The thought led to other children without places to go. This was one area where he agreed with the church: charity and compassion should be practiced by everyone. Wouldn't it be nice if, once Bartholomew was home again, they opened their own charity to house unwanted children? He didn't worry about Mrs. Thomas' reaction, they would probably need to locate it in a larger house somewhere in the city.

Celwyn flicked his fingers, and the swirling leaves outside danced. Like ships upon the waves, they blew across the grounds, riding the crests and falling again. God, he missed the sea. He could admit that he wished he'd stayed behind for a few more weeks on the *Nautilus*. Captain Nemo intrigued him. Even though Phileas Fogg would have to go somewhere else. Perhaps a sojourn in the American desert without a horse. Now that he and Kang had set up funds for the flying machine, the bastard wouldn't be necessary, especially if he should go missing.

The magician glanced at his pocket watch, two hours until dinner. He itched to do something, not just sit here. Celwyn snapped his fingers; earlier, Edward had told him that Annabelle and Patrick had purchased a small calèche.

In seconds, he was on his feet; a quick excursion was in order.

The magician took stock of the inhabitants of Tellyhouse. Like a fine-looking vulture, Qing watched Patrick from his perch atop the armoire, as he slept on the sofa with his mouth open. The women had retired to Annabelle's parlor. That left Kang, who had gone upstairs to compose lesson plans.

Celwyn stopped in the kitchen. He informed Ricardo that he would be back in time for dinner. As he went out the side door, he stopped long enough to add, "If I am not back by then, please let the Professor know that I've gone to the Marlborough Hotel and expect to return shortly."

Celwyn considered that message a full step toward the disclosure and cooperation that Annabelle and Elizabeth expected. He wouldn't be impeded on his little jaunt, yet they would know where he had gone if something went wrong. With the pride of cooperating but not the cooperating propelling him, he hot-footed it down the driveway to the stables, where he found Edward holding a grooming brush.

Edward listened to the magician's request and beamed. "Yes, we have a beautiful new *calèche*. I'll get her ready."

Twenty minutes later, Celwyn climbed in the back of the open two-seater, admiring the feel and smell of the new leather seat. Edward wore a heavy coat as he stepped up into the covered driver's seat.

He jiggled the reins. "There is a rug back there, Sir. It might get a bit nippy by the time we return." He clicked his tongue, and their horse clopped down the driveway toward the street.

Already shivering, Celwyn dug the blanket out from under the seat and heard the springs of the bram creak. When he sat up again, he found Kang sitting next to him.

"I'm sure my invitation to join your little outing, one probably fraught with danger, simply hasn't arrived yet." Kang looked down his nose at Celwyn. "I saw you go into the stables from my window."

"Hmmph." The magician vowed to be more circumspect next time.

The two-seater pulled into the street. As they set off at a good clip, the breeze threatened to steal Kang's hat. After checking for pedestrians, Celwyn wiggled a hand and brought the bonnet up. That helped somewhat with the hat, but the magician still shivered. He added another blanket.

"Where are we off to, and will we be back in time for dinner?" Kang asked as they passed a couple walking a handsome greyhound. "I hear we are having parslied carrots, which you know I enjoy."

"We won't miss it," the magician told him. "This is just a visit to check on Jules. I also want to know more about the *Nautilus* and Captain Nemo."

Talk of the submarine continued until they pulled up in front of the Marlborough's grand entrance. Celwyn told Edward that they would return before the top of the hour. As they mounted the entrance steps, Edward steered the calèche to the carriage park across the avenue.

"Do you think he naps while he waits?"

Celwyn shook his head. "He enjoys word puzzles." He bowed Kang ahead of him. "Are you thinking we should take him with us on these missions?"

"Yes. At least until Bartholomew gets back."

"Then we will do so next time."

They traversed a wide and opulent foyer decorated with potted ferns, statuary, and well-dressed clientele whose only worry might be what wine to choose for dinner. The tile floor had a most intricate pattern radiating from a central star, like a fanciful solar system. Leading off the north side of the foyer, more glass doors led to lush gardens featuring Dutch roses. Overall, a very pretty place for Jules to stay. Upon inquiry at the front desk, they were told the author had been in the bar "for a while."

In the lounge, gilt mirrors and dark wood paneling of an English pub predominated on a grand scale, all without the sludge-like smoke permeating the walls. The bar measured more than forty feet long, with two billiard tables and a row of quiet cubbyholes running the length of the room. From an alcove to their right came music from a piano played by a most bored-looking man in a tuxedo.

They found the author in the farthest cubbyhole.

Several fountain pens poked out from under the stacks of paper that covered nearly all of the table in front of Verne. Beside him, at least a dozen wadded pieces of paper decorated the seat, testimony to a frustrating afternoon. The waiter reached around them to deliver a fresh stein of beer and removed two empty ones. As he and Kang slid into the booth opposite the author, Celwyn placed their order.

Bleary eyes under lowered brows regarded them with a minimal level of recognition.

"Good afternoon, Jules," Celwyn said.

The author put his pen down and burped. "Jonas, did we have an appointment? Dinner, hopefully?"

"We'd be honored if you came to dinner soon," Kang told him.

The author turned to him and pursed his lips. "I know you."

"Yes, you do."

"Jules, can I ask you about the *Nautilus*?" Celwyn tapped the man's wrist to keep his attention. What Verne wouldn't disclose sober, he might reveal while tipsy.

"It is a wonderful ship," Verne murmured.

Celwyn asked, "When was it made?"

Verne stared at him and drank beer. "Damned if I know."

The Professor sent the magician a look that said they were wasting their time.

Celwyn disagreed; he still thought they would learn more from Verne in this condition and about Fogg.

"Do you travel on it often?"

The waiter arrived with their whiskies. When he left again, Kang pulled his close but didn't drink.

"Of course. Nemo is my friend." Verne nearly knocked over his stein and righted it again with exaggerated care. "You are my friends, too." He picked up his pen and looked at it like he didn't know what to do with it.

Kang said, "The *Nautilus* is a big ship. Have you ever been on her when she traveled up underground rivers?"

Verne stopped playing with the cap of his pen. "Shushhhh." He held a finger in front of his mouth. "Who told you about that?" His words slurred. "The *Nautilus* is a secret. Shushhhh."

"We can keep a secret." The Professor lowered his voice. "Tell us about Fogg."

"He is nasty. Méchant." The author drank his stein empty and settled it on top of his pages. "We look for treasure sometimes." He tried to wink, but his fuzzy eye refused to cooperate.

"Those sound like wonderful trips." Celwyn prompted him.

Kang asked, "The Mariana Trench? The underground river of Amol, too?"

"Yes." Verne laid his head on the table.

"You were right, Xiau. This is a waste of time." Celwyn tossed his drink back and stood. He patted Verne's shoulder. "Let's get you upstairs to your room."

Kang held him up while Celwyn swept a hand and collected all the papers and pens into Verne's briefcase. A few minutes later, they ascended to the last step of the grand staircase, then supported the author between them as they walked down the hallway.

"Beautiful carpets," Kang commented.

"And artwork. But I think the underground rivers are a bit more interesting."

Verne burped. "I'm going to be sick."

"Lovely." Celwyn used magic to propel them along to the next corridor. As they rounded the corner, they bumped into a tall, well-built woman in a fur coat.

Verne vomited. Mrs. Karras reared back, as did Kang. Celwyn growled and reached for her, but she knocked Verne into his arms and ran.

This time there weren't hurt boys at his feet, and damn his wound. As the vampire flew down the stairs, Celwyn chased her, running so fast that their feet barely touched the ground. They bounded across the street and through the park. In the gloom of dusk, many residents still walked the grounds. With exclamations of surprise, they scattered behind benches and trees.

Celwyn used magic to keep up and finally reach for the vampire, but she shed her fur into his hands and leaped across a pond full of swans.

Two policemen tackled Celwyn from different directions. He flung them away and got to his feet, but it was too late. Mrs. Karras was gone, leaving him holding her fur permeated with cloying perfume.

"Damn it!"

By the time Celwyn returned to the hotel and up the stairs to the second floor, he had trouble breathing. Kang had moved Verne to the end of the hall and tried to unlock the door while using his elbow to keep the author upright.

"Let me try," Celwyn suggested as he stepped around a puddle of beery vomit. "Again, how lovely." He examined the key. "He gave you the wrong room number." The magician flipped a hand and the room door to the right opened.

"Come on, Jules."

As they bundled him into his room, Kang said, "Mrs. Karras escaped."

"Police intervention helped. Apparently, a man chasing a woman across a park was not to be ignored. After she got away, I made sure they couldn't see me heading back here." They dumped Verne on the settee. "Vampires can outrun me because I can't throw magic at them quickly enough." He toured the room and added, "If I know where they intend to go, it is much easier to catch them."

As he took off Verne's fouled tie, Kang said, "Things have just become more serious, Jonas."

"I know. We'll have to take him back to Tellyhouse." He glanced around the suite, seeing a storm of paper and clothes thrown everywhere. It reminded him of Annabelle's cabin on the train.

"Either Jules is extraordinarily messy, or someone has searched his room."

Celwyn rubbed his face. "I'll go down and tell Edward we're on our way with our new guest. One of us can take a hire coach back to the house." He grumbled, "Jules is not sitting in my lap. Especially in his condition."

"I'll be right behind you after I find him a change of clothes," Kang said and started to rummage. "We can send for the rest of his things tomorrow."

Chapter 50

By the time they arrived at Tellyhouse, dinner must have been waiting a while. Mrs. Thomas met them in the hallway with her lips pressed so tight, she didn't have any. She tramped into the dining room and announced, "They are here. Finally."

Kang and Celwyn approached the table, supporting Verne between them.

"Our apology for the late arrival. We have a new guest." Celwyn hitched up Verne when his knees buckled. "He's a bit under the weather."

Kang said, "Please serve the soup, Mrs. Thomas. We'll take him upstairs and be right back." As they backed out again, he added, "Again, our apologies."

When they reached the top of the stairs, Celwyn elbowed the automat. "We need to put a bucket by his bed."

"Where are the buckets?"

"I don't know. But we'd better hurry."

When they returned to the dining room, they found dead silence filling the room, and each face displayed various degrees of curiosity or annoyance. Mrs. Thomas banged the lid back onto the soup tureen.

Once they were seated, Annabelle asked, "What is wrong with Mr. Verne, Uncle Celwyn?"

"I'm hungry." Zander started to eat his soup. When Otto hesitated, Zander elbowed him, saying in a food-reverent voice reminiscent of Celwyn, "It is very good."

As usual, the boy alleviated a tense situation. Kang bestowed a grateful look on Zander's head. "Mr. Verne doesn't feel well." He waited until both boys looked down at their soup bowls and simulated a drinking motion for the others.

Elizabeth rolled her eyes. "*That* is why you were late?"

Celwyn dabbed his lips with his napkin. "Yes, and since we're all here, I'll mention one more thing before we bring the conversation back to something pleasant." He blocked what the boys could hear, throwing in a few distracting thoughts of puppies. "We discovered Mrs. Karras in the hallway outside Verne's room."

Stunned silence.

"Of all the luck," Patrick growled.

Annabelle's eyes bulged. "Oh, my god!"

Kang said, "We don't know what she wanted, but for his safety, we thought it prudent to bring him with us. We found his room in disarray, and either she searched it, or he is very disorganized."

"And now, let us talk about our day tomorrow." Celwyn removed the block on what the boys could hear. "It is Saturday, and we should do something outside before the colder weather sets in." He asked Otto, "Have you ever visited a zoo?"

The lad shook his head.

"They have a merry-go-round! And a giraffe!" Zander told him.

Kang leaned toward the boys and whispered, "The giraffe looks like Uncle Celwyn."

By the time they were ready for dessert, both Kang and Celwyn had apologized several times to Mrs. Thomas. She hovered and fussed, almost appeased, as Jackson served the bowls of sherbet. "Is that guest of yours staying a while, Sir?"

"Yes. We put him in Bartholomew's room for now," the magician told her. "Tomorrow, please send someone to the Marlborough Hotel for his things." He made sure she was still looking at him as he said, "We appreciate your skill in keeping this house running so well, do not doubt that, no matter how difficult we make things for you."

Mrs. Thomas flushed, then her eyes widened when Kang added, "We should let Francesca and the witches know he is here, too."

Celwyn kicked Kang under the table. The automat had just ruined his peace offering. Mrs. Thomas crossed herself and loaded up the soup tureen onto the cart much faster than usual before pushing it out of the room. With a sigh, Celwyn admitted, "Logical as usual, my friend. And necessary, but good grief, your timing is horrible." He watched Otto as he licked his spoon. "When Jules feels better, we can continue our conversation with him from earlier. I'm especially interested in the voyages of the *Nautilus.*"

"That is the underwater boat you mentioned," Patrick said.

The Professor said, "It is much larger than a boat, more like two tall ships long, and I want to know more about her. However..." he checked to see if anyone had entered the room, "we shouldn't mention it to anyone."

Celwyn spent an enjoyable moment wallowing in his imagination and the sea before finally saying, "I wager Bartholomew will be able to tell us of the underwater adventures."

"Until then, perhaps Mr. Verne will regale us with stories of the places the *Nautilus* visited." Patrick nodded at the boys. "Of course, with a limited audience."

The magician's imagination still swirled. Verne may not be able to tell tales. What if everything Captain Nemo attempted was not legal? What if governments, or the rest of the world, shouldn't know about his adventures? Taking the speculation further, he wondered how much leeway Verne really took in his fiction.

Otto held up his tablet to Kang.

"He asks, 'what is the *Nautilus*'?" The automat handed the tablet back to him. "It is a ship without sails that travels underwater." He held a hand over his mouth. "It is also a secret." Both boys mimicked him and giggled. "Good," he told them with a straight face.

Zander frowned. "Who is Mrs. Karras?"

For his own protection and that of Otto, Celwyn said, "Do you remember that lady with the big red lips who ran out of the restaurant a couple of months ago?" After the vampire had threatened the children, the magician had turned her earrings extraordinarily hot, so much so that she had better things to do than bother them at the moment. After that, things changed.

Zander said, "Yes."

"She is a friend of the 'genie man' that hurt Telly, and she would hurt you or any of us." Kang kept his voice clear and gentle. He agreed; they had to know.

"Including Mr. Verne," Celwyn said.

"She may think Mr. Verne would be an avenue to us." Annabelle speculated with a glance out the window.

Patrick's voice held uncharacteristic anger, and he placed a hand on hers. "I will protect you."

The magician assumed Patrick's past with Mrs. Karras still embarrassed him, and no doubt he dreaded what the vampire might do to his beloved.

Annabelle kissed him, then caught Celwyn's eye and pointed to the boys. He blocked them and nodded.

"I am not afraid for me," she said. "Nevertheless, I am for the boys."

Elizabeth said, "The same here."

"The spell on the house is solid. Edward asked the witches to extend it along the path to the stables, the stables themselves, and the grounds," Patrick told them. "Our peril occurs when we leave the premises. Either Jonas, or one of us, will be with the boys, and you, at all times."

Celwyn felt proud of Patrick. His conviction that their plans would keep them safe caused Elizabeth's anxiety to lessen as she released her grip on Kang's wrist and almost smiled.

Annabelle had a different reaction. Her response sounded part sarcastic and part a happy memory. "I remember Bartholomew promising to teach me how to shoot." She turned to Patrick with her chin up. "How about it?"

Elizabeth sputtered, "But—but bullets don't affect vampires."

"The Professor has silver ones," Patrick said. "We will obtain more of them, too."

Annabelle nodded to Elizabeth. "This time, we'll buy pistols." She fluttered a lace-covered sleeve. "Something small that we can carry with us."

Kang sighed. "I suppose we will eventually be very well protected."

From the automat's face, Celwyn could see that his friend did not like the idea of Elizabeth learning to shoot. Not at all.

When they adjourned to the parlor, Annabelle asked the boys if they'd like to play in their room. They both raced upstairs.

As he watched them, Kang said, "I think Otto is much younger than he told us. He is closer to twelve years old than fifteen."

Celwyn would agree as he poured tea, and the Professor ferried sherry and whiskies around the room. Qing watched him from the top of the armoire, and soon they heard a tinkling, sharp noise, metal on wood. The bird enjoyed tapping on the brass knobs of the furniture and other things. Kang regarded him with a sardonic eye. "We need to get you a new toy. There are more chips out of the whiskey decanter."

From the doorway, Verne said, "I appear to have had an eventful afternoon." He gestured. "This is a beautiful home."

"Our thanks go to Mrs. Thomas, our housekeeper. It is very comfortable," Celwyn said. "Please sit down, and I'll get you some tea."

The author's hair stood on end, but he'd tied his cravat and had both shoes laced. He bowed in front of Elizabeth. "It is nice to see you again, Mrs. Kang."

When he reached the sofa where Annabelle and Patrick sat holding hands, Celwyn performed the formal introductions. "Miss Annabelle Pearse

Edmunds, and Captain Patrick Swayne, this is Mr. Jules Verne. You remember him from the train station." He made the introductions more for Verne's benefit than theirs—the foggy look in his eyes and his movements were testimony to the effects of his afternoon drinking. "Are you feeling better? Perhaps we can have a dinner tray brought to you?"

Verne shuddered. "No, thank you." He still seemed a bit confused as he scanned the room. "Why am I here?"

Kang controlled a smile. "Because when we left the Marlborough bar to escort you upstairs, we found a particularly nasty vampire in the hallway."

"I need to sit down," Verne said, suddenly paler than before. Kang eased him into a chair.

Celwyn said, "I think she was looking for something in your room and would have killed you without hesitation." The magician handed him a cup of tea, and the cup rattled in Verne's hand. Minutes went by without him drinking or moving.

"You seem puzzled," Kang told the author. He spoke a bit louder and slower, "Someone searched your room. We think it was the vampire."

Verne shot to his feet and swayed. "My work! It was with me in the bar!"

"I gathered up your papers." Celwyn settled him back into his chair. "They are here, and the rest of your belongings will be brought here tomorrow." Verne gripped his arm until the magician extracted himself and patted him on the shoulder. "You'll occupy Bartholomew's room until we eliminate Mrs. Karras and the other vampires."

"There's *more* of them?" Verne squeaked and tumbled out of his chair in a faint at Elizabeth's feet. Elizabeth backed away and stifled a giggle.

Kang laughed and tried to cover it. "Sorry, I couldn't help it. Allow me." He dribbled some water from a nearby flower vase on the author's forehead. When Verne sat up again, Kang helped him back into the chair and waited until he'd sipped some of his tea. Annabelle watched the scene with a frown.

"There are several vampires," Patrick told the author. "However, you will be safe here at Tellyhouse. We have numerous spells from the local coven protecting this house."

"Coven? Witches?" Verne paled again.

Celwyn's patience waned. "Do you have any idea why Mrs. Karras would search your room?" He found explanations tedious. "Has anything strange happened in the last few days?"

Verne shrugged. "This morning, a young man asked me if I knew you. He reminded me greatly of that young woman, Mary Giovanna."

"Oh!" Elizabeth exclaimed. "I'd assumed that after yesterday she would have given up."

Celwyn cursed. Kang got to his feet and began pacing.

"What? What is wrong?" Verne demanded.

Annabelle threw up her hands. "That *was* Mary Giovanna. Our danger seems to be increasing." Patrick put an arm around her.

"It is a good thing that you are staying with us, Mr. Verne," Elizabeth told him and removed the teacup from his shaking hand.

Patrick voiced the thought that churned in Celwyn's stomach like the two monsters who had battled in Captain Nemo's underground lake.

"Why were Mary Giovanna and Mrs. Karras both at Verne's hotel?"

Chapter 51

AFTER BREAKFAST, EVERYONE GATHered in the hallway, ready for their excursion to the zoo. Verne had elected to go back to bed and write while he waited for his belongings to be delivered to Tellyhouse.

As the author headed up the staircase, Kang, Patrick, and Celwyn stood at the foot of the stairs and discussed their original plan to entice their enemies out into the open. The Professor was not in favor of dangling the magician in front of their enemies like a choice piece of meat in front of a salivating lion. When the thundering noise of the boys coming down the stairs began, the discussion stopped. Through the fear that filled Annabelle's eyes as she looked at the lads, she nodded in agreement with Kang.

Zander bounced on his heels and threw his hat in the air. Otto caught it and threw it back to him.

He wore one of Zander's coats that looked a bit short and tight for him. Celwyn made the adjustments without the boy noticing, then turned to Elizabeth.

"We are scheduled to stop at the tailor's after the zoo?"

"Yes. According to Annabelle, you will be pleased to know there is a new tea shop next door, too."

Kang stepped up. "The bookshop is after that."

"Of course, it is, dear," Elizabeth told him. "When they," she nodded at the boys, "are not with us, we'll stop at the firearms proprietor. My new pistol will be white ivory."

Kang wore a pained look. "Must you?"

"He says that to me, too," Celwyn informed her.

Annabelle turned away from the hallway window and announced, "Edward just drove up. Are we all ready?"

It only lacked an hour before dinner when they returned to Tellyhouse, tired yet talkative. One by one, they marched down the hallway, each laden with packages like pack elephants in the jungle.

Kang dumped an armload of books on the table in front of the parlor windows. "It was a very good day at the bookstore. Look at this! We were only gone a few months from Prague, and much has been published."

"Such as?" Patrick asked.

"There is a children's adventure, *Alice's Adventures in Wonderland*, and P. T. Barnum's *The Humbugs of the World.*"

Mrs. Thomas herded the boys upstairs to their baths, and Elizabeth came into the parlor behind a maid pushing a tea cart loaded with two pots. Across the room, they could see into the dining room where Verne sat in front of a mound of paper and close enough to hear conversations. Celwyn noted the author had a teacup instead of a libation; a much better choice considering his recent overindulgence.

Elizabeth raided the silver mail tray under the parlor window. She handed Celwyn two envelopes and Patrick two more. The remainder she placed on top of her husband's new books.

"We have a Bartholomew letter!" Celwyn waved it above his head. Everyone stopped what they were doing to listen as the magician read aloud.

> Dear Jonas and everyone,
>
> I am enjoying my time on the Nautilus greatly. I learn something every day and not necessarily about the flying machine. It has been years since university, but along with the Professor's texts and the ones here, I have found many improvements for the flying machine.
>
> Captain Nemo is courteous and helpful. I cannot comment about Mr.

> Fogg other than to see that he bears watching. I do not allow him near me when I leave or enter the ship over the lake where the water dragon lives.
>
> Zander and Otto will be pleased when I return. I have made them some very interesting lesson plans about sea life. It is too bad they cannot ride in the ship. They would find it thrilling.
>
> I look forward to traveling back to Prague soon and participating in the wedding. I have found something for the happy couple that they will enjoy, but I'm not sure they will think of it as a traditional gift.
>
> Ever yours,
>
> Bartholomew

Celwyn quietly opened his other letter while the others discussed some of the shops they'd found during the day. He read it thoroughly and passed it to Kang.

> Dear Jonas and Professor,
>
> I am in receipt of your letter from a few weeks ago.

Your action was a surprise. I never would have dreamed of your generous and welcome gesture. Although I am a wealthy man and with sources of income, building the flying machine is an extremely expensive undertaking. Mr. Fogg's funding came with questionable restrictions. He is an odious man, and I will be glad to be rid of him. Because of our new collaboration, I must dissolve the partnership with Fogg in such a way that he will not retaliate or steal any of the information that we have produced. Above all, I will ensure that he does not hurt Mr. Bartholomew.

We can discuss how much, or little, you wish to participate in funding the flying machine going forward.

I will bring Bartholomew back to you soon.

Yours in appreciation,

Captain Nemo

Chapter 52

December

CELWYN LOUNGED IN FRONT OF THE parlor windows, staring at the softly falling snow. Qing sat on the sill, pecking the swirling flakes through the glass. As the magician stretched, he wondered why he felt an increasing sense of unease over the last few weeks, one that could not be ignored. Even now, a quiet dread seeped down the back of his neck like the tickle of dry, dead fingers.

It had been over a year since Professor Xiau Kang had become his close confidante and friend through many perilous situations. He thought of Bartholomew the same way and knew the big man was happy with his bright shiny new toy. No matter how idyllic everything appeared, the fact that no one had attacked them recently seemed highly unusual. *What were they waiting for?*

Over the last month, absolutely nothing untoward had happened. For several weeks, Zander and Otto had continued their classes while Verne obsessed over his book. Elizabeth and Annabelle fussed over the wedding plans, usually dragging Patrick into the discussions and debates. The wedding dress for the event had arrived and been hung in Annabelle's parlor, its train on a separate hanger off the floor. Qing had been banned from the room after several of the crystals had gone missing from the garment.

Ricardo's culinary creations continued to amaze and delight everyone. Even Mrs. Thomas had declared that everything under her control functioned well. She had confided to Annabelle, with pride and disbelief, that the neighbors admired Tellyhouse with its diverse occupants and unconventional family.

Celwyn could admit that he felt the heavy hand of boredom, coupled with the knowledge that Mrs. Karras and Mary Giovanna still prowled the streets of the city, unsettled him. The magician had tried to find them, but his attempts had been unsuccessful. He felt off-center, not just because of the vampires, and could not pinpoint why.

Across the room, a decorated fir tree reached the ceiling and twinkled with row after row of candles and tin ornaments. A forest of presents covered the floor underneath the tree. The magician happened to know most of them were presents for the boys. He smiled. Xiau would receive a new fishing pole, just like Zander and Otto's. In the spring, they could take a picnic basket with them for a fine outing. The automat would have his favorite trout.

It lacked only a few minutes until four in the afternoon, and already the gloom of dusk made the scene outside even darker, turning the heavy carpet of snow to an icy blue. Inside the parlor, a log fell in a shower of sparks in the fireplace, heralding Kang's arrival. He carried a book under his arm and radiated high spirits like the sun casts a sunrise out of the darkness.

He sat across from Celwyn and eyed him with mischief dancing in his eyes. "If we don't find the vampires before Bartholomew returns, we'll have to move Verne down to your room."

"You don't say?" the magician replied after patting a yawn. "Because?"

"Bartholomew loves his room."

Celwyn enjoyed teasing Kang as much as the automat enjoyed teasing him, but even that seemed stale today. "Don't fret. Verne intends to rejoin the *Nautilus* when we meet them in Odessa."

"You could have just said so," the Professor said. "Anyhow, do you have a date in mind for when we should leave for the rendezvous, especially..." he indicated the scene outside, "with the snow?"

Celwyn sat back and crossed his legs. "From what you've told me, it will take about two weeks to get there. Plus, time to prepare the *Elizabeth*." He got to his feet and crossed to the desk calendar. "We should begin preparations next week so we can be ready to depart."

"Did you consider that we may need to either leave Ricardo here or find a substitute chef?"

Celwyn pursed his lips. "We'll have to discuss it further. Mrs. Thomas won't let us take him." As he spoke, his spirits climbed: they would soon be with Bartholomew again.

The magician decided to celebrate. He caused all the ornaments on the Christmas tree to come to life. Chubby kittens and bears waved paws, and the soldiers tooted their tiny trumpets. One of the dolls blinked her eyes and threw them a kiss as the juggler tossed balls in the air and kicked his legs. When the bear growled, Kang whipped around and spilled his tea.

"Oh, for God sakes, Jonas." With his complaint came a smile of wonder.

Celwyn cleaned up the spill while the tin soldier pounded his drum and marched in place. The fairy's wings fluttered as if she could fly off the tree.

Kang watched them. "Intricate and beautiful."

"So, are we agreed about Nemo?" Celwyn asked. Although he and Kang had conferred earlier in the day and come to a decision, the magician wanted to finalize the plan.

Kang nodded. "Yes. I'll transfer the rest of the money tomorrow to the Captain. Bartholomew would have liked to participate, but he does not yet have the amount needed. After a few years working with the flying machine, he will. Did you tell Nemo?"

"Yes. I wrote to him this morning. Step two of our partnership is ready. The money to buy out Fogg should be there before they depart to bring

Bartholomew to us. I’m not sure if the Captain can unload Fogg altogether, but he will not have to accede to any of the bastard’s wishes ever again.”

“I like that,” Kang said. “If he needs more funds to truly get rid of Fogg, we will do it.”

“Removing Fogg personally would be highly enjoyable. And it wouldn’t cost anything.”

“I’m sure it wouldn’t.”Í

On the tree, the little soldier with a porcelain face tooted his trumpet just as Annabelle entered the room and flounced onto the sofa. She checked the corners of the room for the sound and huffed when she didn’t see anything.

“A cup of tea to fix what is wrong?” Celwyn asked.

“No, thank you.”

She raised her head as the monkey tapped his cymbals together. The miniature trumpet sounded again from the tree. “Oh, my!” She clapped her hands as she watched the donkey buck back and forth and bray. “How delightful…” Annabelle stopped clapping and eyed Celwyn. “I’m not asking how you did that.”

“Of course.” He nodded in understanding.

Kang said, “We were just discussing preparations for the journey to Odessa.”

“I miss Bartholomew terribly.” Her expression took on an obstinate stance. “You know, he would take my side.”

“About?” Kang asked.

“Patrick’s stubbornness.” She pouted, and Celwyn could see how that could demoralize a man as smitten as Patrick. “He won’t allow me to wear my new boots after the wedding. He says the snow would ruin them. Uncle Celwyn, you must fix this."

Bartholomew was known for his negotiation abilities. Celwyn squirmed and wished their friend was home already. Kang took pity on him.

"Tell us more. Perhaps we can help."

Chapter 53

A WEEK LATER, THE MAGICIAN FELT a new sense of purpose as he, Kang, and Conductor Smith set off for the *Elizabeth*. The morning had dawned clear and cold, and now at dusk, the chill seemed to settle over the city like a fluffy blanket, cozy and uncomfortable.

They reached the train yard. Nestled between snowdrifts, the locomotive resembled a beached walrus with her bulbous smokestacks and curved sides. The Conductor led the way as they tramped through the snow to her. He lifted his cap to them and left them to inspect the engines as Celwyn and Kang entered the dining car.

"Mrs. Thomas is a bit miffed that we're leaving again." The automat held the door open for Celwyn. "However, she is very happy she has two weeks to get the train ready for the trip."

"She also wants Bartholomew home again. Have you figured out how we can spirit Ricardo away with us?" Celwyn asked as he walked around the car, verifying that the glassware and bottles hadn't been tampered with. Other than a layer of dust over the table and chairs, it appeared fine. "It is certainly cold in here." He drew his coat closer. The wound in his side hurt more in the cold, reminding him it hadn't healed; in fact, it seemed a tad worse. That bothered him, but he didn't want to make the automat worry more than he already did.

"No, I haven't. Our next stop today is the staffing agency for a chef and more porters." Kang wiped the dust off a lamp. "Since we are leaving Elizabeth, Annabelle, and Patrick behind, we can probably make do with one porter."

"That is true." They moved to the hallway that led to the sleeping compartments. "This will be a quick trip. We will want to visit with Nemo a few days, though." The magician regarded Kang. "What do you want to wager that the water is iced up in the water closets?"

"No bet," The automat replied as they walked past the first cabin and turned toward the remaining compartments.

Celwyn froze.

Kang stopped mid-stride. "I smell something burning..."

They rushed to Celwyn's cabin at the end of the hall. By the time they arrived, acrid smoke billowed out the door.

Atop Celwyn's bed lay the body of a woman engulfed in fire. The flames surrounding her sightless eyes revealed it was too late to save her, as did the frenzied slashes across her body. Celwyn smothered the fire with magic, but it still smoked.

"She looks familiar." The automat held his hand over his nose, crunching across the broken glass from the shattered window above the bed. He drew near the pyre.

"It is the witch who greeted us at Francesca's last month," Celwyn told him. He swallowed a heavy sense of guilt and revulsion and tried to ignore the stench of burned flesh. "Why set her ablaze if she had already been stabbed?"

Kang straightened after examining her torso. "Even more to the point, why stab her if she had already been drained by a vampire?" He pointed to the puncture marks. "No blood in the wounds."

Celwyn rubbed his chin, deep in thought. "I do not know."

Kang's eyes lit up. "Because..."

Behind him, Mrs. Karras burst through the door as three more vampires climbed through the window.

Celwyn shoved Kang out of the way and tore one of the vampires in two. The other vampire arose behind Celwyn and, with an arm around his neck, drove a knife into his side. The magician gasped and turned the knife on the attacker as Kang flung Mrs. Karras against the wall. She screeched and wrapped her hands around his neck. The remaining man jumped on Celwyn, knocking him to the ground as he tried to close his wound, which now gushed blood.

When the magician faced the man on top of him, he stared into Crazy Mary's glazed eyes. Her fangs appeared new and sharp, and the hunger in her eyes was raw and animal-like. He didn't have time for anything fancy or complicated. Celwyn socked her in the jaw. He punched her hard, over and over, until he backed her up and off him. One of the vampires flew by him as Kang kicked him against the wall.

Celwyn elevated both Kang and him to the ceiling as the remaining vampires shredded their pant legs and raked their nails down their calves. One of them slithered out the window. Celwyn felt himself weakening, and they started to fall back to the floor. He used the last of his strength to encircle the rest of the attackers in a net. As he cinched the metallic net closed, their growls escalated.

The magician collapsed on the floor and gasped again. "Make sure ... they burn at sunrise." He fell over.

Kang sank to his knees next to Celwyn and yelled in his ear as the darkness overcame him, "Close your wound!"

Chapter 54

A MOROSE SHROUD OF SORROW COVered Tellyhouse.

Elizabeth assisted Kang as he examined Celwyn. From just inside the parlor door, Annabelle cried softly as she kept the others back. The boys had been sent upstairs by Mrs. Thomas. Abe was assigned to make sure they stayed there. When the housekeeper stomped back into the parlor, she stood in the corner wringing her hands, and a big, fat tear slid down her cheek.

"Where is Patrick?" the automat asked as he cleaned Celwyn's knife wound with little swipes of alcohol. It still bled.

"He and Edward returned to the train," Elizabeth said loud enough for Annabelle to hear, but not Ricardo, Sully, and the others in the hallway. "They are picking up that 'bundle' you left there." She leaned closer, "Is it really full of vampires?" She glanced at Celwyn with concern where he lay on the sofa.

"Yes." Kang broke open smelling salts under Celwyn's nose. He tried to keep his voice steady. "Jonas saved me. Again."

"I can tell that, Xiau, from your shredded clothes and his blood all over you."

The automat returned Elizabeth's look of worry to her. "This is much worse than before." He took a deep breath. "However, he is the most qualified to help himself."

Kang gauged how pale the magician appeared and tried not to think of how ill he had been before this attack. He couldn't think about him dying. Again, the automat shoved smelling salts under the magician's nose and leaned closer until he was an inch away from Celwyn's ear.

"Jonas, it is important that you heal that wound, not just close it." He growled, "Nothing else matters..."

Minutes went by with those nearby unnaturally quiet, unwilling to even whisper for fear of disturbing what Kang was doing. Celwyn's breathing seemed to slow, yet the automat could feel his chest going up and down, only perceptively.

Annabelle began crying again and collapsed in a chair. Behind her, the Christmas tree twinkled with lights and gaiety, mocking the horror in the room. The household staff remained outside the parlor door, as solemn as sentinels in a funeral. Kang looked down, trying to control what he was thinking. Dread grew until it overtook him, and he held his head in his hands.

"Xiau, your arm... your skin is peeled back," Celwyn whispered.

"Jonas!" The automat leaned closer. His color seemed better. "I'm fixable. Stop talking and concentrate."

With a nod, Celwyn did so. A much longer time went by. The magician grimaced and once cried out in pain. Kang grabbed his hand and held on, noticing that the magician's hand was colder than his own.

"I'm here, Jonas. Don't you dare die on me."

Hours later, Patrick and Edward entered the room, nodding to Kang and Elizabeth. Kang still sat by the magician. Sweat poured off Celwyn's brow, but more color filled his cheeks.

Annabelle arrived and closed the parlor doors.

"I finally got the boys to sleep." She looked at Celwyn, and her tears began again. "Is he... he..." In one stride, Patrick reached her and gathered her close.

"We don't know," Kang said.

Elizabeth mopped the magician's brow. "He doesn't feel as cold as before, but this isn't normal either."

Mrs. Thomas and Edward sat on the opposite sofa, side by side, supporting each other. Mrs. Thomas' cap was off-center, and she appeared deflated like a large, discarded doll. Edward said, "If you don't mind me saying so, he looked ill before this."

The automat told Edward, "I agree. His body temp should be the same as most of you." He pulled Celwyn's lids back, looked at his eyes, and then examined the wound again. "This appears better." Jonas always said Kang didn't have a poker face, so he didn't look at them, knowing that his expression would contradict his words.

When Celwyn opened his eyes, only a handful of candles lit the parlor. In the chair to his right, Elizabeth snored as softly as an angel, fluttering the errant curls falling to her shoulder. On the couch beyond her, Annabelle and Patrick leaned together, sleeping. The wall clock had just chimed three times.

Kang sat in the chair at his feet, staring at him with an unreadable gaze.

"Xiau."

"How are you?"

"I hurt. Every time I hurt, I open my eyes, and you are sitting between my feet."

"Did you repair the wound?"

The magician's face contorted as he said, "I think so."

"I sent Edward to telegraph Captain Nemo and Bartholomew to leave for the rendezvous as soon as possible."

"Why?" It hurt to talk.

"Your body is cooling off. Your temperature is even lower than the last time you were hurt." Kang's voice broke. "I am very worried."

Celwyn tried to smile. "I am fine. I…"

"No!" Kang growled. "*You are not.* Don't you want to know why I contacted Nemo and Bartholomew?"

"Yes," Celwyn said as Annabelle stirred and resumed breathing in Patrick's ear. He nodded at them. "That is true love."

"Don't change the subject. We leave in a few days for the estuary near Odessa." Kang's frown deepened. "You will rest until then, and Elizabeth will go with us as your nurse."

"Wouldn't it make more sense to leave me here for when you bring Bartholomew home?"

Kang put his head in his hands and, in a moment, peeked at the others to verify they still slept.

"You remember my private conversation with Captain Nemo in Singapore?"

Celwyn grimaced as he shifted. "Yes."

"He agreed to find the healer Thales for us. For some reason, Nemo likes you."

The automat started to pace beside the sofa where Celwyn lay. "The main, and continuing theme surrounding Thales, is that he is called upon to heal immortals." Kang tried to see outside through the picture window through the darkness but only saw the reflection of the room. In it, Qing peeked over the top of the armoire at Celwyn as he lay below, and if a bird could show emotion, Qing did as he blinked at the magician, tilting his head side to side.

Kang added, "Thales is supposed to be descended from Gaia, one of the original gods."

"An old myth?"

Kang regarded him. "If half of what I heard is true, and we find Thales, you will want to know more about Gaia."

"This is all interesting, but right now, I really want some tea."

"Soon. Tell me how you feel. Is it only your side?"

"Yes, and very sore." Celwyn sighed. "I wish I had been more prepared for what we found on the train."

Kang stood over him and stared without blinking for several minutes.

"I am worried, Jonas. I think ... that you are dying."

"Not yet, I'm not." The magician reached for his hand and patted it. "I have survived hundreds of years."

"Let us hope for hundreds more," Kang said and squeezed his hand in return.

Chapter 55

CELWYN AWOKE AS THE *ELIZABETH* descended into the Gyor valley. They had made good time since dawn with Conductor Smith pulling out all his tricks he'd learned over the years. The magician shifted in his new bed and winced. For his personal bird entertainment, Qing sat on his chest and clicked his tongue in the magician's ear. Since the night the vampires attacked, the mechanical bird had not left his side. Celwyn patted his back, and Qing's glittering eyes blinked slowly. Long ago, Kang had informed him that act was the equivalent of a cat purring. Or crying.

The magician glanced out the window.

In the distance, the mountains seemed smaller under the weight of so much snow. Celwyn sincerely hoped he wouldn't be called upon for strenuous magic—such as making the train fly over an avalanche—until he felt better. He could also admit that if he'd been stronger, he would have dealt differently with Mrs. Karras and Crazy Mary.

As he stared at the scenery, Kang entered the cabin so quietly, Celwyn almost didn't hear him, perhaps hoping the magician still slept. All Celwyn had to do to confirm the seriousness of his condition was to look at his friend's sorrowful face.

"I wager you never can tell a falsehood, Xiau."

Kang's brow furrowed. "What?" He thought for a second and pursed his lips, "Don't read anything into how I look."

"What is that?" Celwyn pointed at a hand crank and rope pulley at the end of his bed.

The automat managed a smile. "My invention. It keeps the constant vibration and jostling of the train from bothering you. The Conductor made it. I use the crank," he demonstrated, "to raise your mattress above the bed. It suspends you in the air so you sway with the bumps, not bounce." The squeaking from the crank nearly drowned him out. "You won't have to expel energy for doing the same thing with magic."

"I see." Celwyn peered over the side of the bed. "The most that can happen is that I get seasick from swinging to and fro."

"Exactly. Jackson will bring in your tea soon, and I have good news."

Celwyn raised a brow in inquiry.

"Ricardo is with us. Annabelle insisted. She said they would endure Sully's cooking until we return."

Celwyn should have been relieved. He felt thankful and said so, but food no longer sounded important.

Kang eyed him. "You must eat. At least a minimal amount."

"How long until we reach the estuary?"

"About six days at this speed. It is a bit closer than Byzantium. I hope Bartholomew and Nemo are there by then." Kang leaned against the cabin window. "I am betting the Captain has a few shortcuts, such as under continents and through underground rivers, that he can take the *Nautilus*."

Celwyn said, "I want to know much more about that submarine."

"So do I." Kang checked the door, probably for Elizabeth. "My wife is asleep. But it upsets her to know I want to visit the ship again." His eyes gleamed. "It is so fascinating."

While he talked, the magician lifted his pajama top and looked at his wound. Exactly in the same place as the Russian's sword had gored him. *Damn.* "It is like I have a blasted mark that tells them to stab me here." He peeled back the bandage and looked underneath it. "I think it looks better."

Kang said, "As your medical advisor, I say that is true of the wound. But," he hesitated, "I am honest with you, Jonas; the rest of you internally seems worse each day."

"It just takes time to heal." Celwyn didn't mention how much weaker he felt or the increasing sense of alarm he couldn't shake. There was no point in worrying Kang any further.

Verne visited him that evening as Elizabeth sat beside him working on her embroidery, occasionally asking him how he felt. Kang was supposed to be resting before he returned for the rest of the night.

As the author sat down, he frowned at Celwyn and said hello to Elizabeth. "If you would like a break, my dear, your husband suggests that you join him in the dining room for a nightcap. I will stay with Jonas."

Elizabeth's eyes darted to Celwyn, who told her, "I'm fine. Jules and I have plenty to talk about."

She checked his forehead for fever and nodded. "I will be back soon, or Xiau will."

"We seem to spend more time on this train than anywhere else," Verne observed as she left.

"Agreed. However, I would prefer to take a long journey in the *Nautilus*." Celwyn sighed, finding it hard to get enough air. "Bartholomew is probably brimming with news about the flying machine."

Verne puffed on his pipe. "Yes. In the only message I've received from Nemo, he says things are progressing well." He opened a portfolio of papers. "I brought along my current book, *From the Earth to the Moon*. It was just published. Would you like to hear some of it?"

"I would, most definitely. But first, where are you and Captain Nemo traveling to after you rejoin the ship?"

Verne chuckled. "I do not know. He always surprises me."

Chapter 56

"The dead will live
The living will die
And music shall untune the sky."

—"A Song for St. Cecelia's Day"
by John Dryden

KANG STARED OUT THE WINDOWS OF the *Elizabeth's* dining room, his thoughts dark as they passed mile after mile of low fields covered in water, the land resembling the bogs of Yorkshire more than anything else. The water shone in the weak afternoon light as long-legged egrets stood in silhouette against the emptiness of the landscape.

The train chugged around a curve, and in the far distance, the tallest buildings of Byzantium could be seen. The automat nodded to himself; when the railroad tracks ended, they would take a coach as close as they could to the estuary.

Elizabeth entered the room from the kitchen and joined him in the other chair. "In case you were offering, I would like a whiskey, please." Kang handed her a glass, and they held hands. "He didn't eat any of his lunch," she said, "and he sleeps even more of the time."

Kang closed his eyes, trying to keep the futility away.

"I know."

"What will happen tomorrow?"

Kang sipped and controlled the urge to wallow in sorrow. "Conductor Smith and Jackson will join us in a carriage as we transport Jonas to the rendezvous. They'll be able to lift him." He looked out the window. "I'm hoping the road gets us as close as possible to the estuary itself."

Elizabeth shaded her eyes and said, "The land is flat here ... and helps to see long distances." She pointed east. "I think I can spy a smidgen of water there."

Kang walked to the window. "I believe you are correct. The estuary is supposed to be five miles north of the city."

"Is that nasty man, Mr. Fogg, still with the *Nautilus*?"

Kang glanced at his wife. He always enjoyed hearing her insights, and her opinion of Fogg matched his own. "I assume so. The good news is that Bartholomew is on his way and will return with us."

She smiled. "That is welcome. I know you two can't wait to talk science and the work he is doing."

Kang hesitated. He hadn't told her much about Thales. And he wouldn't until he knew Nemo had found the healer and that he could save the magician's life.

Ricardo stood on the steps leading off the train, tears dripping off his chin as the carriage pulled away. Kang waved at him and turned back to face the inside of the coach. Under a half-dozen pillows, the magician lay across the opposite seat, with Verne perched under Celwyn's feet. The rest of the party faced them.

Celwyn's sunken eyes shone with fire that belied his wasted body and pallor. His once luxuriant hair lay flat against his skull, and he shivered under the blankets tucked around him. Qing had burrowed under them and occasionally poked his head out to squawk at Kang. He'd become very vocal when the automat had tried to leave him behind.

The automat added another blanket and squeezed Celwyn's hand. "It is a short journey to the estuary. Let us hope Nemo is there."

As dreary as the last few days had been, today had dawned clear, cold, and bright. Kang could see for many miles in each direction and noted the low foothills to the east and the much closer snow-covered mountains to the north.

Like Elizabeth had said, the land leading to the estuary appeared extraordinarily flat, and the water of the inlet seeped gradually toward them. Further away, the terrain ascended to overlook the water, built up high enough to block what lay below. That would be where Captain Nemo would most likely surface. Kang tapped the glass and pointed to the south. From beside the driver, Edward relayed the request, and they joined the road paralleling the estuary.

On Kang's left, Conductor Smith chewed on his mustache and kept worried eyes fixed on Celwyn. Kang wanted to ask him not to, but Celwyn would hear the request. Again, he wondered what the Conductor would think of the *Nautilus*. The automat had given Smith and Jackson a sketchy description, but that was all. He wouldn't have done even that, but he didn't want them to drop the magician's stretcher in their surprise of seeing the submarine for the first time.

Next to him, Elizabeth did her best to smile and announced it shouldn't be too much longer until they arrived. The magician's eyes closed like a flame extinguishing, yet he still breathed.

When they reached higher ground and stopped, Kang got out behind Conductor Smith. "I'll see if they're down there. Please wait a moment."

For each step he took, Kang felt the moment, the intensity, and the importance of what he would find. Above all, he felt the weight of his sadness. He'd done his best to ignore his worry that there was no guarantee that Nemo had found Thales. If he had failed to find him, Jonas would be dead within a matter of days, perhaps hours.

A long time ago, on the *Zelda*, the magician had doubted a mechanical man could feel. Kang stopped walking to get his control back. Right now, the automat knew real sorrow, a wrenching grief that they would lose Jonas. He swallowed hard and trotted faster, climbing to the top of the berm.

There she was! The long black submarine lay still in the water. A single sailor stood on patrol, and another perched in the glass cage on top.

Kang called, "I'll get Mr. Celwyn. Please let Captain Nemo know we're here."

Conductor Smith joined him as they ran back to the coach. The others had seen them and began unloading the magician onto the stretcher that Kang had fashioned for this moment. He skidded to a stop and grabbed Celwyn's hand. "The *Nautilus* is here. It isn't far."

In the distance, a low hum reached them. The sound sputtered and grew stronger.

The magician's eyes opened slowly, like a thread from his memory impelled him to look. Everyone, including Jonas, gazed up at the sky as if they had already known what was coming.

The noise grew louder, and a bright yellow flying machine crested the low hills and headed straight toward the estuary.

"Yes!" Kang shouted, raising his fist in triumph.

The plane swerved to the north, banked, and then flew toward them again in a wide arc.

"Oh, my god! It is Bartholomew!" Elizabeth exclaimed.

Bartholomew wore a broad smile, and his scarf fluttered in the breeze as he sailed over them. He waved. The engine revved as he banked again and turned, descending for another pass. Celwyn raised himself onto an elbow, trying to wave back.

"Hurry," Kang said. "Bartholomew is going to land. We must get Jonas onto the ship."

Chapter 57

Captain Nemo led the way to his study and lifted the magician's legs onto the sofa himself. As the automat tucked blankets around him, Nemo placed more pillows under Jonas' head, and the magician's eyes closed again. Just moving him had depleted him further.

"As you can see, the situation is dire." Kang faced Captain Nemo. "Did you find the healer?"

From his position at the foot of the sofa, Verne's eyes bounced between Captain Nemo and the automat. Before Nemo could answer, Phileas Fogg arrived, joining them as they gathered in front of the magician.

Fogg's demeanor bothered the automat. It showed in the shiftiness narrowing the man's eyes and the assessing looks he aimed at both Captain Nemo and Kang, himself. Before today, he had exhibited a kind of respect for Captain Nemo. At the moment, he didn't seem to have any at all, brushing by him with a haughty glare.

Beyond the tableau, a collection of silvery fish swarmed the glass of the aquatic window as if they, too, could see Celwyn.

When Bartholomew appeared in the doorway, he filled the room with his infectious exuberance. Then he saw the magician.

"Oh, Jonas..." The big man dropped to a knee and smoothed the hair off Celwyn's forehead. In a whisper, he asked, "What happened?" The magician's eyes remained closed, and his breathing shallow.

"He was already sick when we were attacked in Prague." The automat swallowed hard, and looked directly at Bartholomew, and then Captain Nemo. "I think he is dying."

"That is why Professor Kang asked me to find the healer. It is the only chance your friend has." Captain Nemo turned to the automat. "Thales exists. It will take several days to travel to him."

"Jonas..." Bartholomew walked away, his shoulders shaking as he held his head in his hands and wept.

"We need to leave now," Kang said. "He has so little time left."

As Captain Nemo started to speak, Phileas Fogg stepped in front of him to gaze down at Celwyn. With his voice as detached and controlled as a machine, he said, "That is not possible. We will take the flying machine south to Morocco as planned."

"No." Captain Nemo squared off in front of him.

Fogg bristled. "It is *my* money."

Nemo's voice turned as hard as the sides of the submarine. "I am the Captain of the *Nautilus*, and we go..."

Fogg's smile sent chills up Kang's back, and his premonition came too late.

"Perhaps I can resolve this." Fogg removed a pistol from his coat and aimed it at the magician.

"No!" Bartholomew dove in front of Celwyn as Fogg fired.

The bullet hovered before Celwyn's chest, then it crystalized and shattered—the magician's final act. Bartholomew tackled Fogg, and they rolled across the floor. The revolver fell from Fogg's hand as the big man squeezed the life out of him.

The magician sighed and closed his eyes once again.

Into the violence, Celwyn's music began.

Softly, from within the air, as if they too struggled to breathe, the same five notes played so delicately they could barely be heard. The notes faded and stopped, and melancholy overwhelmed them as Qing flew overhead, cawing forlornly.

Grieving.

The violins returned in harmony, strong and pure, the five notes reverberating in the air. From the shadows beyond the bookcases, the strange man that Kang last saw at the café in Singapore, the one who enjoyed manipulating the fish with pig faces, sauntered toward them.

He bowed and regarded Kang as if he was a particularly useful chess piece.

"So nice to see you again, Professor. Allow me." He knelt beside the magician and put a hand over Celwyn's chest. In another second, a sigh escaped the magician's lips.

The man leaned forward and whispered in Celwyn's ear loud enough for them all to hear.

"It wouldn't be seemly for you to die on me, Brother."

Pelaez's eyes gleamed as Celwyn groaned, the music strengthened, and he began breathing again.

"We have so much to talk about, wouldn't you say?"

With an infuriated growl, Bartholomew flung Fogg's lifeless body at Captain Nemo's feet.

Book Club Questions

1. This story includes classic literary characters as well as real authors from history. How does this element affect the story?

2. The plot thickens in this book. What do you think about how the story moves forward?

3. Do you prefer Celwyn, Bartholomew, or Kang to be in charge? Why?

4. If you were making a movie of this book, and Sam Heughan was cast as Celwyn, who would you cast as Bartholomew?

5. Characters spend a lot of time away from one another at certain points. How does this distance enhance their relationship?

6. Who is your favorite minor character? Why?

7. Celwyn and Kang's friendship has grown as they journey together. What do you think about this friendship?

8. Who is your favorite villain in this book? Why?

9. How worried did you get about Celwyn at certain dire moments? Do you worry that your favorite magician will actually die or do you believe in his immortality?

10. The journey in this book covers a lot of different areas. How does this variety of location and places affect the story?

Author Bio

EARLY WORK WAS HORROR AND SUSpense; later work morphed into a combination of magical realism, mystery, and adventure painted with a horrific element as needed.

I'm one of those writers who doesn't plan ahead—no outlines, no clue, and I sometimes write myself into a corner. Atmospheric music in the background helps. Black by Pearl Jam, especially.

More information is available at LouKemp.com. I'd love to hear from you and what you think of Celwyn, Bartholomew, and Professor Xiau Kang.

Milestones:

2009 The anthology story Sherlock's Opera appeared in Seattle Noir, edited by Curt Colbert, Akashic Books. Available through Amazon or Barnes and

Noble online. Booklist published a favorable review of my contribution to the anthology.

2010 My story, In Memory of the Sibylline, was accepted into the best-selling MWA anthology Crimes by Moonlight, edited by Charlaine Harris. The immortal magician Celwyn makes his first appearance in print.

2018 The story, The Violins Played before Junstan is published in the MWA anthology Odd Partners, edited by Anne Perry. The Celwyn series begins.

More books from 4 Horsemen Publications

Fantasy, SciFi, & Paranormal Romance

Amanda Fasciano
Waking Up Dead
Dead Vessel

Beau Lake
The Beast Beside Me
The Beast Within Me
Taming the Beast: Novella
The Beast After Me
Charming the Beast: Novella
The Beast Like Me
An Eye for Emeralds
Swimming in Sapphires
Pining for Pearls

Chelsea Burton Dunn
By Moonlight

Danielle Orsino
Locked Out of Heaven
Thine Eyes of Mercy
From the Ashes
Kingdom Come
Fire, Ice, Acid, & Heart
A Fae is Done

J.M. Paquette
Klauden's Ring
Solyn's Body
The Inbetween
Hannah's Heart
Call Me Forth
Invite Me In
Keep Me Close

Jessica Salina
Not My Time

Kait Disney-Leugers
Antique Magic

Lyra R. Saenz
Prelude
Falsetto in the Woods: Novella
Ragtime Swing
Sonata
Song of the Sea
The Devil's Trill
Bercuese
To Heal a Songbird
Ghost March
Nocturne

Paige Lavoie
I'm in Love with Mothman

Robert J. Lewis
Shadow Guardian and the Three Bears

T.S. Simons
Antipodes
The Liminal Space
Ouroboros
Caim
Sessrúmnir
The 45th Parallel

Valerie Willis
Cedric: The Demonic Knight
Romasanta: Father of Werewolves
The Oracle: Keeper of the Gaea's Gate
Artemis: Eye of Gaea
King Incubus: A New Reign

V.C. Willis
The Prince's Priest
The Priest's Assassin
The Assassin's Saint

Cozy Mysteries

Ann Shepphird
Destination: Maui
Destination: Monterey

Crime, Detective, and Noir

A.K. Ramirez
Secrets & Photographs

Joe Davison
Journey to Hell

Mark Atley
Too Late to Say Goodbye
Trouble Weighs a Ton

Fantasy

D. Lambert
To Walk into the Sands
Rydan
Celebrant
Northlander
Esparan
King
Traitor
His Last Name

Danielle Orsino
Locked Out of Heaven
Thine Eyes of Mercy
From the Ashes
Kingdom Come
Fire, Ice, Acid, & Heart
A Fae is Done

J.M. Paquette
Klauden's Ring
Solyn's Body
The Inbetween
Hannah's Heart

Lou Kemp
The Violins Played
Before Junstan
Music Shall Untune the Sky

R.J. Young
Challenges of Tawa

Valerie Willis
Cedric: The Demonic Knight
Romasanta: Father of Werewolves
The Oracle: Keeper of the Gaea's Gate
Artemis: Eye of Gaea
King Incubus: A New Reign

Discover more at 4HorsemenPublications.com